DEBORAH

ESTHER SINGER KREITMAN

Translated from the Yiddish by Maurice Carr

Introduction by Ilan Stavans

Afterword by Anita Norich

THE HELEN ROSE SCHEUER JEWISH WOMEN'S SERIES

THE FEMINIST PRESS AT THE CITY UNIVERSITY OF NEW YORK
NEW YORK

Published by the Feminist Press at the City University of New York
The Graduate Center, 365 Fifth Avenue, New York, NY 10016
feministpress.org

First Feminist Press edition, 2004

08 07 06 05 04   5 4 3 2 1

Published simultaneously in the UK by David Paul, 29 Redston Road, London N8 7HL
davidpaulbooks.com

This book was originally published in Yiddish in Warsaw in 1936 as *Der sheydim tants*. The
first English-language edition was published in 1946 by W. & G. Foyle Ltd, London.

Library of Congress Cataloging-in-Publication Data

òKreyòtman, Ester, 1891–1954.
        [Sheydim-òtants. English]
        Deborah / Esther Singer Kreitman.— 1st Feminist Press ed.
                p. cm. — (Helen Rose Scheuer Jewish women's series)
        ISBN 1-55861-469-9 (Hardcover : alk. paper)
        I. Title. II. Series.
        PJ5129.K665S413 2004
839'.133—dc22   2004008829

Steven H. Scheuer, in memory of his mother and in celebration of her life and the 100th
anniversary of her birth (1995), has been pleased to endow the Helen Rose Scheuer Jewish
Women's Series. *Deborah* is the tenth named book in the series.

Text design by Dayna Navaro
Printed on acid-free paper by Transcontinental Printing, Inc.
Printed in Canada

INTRODUCTION

Half the sorrows of women would be averted if they could repress
the speech they know to be useless; nay, the speech they have
resolved not to make.

—George Eliot

My yellowed paperback of Isaac Bashevis Singer's *The Séance*, which
I acquired in the late eighties in an antiquarian bookstore in
Connecticut, carries the following dedication: "In memory of my
beloved sister MINDA ESTHER."

Somehow I caught the typo already then, circling in pencil the
upper-case name. It was an unpleasant coda to a troubled relationship, I would come to realize, not only between the Nobel Prize win-
ner and his forgotten older sister, Esther Krietman, but between her
and the entire Singer family and even with the Yiddish literary establishment as a whole.

Kreitman was known in Yiddish as *Hinde* Esther.

The typesetters had made a mistake in *The Séance*, which isn't at all
surprising. For the brilliant Kreitman suffered bad luck throughout
her life. She was never recognized on her own terms. Her books were
perceived as strange. She failed to receive the love she deserved from
her parents, siblings, and husband. She weathered recurring illnesses.
World War I pushed her to exile and World War II to despair.

Since her death—in London at the age of sixty-three—she
remains eclipsed, a mere footnote in the history of Yiddish literature
for too many readers.

"There are two Singers in Yiddish literature," critic Irving Howe wrote in 1980, referring to the brothers Israel Joshua and Isaac Bashevis, "and while both are very good, they sing in different keys." He should have known better, for there are *three*: in spite of her misfortunes, Kreitman, in less than fifteen years, managed to publish a literary triptych made of two novels, *Der sheydim tants* (1936) and *Brilyantyn* (1944), and a collection of stories, *Yiches* (1949). That Howe, a life-long Yiddishist responsible for the Pulitzer Prize-winner *World of Our Fathers* endorsed her anonymity is inexcusable. He surely knew better. But he too was a link in the all-male club that dominated modern Yiddish literature since its inception in the eighteenth century. Open any history of the tradition composed prior to 1960 and you'll find a huge hole. Half of humankind is omitted. (By the way, Howe was once asked why he didn't call his book *World of Our Fathers and Mothers*. "What I needed was a title," he answered, "not a political slogan.")

Years of research have begun to correct the anonymity and neglect with which female authors were treated. We now have at our disposal parts of the oeuvre of Dvora Baron, Kadya Molodowsky, Rokhl Korn, Celia Dropkin, and Yente Serdatzky, among others. If none of them was as accomplished as the old masters of Yiddish literature— Mendele Moyker Sforim, Sholem Aleichem, and Isaac Leib Peretz— it is because Jewish women in Eastern Europe between 1860 and 1940 were discouraged from embarking on artistic pursuits.

Esther Kreitman symbolizes that discouragement. Her mother Batsheva was said to be disappointed when, at Kreitman's birth, she didn't turn out to be a boy. Her father Pinchos Mendel, a rabbi, precluded her from a formal education. In general the Singer family ostracized her, first in the Polish *shtetl* of Bilgoray, where she was born, then in Radzymin, where the family moved to after Pinchos Mendel became the head of a local yeshiva and unofficial secretary to the rabbi, and finally in Warsaw. In fact, so unhappy was her mother with Hinde Esther that she sent her away to be raised by a wet nurse and had her sleep in a cot under a table. The rest of the Singer clan were male—aside from I. J. and I. B., there were two

Introduction

daughters who died at a small age on the exact same day of an out-
break of scarlet fever, and then came Moishe, the youngest in the
family, who perished with his mother in the Holocaust—and she was
invariably compared to them. No wonder talented women like
Kreitman committed themselves to literature through a side door,
favoring the domestic and erotic realms, and often writing of women
with tragic fates.

Kreitman's domestic novel is a thinly disguised autobiography
about a woman (daughter, sister, wife) in search of a place in the
world. Kreitman's native Leoncin is Jelhitz; Radzymin, where she
grew up, is R.; and Krochmalna Street, the street in the Jewish slums
that I. B. made immortal, is the novel's Warsaw setting. Avram Ber is
Kreitman's father, Pinchos Mendel; Raizela is her mother; Israel
Joshua is Michael; and Deborah herself closely resembles Kreitman.

"Ever since childhood," the reader is told, "[Deborah] had longed
to receive an education, to cease being a nonentity of the family."
And later on it is said: "Deborah—the girl who, as her father had
once said, was to be a mere nobody when she grew up—would be a
person of real consequence." To achieve this end, she escapes and
returns home, being ambivalent about almost everything. She also
embraces Socialism, an ideology she later finds empty. "It would
probably be as easy to talk her into Zionism as it had been to convert
her to socialism," Kreitman writes. "She was the sort of person who
had to cling to something or other—anything would do, but, of
course, a lover would be best of all! True, she had the makings of an
idealist—an idealist without a definite ideal."

I. B.'s obliquely feminist story "Yentl, the Yeshiva Boy" is loosely
based on Kreitman's odyssey. Yentl rebels against her father and
against the divine for having made her a man in a female body. I. B.
described his parents in the same terms and declared them "a mis-
match." Batsheva had the mind of a man and Pinchos Mendel the
sensibility of a woman. The unhappy housing of male ambition in a
female body was the curse of both Yentl and Kreitman—except that
Kreitman needed to live within the social constraints of her time and
paid a heavy price for it. Hers wasn't a Hollywood-made life. She was

forced to marry Avraham Kreitman, a Belgian diamond cutter, whom
she came to despise. The marriage was both an escape and a torture.
"You're sending me away because you hate me!" she screamed at
Batsheva, according to I. B., just before the ceremony was about to
take place. But then she consented: "I'd rather go into exile. I'll disap-
pear. You won't know what happened to my remains."

To exile she went . . . Kreitman lived with her husband in Antwerp,
where they had a child: Morris Kreitman, later known as Maurice Carr,
a journalist and the translator of *Deborah*. But her liaison was hellish,
so in 1926 she returned to Warsaw with her son. I. J. allowed them to
live in his summer home for three months. But Kreitman, ambivalent
again, returned to Belgium. When the Germans invaded, the family fled
to London, where they settled for good. She and Avraham Kreitman
lived uncomfortably together, on and off. Eventually, in spite of the
scarce income it provided, she dedicated herself to literature, doing
translations (she is responsible for the Yiddish renditions of Charles
Dickens's "A Christmas Carol" and George Bernard Shaw's *Intelligent
Woman's Guide to Socialism and Capitalism*) and writing fiction.

Disturbances of mind and mood were her plight. Since childhood
Kreitman had suffered epileptic spasms. In his memoir *In My Father's
Court*, I. B. described her as often laughing profusely and then faint-
ing. At one point a London psychologist diagnosed her as neurotic
and not as psychotic, which meant, Maurice Carr was told, that "she
posed harm only to herself." Was her paranoia anatomical? Had it
been accentuated by the antagonistic environment in she grew up?

In families like the Singers, the line between genius and mental illness is a thin and tortured one. The list of cases is long: think, for example, of Albert Einstein's vanishing anonymous daughter. And of Alice
James, whose diaries and letters are a painful record of the metabolism
that propelled her siblings, psychologist Williams and novelist Henry,
to stardom and her to despair. Kreitman shares with them the pathos.
As she grew older, she became delusional, believing that demons, gob-
lins, and dybbuks were out to get her. She asked to be cremated so as to
avoid the evil forces that could overwhelm in death as they had in life.

Such has been Kreitman's eclipse that English-language audiences have had to make due with a partial, elusive view of her work. This is in spite of the fact that she made her debut in Shakespeare's tongue before I. B. (I. J.'s *The Brothers Ashkenazi* was published by Knopf in 1936.) A bunch of Kreitman's tales are available in anthologies like *Beautiful Moon, Radiant Stars,* edited by Sandra Bark. *Deborah* appeared in London in 1946. After receiving conflicting reviews (including a decidedly mixed one in *The Jewish Chronicle* by a mysterious I.B.S.), it quickly disappeared from sight. It was in 1983, with a rise in interest in women's literature, that *Deborah* was reprinted by Virago Press. And now Kreitman's novel comes back to us again, from the Feminist Press, giving us a chance to reevaluate her work in the very year when international celebrations will mark I. B.'s centennial.

Have we learned to appreciate Kreitman's place in Yiddish literature? I trust we have. Critical responses to her have mushroomed in the last few years. Plus, the other two components of her triptych, also autobiographical in nature, with protagonists that take Deborah's journey a step further, are now, or will soon be, available in English from London publisher David Paul: the novel *Diamonds* (forthcoming, 2005), translated by Heather Valencia, and *Blitz and Other Stories* (2004), translated by Dorothee Van Tendeloo.

Deborah is the main course, though. Far from being a confession of madness, it is a critique of the forces that crush women and catalog them as "crazy." In the scholarly essay that serves as afterword to this edition, Anita Norich studies the stark difference between the Yiddish and English versions, asking important questions: why did Maurice Carr translate the novel if Kreitman was fluent in English? Did the tension between mother and son affect any editorial decisions? How come Kreitman gave up the more emblematic Yiddish title *The Dance of the Demons* in favor of a colorless one? And why did she extricate entire passages?

Almost seventy years after its original Yiddish appearance, is it worth the effort? My answer is a categorical yes. Kreitman isn't a proverbial storyteller. Her narrative structure is prismatic, even erratic. Her atmospheric descriptions are pungent yet disorienting. The reader has difficulty warming up to her awkward style. But in her case the silences, deliberate and unconscious, are the message. She explores the predicament of women in orthodox families with enviable urgency. The surviving members of the Singer family uniformly moved from religiousness to secularism. But not everyone enjoyed the fruits of freedom and education.

Almost seventy years after the novel first appeared in Yiddish, some orthodox Jewish wives and daughters are still considered sheer companions of their spouses—a fixture of the environment. Their intellect is unworthy of cultivation. Metaphorically, they are, like Kreitman, but a typo. My copy of *The Séance* is proof of it.

At the end of *Deborah*, the protagonist, in a mesmerizing scene, is overwhelmed by a dream in which she returns from Antwerp to her parent's home in Warsaw . . . only to find the house empty. Empty and silent.

A disappearing act. But by then, unfortunately, she is past caring.

Ilan Stavans
Amherst
May 2004

CHAPTER I

It was the Sabbath. And even the wind and the snow rested from their labours. The village of Jelhitz, a small cluster of wooden cottages and hovels, stood hidden away from sight at the edge of the Polish pinewoods—to all appearances nothing more than one of the many snowdrifts covering the land. But within Jews were comfortably asleep in their beds after the heavy Sabbath dinner.

All was silent in the village, but nowhere was the quietude so impressive as in the large house by the synagogue which stood facing the common meadowland and the frozen river. Here lived the Rabbi, Reb Avram Ber, and unlike most of his flock, he did not snore in his sleep. As for Raizela, his wife, her breathing was so gentle, that whenever Deborah peeped into the bedroom to see whether her parents were astir yet, the fourteen-year-old child grew anxious, wondering whether her mother was breathing at all.

The warmth and the shadowiness of falling dusk were cosy inside the Rabbi's house, but Deborah, as she sat beside the tiled stove, reading, felt lonely and sorry for herself to the point of tears.

Earlier in the day she had overheard her father say:

"Michael is showing great promise in his studies, the Lord be praised! One day he will be a brilliant Talmudist."

Michael was her younger brother who, in accordance with the centuries' old custom of orthodox Jews, was being brought up to spend all the days of his life in the study of the Talmud.

"And father, what am I going to be one day?" Deborah then suddenly enquired, half in jest, half in earnest, for, as long as she could remember, never had a word of praise fallen to her lot.

Reb Avram Ber was taken aback. It was an accepted view among pious Jews that there was only one achievement in life a woman could hope for—the bringing of happiness into the home by ministering to her husband and bearing him children. Therefore he did not even vouchsafe Deborah a reply, but when she pressed him, he answered simply:

"What are *you* going to be one day? Nothing, of course!"

This response did not at all satisfy Deborah. It was quite true that most girls grew up only to marry and become drudges, but there were exceptions, such as her own mother, Raizela, who was highly educated, a real lady, and as wise as any man.

To be sure, in his heart of hearts Reb Avram Ber disapproved of his wife's erudition. He thought it wrong for a woman to know too much, and was determined that this mistake should not be repeated in Deborah's case. Now there was in the house a copy of Naimonovitch's Russian Grammar, which Deborah always studied in her spare moments, but whenever her father caught her at this mischief he would hide the book away on top of the tiled stove out of her reach, and then she would have to risk her very life to recover it. She would move the table up against the stove, set a chair on the table, herself on the chair, and after all that trouble, clouds of dust and loose leaves from torn books, disused feather dusters and God knows what else would come fluttering and tumbling down—everything, in fact, except the Russian Grammar. Nevertheless, during her fourteen years of life, she had managed to learn all its contents by heart, and still she was dissatisfied. How tediously morning changed into afternoon and evening into night! How wearisome was her housework, and yet, beyond that, she had few real interests. She was forever lacking something, herself hardly knowing what. A strange yearning would stir in her, an almost physical gnawing sensation, but it had never before been so painful as on this wintry Sabbath afternoon, when all was quiet within and the world outside was muffled with snow.

She sought refuge in daydreams. She recalled how the family had first come to Jelhitz many years ago, arriving at nightfall; how the bearded pious Jews, in long gabardines, black top boots and peaked cylindrical caps—a fashion surviving from the Middle Ages—came forward with lighted candles to greet their new Rabbi, crying in unison:

"Blessed be thy coming!"

What a splendid figure Reb Avram Ber had cut in his rabbinical garb—black buckled shoes, white stockings, satin gabardine and broadbrimmed black felt hat.

As she remembered all this, and saw again the smile—grateful and almost childish—that had settled in Reb Avram Ber's longish fair beard, hot tears slowly trickled down her flushed cheeks, senseless tears for which she could find no justification.

When Michael burst into the room and found his sister crying, a psalter in her hand, he laughed so boisterously, that his parents woke up in the next room. Michael and Deborah were never on very friendly terms. And he snatched this opportunity of poking fun at her, calling her a fool for staying indoors, for poring over the Psalms with tears in her eyes like a miserable old sinner whiling away dull old age with penitence. As for himself, he had been out on the river, which stretched away frozen, hard as a sheet of steel, with snow-covered fields all around, with a blue, transparent, Sabbath sky hanging above wonderfully silent. After his exertions, Michael's cheeks were flushed, his ears tingling with frostbite, and the bright gleam in his eyes flashed with ever-changing tints—now black, now brown, then coppery. He had come back brimming over with life, and his sister, who always stayed indoors and meekly bore the stagnation of their home-life, seemed to him now more pitiful than ever.

He became more subdued when his father entered the room.

"Have you been getting on with your studies, Michael?" Reb Avram Ber asked with a sleepy yawn.

"Yes, father."

Deborah gaped. She endeavoured to catch Michael's eye, but he was reading some religious tract very studiously, and there was nothing in his now thoughtful face to betray his lie. Good God, what a wicked boy! And what was worse, he thought himself so clever and dared to make fun of her. She had a good mind to give him away. But

Reb Avram Ber was asking her for a glass of hot tea, and seemed to have forgotten all about Michael by now.

Anyhow, not that her own conscience was any too clear! Exchanging one of her father's religious books for a work of fiction was surely an even more heinous sin than going for a slide on the ice on the Sabbath. If her father was to know of it, he would—she could not imagine what he might not do . . . Good God! How awful to exchange a holy book for a story book! Conscience-stricken herself, she kept her tongue, but as she poured out the tea she reflected that had she been a boy instead of a girl, she would not have found herself driven to commit such iniquities. She would have spent all her time in the study of the Talmud. But hers was a dreary lot, and even when she erred, life was still maddeningly dull. As for the chapman, he only came down to the village once in every four weeks, on market-day.

That was the only day which broke the humdrum silence of the village. When she woke up on market-day, to the rumble of spring-less peasant carts and the sound of strange voices, a thrill passed through her, as though having gone to sleep in an isolated hut far from all human habitation she had suddenly awakened to find herself in new surroundings, where life simply tumbled over itself. Indeed, Jelhitz was unrecognisable on market-day. Gone was the sovereignty of the ragged goats that otherwise rambled about the village as if they were the masters of all they surveyed. All was transformed. Even the leaning houses seemed to wear an air of alertness on market-day. Pedlars did not leave by candlelight, in the dark before dawn, to tramp the surrounding farms. None of the menfolk idled their time away in the warmth of the synagogue, relating strange tales of events in the unknown beyond. The very womenfolk had no time for the least tittle-tattle. The blanket of snow that stretched away from Jelhitz to the forest and to the horizon was broken by countless footsteps and wheel-ruts. And peasants, in carts, on foot, crowded into Jelhitz, driving cattle before them, or dragging unwilling pigs behind them; with their wives accompanying them in festive attire. While competing merchants from closeby villages brought their own wares—anything from lace veils to top boots, carved crosses to sheepskin jackets, sweetmeats to quack medicines. Gipsies were there, and conjurors, and drunkards, and idlers and loungers. And lastly came the chapman, whom Deborah sought out with more eagerness than the rest, only to be bitterly disappointed. For, as it always turned out, he had nothing of real interest. His was a burden of holiness: prayer-books, praying-shawls, ritual fringes and a miscellany of religious tracts. Only by chance would a profane book get mixed up with this spiritual load. So during the intervals of waiting she would have to read "The Fate of the Enchanted Princess" or "The Tale of the Three Brothers" ten times over, and in the end return to the wrinkled pages of the psalter after all!

The wintry light was beginning to fail by the time Raizela joined the family in the living-room. She got out of bed and immediately climbed on to the couch by the window, where she spent most of her waking-hours, absorbed in philosophic and religious books. Absentmindedly the family drank their tea, all of them except Deborah preoccupied with their reading. And yet, though they all seemed to be unaware of each other's presence, every one breathed a breath of gentle disapproval on his neighbour. Michael was grieved to have to stop indoors under his parents' eye, and indeed, as soon as he could, he slipped out unnoticed. Deborah felt slighted by them all. And husband and wife were displeased with one another on an old, old score.

Raizela was accustomed to a different life from that which she had been leading during the past ten years in Jelhitz. She had been brought up in a house of plenty—plenty, in the material as well as the spiritual sense of the word. Her father was one of the best-known Rabbis in Poland and perhaps the most learned Jew of his day. His very presence commanded the reverence of all who saw him—even of such plain folks as live by the sweat of their brow and usually feel nothing but contempt mingled with hatred for those who do no work but "wear out the seats of their pants" over the Talmud. He was very tall, with a dark lean face, magnificent black silky beard and large black eyes which showed a fine sense of humour that was eternally being stifled by a stern sense of duty and of the Holy Presence. He rarely spoke, only studying from early morning till late at night, with many scholars, or rather disciples, some of them middle-aged men, at his side, and around him in the house moved his many sons and daughters and grandchildren. It was the custom of pious Jews to marry off their children at the age of fifteen or so, and then to keep them at home until they became self-supporting.

Also Raizela, his favourite daughter, had been wed at the age of fifteen. And the husband chosen for her, a youngster a year older than herself, was Reb Avram Ber, because of his great learning and the renown attaching to his name. Some of his ancestors were among the great of Israel, household names in the Jewish world, and moreover he claimed descent from King David. So it had seemed a promising match. However, Reb Avram Ber turned out to be a failure. True, there were few to compare with him in learning; but he was unworldly, needed looking after like a child. Beyond the realm of the Talmud, he was just a simpleton.

He went on with his studies in his father-in-law's house until he was himself a father of two children, and still he gave no thought to the future. At length it was decided that Reb Avram Ber must set up for himself. The only course open to this simple-minded young man was to become a Rabbi, but in order to qualify for such a position in a town of any importance he was required by the law of that time to pass an examination in the Russian language and in other temporal subjects, so that he might combine the functions of registrar of births, marriages and deaths with that of Rabbi.

After much persuasion, Reb Avram Ber was finally torn away from the Talmud and made to journey to the town of Plotck, where he took up residence with a tutor who specialised in preparing future Rabbis for the official examination. With thoughtless willingness he paid the full fee in advance; with thoughtless reluctance he turned to his new subjects. And still all might have gone well, but for the chance arrival of another future Rabbi—a handsome young man with cute, twinkling eyes, a cynical mouth and a delightfully pointed silken little beard. This young man was soon on friendly terms with the tutor's wife and, among other things, told Reb Avram Ber that this woman wore no wig, as prescribed by Jewish law, according to which no married woman may expose her hair lest the charm of her tresses provoke sinful thoughts. In any case, Reb Avram Ber was tired of the whole business. He simply could not concentrate on the new, queer education. Nor did he relish the tutor's continual reproaches about not doing as he was told. He was weary to death of the uncongenial surroundings generally, but when his eyes were opened and he saw that the tutor's wife was not wearing a wig as prescribed by Jewish law, that was the last straw.

For once in his life he became a man of action—and he ran away. Lacking courage to return to his father-in-law's house, he decided to go into the "wide world." The "wide world" was the nearest village to Plotck. The Jewish inhabitants, finding a stranger in their midst, shook hands with him, bade him "Peace!"; then asked him who he was, what was his business, whence had he come, whither was he going. And many more questions besides did they ask him, as the custom is. But Reb Avram Ber answered briefly. He merely begged the beadle to announce that a preacher had arrived and would deliver a sermon immediately after the evening service.

Reb Avram Ber was well versed in parables, and his rambling sermon, full of deep knowledge of the law, was mingled with many fascinating tales which held his audience spellbound.

"His words flow sweet as wine!" said the womenfolk, not a little impressed by his good looks.

"A great scholar!" declared the menfolk.

Thus it was he went from village to village, until he at last came to Jelhitz, which had been without a Rabbi for some time past. And Reb Avram Ber found great favour in the eyes of the Jews of Jelhitz. The community of three hundred souls determined not to let this erudite young man continue on his travels. After several heated meetings, at which everybody tried to speak at the same time, Reb Avram Ber was appointed Rabbi of Jelhitz.

But Raizela never forgave him his escapade. And on this wintry Sabbath afternoon it all came back to her. The family were in great distress. The stipend paid by the community was far from adequate, and driven by the sheer force of circumstances, Reb Avram Ber was that evening going to ask for an increase.

Earlier in the week he had consulted her how to go about it. She was his adviser in all secular matters. Reclining on her couch, ailing and feeble, she would turn his problems over in her mind and drop words of counsel.

"Whatever you do, don't be apologetic," she had said in a quiet voice that seemed to heighten her frailty.

"Oh no, I'll be very firm with them this time," replied Reb Avram Ber.

Raizela's thin lips spread into a faint smile. She could not help thinking that her husband looked rather ridiculous promising to be firm, with his blue eyes so gentle, with so pleasant a smile playing on his face.

Reb Avram Ber, usually short-sighted and unobservant of what was going on around him, had by this time learnt to interpret that flickering little smile as a bitter reproach to himself for his past errors, and whenever he noticed it he began to defend himself stoutly, as though her thoughts had been audible. And then, when Raizela made no reply, he invariably transferred to his father-in-law that flush of anger which had risen in him momentarily against his wife. He blamed the father for having encouraged the daughter to study, for having supplied her with reading-matter (orthodox books, of course, though afterwards it was whispered that she read all sorts!) and for generally having taken her—a mere female—into his confidence.

With that the "scene" always ended, and calm was restored to the home. But now, on this wintry Sabbath afternoon, when any talk on worldly matters was out of place, husband and wife were again having the same old quarrel, even though not a word passed between them. And Reb Avram Ber felt relieved when the time came for him to put on his overcoat and go into the synagogue, only a few steps away, for the evening service.

In a hushed murmur the sound of prayers reached the house.

Deborah listened intently. In her imagination she saw the all too familiar bearded faces of the congregation in the candle-lit synagogue, and she wondered what the heads of the community would say to her father's request. But Reb Avram Ber returned immediately the service was over. He looked very grave, and he brought bad news.

One of the villagers' children, who had been slightly ill for some time, had suddenly taken a turn for the worse. The father, Mendel, nicknamed "Big" Mendel, one of the wealthiest men of the tiny community, was travelling to the town of R— to ask a *Tsadik*, a holy man, who dwelt there, to pray for the recovery of the infant. Another villager, whose wife was with child and was troubled with presentiments of disaster, was accompanying "Big" Mendel, in order to beg the *Tsadik* to drive out the evil spirits responsible for the presentiments, and Reb Avram Ber proposed to go too. He would thus have to postpone his request for an increase in his stipend until some other, more propitious time.

Raizela was displeased. Like her father, she was not a believer in *Tsadikim*, professional holy men, who, because of their purity, were reputed to stand in closer communion with God than the ordinary mortal. She often tried to enlighten Reb Avram Ber, ridiculing in her quiet way the possibility of any man being holy by profession, the sophistry of such a man wielding occult powers to heal and to wound, to create and to destroy, in return for temporal might and wealth. These *Tsadikim* lived in great style, holding court like kings and branching out into great dynasties, the sons inheriting the holy spirit from their fathers.

But Reb Avram Ber was not to be deflected from his faith. He was a staunch follower of the *Tsadikim* and their movement of *Hassidism*. He never doubted that the *Tsadikim* were righteous men, and he loved the cult of *Hassidism* which declared that life being God's most precious of all gifts, it would be sinful for man not to delight in this gift. He loved to serve God by being merry, and he loved to travel to the courts of the *Tsadikim*, where he met other *Hassidim*, pilgrim believers, from all parts of the country and from all stations of life, where he could mingle with his fellow men in an atmosphere of mystical rejoicing; where he could join in the dancing, the singing and the prayers of the masses; where he heard strange new stories, picked up haunting new melodies and received fresh inspiration for even more steadfast application to the Talmud and the mystical Cabala.

With eager anticipation now he dressed up in his warmest great-coat, tucking his beard into the lapels, and by the time "Big" Mendel's conveyance had drawn up outside the window, he had quite forgotten about the financial straits of the family and his promise to be firm.

"Big" Mendel entered with pale face. Usually beaming, he was very grave now, and he chilled everybody's heart. Reb Avram Ber hastily bade the family good-bye. Raizela was cross and returned her husband's farewell without even raising her eyes from the book she was reading.

The wheels crunched on the snow outside, and Reb Avram Ber was gone.

CHAPTER II

It was on a Thursday, about ten o'clock in the morning—Raizela had just made her mind up to send off a telegram, for never before had Reb Avram Ber spent such a long time at the *Tsadik*'s court—when the door opened and in walked Reb Avram Ber himself, beaming with joy, his whole person wrapt in an air of mystery. He entered wiping the perspiration from his face with a red-spotted handkerchief, although the weather was still cold and wintry. His eyes sought a chair. Deborah brought him up a stool and placed it opposite her mother lying on the couch. Reb Avram Ber seated himself, unbuttoned his overcoat, removed his hat, adjusted the velvet skull-cap on his head, stuffed his handkerchief back into his pocket, and exclaimed:

"I have news for you!" And then—"All's well, the Lord be praised! All's well!"

He turned to Deborah, in whom he hoped to see a bright reflection of his own happiness. Deborah, finding her father in such high spirits, anticipated that he had brought home a larger sum than usual, given to him as a parting gift by the *Tsadik*, and she rejoiced. They were in a bad way, deeply in debt. And she waited impatiently for him to name the amount. Then, recollecting that he had mentioned "news," she was all agog to be let into the secret. But as if on purpose to tantalise her, all at once Reb Avram Ber turned very deliberate. He released his beard, took out his pipe in leisurely fashion, knocked it on the leg of his stool, filled it with tobacco, pulled large puffs of smoke to get it to light properly, and at length he said:

"How would an offer of fifteen roubles a week, with free accommodation, appeal to you, I wonder?"

Raizela's eyes opened wide with astonishment. She looked at him for some time and made no answer.

"Aha, you are surprised? Well then, let me tell you all about it."

Deborah sat down on the edge of her mother's couch in silence. She did not know whether it was best to look solemn, like her mother, or happy, like her father.

"Now you've heard of the new *yeshiva*, the Talmud-academy, which the *Tsadik* is building at R—?"

"Yes, I've heard. I know all about it," Raizela answered sharply, angry with Reb Avram Ber for having caused her so much anxiety by his prolonged absence.

Reb Avram Ber explained that he had been offered the post of principal lecturer at the *yeshiva*. Strangely enough, she did not seem at all pleased with the prospect of fifteen roubles a week. She had no faith in the *Tsadik*, and she told Reb Avram Ber as much in plain words.

"You're always the same!" said Reb Avram Ber, waxing angry. "I do believe you wouldn't trust your own shadow!"

Here was he out of breath after tearing through the village high street, the sooner to bring her the glad tidings, and now nothing but disappointment—no response whatever. . . . But he was soon appeased. She was poorly, she should have been spared the worry of the past few weeks, he excused her in his heart.

"As you know," he continued, "for some reason or other the *Tsadik* treats with me with the greatest consideration. Whenever I pay him a visit, he showers gifts on me and insists on my accepting them. And if it wasn't for his kind help from time to time, I don't know where we should be. Well naturally, the moment he saw an opportunity of giving me a secure livelihood, he was delighted. I was the very man for the job. The *Tsadik* has a heart of gold, really he has. When he asks me how I am getting on, and I tell him that you are ailing, that the children too are in delicate health, and that our livelihood is only so so, it simply breaks his heart."

Raizela gave a faint smile. Reb Avram Ber noticed it.

"Well then, *you* tell me why he insists on giving me money! Does he profit by it in any way? Now I ask you, why?"

"Since you ask, I shall tell you. The *Tsadik* of R—, you see, unlike most other *Tsadikim*, has very few learned *hassidim* among his followers, not to mention Rabbis of course. Well naturally, he likes to see a full-blown Rabbi mingling with his crowd for once in a while. Don't you always tell me how reluctant he is to let you go, and how he keeps delaying your departure as much as ever he can? Only that explains why he is so eager for your company, and that is why he invites you to come the oftener the better, though every visit you pay him is so much extra expense to him. You know quite well that a *Tsadik* always accepts gifts, but never offers any. It's obvious! You don't see it—I do!"

Reb Avram Ber reached for his beard again, and began striding hastily up and down the room.

"You're a sceptic! You're no better than your father! You are calumniating a holy man. A sceptic is capable of blaspheming our very Father in heaven and the Messiah. I always said that your father made a very great mistake in giving you an education."

Now, as ever, Reb Avram Ber transferred his wrath to his father-in-law. . . .

Thereafter never-ending discussions took place between father and mother. As the town of R— was of course much larger than the village Jelhitz, both Deborah and Michael hoped that for once father would have his own way. Then they would at last be rid of sleepy lit-

DEBORAH

tle Jelhitz, and with Reb Avram Ber installed as head of the *yeshiva* at R—, a new and glorious life would begin.

Reb Avram Ber scarcely applied himself to his studies. He was forever arguing with Raizela, who never once wavered in her opinion that the *Tsadik* was not a man to be trusted—she had the less faith in him because of his gifts! On the other hand, Reb Avram Ber did his best to convince her that here indeed was the finest possible proof of the *Tsadik*'s great-heartedness, holiness and generosity, quite apart from the fact that the post had to be filled by someone—and the academy was going to be one of the finest in the whole of Poland and even Lithuania.

"Moreover, the Rabbi of that town is almost eighty, and when his time comes, will have no heir to succeed him. Not that that matters. May he go on living to a great old age, until the coming of the Messiah!"

Deborah and Michael were in entire agreement with their father.

The most prominent members of the Jelhitz community began calling on Reb Avram Ber in an endless succession, in an endeavor to deter him from taking the proposed step. They made him many tempting promises, invented all sorts of fairy tales, and insisted that for a long time past they had been thinking of increasing his stipend; but finding him adamant they tried their luck with Raizela. In honour of their visit Raizela sat up on her couch, heard out patiently all they had to say for themselves; she nodded her wise head and inwardly thought that they were liars no less than the *Tsadik* himself.

Very soon a go-between, acting on behalf of a young man of a neighbouring village who had cast an eager eye on the vacancy which Reb Avram Ber would leave, began making ever more frequent appearances in the home. Michael rejoiced anew each time the man called, although in himself the stranger was not such as to rejoice one's heart, for there was a wild, greedy-needy look in the fellow's eyes; his beard was unclean and tufted; he wore a gabardine which was so old, it must have belonged to a distant ancestor—apart from being greenish, greasy and shiny through age, it was bespattered with mud up to the girdle; and over his top boots he wore a pair of sloppy, squelching galoshes, which he did not trouble to remove even when coming into Reb Avram Ber's study. He announced himself by wafting a strange aroma into the house, partly due perhaps to the evil-smelling pipe and cigarette ends rolled in ordinary newspaper which he was in the habit of smoking. Deborah and Michael could not bear the sound of his voice, nor his manner of arguing, nor the way he gesticulated with hairy hands and filthy finger-nails. But most repugnant of all was his grin, revealing his teeth—brown, chipped and in parts black as coal. And as if that in itself were insufficient, a slight foam would play on his mouth whenever he grew excited. No, there was nothing very esthetic about him. Yet how they exulted to see him!

Strangely enough, neither Deborah nor Michael ever dreamt of feeling disgusted with Hannah, the "daily woman," notwithstanding that the greasy folds of her dress absolutely clung to her hips in their stickiness: to her they were accustomed. Indeed, Deborah was perfectly content if she was left in peace by Hannah, who was forever muttering and grumbling about never receiving a helping hand, forever nagging at that "lazy idle girl" who refused to run an errand but gave herself a holiday the moment she, Hannah, entered the place. Of late Deborah had in fact avoided the woman, not that she minded the work. But for some time now Hannah had been at loggerheads with the world, testier than ever. As she dragged herself from one task to the other, dark clouds continually frowned and threatened down from her aged face. The dark furrows around her neck had grown even deeper, and the swollen wrinkles in her cheeks and round the corners of her mouth even flabbier. Her tiny beard had greyed of late together with the wisps of hair showing through her wig. She would give the family no more cooked dinners. No use reasoning with her, pleading with her. She would listen, shake the empty skin-bag under her chin, mutter something through her drawn, toothless mouth, and take not the slightest heed.

In the end Raizela decided that, weary as she was of Jelhitz, she had after all but little to stake: she would therefore entrust herself to the mercy of the Lord, and maybe everything would turn out for the best. That settled, she curled herself up more resolutely on her couch, wrapped herself tighter in her black velvet jacket, continued her reading more intensively than ever, and left the matter entirely in Reb Avram Ber's hands—an occurrence which was without precedent.

Unexpectedly, Michael began to chum up with Deborah. He knew that she felt about the matter as strongly as he did, and would therefore sympathise with him. He went to her complaining how unreasonable was the attitude of their mother in refusing to meddle in the whole affair; thanks to her lack of interest, it would be a long time before anything was settled, if ever. Both brother and sister were filled with longing to leave the stagnant, sleepy village behind them, to get rid of old Joel, the beadle, of the everlasting loneliness and dreariness, of the unpleasantly familiar atmosphere, of Hannah, of the long, empty days, and above all—of mother's couch, which they hoped Reb Avram Ber's successor would take over together with the rest of the furniture. . . . Although Reb Avram Ber visited the *Tsadik* twice in the course of three weeks, and on each occasion returned with renewed enthusiasm—the roof was well-nigh finished, students were beginning to arrive, they were meantime studying in the *Tsadik's* own synagogue, the *Tsadik* was now promising twenty roubles a week—in spite of all this, both Deborah and Michael were still very dubious, for did they not clearly see how indifferent their mother was to the whole business?

However, one fine morning after Purim, when the door opened and in walked a stranger, short, stout and middle-aged, with an expensive fur collar on his huge black greatcoat, and in his wake a pale young man, tall and thin, with sharp, nervous eyes overcast by dark, bushy eyebrows, with long black sidelocks (which he was in the act of disentangling from the rest of his hair), only then did Michael begin to feel a certain conviction that negotiations were well advanced, and he could not resist sharing his glee with Deborah, who was even more exultant than he.

Reb Avram Ber received his visitors with a hearty welcome— "Peace unto you!"—as was his custom. He pulled up chairs for them at the table in person. The short stout man sat down with a thud, unbuttoned his greatcoat, caught his breath, glanced at his solid gold watch and returned it to his waistcoat pocket. The pallid young man looked around him as if seeking a place where to deposit his suitcase, and finally he stood it under the table, seated himself respectfully and glanced across at his father-in-law. Suddenly the go-between appeared as from thin air (he had come in quite unobserved), and he too took a seat—without being asked. Also he unbuttoned his overcoat, and having made himself quite comfortable, gazed up at the ceiling. Only when Reb Avram Ber had told Joel to tell the woman to be good enough to bring in tea, did the fellow suddenly remember his duty of introducing the guests. Whereupon Reb Avram Ber again asked them how they were, and how did they like the village. The conversation turned on Jelhitz and the benefice. It transpired that the young man had only four hundred roubles at his disposal—his entire worldly fortune. Reb Avram Ber felt awkward and disappointed. Only four hundred roubles! And he had himself heard Raizela say that at eight hundred roubles the house with the goodwill of the benefice would be a real bargain. Those were her very words, and now she refused to have anything to do with the whole business; but without her he was completely at a loss. He grew weary of the conversation, and in the end started debating a point in the Talmud.

The colour suddenly rose to the pallid young man's face. He stood up and he sat down. He warmed up to the discussion. His eyes began to glow; he tingled all over. New life welled up within him, there was nothing apathetic about him now, he was quite a devil of a young man. . . . Serenely Reb Avram Ber stroked his beard, serenely he sipped his tea, serenely he listened to all the young man's arguments, and then at one stroke he shattered them out of existence, mercilessly dashing to pieces the intricate structure of logic which the young man had built up with so much toil and care.

The short stout man followed every movement, every gesture of his son-in-law. He could not make out what those two were wrangling about: why was the Rabbi so cold-bloodedly tormenting his, Gimpel's, son-in-law, and why had the latter got so excited? He smiled, not that he saw anything to be pleased about or otherwise. As for the go-between, he did not even watch the pair.

"Bah!" he said.

Meanwhile Joel had slipped into the kitchen for a chat with old Hannah, trying to coax a little bit of prophecy out of her as to whether anything would come of it all.

The go-between began to calculate his hoped-for commission, chalking various sums on the table; then he counted the tassels of his ritual fringes; he was bored.

The young man was feverishly engaged in untwining one end of his youthful sprouting beard. He rose and began striding hastily over the room, to and fro, backwards and forwards. Suddenly he paused in front of the bookcase. Mechanically he took out a volume, *Pri Magudim,* and pored over it a while, without seeing a word. His thoughts were far, far away. He continued his pacing up and down, and then stopped at the window. He looked out, with his deep-set eyes opened wide, as if there on the crumbling roadway lay the solution to his knotty problem. Now he was simply tearing his girdle into shreds. His father-in-law went up to him and rescued the girdle from out of his hands.

"Calman, what are you doing? You're spoiling your girdle."

Already Reb Avram Ber was sipping a second glass of tea. Reb Avram Ber was at home in the Talmud. He had no need to get excited.

"Yes, yes, it is so!" Reb Avram Ber agreed with his own thoughts.

But at that moment a smile spread over Reb Calman's face. He took out his handkerchief, wiped his face, and delivered himself of so powerful a dissertation, that at first Reb Avram Ber was at a loss for a reply, let alone for an argument with which to shatter his opponent. Finding himself in difficulties, Reb Avram Ber rose to his feet, reached for his beard and this time he too became a little heated. A struggle for life or death ensued. . . . In the end a smile settled on Reb Avram Ber's face.

Exhausted, the young man sat down. Abashed, defeated, completely disarmed now, he also smiled, but sad was the smile.

"You showed great knowledge, Reb Calman. I see that you are a great Talmudist, the Lord be praised. Indeed, you showed great insight," said Reb Avram Ber. He could afford to show tolerance towards the vanquished. "Tell me, where did you study?"

"In Suddiger."

"Ah, I presume you are a *hassid* of the Suddiger *Tsadik*? So! And your father-in-law, which *Tsadik* does he give allegiance to?" asked Reb Avram Ber, not wishing to ignore Gimpel altogether.

Reb Calman looked across at his father-in-law. The latter did not quite grasp what Reb Avram Ber meant. Reb Avram Ber guessed that Gimpel gave allegiance to no *Tsadik*, and exchanging a glance with Reb Calman, they dropped the question.

By this time the broker had lost all patience.

"Reb Calman's father-in-law," he began, taking advantage of the momentary pause, "wishes to take over the benefice and the house."

Reb Avram Ber could not help smiling.

"Really? How wonderful!"

Reb Calman also smiled. His father-in-law was to take over the benefice—that was excellent!

Gimpel looked first at one, then at the other. What was the joke? Funny creatures, those two! First they disputed, then they exchanged knowing smiles! But not to be outdone, he grinned broadly. The broker alone would not smile. He wiped his mouth with the flat of his hand and got ready for some practical work.

"Saving your reverence," he said, "but it's getting late. It's time we came down to business!"

Rev Avram Ber excused himself. He retired to Raizela's room. Raizela wrinkled her forehead. She gazed at him with her large, gloomy eyes.

"So you are really going to take the leap?" she said.

"Why, of course! And, please God, we shall have no reason to regret it. The only trouble is that the young man is short of money."

"Nonsense! The young man may be short, but his father-in-law has plenty. If you were to agree to seven hundred roubles, that would be very moderate indeed. And we must not forget that in a few years we shall be needing a dowry for our daughter. Besides, the house alone . . ."

She could say no more. A lump rose in her throat, stifling her words. She had spoken softly, and her voice had sounded hollow, as if it came from nowhere. She lay back on the couch. Reb Avram Ber stood there a while, waiting for her to go on. She said nothing further. At last he returned to his study, paced up and down several times, and then repeated word by word Raizela's point of view.

"Seven hundred roubles!"

He felt better. Thank goodness that was over!

Gimpel whispered into Reb Calman's ear that he was not in a position to make up the difference of three hundred roubles. The go-between wriggled like a worm. On the quiet he told Reb Avram Ber how shocked he was to hear the price—perfectly extravagant!—and on the quiet he tried to talk Gimpel into believing that this was the greatest bargain one could hope to come across in a lifetime.

Reb Avram Ber told Joel to call in Raizela. This annoyed her. Preparing a little speech for Reb Avram Ber when he had to face the village council, well, that was one thing, but haggling with a merchant on his behalf was another—no, she would not lower herself to that. She scribbled down a few words and sent them in with Joel. Reb Avram perused the scrap of paper. A smile settled in his beard.

"Well, gentlemen," he said, "I shall now accept six hundred roubles, and here's good luck!"

"Amen!" howled the go-between, as if he had suddenly had a tooth wrenched out.

Gimpel began to bargain with renewed fervour, in an attempt to bring the price down lower still. But Reb Calman spoke several urgent words in his ear, and he stopped. He then demanded to be shown round the house. He wished to inspect it. Now this was Michael's responsibility. From behind the kitchen window, Deborah gloated over them. Finished with the exterior, Gimpel insisted on being shown round all the rooms. Here Deborah came to Michael's aid, and together they passed from chamber to chamber. Gimpel critically examined the walls, the ceilings; he knocked at the stoves, as if they were doors; rattled the windows. Only the panes and echoes responded as he endeavored to find fault. Even so, he now felt pleased with himself. At last he was in his element. Now *he* was the man of the moment. Afterwards, it was arranged to summon the elders of the Jelhitz community, in order to talk the matter over with them and obtain their approval that very same evening.

Joel, the beadle, returned tired and perspiring, quite out of breath.

"Phew! My word, I've had a run for my money—rushing all over the place! I had to keep calling and calling before I could find anyone at home."

"Well, and did they promise to come?"

"I should say so! Ha, you leave it to Joel! My good point is that I know exactly what to say. Of course, I never told them what they were wanted for. He, he! I know the right thing to say, just leave it to me! He, he, he!"

"What do you think, Joel, will this young man appeal to them?"

"Will he appeal to them? Of course he'll appeal to them! He's a gent, that's what he is! The only trouble is that they don't feel like parting with you at all."

"Well, yes, but you can't expect me to stick in this hole of a village for ever," said Reb Avram Ber, as if apologising to Joel, and he told the beadle to ask the woman to be so good as to bring in a glass of tea.

Joel warmed his hands over the coals of the samovar, and thought it a pity that Hannah was getting older every day, and the older—the crosser. Nevertheless, he liked the idea of having a little flirt with her, of tickling her under the chin, of placing his ancient hand on the back of her parched, wrinkled neck, and he did not stop at the mere idea. Hannah nearly overturned the samovar, and as was her wont when Joel became frolicsome, she scolded him most vehemently, told him that he was nothing but an old fool, while memories came back to her of times which seemed to be of yesterday and of long, long ago.

Towards evening the elders began to arrive one by one, until Reb Avram Ber's study overflowed with them. Most conspicuous of all were the two Mendels, "Big" Mendel and "Little" Mendel. The former was tall but with a bad stoop (as if ashamed of his great size!), and his head, supported by a brown curly beard, reared itself above the whole assembly. He wore a fur collar and long fur gloves, which hampered him as every now and then he tried to twirl the ends of his long drooping moustache. He had apparently just returned from the forest and had not had time to change. Then "Little" Mendel—a tiny fellow, with a tiny pinched nose perched on a tanned face, with a tiny roundish beard, and with two sparkling black eyes that were quite immense for so miniature a creature. These eyes of his never kept still for a second. At one moment they would penetrate into your innermost soul, read all the secrets hidden there, and at the next, in passing, they would peep in to see what was happening within your neighbour. He was quick to find his bearings, and knew everything. You could not deceive him. Dressed in a somewhat worn black cloth coat, a pair of childish galoshes (which, like the broker, he did not take off when coming into the room—lest they should be gone by the time he went out), enveloped in a large red woollen scarf taken from his own shop (where the stocks verily reached the low ceiling), he did not in appearance betray that great wealth with which the villagers credited him. He was held in great esteem because of this belief—and he knew it.

The two Mendels formed the core of the congregation. The rest had come more or less for the sake of propriety. They said very little, but listened attentively to what the two had to say. To-day, possibly for the first time in his life, Reb Calman was suffused with a deep red from the nape of his neck to the tips of his ears, for "Little" Mendel, contrary to his custom, gave him a long and searching look before he could make up his mind about him. However, by way of compensation, he darted only a fleeting glance at Gimpel and immediately recognised his man. Gimpel returned the glance with interest. He could not make it out why that tiny mite had stared so curiously first at his son-in-law and then at himself. What did that little doll mean by it?

"Gentlemen!" said Reb Avram Ber, looking down first at "Little" Mendel and then up at "Big" Mendel, then at the general assembly. "Gentlemen, as you see, I must leave you. It is so ordained by God, for man does not make the slightest movement, does not stir his little finger, without that it has previously been determined in the heavens. I—," said Reb Avram Ber; but at this point "Big" Mendel exchanged a look with "Little" Mendel, whereupon the rest of the throng looked round themselves significantly and waited for one of the Mendels to speak. Reb Avram Ber's study was filled with the sound of breathing. No one uttered a word. Reb Avram Ber took advantage of the silence and continued:

"You see this young man, Reb Calman, here? Well, Reb Calman is, the Lord be praised, a profound Talmudist. More, he is—one might say—a sage, well versed in our Holy Knowledge. We have only just had a discussion, and I must admit that he wore me out."

Reb Calman gazed intently into an open book lying on the table and never lifted his eyes. Gimpel gathered that he had reason to be pleased with what Reb Avram Ber had said concerning his son-in-law, and he looked at Reb Avram Ber with an expression of animal gratitude. All eyes turned upon Reb Calman. Reb Calman smiled faintly in recognition and quickly lowered his eyes again. "Big" Mendel, "Little" Mendel and—for the sake of appearances—the rest of the elders approved Reb Avram Ber's negotiations with Reb Calman for the disposal of the benefice. Joel brought in a bottle of whisky and beakers. The crowd wished them both luck, and chatted a while. Reb Calman exerted himself to exchange a few words with the elders of his new flock.

Before taking their leave the villagers went into Raizela's room, paid her their respects, wished her happiness, and one by one they left for home.

That evening left a deep impression on both Deborah and Michael. They remembered it all through the years to come.

As soon as the villagers had departed, Reb Calman drew himself erect and squared his shoulders, as porters do after throwing down a heavy load from their backs. From under his black bushy eyebrows he threw a look of gratitude to Reb Avram Ber.

"Well, Reb Calman, you will soon be assuming your new duties. I am sure you will be a success."

Reb Avram Ber held out his hand. Reb Calman took it and pressed it with such warmth, that even Joel felt the glow of that handshake.

DEBORAH

Raizela came in. Pale, thin, and with those large grey eyes of hers, she looked like a Talmudist who spends his days and nights and years in study, rather than a woman. Even the black dress and velvet jacket she had on scarcely betrayed her. Reb Avram Ber pulled a chair up for her and politely bade her be seated, as if she were his guest.

"You know, of course, that the elders, that is to say, Reb Mendel and er . . ." Reb Avram Ber had almost said "Little" Mendel, but he checked himself in time. He racked his brain for the correct surname, but could not remember it. At last he cried out gleefully, "and Reb Mendela Shvairdsharf, they have both, the Lord be praised, given their consent."

"I know. Congratulations!" Raizela said quietly to Reb Calman and Gimpel. The latter watched her with the expression of a cow when it turns its head to discover by whom it is being milked. A thought crossed his mind that she it was who was now depriving him of a little fortune; then another thought, that possibly he could bring the price down once more if he tried. He tried.

It had always been the broker's misfortune that when a transaction was all but completed—all that remained for him to do was, seemingly, to stretch forth his hand and pocket the commission—then some hitch occurred unexpectedly and everything ended in smoke. For this very reason he had viewed the present negotiations with a sceptical air, notwithstanding his mannerism of chalking up on the table the interests that would accrue from the commission. At Gimpel's essay, and flushed as he was with his rare success, he now became so confused and flustered, that spots began to dance before his eyes. He lost his head entirely. Catching sight of Raizela's wan features, he decided that she was to blame for everything: calculating and cruel, she would at a touch destroy all the fruits of his victory. He failed to see that it was Gimpel who had started his haggling all over again.

Clutching his ritual fringes, the broker frenziedly lashed the air and cried out "For shame, Madam! It is very wrong of you! The Rabbi himself will tell you so. Saving your reverence, but it really is very, very wrong of you! Very! Why, what we're offering you is a little fortune!"

"This is no market-place!" Raizela said to Gimpel with cold contempt, and made as if to walk out.

Seeing Raizela rise from the table, the broker became so alarmed, that he flew to the door, planted himself there firmly, prepared to let no one pass, and he screamed almost at the top of his voice:

"For shame! We are Jews, aren't we? Well then, we must settle the matter peacefully, here and now—and let's get it over!"

Raizela smiled her wise smile. She wanted to please him, this poor comical man. So she sat down again. Gimpel scarcely dared to breathe. Fear mingled with respect, an unaccountable feeling of awe dumbfounded him now as he looked at her once more.

"Well, here's luck!" Joel suddenly interposed, drowsily rubbing his eyes.

"Here's luck!" the company echoed his words, all except Raizela, and thereupon it was agreed that Reb Avram Ber was to receive a deposit within the next few days, the balance to be paid at the date of moving. And the price, of course, remained as stipulated by Raizela—six hundred roubles.

Only on his way back to the inn did Gimpel, who was a keen bargainer and indeed always bought cheaper than his competitors, begin to wonder why he had withered under Raizela's gaze, accepting her demands without a whisper. What had made him so afraid of her?

"A very funny woman!" he remarked to his son-in-law, with a pang of regret.

"A very clever and worthy woman!" retorted Reb Calman, and softly, quite softly, he added, "Of course, she comes of good stock . . . the daughter of a learned man . . . What a difference! . . ."

CHAPTER III

When the last of the strangers had gone, the family grouped themselves in a corner of the living-room to discuss the events of the day in unwonted intimacy. Raizela felt as if some great change had, of its own accord, descended upon their modest way of life, and she could

not accustom herself to the thought that it was she who had consented to it all. Nevertheless, had the occasion arisen, she would
again have given her consent—and again rather reluctantly.

A bitter-sweet mood took possession of them directly the
strangers left, a sort of yearning for the past and a misty vision of the
future. Even Deborah and Michael's jubilations were forced. No one,
however, revealed his feelings to the other, nor gave the slightest hint
of them. The family talked far into the night, recalling every incident,
laughing heartily over many of them, and outwardly everybody
seemed quite cheerful.

It was four o'clock when they went to bed. In spite of the lateness
of the hour, sleep would not come. Only towards dawn did the first
snores rise up from the beds, and a faint odour of perspiration and
warmth filled the air.

Deborah was unable to fall asleep even towards dawn. She tossed
about in her bed, smothered herself up completely in the feather bed,
but to no avail. If she could only talk to the night watchman out on
his beat and induce him to stop pacing backwards and forwards on
the crumbling roadway outside her window, perhaps by offering him
some of her father's tobacco. Every crunching step he took in his
heavy boots was simply torture to her. In the heated turmoil of her
mind she imagined that it was he who prevented her from falling
asleep. . . . How terribly dark and thick the air was, as if the Night
had poured barrels of pitch over the whole world. And it seemed to
be getting darker still. What a long, long night! And they had gone to
bed so very late. She dug herself into the hot bedclothes, tucked her
head in and drew up her legs, so that her hair and knees rested upon
her belly, but that did not help.

"No wonder mother calls me a silly wild goose! No wonder! The
rest of them are all asleep. They didn't work themselves up into a
frenzy. Deborah, you're mad!" she cried into a mouthful of bedding.
"Go to sleep, will you?"

In the end, when all her self-remonstrances proved unavailing, she
slipped out of bed, lit the tiny paraffin lamp and tried to read a frag-
ment of newspaper which one of the elders had forgotten on the table

and which she had hidden away as a rare treasure. The shadows on the wall trembled. A stifling sickly stench spread over the room. She turned down the offending wick, hid the paper under her pillow, and when the light of morning was waxing strong, she finally dozed off.

It was mid-day when the family awoke. They dressed in haste.

"Dear, dear, what a time to get up! Pish, pish!" said Reb Avram Ber.

Deborah awoke gaily. The few hours of sleep had refreshed her. All that had passed yesterday came back to her. Well, the momentous step had been taken.

Hannah came in. Deborah caught her round the waist and impetuously danced her round the room. Hannah flared up. Her seared face assumed an even grimmer expression than usual.

"Let me be!" she cried, pushing her away. "I'm in no dancing mood, not me! And what's the matter with you, anyway? What have you got to dance about? Nothing, believe me!"

Deborah stepped back in confusion. Hannah's words had pricked her like a needle. She wandered away gloomily, but since Michael was still on the most friendly terms with her, it was not long before she left off moping because Hannah would not share her joy, and after breakfast brother and sister repaired to the river like true comrades (an occurrence without precedent), there to build plans for the future. She quite forgot that such a woman as Hannah existed. There on the river, which still stood frozen and firm although spring was at hand, Michael gave boisterous expression to his great, great joy.

The Passover holidays were over. The family were packing. The home was topsy-turvy. Michael refused point blank to have any truck with his old overcoat: he would leave it behind. Deborah pointed out that it might come in useful, but Michael paid no heed.

"Rot!" he said. "Who wants a shabby old coat like this? Old rags!"

He was now wearing his new gabardine. What did he care if he might soil it? Not a bit! Deborah protested. Why had not *she* put on her new frock? Had they not had all their new clothes made specially for their new home?

Raizela was no longer reclining on her couch.

Reb Avram Ber was helping Joel to transfer the books into large wooden packing-cases. He was perspiring freely, and constantly mopped his face and beard. Joel was working sluggishly, as if he did it only to keep up appearances. Soon he would be beadle to Reb Calman, soon he would have new duties thrust upon him and he deemed it best to spare his strength.

However, a few villagers showed up and offered to lend a hand. They abused him for his laziness, then told him to get out of their way, and they set to work with a will. Reb Avram Ber watched them, and wiping the sweat from his forehead, he marvelled at their skill. He smiled with contentment as he smoked his pipe and breathed huge clouds of smoke.

"Pish, pish!" he exclaimed with admiration. "Just look at them!" He stroked his beard.

The villagers did not trifle. Clip-clap! Clip-clap!—and there stood the cases all nailed up and fastened with rope, and there were the bedclothes and other household articles packed in huge wickerwork baskets or bundled up in sacking. Reb Avram Ber felt so grateful to them. How could he ever thank them? His gentle face simply shone with pleasure, there was such a good-natured look in his eyes, and his smile was so infectious, the very pipe in his mouth seemed to be smiling too. Inspired by Reb Avram Ber, the villagers flocked into the kitchen to offer their help there. They would not allow Raizela to touch a thing.

"No, you know how delicate you are," they said to her, "You must be careful. If only Deborah will be so kind as to tell us what to do, you can leave it to us—we'll do it!"

Hannah was indisposed. Her head bandaged up with a filthy handkerchief, she lay upon Raizela's couch and from this point of vantage watched the villagers at their labours.

"Let 'em get on with it! It'll do 'em good! Oh Lord, give them my headache, will you?"

She was in a black study, her mind racked by doubts as to whether the new Rabbi's wife would engage her. But she consoled herself with cold comfort. She sighed:

"Ah well, something is sure to turn up. Anyway, one last shirt and one last hope are worse than useless!"

Mottel, an orphan who was supported by the community so that he might study in the house of worship and who, when assistance failed him, took his meals at Reb Avram Ber's table, was busy too. He was rejoicing, for yesterday Reb Avram Ber had informed him that he might accompany the family to the town of R— and there enter the new *yeshiva*. He was showing great industry and constantly busied himself over tasks which brought him close to Deborah. Occasionally their eyes met. Once he had even touched her hand. A shiver had gone thrilling through his body. It was as though something were running down his spine. He too was dressed up in a "new" gabardine, one that Reb Avram Ber had obtained on his behalf from "Big" Mendel's clerk. He also had a new hat. They were rather a tight fit for him, but then he looked quite the young spark in that grey gabardine, with its tails and two grey buttons on the back. As for his spectacles, he had given them such a brilliant polish that day, that no matter what Deborah did, she could not help seeing herself reflected in the lenses.

A crunching of wheels and a clinking of harness announced the arrival of Abbish. He had two carts, one for the passengers and another for the luggage. Almost the whole village had assembled outside the Rabbi's house. The boys had a day off from school and they were kicking up a shindy. They clambered on to the carts, stood up on the spokes of the wheels, got cuffs and kicks from Abbish and his man Itchela, but what did they care? It was better than being whacked by the schoolmaster.

Already Abbish was hitching up the rope on top of the tarpaulin that covered the chattels in case of rain. He gave the final touches, and now they were off. Michael exulted. How his pals and even the grown-ups envied him! He was enjoying himself. A cluster of small boys was hanging on to the tailboard. Michael drew Abbish's attention to this churlish conduct. Abbish felt for his whip and the youngsters all scattered, but were all back again the moment he turned his head. The wheels ploughed through and churned up the earthen village road-way.

Raizela was by now weary of nodding her head to right and to left, weary of smiling in acknowledgment to farewells and parting bless-ings showered upon her by humble women who had been lacking in courage to come and say good-bye personally and did so now *en pas-sant*. Half the village, at the very least, men and women and children, escorted the family a goodly distance, all the way to the meadows by the river. They walked step by step with the horses, talking and laughing, giving counsel and blessings. The horses accompanied the uproar with the rhythmical stamp! stamp! of their newly-shod hoofs. And at every renewed outburst of womanish sentimentality, they lifted their heads and uttered a loud neigh, as if they too wished to put in a word, or give their blessing or perhaps even give some coun-sel—counsel to the women that they were overdoing things, that it was no good going on for ever. In the end the women themselves realized that it was no good going on for ever, and at last after a few final exchanges, they turned for home. Abbish climbed up on to his seat, made himself comfortable, swished his whip over the horses' heads and cried:

"Gee up! Come on now, me hearties!"

This was what the horses had been waiting for. High-spirited after many days of inaction, they let themselves go, and how they gal-loped! The cart swayed and jumped and with a great clatter and thunder of hoofs it seemed to leave the ground and simply flew through the air. Reb Avram Ber became alarmed lest it should over-turn, and Abbish was obliged to slow down somewhat.

Soon the village was out of sight, but after going only five or six miles they came upon a Jewish hamlet, Senzimin. Here they stopped, for Reb Avram Ber would not dream of passing without so much as saying good-bye to the inhabitants who were his parish-ioners. Abbish pulled a wry face. But he had to yield: Reb Avram Ber was the master! . . .

During the halt the horses gulped down a pail of water each, then buried their muzzles in the thick grass and resigned themselves to the inevitable. It was no use showing impatience: Jews would be Jews, and *would* have their own Jewish way! Deborah fretted. She would have loved to be off again, to draw ever nearer and nearer to R—. But the menfolk of Senzimin, and more so the womenfolk, were people with secret longings and yearnings of their own, and had to give expression to these feelings for once in a while. After all, surrounded always by peasants, cattle and sheep, they never saw a new Jewish face from one year's end to the other, except when they went to Jelhitz for the High Festivals, and now that such a golden opportunity had presented itself—the Rabbi himself and his family (God bless them!) here in the hamlet—were they going to let the occasion pass without due celebration? It was not as if they saw a really respectable Jew every day of the week or every week of the month. What if Hershl Stock did tramp into the hamlet regularly each week, with his exposed chest all hairy, like a peasant, with his muddy top boots slung over his shoulder, with his long shaggy beard and his hand gripping a stout, knotty stick that had a large nail protruding at one end, looking for all the world like a highway bandit, but coming only to buy pigs' bristles—could one call him a Jew? Was he a Jew worthy of the name? So the present occasion was indeed one to rejoice over, and they made the most of it.

The greatest joy and honour fell to the lot of "Uncle" Jonah, whose custom it had been to bring Raizela some gift early each autumn, such as a sackload of potatoes, carrots, beetroots and other vegetables which would keep during the winter. To be sure, it was no mean privilege to have the Rabbi greet you and clasp your hand before turning to the other farmers of the hamlet, and to give you such a radiant smile that it made you tingle all over. His good wife, leaving him in a state of bewildered festivity, meanwhile slipped into her cottage, rummaged about in the pantry and soon returned with a round of dried yellow cheese made almost entirely from cream, and with a pound of yellow butter patted in between two newly plucked green leaves. Both the butter and the green leaves were moist with silvery drops of water so bright and pure, it verily made everybody's mouth water.

Youngsters from afar, noticing that something was afoot in the hamlet, something which might very well concern themselves, promised their Christian comrades a lump of sweet white Sabbath bread, and entrusting herds of cattle, sheep and goats to their care, rushed home to welcome—whom, they did not know.

Other women followed the example set by Jonah's wife. They brought to light whatever treasures they had: a pot of cream, or home-made preserves, or a bottle of raspberry-juice, things that were not to be touched in the ordinary way but were kept in reserve for special occasions, such as a wedding or (God forbid!) an illness. Raizela protested. She thanked them, but what would she do with all these delicacies? She pleaded with them, but they were deaf to her entreaties. They simply put the gifts into the cart, tucked them up in straw, and hoped that the Rabbi and his family would enjoy these refreshments on their journey.

The horses having drained the remaining water in the pails, again held their heads out uncomfortably as Abbish led them by the halter. Again there was the stamp! stamp! of powerful hoofs, again a shower of blessings and counsels, but now these homely folk were waving the last farewell. When the hamlet was left behind, Reb Avram Ber suggested that he and Raizela should move over on to the other cart.

"We won't get bumped about so much," he said.

Raizela consented: she would be able to get on with her reading in greater comfort. So Itchela adjusted some soft bundles for them to sit upon.

The "children" now had the cart all to themselves. That was magnificent. Magnificent was hardly the word for it!

The air was laden with the scent of fresh grass. The trees were showing leaves already—so bright and green and tender. On some trees there were full-grown leaves hanging among hosts of heavy reddish buds which seemed ready to burst into blossom and to cover the dark, lush boughs at any moment. The sky here was infinitely loftier than in Jelhitz or even Senzimin, and was steeped from horizon to horizon with a brilliant golden light. The sky rested motionless over the world. And if, at times, a tiny white cloud emerged, it was powerless to stir, for all was at peace. The sun poured its rays down upon the bare fields, pierced the scattered trees and splashed its brilliance over the peasant huts and hovels, which, strewn over field and meadow, and half sunken into the ground, looked like strange plants growing out of the spring earth ready whitewashed by nature. They hugged their shadows tight. All was at rest. All was radiant, fresh and alive with the life of early spring.

"God bless your labours!" Abbish called out to peasant men and women engaged in ploughing and sowing with an intent and eager air. Small thin-legged horses were stubbornly dragging shiny ploughs, under which the soil sprang up black as soot. Every movement of the labourers rippled with health and vigour.

"May God give you health!" the peasants responded, making the sign of the cross.

Reb Avram Ber could not understand Polish, but he guessed that greetings were being exchanged. And he felt a keen desire to say something himself. He might have managed a few words in Russian, for had he not once spent two whole weeks studying the language? There were still a few phrases he remembered. Suddenly he was overcome by a passionate feeling of love towards those strangers in the fields at their healthgiving and useful toil.

"Man was created for labour," he quoted.

Everything around him was so full of love and beauty. His feelings mastered him, and he began to sing joyfully: "How glorious and pleasant, most holy, are Thy . . ." He forgot that it was the season of *Sfira,* when music is forbidden, but Raizela immediately pulled him up. Reb Avram Ber broke off, the sudden interruption leaving a trace of sadness on his face. But no man, least of all Reb Avram Ber, could remain downcast for very long on such a glorious day.

The carts rolled on. The peasants were lost to sight; the hammock suspended between two trees, the sleeping child, the linen spread out on the ground for bleaching, vanished. The fields were now vast and solitary: not a soul was to be seen. The soil was black and furrowed, but already it was showing signs of birth—tiny green corn blades.

Reb Avram Ber felt restless. His heart thumped and trembled in exultation. He began humming again, but checked himself.

"*Sfira, Sfira!*" he murmured.

Suddenly he felt he would like to embrace Raizela and kiss her. But, for one thing this was not the place—absurd to think of it!—and for another, Raizela was so deep in thought, she looked so terribly solemn. . . . The cart swayed on and on, and after a time Reb Avram Ber dozed off. Raizela's eyelids too were drooping and viscid. She had strained her eyes with reading. (Incidentally, she had noted and taken in the wondrous beauty of the day as sensitively as the others and perhaps even more so.) She fell asleep.

Michael was whistling as loudly as ever he could. He sat on the driver's seat, beside Abbish, and fingered the reins. Every now and again he egged the horses on in a truly professional manner, although they still trotted along with great briskness and needed no constant "Gee-ups!" or clicks of the tongue by way of encouragement. However, since it gave Michael pleasure to do so, Abbish was not going to deprive him of his fun.

All this time Mottel kept squirming as if he had the itch. Empty though the cart was, he could not settle down. He was continually edging towards Deborah. Now he sat so close to her that she could feel the warmth of his young boyish body. A shiver ran through her and a sensation which she knew she ought to be ashamed of, to conceal. So she crimsoned, and thus only revealed her guilt all the more. She moved away; but Mottel persisted. He wriggled and writhed and sidled up. He hardly noticed the beauty of the scenes through which they were passing. Deborah engulfed him completely. Suddenly he whispered something to her, so softly that she heard it only by the promptings of her instinct. She made no reply, but moved away. Mottel snuggled up against her. Suddenly she felt that he had enclosed her hand in his big palm, and it scorched her, it was burning hot. She tore her hand away and flushed crimson all over. Her eyes filled with mist. And how fortunate it was that she had kept her presence of mind, for at that very instant Michael turned his head. If he had caught them in the act! . . . Another three hours went by, and already the sun was low in the skies. Faraway horizons grew still remoter. Small wisps and whole mountains of burnished copper clouds moved in stately fashion over the clear blue sky, growing larger and shinier with every passing minute. Distant treetops seemed to catch fire and to approach. Peasants began to make for home across the footpaths, hatchets and saws in hand or slung over their shoulders. Some called out a friendly word of greeting, others just stopped to watch the two carts go by. Felling trees in this early hot weather was no joke, and coarse linen shirts were clinging, quite drenched, to aching backs. Large drops of sweat were poised on bulging temples. Youths uttered long, low whistles every now and then in exultant anticipation. They felt the pangs of hunger through the livelong day. The cattle too were unable to eat their fill in the meadows, with the grass so young. Hence they were all wending their way home with hearty appetites. The girls had gone before them to prepare supper, and from low chimneys there rose white coils of smoke and blue coils of smoke— a promise of cooked food, hard welcome beds and sweet sleep.

At length Abbish decided to halt. Itchela slipped the nosebags over the horses' heads. But the animals chewed the fodder reluctantly, every now and then lifting their heads out of the bags to turn them this way and that, as though with an air of disapproval. They had their tongues hanging out and halfheartedly tried to swallow the morsels caught in saliva. Their viscid nostrils dilated as if endeavoring to sniff something in the air. Itchela came back from a nearby pond, with a bucket of water in either hand. The horses snorted, reared, and almost overturned the buckets as they thrust in their eager heads. In a moment the buckets were emptied. The water was still dripping freely from their muzzles, when Itchela was back with two more—this time for his own horses, and Abbish immediately set off to get a fresh supply himself. On this occasion the water did not meet with such a lively reception, but it was accepted nevertheless. Abbish replaced the bags, Itchela did likewise, and seeing with what relish the horses were now munching their oats, it whettened their own appetites. Abbish tossed a hefty lump of black rye bread over to his mate, followed by a large piece of dried sausage, and the two of them did themselves justice. Raizela called up Michael. She handed him a parcel. What treats that parcel contained!—pancakes, cheese, gingerbread, large juicy pears, all kinds of fruit juice, and what not? Reb Avram Ber muttered grace after grace over each separate victual. As for Raizela, she seemed to busy responding "Amen!" to partake of very much herself. Abbish wiped his moustache, picked the crumbs out of his beard and thanked the "children" for all the delicacies to which they had treated him. He handed Itchela a flask of water, climbed up on to his seat and gaily called out to the horses:

"Now get a move on, me beauties!"

But apparently Abbish had never been that way before, for with the best will in the world the horses could not now comply with his behest. The road ended abruptly in a stretch of soft clay. For quite an hour the wheels struggled in the mess, now sinking to the axle, now dragging themselves out again, only to go under once more, until at last the outskirts of the forest were reached, which all this while seemed so close at hand, one had only to put one's fingers out to grasp the twigs of the foremost trees. . . . A sorry illusion, for the fight took a whole hour, and with every inch of ground gained, the going got heavier—a veritable little wilderness barring meadow from forest.

"Come on, you cripple, shift yourself!" a burly young giant with a large round face and sinewy arms bawled at a small emaciated horse which had got stuck and seemed to be using its prominent ribs rather than its legs as it strained at the cartload of clay to which it was harnessed. It was doing its best to please its master, a bony peasant with a clay-besmeared face and clayey beads of sweat as big as peas on his upper lip, but the peasant flogged the animal furiously. The young giant who was looking on, himself fresh and still bursting with energy after the day's toil, put his hack and saw on to the cart, and digging himself in, put his shoulder to the cart. It bumped out of the ruts and was soon standing safely on firm ground.

Abbish was whacking his horses for all he was worth. The young giant glanced over his shoulder at him. "Jewish horses!" he muttered, and slinging his hack over his shoulder, went on his way.

Abbish lost his temper. He cursed Itchela for ill-treating the horses.

"They're not yours, are they, you big lout? You don't care if you cripple them, do you? If you weren't such a lousy, clumsy blockhead, we'd have been miles away by now."

He conveniently overlooked the fact that he was in the lead himself. The ordeal was over at last. At last they had entered the forest. They all retook their places in the carts, which stopped a while to give the horses a rest. Abbish wiped the sweat off himself and off his horses with the same dirty piece of cloth. The animals blinked and looked back at him with gratitude in their yellow eyes.

The forest was entirely ablaze. The tops of the fir trees loftily reached for the sky, which although was still a translucent blue, was scarcely noticed here.

Abbish was back on his seat, and he sent Michael packing.

"You get off of here, and stay where you belong to, and stop making yourself a nuisance!" he fumed, quite forgetting that this was not Itchela whom he was addressing. Michael did as he was told. He had had enough anyway.

Already the outer belt of the forest, on which clearing work had been begun only the week before—and it was still pretty dense—was in full retreat. The sturdy pines and slender firs were recoiling, and above the sky had emerged once more over a wide belt of whitewashed saplings—and the going was good. A pale slice of moon had come out, and soon sparkling stars were assembling, playful, frolicsome and young—just like the saplings.

But then they came to a dismal stretch of woodland. Here the corpses of once living trees stood all in disorder, their knotty backs bent, the tracery of their branches disheveled, their hideously drooping boughs all bare, so that they inspired one with dread, with terrible forebodings. These trees looked like crafty, hulking old men, and their boughs like trembling hands stretched forth, secretively, to capture something in the gathering dusk. Fear crept over Deborah, fear mingled with loathing, and she was glad when they finally came into the forest proper.

On either side of them it stretched dense and dark. The track, beaten by hoofs which had passed this way before, grew narrower and darker the deeper it penetrated into the forest. The air was perfumed, far sweeter than any honey.

"Ah! Ah! Have you ever smelt anything like it?" an unspoken question hovered on all lips, but there was no breath to spare for speech. Everybody was silent and drank in the scented May air of a Polish forest at night.

"Look, a rabbit!" cried Deborah.

Michael turned his head, but too late—the rabbit had vanished.

"What a shame, you should have seen it! It simply flew along as if it had wings. It did look dainty!"

"Ha, ha! Ever seen a rabbit look dainty?" Michael scoffed. "You're a real joke, you are!"

"You should have seen it!" Deborah persisted.

"Oh, give the rabbit a rest! I don't want to see it," said Michael, while his gaze eagerly sought the ground.

Reb Avram Ber, having said his evening prayers, decided that it would be safest for them to travel all in one cart overnight. He tugged the hem of Itchela's jacket, Itchela turned his head and listened. The uncouth fellow did not appear impressed, he disposed of Reb Avram Ber's fears with a wave of the hand, but had to yield in the end and he shouted over to Abbish to stop. Again Raizela climbed down from one cart and on to another. She did not seem very pleased about it. Abbish shared her displeasure.

"A forest," said Abbish, "is a very funny place. To dilly-dally in it is asking for trouble. The Polish forests aren't so safe as they used to be, especially at night. No, sir!"

Raizela gave him a searching look, but did not comment on his heavy sarcasm.

"That's the reason why I said it was best if we all travelled together. And we ought not to fall asleep, either," said Reb Avram Ber.

"If we do that, maybe robbers will seize us, take all our belongings and rip our guts open!" Itchela put in teasingly.

"If you keep awake," said Abbish, trying to make good Itchela's clumsy jest (that fellow was a lout!), "if you keep awake, you can always ransom your lives."

"Very comforting!" thought Raizela.

"If you don't keep awake, you may get up in the morning and find your heads lopped off, and worse still, find all your belongings gone," chimed in Michael with a great air of bravado, but he turned his face to hide the signs of fear on it.

"Michael, hold your tongue!" Reb Avram Ber admonished him, in his "sternest" manner. "Open not thy mouth unto Satan," he added in a soft, tremulous voice.

"Be quiet, idiot!" said Raizela.

Deborah shrank into her coat. Mottel closed his eyes. Michael now deeply regretted the words he had uttered. Somehow, they seemed to have intensified the hazards and perils.

When they were all in the one cart, Abbish cracked his whip, and they proceeded at a trot through the very heart of the forest. The heavy odours of the night were intoxicating. The cart rocked, swayed, and the passengers, in spite of their resolve not to fall asleep, let their heads droop one by one, raising them every now and again in an attempt to resist slumber, but weariness triumphed, and they slept soundly.

It was only when the carts had come to a standstill at R——, that everybody woke up with a start.

CHAPTER IV

The sun came up like a clot of blood, with promise of another brilliant sunny day. Deborah felt bewildered. When had they left the forest? She rubbed her eyes. Surely she had not dropped off to sleep?

They were in R——. The one-storied houses of the main street, where Abbish had pulled up to enquire from Reb Avram Ber the whereabouts of the *Tsadik*'s court, looked to her like soaring skyscrapers in her drowsy state of mind. The town slept. The windows were all draped, some with rich curtains, or embroidered blinds, others with cheap but clean half curtains, others again with sheets and even pinafores. Here and there the light of a lamp-post glowed feebly, ineffectively.

Somewhere on a bench in the open lay the sleeping figure of an old Jew—or was it a Gentile? She could not tell. He lay there all of a heap, with his head between his hands. Deborah shuddered. Never before had she seen such a pitiful sight.

Fuisher, Jelhitz's own madman, came to her mind. Even he had his couch in a loft up in the synagogue. True, there were occasions when he never went to bed, but stood slamming the door all through the night, crying that it was his mother (who was long dead) that was pushing the door to and pinning him down by his lungs and his liver every time he tried to get away. He would weep and whine, complaining that his mother was too quick for him. Ghostly the bang-bang of the door and the frenzied shouting would ring through the night-smothered village. Only with the first streaks of morning would he leave off and, exhausted, sink down into oblivion in the doorway of the synagogue. Well, he was a madman; but the huddled up person on the bench over there, one could tell—even as he slept—that that was no madman. Such a wave of pity passed over her for the poor destitute white head of hair, that a pang of hate was born in her, hatred of the town where such a sight was possible.

The carts passed slowly through the tortuous streets, and after much pother turned into a small square courtyard. Abbish and Itchela between them unloaded the cart and carried the goods away through one of the doorways in the courtyard.

"Hallo, Deborah, what are you gaping at? Don't you see, this is the end of the journey?" said Reb Avram Ber.

Deborah hardly paid any attention. She stumbled along and gazed upwards at the veiled windows. So many rooms in that one house alone, and yet there was an old man sleeping out in the street. Her people were calling her, so she went in.

"Anyhow, it's a good job there's that bench by the pump for him to sleep on," she thought, trying to console herself, but it was no use. In the end she decided that he must be a lunatic too, and she was comforted.

Soon she was engaged in viewing the rooms of their new home. All was so different from Jelhitz. The ceilings were whitewashed, but not the walls; these were painted over with a pattern of brown flowers on a blue background. Brown flowers! She could not help laughing. No wonder they were brown, growing on brick walls . . .

She paid a visit to all the three rooms and the kitchen. It was a splendid flat, with large windows, lofty and airy.

"What are you wandering around for, Deborah? You'd better help your mother arrange something to sleep on. She is so tired. And you could do with some more sleep yourself. It's only about five o'clock."

Deborah undid the bundles of bedding and rigged up two "couches" on the floor. Her mother laid herself down. Reb Avram Ber said his early morning prayers and followed her example. Ah, it was good to be able to stretch one's limbs once more! Deborah lay with her head resting on her mother's pillow.

Their first day in the small town of R—, the day which had been the focus of so many of Deborah's dreams, passed away quite unexcitedly. The family just drifted into their new life, and the only strange sensation was a certain unpleasant feeling of loneliness . . .

Reb Avram Ber was the first to awake.

"Where's Michael?" he said, rousing Deborah.

Raizela heard him in her sleep.

"Oh dear, what's happened to him?" She wrung her hands. "Where could Michael have got to? He'll lose himself in this strange place."

As he was nowhere to be found in the courtyard, nor in any of the closets, there would have been quite a hue and cry, had not Michael turned up at that very moment, his face all beaming. He failed to see the black looks which were given him, in which joy mingled with dark threats. He rushed into the room where Mottel was lying and gave him a kick. Mottel opened a pair of sleepy, rather bad-tempered eyes, which stared at him in amazement.

"What a lot of sleepyheads!" cried Michael, actually referring only to Mottel. He said "a lot," because it added emphasis. "If you had only seen what I've seen! Crumbs, what a town! What a town! Just like Jelhitz, and I don't think!"

"Where have you been, eh?" asked Reb Avram Ber, trying to be stern.

"Nowhere!"

"Where's nowhere?" interposed Raizela crossly.

"I was in the courtyard."

"But you weren't in the courtyard!"

"I was!" persisted Michael.

"Well, what's the use? So long as he's back, the scamp!"

Reb Avram Ber felt that it was incumbent on him to act the host here. He conducted Raizela round the rooms. Although he had seen them before, he studied them with fresh interest and drew her attention to all the good points. Raizela did not show the least sign of pleasure. She looked vexed and grieved, although there was nothing she could find fault with. All was admirable. The walls were freshly done up, the ceilings spotless and smooth—vastly superior to Jelhitz, but somehow the place did not appeal to her. At least in Jelhitz one had had something tangible to disapprove of.

"Good, eh?" inquired Reb Avram Ber with much satisfaction.

An ancient knee thrust open the front door, and the owner of the limb appeared, bearing a tray in his flabby old hands that trembled palpably. The tray was crowded with tumblers, spoons, a jugful of warm milk, a bowl of sugar, several gingerbreads and a steaming kettle. The old man staggered up. He deposited the tray, rectified his crooked back somewhat, and still panting breathlessly, fumbled for something in his pocket.

"The *Tsadik*, that is to say the old lady, his mother, sends you these refreshments, with her compliments," he said, helping himself to a pinch of snuff.

"Thank you," said Raizela.

"He, he! No need to thank *me*! If the *Tsadik*, that is to say, the old lady, his mother hadn't sent me—he, he, he!—I can assure you I wouldn't have brought you all this of my own accord!"

Even Raizela condescended to smile. Reb Avram Ber was delighted.

"Well, Reb Baruch, do you think we shall be comfortable here?"

"Why, of course, you will, of course! I wish I was in your shoes. You know, the *Tsadik* himself sent in word to his mother, telling her to tell the—atchoo!—the beadle to tell the cook to hand me . . . Atchoo! Atchoo!!"

Michael was struggling with inner mirth—this was evident from the concerted twitching of his features. He was either going to laugh or make some very witty remark. But he was afraid to chance it in front of a newcomer in a new town. . . . He held his peace.

"Take a seat, Reb Baruch!" Reb Avram Ber invited the old man to join them, forgetting the while that there were no chairs.

The old man glanced about him.

"Why, you've nothing to sit on yourselves."

"That's all right, we'll soon remedy that," said Reb Avram Ber, himself pushing a box up.

They all settled down on cases and bundles of bedding. Deborah poured out the tea. Mottel felt that it was good to be alive to-day. He was like one of the family. Reb Avram Ber pressed the old man to accept a glass of tea. Raizela moved away on to the farthest bundle, and eagerly drank from her glass—her throat was parched. The old man, feeling Reb Avram Ber's friendly gaze fixed on him, began telling them all about the *yeshiva*. Reb Avram Ber exulted. Every now and then he cast a glance at Raizela to see if she was impressed.

The repast over, Reb Avram Ber passed his red-spotted handkerchief across his moustache. Their visitor, helping himself to more snuff, also wiped his mouth dry—with the flat of his hand. Then he accompanied Reb Avram Ber to the synagogue.

"Good morning!" the old man stuttered at the door, just managing to hold back a sneeze.

"How about you, Mottel? I expect to see you at the synagogue soon. And you too, Michael, I don't want you to dawdle," said Reb Avram Ber from the threshold.

Mottel slipped into the kitchen where Deborah was sulking in a corner. Mottel knew the cause of her bitterness: he had overheard Raizela scold her without any justification whatever, whereas Michael, who had been playing truant, had been let off without so much as a word. Favouritism, thought Mottel, not without indignation.

"How do you like it here?" he asked, because he wanted to say something to her, and immediately a thought struck him that this was a stupid question, for as yet they had seen nothing of the place either to like or dislike.

"So-so!" Deborah answered him morosely.

"What's the matter?" Mottel persisted, feeling more awkward than ever. Perhaps he ought not to have asked any questions?

"Do you believe in luck?" Deborah asked.

Now that was a peculiar question! It was so unexpected.

"Why, yes!" he said. And perhaps there was no such thing after all? Anyhow, none of it had ever come his way.

About two in the afternoon a rosy-cheeked girl with short chubby arms and gay eyes knocked at the door.

"The *Tsadik*'s mother has asked me to come along and help you put things straight," she announced.

This was a welcome visit.

Reb Avram Ber came home for a few brief minutes to have his lunch, and then went off to the *yeshiva* to deliver his first lecture.

"It would be a pity to waste any time," he told Raizela apologetically.

The maid set to work with a will. Now she was cleaning the windows and soon she was scrubbing the floors. Deborah offered to lend a hand, but quite offended her. Raizela was not a little amused by the girl's vanity. It was inconceivable that she always toiled with so much zest, but that she was no slattern like Hannah, that much was clear.

"Now I'll go and fetch the dinner," she said, unpinning her tucked up frock. She combed her hair with a broken comb, wiped her face on the edge of her pinafore and studied her reflection in the gleaming windowpanes. She returned with a heavy load of many dishes. The table-cloth, which Deborah had found for her, she spread out over several cases pushed together, and this hilly table she laid with massive silver cutlery and a fine porcelain dinner-service. Nothing was omitted, not even the pepper-pot.

While going about her task, with a more leisurely air now, she informed Raizela that the *Tsadik*'s wife—the "young one," as she called her—was a real diamond, and that his mother, the "old one," ought to take a lesson from her in good manners. If she, the maid, had been born under a lucky star and had not been an orphan, she would have entered the service of the young one and not the service of the old one. She collected the tea-things, and after being very strongly pressed by Raizela, departed with fifteen kopecks in pocket.

A few days later, Laizer Nussen, the elder of the *Tsadik*'s five personal attendants, and the most insolent, the most blackguardedly of them all, appointed himself—quite against Reb Avram Ber's will—as his right hand. He got hold of Reb Avram Ber's money for the purchase of furniture, ordered goods according to his own taste, consulted no one but himself, and spent just as much as he thought he would. Raizela hated the fellow; but such trivial matters as love and hate impressed Laizer Nussen not at all. He was nothing if not hardheaded and practical. Raizela's cautions to Reb Avram Ber not to trust him proved of no avail. He simply had to trust him, for such was Laizer Nussen's wish, and when Laizer Nussen wished a thing, he had his way with folks far wilier than Reb Avram Ber.

However, when the time came round for erecting the furniture, Laizer Nussen considered his duties at an end and he charged Reb Baruch to accomplish the task with the help of Zelik, the *Tsadik*'s manservant.

In spite of the fact that old Baruch was forever protesting that by rights none other than himself was the elder of the *Tsadik*'s personal attendants, and that had the father of the present *Tsadik* survived (his memory be blessed!), none other than he, Baruch, would have lorded it in the Court, with Laizer Nussen a mere nobody—but the old *Tsadik* (his memory be blessed!) had departed this life many a year ago and was probably now holding Court in paradise—in spite of all this, Baruch was under the orders of Laizer Nussen, always at his beck and call, and all he could do to express his rightful indignation was to take a pinch of snuff. To be sure he also found consolation in whisky taken neat. But old Henya, Baruch's wife, always maintained that it was only since he had been deprived of his mantle of glory by Laizer Nussen that he had taken to tippling, and she denied the assertions of certain old inhabitants who would have it that Baruch had been addicted to his drop of whisky even at the best of times. Anyhow, a grand old man was Reb Baruch, never drunk, though always drinking, and even though oftentimes, when he drifted away into dreams of the days gone by, when he romanced over tales of yore, he would lie on a shocking scale, giving the most fantastic descriptions replete with the minutest details to stamp them as authentic, still you could not help liking him and, what was more, became deeply absorbed in his yarns. One look at Reb Baruch was enough! It was fascinating to see him go into raptures, see his dim old eyes light up again and a smile play on his lips, himself fully believing in all those strange events and miracles which happened in the lifetime of the old *Tsadik* (his memory be blessed!), when he, Baruch, had bossed it in the Court, with Laizer Nussen still unborn. Deborah adored these yarns, as she did the teller of them. And she positively came to hate Laizer Nussen for having usurped old Baruch's authority. Even Raizela was well disposed to him. She only used to marvel how so old and flabby a man, with one foot in the grave, came to be possessed of so fertile an imagination.

Zelik put up the beds—wooden beds with carved tops—beds that were remarkable in many ways. For one thing they looked distinctive, and for another they were dirt cheap, costing (as Laizer Nussen said) next to nothing. Actually, of course, twenty-five roubles for a couple of beds was a tidy bit, but then (as Laizer Nussen said) there are beds and beds. What beds! What a polish and a glitter, and the workmanship put into the carvings!

"Don't you like them?" said Laizer Nussen to Raizela. "What, you think the wood cheap? Well, what of it? You don't mean to tell me that it's the wood that counts. Rubbish, you're not going to fight the beds! Ah, may the Lord grant you good health and happiness in them!

"What's that? They'll start groaning later on when you get into them? Nonsense! Give them a dose of oil and they'll soon be cured. Ha, ha! Surely they're no better than mortal men," Laizer Nussen philosophised, and took his leave after repeating his instructions to Zelik.

Baruch rendered help by croaking to the rhythm of Zelik's hammer and by handing up the wrong tools. When the pincers were wanted, he delivered a screwdriver. This rather annoyed Zelik, but he refrained from rudeness. After all, Baruch was one of the *Tsadik*'s personal attendants and an old man besides. Indeed, Baruch had grandchildren who were of the same age as Zelik. Furthermore, he had a warm corner in his heart for the old man.

When he had done with the beds and had given them a shaking to test their strength, Zelik turned his attentions to the wardrobe; this too had its good points if one looked for them.

"It's just a bit on the narrow side," said Zelik, "and it's too much of a featherweight. Why, you could carry it off on your back."

However, the table eclipsed and atoned for everything: it was large and robust, with a high polish through which biggish inkstains were visible—apparently second-hand, but that was a detail. It was a table not to be compared with other tables. When a man could sit at a table like that, with its legs planted firmly on the floor like a bear's paws, with its edges a mass of carving, with its polish positively dazzling, and yet the whole so massive, so solemn, it gave him added inspiration for the study of the Talmud (said Laizer Nussen), and even food, when served on such a table, gained added relish. On the other hand, the kitchen table was brand new. So was the kitchen bench. The dresser was spick and span and had a commanding position opposite the door. As for the bench, that was finished off at either end with scallops. In each scallop a hold had been bored most artistically, and from under each hole a brass button sent forth a golden glitter.

"A pity they're not varnished. If I were you I'd have them varnished," said Zelik thoughtfully to Raizela. "Like this they'll get dirty in no time."

"Don't be an ass!" Baruch put in, to the accompaniment of a pinch of snuff. "Varnish-shmarnish! It's when they get dirty that you want to varnish them, not before! Ass!"

Zelik categorically refused to accept any beer-money.

"May you enjoy it all in the best of health," he said and, collecting his tools, went off. Baruch followed him out, and now once more the family were installed in a home of their own, for which the Lord be praised.

Raizela had everything new: new furniture, a new home, a new town, a new life . . . But with all this newness something else that was new stole over her—a new feeling of gloom, which depressed her without cause, a sense of oppression that grew heavier day by day, whilst Raizela's purse grew lighter day by day. Not that this was the source of the strange misery lurking in their new home, which Deborah tried for the time being at any rate to keep as prim as possible.

On the other hand, Reb Avram Ber daily returned from the *yeshiva* with fresh tidings of joy: students were flocking in from all parts of the country; the *yeshiva* was already one of the most important in Poland; soon there would be no vacancies for fresh arrivals, and they would have to be turned back, unless a new wing was added to the building.

On the previous Sabbath, at his usual banquet, the *Tsadik*, while expounding the law, had introduced many scripture texts, allusions and insinuations in his sermon to demonstrate how great were the heavenly rewards bestowed upon the charitable of the land who enabled poor Jewish students to pursue their studies of the Talmud. He begged—nay, commanded—every inhabitant of R— to make certain of securing such heavenly reward by inviting students to share the family board for at least one day in the week, as is the custom among pious Jews. This noble deed could be rendered nobler still by well-to-do people who could afford to share their board with students several days during the week. The *Tsadik* stated that for the time being the students were being fed in the communal kitchen established in the Court, that the kitchen would be maintained hereafter as heretofore, but that to further the work of the *yeshiva,* it was essential that outside assistance should be volunteered, and solemnly he charged his followers to participate in his most holy mission. Solemnly two rows of beards pointed downwards at the long table. Solemnly the throng of *hassidim* standing around the table shook their heads. After this the *Tsadik* returned to his usual preachings, and went off into celestial raptures . . . The

Tsadik's appeal soon spread all over town, and Jews freely offered their hospitality to the students—not for several days in the week, to be sure, but a large number invited students home for one day in the week.

Reb Avram Ber delivered his lectures day by day. Michael attended in the company of students many years his senior, but he was not a jot behind them. Deborah had plenty of housework to keep her occupied. Raizela alone found the time hanging heavy on her hands. Somehow she could find no relish in any of the books she picked up; she had not settled down yet, had not become accustomed to the feel of the new couch, which incidentally, like herself, had a very feeble constitution.

"You know, you would be well advised to pay a call on the *Tsadik*'s wife. It would make a delightful change. She's quite an exceptional person—a person of real dignity. She comes of a very good stock—the Balzaker *Tsadik* is her father—and she's very clever. Moreover, she's a learned woman," said Reb Avram Ber, and as he said these last few words, he scanned Raizela's face to see how they would impress her. Raizela smiled. She reflected that it would be well if some fitting occasion were to arise.

It arose very simply. One sunny morning the *Tsadik*'s wife sent her maid in with an invitation to Raizela. The girl did not look like a servant at all, dressed as she was in a neat white frock with a little white starched pinafore over it, and patent leather shoes on her tiny feet; nor did her face betray her—a pretty blonde with a captivating smile. As she entered, she simply brought new life into the place.

"The *Tsadik*'s wife begs you to be good enough to call on her for tea this afternoon," she said to the accompaniment of such a radiant smile, that even Raizela's thin lips parted.

The *Tsadik*'s wife, clad in a long black silk dress, with a long string of costly pearls round her white, plump throat, rose to her feet when Raizela entered, also clad in a black dress, but without a string of pearls on her thin, skinny neck. She came forward to welcome her visitor, bade her be seated, and directly created a favourable impression on Raizela. The woman's frank, clever expression, especially the eyes, were bound to please, and certainly Raizela was a keen judge of character. For the rest, everything in the chamber was set out so originally, with so much good taste, the mistress and her surroundings harmonised so perfectly, that the effect could not but please. The drapings on the walls, the silk curtains by the door and windows, dark blue and quiet; the furniture simple and yet artistically splendid—all was at one and endowed with her spirit. The atmosphere in the chamber was caressingly gentle: it did one's heart good, soothed the heavy spirit, dispelled oppressive thoughts, and characterized the individual who had known so well to arrange it all. Raizela felt at ease—in her own element. This was the milieu she was always pining for.

The *Tsadik*'s wife showed her a copy of a newly published book which had reached her only that morning and which had been sent to her by a nephew, who incidentally was its author. Afterwards she led her to the book-case, opened the glass panel and introduced her to what she called her "friends"—a rare collection of books in which she took great pride. She considered herself something of a connoisseur, and proved as much to Raizela by indirect means. . . . In front of this imposing array of books, Raizela felt sorely tempted, as though she had suddenly entered a large garden full of all kinds of fragrant flowers, none of which she could pluck, even though the mistress politely offered them to her. The *Tsadik*'s wife closed the book-case again. They returned to their seats, and the maid with the pleasing frank face served tea and biscuits on an engraved silver tray which was deeply wrinkled with age. The spoons, the sugar bowl, the tongs, all bore the same blazonry as the tray and all showed the same signs of antiquity, bearing tribute to their common descent from an old and powerful family.

"Why, you haven't touched your tea yet. Please don't let it get cold. Would you rather have some fruit juice?"

"Oh no, thanks, please don't trouble!"

"As I was saying, we can never be lonely when we have our books, that is of course the right type of books," the *Tsadik*'s wife resumed, speaking for Raizela as well as for herself and again hinting that

Raizela could have free access to the library if she wished. "You see, I know all about you. The Rabbi (Reb Avram Ber) has told me all, and a passion for books is a fault we both of us share."

Raizela smiled with real pleasure.

When she returned home and told Reb Avram Ber where she had been, adding that she had found the *Tsadik*'s wife pleasant company, Reb Avram Ber stroked his beard with such an air of rejoicing, he could not have been more pleased if an unknown uncle had left him a million roubles.

"And what a wonderful collection of books she has!" said Raizela as an afterthought.

"You see! Didn't I always tell you that you would be far happier here than in Jelhitz. You never had anyone to exchange a word with in Jelhitz, but here you already have such a splendid friend. She's a very fine woman! So gentle . . ."

"True!" Raizela agreed.

"At present you only have a first impression. You'll think even more highly of her when you get to know her well," said Reb Avram Ber, his face wreathed in smiles, and he went on to say how the *Tsadik*'s wife was so esteemed by her husband's *hassidim*, that many of them would not dream of paying him a visit without calling on her to pay her their respects.

"That shows how much they think of her. And to tell you the truth," added Reb Avram Ber, dropping his voice as though he feared the walls might hear him, "I've come to the conclusion that she's more deserving of respect than is . . ." Reb Avram Ber did not finish the sentence.

But Raizela understood. She was silent.

In the *yeshiva* all went smoothly. It stood in a corner of the spacious courtyard of the *Tsadik*'s residence full of majesty with its new bricks a fiery red and its corrugated iron roof glowing beneath the sun's scorching breath. The large windows were all flung wide open, and from them issued a sweet, melancholy chant which floated over the courtyard, turning and twisting and swelling, till it reached the street; then suddenly it withdrew, curling itself up secretly, full of mystery, but soon it rang out again boldly through the whole courtyard, and above all the voices that melted into one chant could be heard Reb Avram Ber's gentle and fatherly "*Yesh Omrim . . .*"

Mottel rejoiced in the unlooked-for opportunity that came his way one morning when Reb Avram Ber, having left his pipe at home, picked on none other than Mottel to go and fetch it for him. Mottel, now taking his meals in the communal kitchen, had not been to Reb Avram Ber's house for a long time. He had hoped that one day he would receive an invitation, but that had not occurred to Reb Avram Ber at all, for he saw the boy every day, and how was he to guess that Mottel was simply burning with desire to see Deborah? Mottel set out for the pipe like a pirate for hidden treasure, but fate was against him. It so chanced that on the very same morning Deborah had decided to go along to catch a glimpse of the *Tsadik*. She had not yet seen him in the flesh, and having learnt that he was due to deliver the first of a series of weekly lectures at the *yeshiva*, she lay in wait for him in one of the many doorways of the spacious courtyard. The place was quite empty, save for a few old women who waddled in like ducks, then waddled out again, leaving a void once more, and for an excited-looking youth, bearing a strong resemblance to Mottel, who rushed out of the *yeshiva* as though the building were on fire.

Time wore on and still nothing happened, until she began to think that she had come on a fool's errand. A faraway clock struck the hour—eleven peals floating through the quiet air. The last stroke had scarcely died away, when the *Tsadik* suddenly appeared in the court-yard with one of his personal attendants. His tread was firm and strong, and his boots met the cobbles fairly and squarely, resounding through the huge square courtyard like the pounding of a horse's hoofs. Deborah recoiled, as though afraid of profaning a holy pres-ence, but on giving him a second furtive look, it was a feeling of alarm and not of awe that took possession of her. The man fright-ened her by his very size. Never in all her life had she seen such a gigantic Jew. What a height! What a girth! And what a belly! Never before in all her life had she seen such a tremendous creature. His shiny black silken gabardine was unbuttoned, and on his projecting paunch the white ritual fringe garment with its wide black stripes billowed out as though filled with a strong breeze. His beard was terribly long, it reached down to his waist. And his face was a shining red mass of flesh—utterly coarse! There was nothing holy about his appearance, in spite of the great length of beard. There was a crafty and self-satisfied twinkle in his luminous eyes. Deborah gaped. Could this really be the *Tsadik* himself? She compared him with the image of her grandfather, of her father. How utterly different! There was no comparison. A strange *Tsadik* indeed!

Suddenly, as she stood musing over the *Tsadik*, vainly trying to recover from her amazement, she became aware of two blazing dark eyes fixed upon herself with a look that touched her to the quick; a tall and lean young man was approaching, clad or rather wrapped up in a long, shabby gabardine encircled by a half-torn sash. He went by swiftly, seeming to float over the ground. His eyes were large and deep-set in a lean pale face all cheekbones. In passing, the eyes gave her another flash, which stirred her to the depths, and then this young man too vanished in the doorway of the *yeshiva*.

"Now that's a funny looking *Tsadik*!" said Deborah to herself, trying hard not to think of the young man. Perhaps she had been mistaken? Perhaps that big fat man was only one of the attendants? But no, an attendant would not be wearing a silken gabardine on a weekday, nor would he have on a rabbinical fur hat. That hat was easily thrice as big as her father's and how comically it was perched on the head. Both the hat and the head had a knowing air, as though the two of them were in a conspiracy.

She laughed aloud.

Now that young man with the blazing eyes looked more like a real *Tsadik*. At this thought she crimsoned. But undeniably there was something deeply spiritual and intellectual about that lanky figure.

On the way home she stopped at the butcher's to get some chops for dinner.

Later on in the day, when she attempted to picture the *Tsadik* to her mother, a new surprise lay in store for her. Raizela showed not the least sign of astonishment. She just listened with an amused smile.

"Well, that's splendid! I am glad to hear that the *Tsadik* is looking hale and hearty. Splendid!"

That was her mother's sole comment. It was all very weird. . . .

CHAPTER V

The weeks passed into months and Raizela's purse dwindled until it was positively consumptive. There was scarcely enough money to buy food with, and still the *Tsadik* neglected to pay any stipend. By this time even Reb Avram Ber, who had imagined all along that it was the *Tsadik*'s intention to make payment in a lump sum, began to grow uneasy and at length he approached him about it (although he had to fight a bitter struggle before he could bring himself to do so).

"Give me a call at five o'clock, and then we shall see what we can do for you," was the *Tsadik*'s reply, as though he were answering an appeal for charity.

Reb Avram Ber smarted, but did as he was told. One must live . . . There was the family to think of . . .

The *Tsadik* asked him to take a seat. Then he informed Reb Avram Ber that shortly he would be going away to take the waters. In a peremptory tone of voice he charged Reb Avram Ber to keep the *yeshiva* up to the mark and to maintain discipline among the students. After that he turned to the subject of the communal kitchen, intimating that in the absence of his mother, who was accompanying him to the watering-place, the establishment would be run by Laizer Nussen's wife. Money would be provided by himself for the purpose. Next he discoursed on a knotty Talmudic problem, racking his brains all the while for some subterfuge to escape his obligations. Then came a brooding silence; in the end he vanquished his own reluctance. He rose to his feet, drew aside a dark green plush curtain and vanished into a chamber, the existence of which Reb Avram Ber to-day discovered for the first time. He heard the *Tsadik* jingle a bunch of keys, and there was a turning of heavy locks. When the *Tsadik* emerged, he hurriedly stuffed two paper notes into Reb Avram Ber's hand together with some silver coins. Reb Avram Ber handed them over to Raizela after evening prayers—five and twenty roubles in all. This restored confidence in the home.

"He seems to prefer paying a lump sum," said Reb Avram Ber.

"I don't see how you make that out," Deborah put in. "Why, there's over a hundred roubles owing already."

"Don't be silly. This is obviously just something to get on with," Reb Avram Ber reassured her. "I'm certain he'll let me have the rest before he leaves."

Meanwhile in the *Tsadik*'s Court preparations were in full swing for the coming departure. Again several weeks went by without Reb Avram Ber receiving any further payment. The family were beginning to feel the pinch; each passing day brought them nearer to destitution. Reb Avram Ber could not understand it at all; but the *Tsadik* could—only too well! He held forth on the achievements of the *yeshiva* almost daily, impressing on the public how holy a mission this was and how it was incumbent on them to do everything in their power to support the institution's material welfare. He quite worked himself up into a frenzy when appealing to the inhabitants of the town to accommodate in their homes as many of the students as possible, in order to lighten the burden on the communal kitchen. The whole court was echoing with appeals. Now at last he was on the point of departure, and still Reb Avram Ber heard nothing from him. When Reb Avram Ber, after many broken resolutions, finally brought himself to speak to the *Tsadik* about it, the *Tsadik* airily dismissed his request with a promise to attend to the matter in the near future. Time wore on, and still nothing happened. For some reason or other, the proposed journey was put off, no one knew why. Reb Avram Ber remained hopeful.

Then, when all preparations were complete down to the last detail, the *Tsadik*, surrounded by a veritable army of personal attendants and manservants, even including a ritual slaughterer, took his departure without giving any notice, and Reb Avram Ber was left behind empty-handed. The *Tsadik*'s mother went off with her own personal suite, his wife left soon after with hers. When bidding good-bye to Raizela, she asked her whether she was going away this summer. Somehow the *Tsadik*'s wife had guessed that all was not going well with the family, and she purposely put this question to test her suspicions. The whole truth of the matter, that her husband had left Reb Avram Ber absolutely penniless, was so improbable as not even to enter her mind. Raizela said in reply that she had not quite made her mind up yet. From this the *Tsadik*'s wife inferred more than Raizela would have had her infer. She sent for Reb Avram Ber, offered him a loan of twenty-five roubles, informed him that she would have a talk with the *Tsadik* about his obligations, although she could not say that she exerted any great influence with him, and—but here her voice faded into a murmur inaudible to Reb Avram Ber . . .

There was unrest in the *yeshiva*. There was anger at the *yeshiva*. The hospitality extended by the townsfolk to the students was far from sufficient for keeping them fed day by day or even every other day. As for the communal kitchen, the soup served there grew thinner from mealtime to mealtime, as did the students. They began to look haggard through under-nourishment. Many of them left the town. Reb Avram Ber was, of course, powerless to hold them back. Nor could he infuse those who remained with any zest for their studies. So the Talmud suffered too . . . Laizer Nussen's wife showed no inclination to expend any of her own money on the kitchen. The trifling sum the *Tsadik* had left in her care was soon consumed. The students clamoured for food, but there was none to be had. The butcher, the baker, the grocer—every one of them, to a man, refused to grant any credit. They were not going to give their goods away and then have to go cringing to the *Tsadik* for their due, following him about like beggars seeking alms, such was their unassailable argument.

The *yeshiva* went to pieces. If a student had a home to go to, he did not think twice about leaving. Reb Avram Ber's mind began to wander: it was all like a nightmare and he saw no means of shaking it off.

Again Raizela spent whole days on end reclining upon her couch. Deborah had become, not merely the housekeeper, but the family charwoman and washerwoman. She was taught her work by the neighbours, who never wearied in telling her that an honest day's toil never did anyone any harm, it was good for a girl, and what was good for their own daughters was good for her too. Deborah came to hate them. It was obvious that the neighbours took great pleasure in seeing her upon her knees, and she wondered why it should afford them so much joy. What gratification was there in the sight of her scrubbing a floor?

Mottel again took his meals—such as they were—with the family. He abused the *Tsadik* most vilely (not, however, in the presence of Reb Avram Ber, who would not allow it in spite of everything). Michael came home from the *yeshiva* every evening with a new store of jokes at the *Tsadik*'s expense. These witticisms grew funnier and more biting as the plight of the students became worse. Michael was himself the author of many of them. He also gave imitations of the *Tsadik* making a propaganda speech on behalf of the *yeshiva*, his voice quavering rapturously and his hands flung above his head in a frenzy of holiness. In this Michael was inimitable, and his efforts were greeted with hysterical laughter. It was the sole ray of cheerfulness that pierced the heavy gloom. Thanks to Michael, not only Deborah and Mottel, but also Raizela would laugh, thus forgetting her troubles for a little while.

Also, the young man with the luminous dark eyes and prominent cheekbones, the one whom Deborah had seen go by on that disturbing morning when she had been out to catch a glimpse of the *Tsadik*, now frequented their home as the personal guest of Reb Avram Ber. Deborah felt that there was something mysterious about him. For one thing, he consistently refused food, always saying that he had just finished a meal somewhere or other. Discussion, that seemed to be his passion—Talmudic debates with her father. She did not know the reason why, but whenever he visited the home, everything seemed to brighten up, all worries were forgotten and life became delightful. He introduced a strange, as it were rarefied atmosphere in the house, dispelling all cares. And yet in himself he was far from cheerful. He seemed to be of a rather gloomy disposition. Even Raizela was impressed by him, saying that it was a joy to hear him talk, although of course he barely exchanged a word with the womenfolk. He was extremely aloof, keeping himself to himself even when he was at a person's side. Deborah came to the conclusion that he must be fanatically religious. As for earning her mother's admiration, that was indeed an achievement, which caused Deborah both pain and pleasure—pain because she was herself so little thought of by her mother, and pleasure because . . . simply because it pleased her! She had once overheard Raizela sing his praises to Reb Avram Ber.

"A young man of exceptional spirit," her mother had said. "He obviously has great powers of intellectual concentration, and there is nothing boastful about him. It's quite a treat to have him here."

"Well, he's far away the most brilliant student we have, you know. He's a wonderful boy. I only wish I had the means, I'd take him as a husband for our daughter."

That always made Deborah laugh. It would be quite a joke, getting engaged. Ah, how her former friends would all envy her! And that woman Surka in the grocery shop would not dare to be so rude to her any more. Deborah could just fancy herself as a bride . . .

Only in some ways he seemed rather unreasonable. Why was it that he could never walk along deliberately like other people? What made him rush so? And what thing was it that his eyes were forever seeking? When he discussed the Talmud with her father, why did he have to be so intent and cutting? At such times his eyes seemed to become an even deeper black, and they bulged from their sockets, flashing fire. But even when he was only listening his eyes were different from other people's. But there was a strange beauty in them, and they held some secret also. Peculiar eyes! He was handsome. If he were better dressed, she thought, he would be exceedingly handsome . . .

Undeniably her spirits rose to festive heights in his presence. She would become so absorbed, that she never even noticed Mottel's

jealousy. He would turn green with envy when that radiant look
came to her face directly the stranger entered. Now, she had a liking
for Mottel too. He supplied her with books, and had talks with her
whenever he got the chance. He once lent her a book which he cau-
tioned her to read in dead secret. She must never in all her life tell
anyone about it, nor in any circumstances divulge its source. He
impressed upon her that this was the only type of book an enlight-
ened person should read. Not only did one derive much benefit
from the reading of such books, it was one's sacred duty to read
them. And then he confided to her, as a solemn secret, the fact that
it was the dark-eyed stranger who distributed this literature. This
came as a terrible shock to her. But little by little the surprise wore
off. Mottel told her incidentally that the stranger was a freethinker.
She never repeated a word of all this. She had given her oath not to.
But it was most unfair of Mottel to have let out such a secret in the
first place. Perhaps that was why she felt more attracted to the
stranger . . .

As the summer wore on, a number of fires broke out in the
Tsadik's Court. They were not of a very serious nature, and were
soon extinguished. But they developed into a little epidemic, hardly
a week passing without its fire. Here an overturned candle was found
blazing on a table. There a dropped cigarette end had set the wooden
floor smouldering. Next the cloth on the mantelpiece over the grate
in the communal kitchen caught light. Flames might shoot up anywhere. No one could understand it and there was a great deal of
speculation. Nothing like it had ever happened before. However, as
the fires were always quickly got under control, with little serious
damage done, the Lord was praised for His clemency as well as being
thanked for His little mercies in providing the townsfolk with a topic
of conversation on these drowsy summer days when no one had any
inclination for work and besides there was none to be done. The
Tsadik and everybody else that mattered were away, the flow of *hassidim* had ceased for the time being, the communal kitchen was as
good as closed. Actually, therefore, the fires were a blessing in disguise, occupying the minds and tongues of neighbours lolling in the

narrow streets and courtyards under a fierce sun which sent the whole town to sleep.

Deborah found more variety in life than ever she had done in Jelhitz. There the days used to pass with a greater sense of security, with no expectancy of strange things to come; from morning to night and from night to morning time used to go its irksome way with unbroken monotony. Now life was unsettled, harsh circumstances played havoc with it. Trouble and cares descended on the family from all quarters, came swarming in like vermin from the walls of a rotten building, creeping forth from every chink, and each time one chink was stopped up, two others appeared in its place. . . .

But matters came to a head when one morning a woman dressed all in black came to their door and, announcing herself as the landlady, vociferously demanded the rent. Now that was something they had not bargained for at all. All this time Reb Avram Ber and his family had laboured under the illusion that the house they were living in was the property of the *Tsadik*, and that, in accordance with his promise, they were entitled to their flat rent-free. He had never said a word about the payment of rent and of course no such possibility had ever entered their minds. It transpired, however, that Laizer Nussen had paid for the first quarter in advance, and the next payment was now overdue. The house actually belonged to this widow in mourning, who at the end of each quarter would come down from Warsaw to collect her rent. Madam was a shrew. She did not believe in sparing anyone's feelings. Raizela assured her for the hundredth time that it was the *Tsadik*'s liability, not theirs, and that he was sure to pay in full on returning from his holidays. But the woman refused to listen to reason.

"Whatever arrangement you have with the *Tsadik*, is *your* affair, I'm not interested. All I know is that you live here and therefore you must pay the rent," she said with an air of finality, and nothing would move her.

"But why didn't you ever show up before, why didn't you get in touch with us in the first place? Then we should have avoided all this unpleasantness," Raizela pressed the woman, but she, taking a seat by the window, unbuttoned her costly black coat, detached the black veil from her black hat, put her black kid gloves upon the table, crossed her black silk-stockinged legs, and settled down as if she would wait for ever—unless she got her rent, that is.

Reb Avram Ber was lecturing in the *yeshiva* at the time. Deborah ran to fetch him. She told him the story hastily, in as few words as she could.

"Mamma is quite distracted. Something must be done quickly. The woman won't go away, she won't go away!"

"Hm!" Reb Avram Ber muttered, looking first one way, then the other, as if he had lost something. "Oh merciful God, creator of the heaven and earth and all that in them is, do not forsake me! Pray help me, help me!" Reb Avram Ber pleaded, like a child pleading with its father, and shattered by the news—the last thing he could have expected—a broken man, he hastened home.

"Good morning!" he said, partly addressing the woman, but with his eyes fixed anxiously on Raizela.

The woman stirred.

"Pray be seated, be seated," Reb Avram Ber said, still the perfect gentleman.

She kept her seat.

"Couldn't you possibly give us a few weeks' respite? God willing, we shall not keep you waiting very long, and I assure you that not a single groschen will you lose."

Neither Reb Avram Ber nor Raizela had kept their wits about them sufficiently to realise that this woman had no legal claim upon them, since Laizer Nussen had rented the flat on the *Tsadik*'s behalf. The woman knew this full well, but was trying her luck. She might as well get her money now as later.

"You see, I am a widow. God grant that you may never be one yourself! Just a poor widow," she explained to Reb Avram Ber. "And it wouldn't be right to keep me waiting for my money, now would it? A lonely widow, that's what I am, and I have no one to care for me. And that's why I . . ."

"Up above," said Reb Avram Ber, and he involuntarily raised his eyes heavenwards, "up above widows and orphans are guarded over."

He uttered these words with such fervour, that the set of the woman's mouth, with its heavy furrow on either side, softened somewhat, and a glistening moisture even entered her eyes. She rose from her chair, put on her hat and lowered the crepe over her face.

"Well, then I have your promise, Rabbi, that you will let me have payment within the next four weeks?"

"Yes, God willing! But I never said how many weeks. For all I know I may be able to let you have the money before then—everything is possible with the Lord!—but maybe it will take rather longer than that. He is almighty!" Reb Avram Ber added, as though speaking to himself.

The woman slipped a black glove on to her fingers, making her apologies to Raizela the while. Had she not been a widow . . .

"Now what are we going to do?" Raizela demanded of Reb Avram Ber, who, as it happened, was at that very instant putting the very same question to God Almighty. "The strange part about it is that this woman should have left us in peace all this while. It's not like her to miss any of her tenants. Of all our afflictions, I never dreamt, never imagined, that this one would be coming to us. Never! Well, I suppose we owe that woman a tidy sum of money now."

"Yes, but the *Tsadik* promised to give us free accommodation, and I scarcely think he would care to compromise himself with such a woman, who would certainly not hesitate to damage his good name. She's the more dangerous because she does not live in these parts, and I think that when he comes back he'll let her have the rent without further ado."

This did not seem altogether unreasonable to Raizela, but was there any certainty?

"Have you anything in writing to support your claim?" Raizela inquired, merely for the sake of saying something. She knew full well that Reb Avram Ber had no such thing and would scorn the very idea of it.

"Of course not! You don't imagine I would ask the *Tsadik* for a written agreement!"

"Of course not," Raizela repeated Reb Avram Ber's words, and turned away from him. She picked up a book, but not a single word could she understand, nor could she repress the nervous tremors of her emaciated body, which, like a thing apart from herself, quivered violently and would not be soothed.

"Will you have something to eat, father?"

"I have not said my morning prayers yet," Reb Avram Ber replied, as he wandered up and down the room with knitted brow. He kept tugging at his beard and muttered something inarticulate to himself all the time.

"Do be calm," he said finally, approaching Raizela. "The Lord will not forsake us. Believe me, everything will turn out for the best. These troubles will pass, and meantime you mustn't destroy yourself with worry."

His plea remained unanswered. He went back to the *yeshiva*.

"Deborah, can you hear someone screaming? I wonder what's happened?"

"It's nothing, Mamma. It's only that woman again, kicking up a row."

"Yes, but I can distinctly hear Polish?"

"It's her all right! Only she's giving the neighbours a piece of her mind in Polish. I suppose she thinks she'll get her rent quicker that way," Deborah explained, and could not help laughing.

Then a thought crossed her mind that the woman might yet return. She did not mention this fear to her mother, but all mirth was stifled. Nervously she followed the woman's screams all through the house . . . Thank God, they had ceased!

"Ugh, what a horrid woman! Don't you think so, mamma?"

Raizela made no reply.

So it had come to this! This! The image of the woman all in black still haunted her, still sat on that now vacant chair by the window.

In Jelhitz, at least, Raizela had had a little nest of her own, a little peace and security. There she had never had any cause to tremble lest a threatening black crow might descend upon the home to scare the family out of their wits. There the roof over their heads had been their own, and it all came back to her how, by a strange chance, a long cherished ambition had been realised, how a house had been built up on the foundations of a passing thought. It had all happened most unexpectedly, and the memory of it now rose clearly in her mind.

It had all started with the wealthy villager Hershl Shveiger taking it into his thick head that Solomon, his son (who was no less thick-headed than the father) must at all costs become a scholar. And when, on approaching Reb Avram Ber, he obtained a ready promise that the boy would be taught all that he possibly could be taught, Hershl Shveiger was seized with such transports of delight, that he pressed Reb Avram Ber to accept an advance fee of one hundred roubles. That was how it began. Then she, Raizela, humorously told Reb Avram Ber that she would invest the money in a cottage, and she immediately forgot all about this chance remark. But Reb Avram Ber passed it on to "Big" Mendel, who laughed heartily and jokingly informed the congregation after prayers in the synagogue that the Rabbi was going to build himself a house for a hundred roubles. "How's that for a brainwave?" he asked, and everybody chuckled. But Reb Joseph Cahn, a man who owned vast tracts of forest and who only came down to the village to attend divine service on the anniversaries of his parents' death, took this jesting in bad part. Without saying a word at the time, he silently made a resolve to translate this dream-house into reality, and a few days later he sent down a huge load of timber with his compliments to Reb Avram Ber. Now Reb Joseph Cahn was a man of great influence, and when he did a thing, everybody else did the same, and soon gifts were pouring in from all quarters. Someone sent in a load of tiles, a timber merchant drove up with a cartful of beams, a few of the villagers gave cash. Within a short time there was more than enough building material, and all that Raizela had to pay for was labour, locks for the doors, window panes, cement and other small sundries. And thus a joke gave rise to a handsome cottage! But matters did not end there, for fortune had deigned to smile and it so chanced that Joshua Glisker, who managed the squire's estates, one day told the squire the curious tale of how the Rabbi was building himself a house for a hundred roubles. The squire was very much struck with it. He laughed merrily, and taking Joshua Glisker along with him, paid the Rabbi a call.

Raizela saw it all again in her mind's eye as she lay huddled up now on her couch. She had only just got out of bed. Reb Avram Ber was away at the synagogue at the time, when in walked Joshua Glisker to announce that the squire was desirous of speech with the Rabbi. This news quite startled her. What business could the squire have with the Rabbi? It occurred to her that in all probability he was engaged in some dispute with some Jewish merchant, and having lost his case in the courts, now wished to arrange for Jewish arbitration, for this was a customary procedure with the Polish gentry. It transpired, however, that the squire had no disputes with anyone. All he wanted was to speak to Reb Avram Ber on a matter touching his person. Joshua Glisker knew what this matter was, but not a word could she wring from him. He was determined to lend a sharper edge to the surprise that lay in store. Now, she remembered her introduction to the squire, who, tanned and humorous-eyed, opened wide his grey eyes with astonishment on seeing that this was the Rabbi's wife, but he immediately made a deep bow and allowed the smile, which always lurked on his stern face, to come to the surface, in an endeavor to cover up his surprise.

Reb Avram Ber hurried home from the synagogue white as a sheet. He was quite distressed, especially as the squire had not stated the purpose of his visit. But when the squire greeted him with a smile from afar, and finding that Joshua Glisker was there too, Reb Avram Ber was somewhat comforted.

Puzzled as she was herself, her puzzlement grew when the squire, after first shaking hands with Reb Avram Ber, briefly stated that he had heard the story of the house that was to be built and wished to offer a site for its erection, free of charge and exempt from all tax. She remembered how the squire had firmly declined their invitation to step inside, for which she was very thankful, because the place was in such fearful disorder. How, after he was told that they would like to erect their house next door to the synagogue, the squire's face became wreathed in smiles and he commended the Rabbi on his good taste in choosing to live on the outskirts of the village facing the meadow. . . . Thereupon they all trooped off in a procession— herself, Reb Avram Ber, the squire with his manager, and a large brown long-haired dog that kept wagging its tail, as if the animal too was delighted with Reb Avram Ber's good taste.

A smile came to Raizela's lips as she saw again Reb Avram Ber shrinking into himself and dodging this way and that to avoid the dog, which, unfortunately for him, happened to be in high spirits and gave vent to them by dashing from person to person. Then Joshua Glisker produced a wooden yardstick, which had been folded up in his pocket, and squatting on the ground, he made various measurements, drew chalk-lines, uttered comments and looked out of a corner of his eye all the while, as though to say:

"If you please, I'm a business manager; but if the occasion arises, I'm equally good as a surveyor, and pray tell me, is there any task in the world I could not do better than any other man?"

And there stood the squire, tall, erect, fair-headed, his hair glinting in the sun, his nose longish and, as it were, smiling. He bored holes in the ground with the end of his cane to mark the chalked-in grassy plot, then turned to her and said that she could consider this her property for all time. Reb Avram Ber, moved by gratitude, clasped the squire's hand and pressed it with all the warmth he could muster. Then a red-haired youth with stupid wooden features brought up two sleek black horses with extraordinarily thin legs, narrow heads and docked tails. How adroitly the squire and his manager jumped on to the animals' backs, and, after a final deep bow to herself, went off in such a gallop, that Reb Avram Ber was lost in amazement for a long while after.

"Dear, dear, just look at them!" he said.

Raizela broke into a smile on her couch, but only for an instant. The heavy curtain of gloom enveloped her once more, choking her, numbing her. And now it had come to this! This! Now she was at the mercy of a pitiless shrew, whose very presence chilled one's heart. . . .

What little shelter the family had had was all swept away. It had been thoughtlessly dissipated. Nothing was left to them, but a few sticks of furniture. And what did the future hold in store now? . . .

After many trials and tribulations Reb Avram Ber succeeded in obtaining a loan of ten roubles and with this he silenced the woman in black when, sure enough, four weeks later, she turned up to get whatever she could from the family and to find out if the *Tsadik* was back in town . . .

CHAPTER VI

Towards the end of summer two sturdy grey thoroughbreds came dashing through the streets and alleys of R—, to pull up with a great flourish in the courtyard of the *Tsadik*'s house, where preparations were in full swing for the reception of the holy master. And everybody knew at once that he had come, he had arrived!

Reb Avram Ber, who happened to be leaving the *yeshiva* at the time, unwittingly came face to face with him. But the *Tsadik* gave no sign of recognition, and accompanied by two of his personal attendants, went straight indoors to seclude himself in his sanctum.

A crowd of sightseers quickly gathered in the courtyard—Jews, old and young, and women and children, with even a few Gentiles. And reverently they eyed the *Tsadik*'s horses, which, with their heads plunged deep into their nosebags, calmly went on chewing their oats, without so much as condescending to give the rabble a glance.

Towards the end of summer he returned, with all his suite, from the watering-place. His mother came back too, with her own suite. Only his wife had been left behind: she had not finished taking her cure yet.

Once more the Court began to throb with life.

Again the *Tsadik*, with just a little less fat on him, his face scorched by the sun and the skin of his shiny nose in tatters, mounted the "throne." Again his attendants went about the Court with an intent and mysterious air.

No longer were common maidservants to be seen reposing on balconies on high, no longer did they gaze down from the holy of holies, carrying on flirtations with romantic young men on the cobbles below. The old life began anew. Tiny men kept dragging big baskets of victuals into the Court. Restaurants re-opened their doors. And Hersh Laib's talkative wife again stood airing her old grievance to her old audience about her husband's irksome duties. His was the distasteful task, as the *Tsadik*'s youngest attendant, of taking the *Tsadik* to the closet. It was not the right sort of work, she protested, for so handsome fellow with such tidy habits and such a lovely curly little beard. . . .

"The *Tsadik* is tired and he can receive no visitors," was Laizer Nussen's stern reply to all those—personal friends even—who presented themselves to welcome the *Tsadik* on his arrival.

The *Tsadik* will now receive visitors," was the news which a little later rejoiced the hearts of those personal friends who were just thirsting for a glimpse of the holy man's greasy sunburnt face.

Reb Avram Ber was not among them, even though officially he was still the *Tsadik*'s closest confidant. He had no desire to see the man, still less inclination to bid "Peace!" unto him at a time when sorrow, distress and bitterness racked his own soul. Because of this man, he had lost his old naive confidence in humanity. Reb Avram Ber was vaguely aware of this, and withal unconsciously, deeply mourned the loss. Because of this man, also, he knew for the first time a terrible feeling of self-disgust. He could not face Raizela without a sense of shame, without wincing. It agonised him horribly to see her suffering, suffering in silence. Never had he brought anything upon her but suffering! First he had taken her out of a house of plenty to lead a cramped, miserable existence in Jelhitz, then he had persuaded her to accompany him to a "promised land," but here, instead of a change for the better, destitution had come upon them: the *Tsadik* had shattered their lives, taking them away from a position where their bread and butter was assured and literally leaving them to starve, as if they were nothing better than toys, playthings for the *Tsadik* to do with as he pleased. . . .

On the third day after his homecoming the *Tsadik* sent for him.

"Peace unto you, *Tsadik!*"

"Peace be unto you! Now tell me, what have things been like in my absence?"

Reb Avram Ber lost his temper. He was overwrought. The *Tsadik's* fat, beefy face and sanguine complexion got on his nerves. Reb Avram Ber had changed.

"Things have been unsatisfactory, as was only to be expected."

"Why, what on earth do you mean?"

"And what on earth do *you* mean by looking so surprised? The students were left unprovided for, they were hungry and ran away. 'No bread, no *Torah,*'" Reb Avram Ber retorted with ill-concealed anger. He was about to make a direct demand to the *Tsadik* for a settlement of the outstanding debt. The *Tsadik* felt it coming, he had foreseen it. Plunging suddenly into deep meditation, he began pacing the room. Without stopping, he harangued Reb Avram Ber:

"Yours was a precious trust. I left the *yeshiva* completely in your trust, and I must hold you responsible for what has happened. Had you used your full powers, there would not have been this mass-desertion on the part of the students. Within a few weeks you have managed to reduce the *yeshiva* to a miserable skeleton of its former self. It's a pity, a terrible pity!"

"But the students were left to starve. There was no money in the cash-box to keep the communal kitchen going, and failing charitable support from the townspeople, the position was hopeless."

"Pshaw, nonsense!" the *Tsadik* exclaimed, and his face turned as red as if it had been boiled.

He resumed his pacing of the room. From the back pocket of his gabardine the end of a large handkerchief peeped out and kept wagging up and down like a scornful finger. A silver snuff-box was clutched in his hand. He made a gesture, as if dismissing an unpleasant thought from his mind, and turned his back on Reb Avram Ber without a word. There was nothing left for Reb Avram Ber to do but to go. He went, in silence.

Again several uneventful weeks went by. Some of the old students returned to the *yeshiva*. New ones were recruited, especially among young married men of the upper middle-class, eager to escape the black looks of angry fathers-in-law, whose hospitality they enjoyed. Having been given wives at a very early age, in accordance with ancient tradition, and then carefully looked after until such time as they might be able to support themselves, when they came of age they often resisted strongly any attempts to be converted into responsible husbands, and large numbers of such young men flocked to the *yeshiva* to take the air and to continue their leisure in the beautiful hygienic building. Some of them actually were serious students. As for those young men who thought nothing of going without food for days on end, they had not left the *yeshiva* in the first place. The *Tsadik* found a new ornament for himself in the form of a magnificent-looking Rabbi, who knew all the tricks and who fleeced the *Tsadik* with all the cunning he could muster.

Michael's hatred of the *Tsadik* was quenched. The man was simply a prosperous sharper and Michael accepted him as such. This realization greatly tickled his fancy, lending an even keener edge to his everlasting jokes at the *Tsadik's* expense. This new air of detachment made his witticisms irresistible and they flashed like lightning through the blackest of clouds, piercing the heaviest of gloom. Thanks to his gift of mockery, Michael became the most popular student in the *yeshiva*, though the youngest.

"Come on, Michael, do your stuff! We're just about fed up to the neck!" his companions would demand entertainment, as if he were a professional clown.

Michael was never caught unawares and before long he had the *yeshiva* resounding to shrieks of laughter. Ha, ha, ha! Ha, ha, ha!

"Good, Michael! Bravo!"

Reb Avram Ber, in spite of everything that had happened, continued to deliver his lectures with unflagging zeal. He and his family had nothing to eat, but still he went on giving his lectures day after day.

And now the High Festivals were at hand. The strips of sunlight, which all through the summer had settled expansively in between the benches and desks of the lecture-hall, began to shrink with each passing day. The sky above hung lower over the rooftops. But the hot weather lingered on, as though oblivious of any change in the seasons. Indeed, the heat became more stifling than ever.

One Friday afternoon, when the cooks in the Court were hard at work and when Deborah had finished her scant preparations for the Sabbath; while Michael was resting on the grass in a meadow outside the town, close by a bridge over the river, where the sight of girlish bare feet and of naked sunburnt arms bearing baskets of mushrooms, kept his eyelids from drooping, and Raizela was reclining at home on her couch, feebler than ever; when Reb Avram Ber had just come back from the ritual bath-house, with water trickling from his beard and sidelocks—all at once a smell of burning filled the *Tsadik*'s Court.

His mother was the first to notice the fumes. Clad in a trailing black silk dress, with a big flowery bonnet on her head, she ran out into the centre of the courtyard to raise the alarm, screaming herself hoarse before she could make herself understood. Soon the whole atmosphere was contaminated with this acrid odour, but the cause of it was a mystery until suddenly the large open windows of the *yeshiva* began to belch forth huge clouds of smoke. Panic broke out. Crowds flocked into the courtyard from the numberless doorways and from the street gate. The people shouted, they flung up their arms in despair, until an insistent voice suggested that the fire brigade should be sent for. By the time they arrived, the impenetrable black mass of smoke inside the *yeshiva* had begun to vomit up half-smothered flames and sparks. Within a few minutes the entire Court stood brightly lit up.

The *Tsadik*, accompanied by Hersh Laib, the youngest of his personal attendants, arrived on the scene. He had been to take a ritual bath, and gleaming drops of water still lingered on his long beard and his sidelocks were dripping. His face and bare throat were flushed as if they had been scalded with boiling water; in contrast, the colour of his shirt was dazzlingly white.

"My good people, what's the matter with you? Why don't you do something?" He uttered a cry like a wounded creature, and as if to set an example, he began to sprint across the courtyard with the agility of a boy of twelve—there was nothing of the fat old man about him now—making straight for his sanctum.

A great uproar ensued.

Someone shouted out: "The *Tsadik*!"

The multitude began to chant: "The *Tsadik*! The *Tsadik*! The *Tsadik* has gone into his sanctum! Help! Save the *Tsadik*!"

Jews ran helter-skelter with dishevelled beards and outspread hands to join the *Tsadik* in his peril. Women ran helter-skelter to join the *Tsadik* in his sanctum. Bundles of bedding, clothing and all sorts of knick-knacks tumbled helter-skelter from windows outside the danger zone, sparks shot up helter-skelter from the stifling fumes, and helter-skelter came the *Tsadik*, back from his sanctum, with a large leather portfolio under his arm and his mother hard on his heels.

And climbing on to a heap of bedclothes, he sat down, surrounded by his valuables and the salvaged holy scrolls, which had been carefully wrapped in cloth like coddled babes—sat motionless like a statue in bronze.

The firemen were unable to make much impression on the blaze. The flames went from strength to strength, growing more brilliant as they ate their way through the building gluttonously, pausing only now and then to lick their meal with relish. The *Tsadik*'s mother stood wringing her hands. The sky, aglow with the setting sun, was now illumined by two conflagrations. In the narrow street outside the Court there was a constant wailing. Women, overcome by fear that the whole town might be swept by the flames, fainted away on the pavement. Youngsters shrieked. The menfolk carried them away from the scene of the fire.

Still the *Tsadik* sat upon his pile of valuables, and nothing could move him. All the worthies of the town tried their powers of persuasion on him, pleading with him, imploring him to accept their hospitality, but he refused to climb down. Then the common folk approached him, after everybody else had failed, but it was no use. Reb Avram Ber was quite heartbroken at the pitiful sight. He inwardly pledged the *Tsadik* forgiveness, but what did forgiveness avail the *Tsadik* who was clinging stubbornly to his perch like an out-cast? Like a creature forlorn he sat there, surrounded by his treasures. The manuscripts and priceless diamonds, which were locked up in his portfolio, he stealthily transferred to his deep bosom pocket. His mother, whose diamonds they were, loyally remained at his side, and thus they sat hour after hour keeping guard.

Later on when twilight descended on the courtyard (the rest of the town was long since wrapt in darkness), he arose, and, with a con-gregation of a few score Jews behind him, said his evening prayers. The womenfolk and the Gentiles withdrew respectfully, and contem-plated the awesome scene from afar. Above, the sky was perfectly dark, now that both conflagrations were extinguished. The holy scrolls were taken into the little old synagogue, which stood quite unscathed. The Court as a whole had not suffered much damage, but the *yeshiva* was destroyed completely; the sole visible trace of it was a tangle of girders, a heap of black rubble mixed with wet cinders, the whole studded with glowing embers. The *Tsadik* had his property taken back indoors, under his personal supervision. His eyes, though so deeply embedded in flesh, were keen and all-seeing.

For a very long while to come the *Tsadik*'s personal attendants and the local restauranteurs would pour wondrous tales into the ears of the faithful, how the *Tsadik* had braved the flames, how, imbued with a holy spirit of martyrdom, he had staked his life on salvaging the rare manuscripts and tokens that had been bequeathed to him by his father (whose memory be blessed!) and many other marvellous things did they recount; many were the miracles that the *Tsadik* had wrought on that memorable Friday afternoon.

His persistence in clinging to the pile of valuables in the courtyard was interpreted in a variety of ways. One school of thought insisted that his action was a demonstration of submission to the heavy hand of Providence. But others insisted that he had behaved thus through sheer modesty. A third explanation was that having been temporar-ily rendered homeless together with the holy scrolls, the *Tsadik* had taken this opportunity of publicly lamenting the exile of the

Children of Israel. As for the fire, although there was much speculation, no one knew for certain how it had started. There were mur-
murs that the *yeshiva* had been deliberately burnt down, that one of
the students did it in revenge. It was known that feelings had run
high among the students when the *Tsadik* went away to take the
waters, while he left them to starve. And many of the townsfolk
thought this theory reasonable. Others pooh-poohed it. The whole
thing remained a mystery.

The High Festivals were but a few days away. And this was the
Tsadik's busy season. A multitude of Jews from far and near came
flocking to him to secure his blessing.

The Court and the narrow streets around it were packed. There was
a coming and going of people from morning to night. The town saw
many strange faces—the careworn, perspiring faces of hardworking
Jews. Many of these strangers were wearing their working clothes.
Cobblers smelt of leather, tailors had threads all over them, and
millers were coated from head to foot in flour. They had neither the
time nor the inclination to change. The pilgrimage to R— was a luxury they could ill afford, although the journey only took a few hours
from Warsaw and other populous Jewish centres. When a man has a
family to feed, he must keep his nose on the grindstone all the time,
and the *Tsadik* must wait. But on the eve of the High Festivals hard
hearts softened. The voice of the soul made itself heard above the din
of the daily round. What was the use of satisfying the flesh, if the soul
went hungry? The flesh would perish, the soul would live for ever.
And Jews, hearing the call, jumped on to carts and into trains, and
came flocking to the *Tsadik* (God bless him!) to ask him to pray for
them, to ask him to save their souls, which, hidden under shabby
working clothes, were pining for spiritual succour. And everybody
rushed about as if in a trance.

The *Tsadik*'s personal attendants were overwhelmed, in a perfect
sweat over their dual task of writing out cards of introduction for the
visitors and quietly pocketing tips . . .

Meanwhile *hassidic* devotees who at all seasons heard an inner voice say—*it is not this frivolous mundane existence which matters, it is not lowly flesh a Jew must care for, but the soul, aye, the great and mysterious hereafter when the soul shall live for ever;* devotees who were not in the habit of snatching a mere day off to see the *Tsadik*, but would come to rejoice in his holy presence time and again; such devotees sauntered about the Court with an air of perfect leisure, like men at home. And loftily they viewed the common herd waiting in the queue with piously inflamed faces to see the *Tsadik*—to see him for a fleeting moment, hand him a donation and then fly off home again to their wives and children, to their mean occupations in the quest of nothing better than bread and butter . . .

Every single inn in the town was packed, there was not a bed to be had anywhere. The prices of foodstuffs were soaring hourly. The innkeepers and their families were run off their feet by day, and when night came they had no pillow to lay their heads on. Traders forsook their usual posts in the market-place and invaded the streets around the Court, where business was flourishing. Loudly they cried their wares, consummating the general din and confusion:

"Buy, my good people, buy, buy! This is your last chance before the prices go up! Come on, what would you like?"

"Ten groschens for two boiled eggs! Boiled eggs, straight from the fowl, all new-laid, all hot!"

"Lovely apples! They're a tonic! Pears, four groschens a pound! Four groschens only!"

"Anybody wanna 'ot cheese cake? Speak up! I'm givin' em away for nothin'! That's right, put down five groschens and see for yourself!"

This last wisecrack was being shouted at the top of her voice by a woman of gigantic stature, who was doing a roaring trade. It caught Michael's fancy while he was out sightseeing. In the flood of craziness that was pouring through the town, this mountain of a woman with her amused smile seemed like an island of common sense which would never be submerged. Never before had Michael seen such a torrent of hurrying fools! They were streaming in, to cleanse their souls in the mud! . . .

Michael missed none of the sights and then went home to play-act the more comical scenes for his mother. He mocked the humble mien of those waiting in the queue, beseeching Laizer Nussen to accept their money; how Laizer Nussen quelled them with a glance, even while he pocketed their coins.

"Michael, will you do me a favour and shut up," said Raizela. "I've a terrible headache, and I'm not going to have it made any worse through listening to your everlasting nonsense about the *Tsadik*. Keep quiet!"

"All right, Mamma, but you should have seen Laizer Nussen. You ought to have seen him, he was wonderful. He had the whole mob completely under his thumb, and they all insisted on having their cards of introduction written out by him. The other personal attendants were ignored, and stood by helpless, and were they looking blue! Watch, Mamma, this was the expression on their faces! As for poor old Baruch, he was perfectly wretched. Poor fellow, he hasn't done a stroke of business all day. The mob had all made their minds up to be fleeced by Laizer Nussen and by no one else."

Deborah was angered by Michael's derision of the "mob." Ignorant and simple-minded, they were bamboozled, made nought of; but no one ever tried to enlighten them, no one ever ventured to expose the *Tsadik* and his confederates for what they were, and so the "mob" continued to lavish luxuries upon him in all innocence.

"But you can't expect these plain honest people to know any better," she argued with Michael. "Wasn't Papa just the same? Didn't he used to think a lot of the *Tsadik*?"

Deborah felt hurt for her own sake as well as theirs. She shared their fate. She was a drudge, treated with contempt by those upon whom she danced attendance, and if ever she tried to shake off her responsibilities, protesting that she was made for something better, they asked her with a sneer:

"Don't you think housework is good enough for you? Well, why don't you study the Talmud, and one day you'll be a Rabbi maybe?"

Such was life, Deborah mused bitterly. People were derided, but never shown their errors.

As for Michael, this crazy rush to the *Tsadik* was to him nothing but an inevitable manifestation of incorrigible human folly, and he was duly amused. He left Deborah to get on with the moralising.

"Mama, why doesn't someone tell the common people the truth about the *Tsadik*? Why shouldn't they know that he's a scoundrel?"

"Yes, but who's going to tell them?"

Deborah reflected.

"Why doesn't Papa do it?"

"Don't be absurd!" said Raizela, and she relapsed into her former pensiveness.

"No, go on, Mamma, tell me, why can't Papa do it?"

Raizela was silent for a while. Then she remembered that she had not answered Deborah's question.

"What is the use of telling them the truth, if they're not going to believe you in any case?" said Raizela. "They would certainly go into a frenzy and might even assault you. You see, they're rather feeble-minded, and they can't help clinging to one support or another. If it wasn't the *Tsadik*, it'd be somebody else. They must have an idol to pay homage to. The *Tsadik* is their golden calf."

"They put a rouble in the slot and out comes the fattened calf!" Michael put in through the open door of the next room.

"And what a calf!" said Raizela.

"A regular bull!" Deborah laughed.

"Who's a bull?" demanded Michael, rushing in again to join the conversation. "You can't call the *Tsadik* a bull. He's a slaughterer, and his crowd are cattle. Cattle, that's what they are, and that's what you are, too!"

"Stop! That will do! I don't want to hear another word about the *Tsadik* and his flock. It's no affair of ours."

"But how is it that learned Jews believe in him as well?" Deborah persisted.

"Enough, I say!"

"No, but tell me, Mamma, why is it?" Deborah went on undaunted.

"It's because the so-called learned Jews who hang round this *Tsadik* are really only mediocre Talmudists. He has a big, but a poor, following, and so with what little knowledge they have they shine here and play the part of venerable men who are the confidants of the *Tsadik*. Elsewhere they would receive hardly any attention at all."

"Yes, but even so, would they still remain loyal if they were told that the *Tsadik* is a downright liar?"

"For goodness' sake, stop! You're an utter fool!" Raizela snapped back at her, having completely lost her patience. "No wonder it is written in the Talmud that *an ignoramus will ask questions for the mere sake of asking*," she turned to Michael with a smile.

Deborah did not understand this Hebrew quotation, but instinctively gathered the gist of it. She turned away shamefaced and with a vow that never again would she humbly serve the "great," only to be scoffed at, like those poor crowds that were struggling to see the *Tsadik*. . . .

Almost every night, in bed, she firmly resolved to give up her duties of keeping house, and to become a student instead. Ever since childhood she had longed to receive an education, to cease being the nonentity of the family. She would learn things, gain understanding, and then not only would papa be a great Talmudist, not only would her mother possess a boundless store of knowledge, not only would Michael be a brilliant student, but she, Deborah— the girl who, as her father had once said, was to be a mere nobody when she grew up—would be a person of real consequence. She would make her own life. But these thoughts were all very fine at bedtime. When she got up the next morning, she was drawn irresistibly into the usual drab routine, and each day was like a wretched repetition of the one that had gone before it. Again she managed the home, again she assumed the burden of responsibility that weighed so heavily on her childish shoulders. She was lacking in courage and too sentimental to leave her ailing mother to get on with it, and so—without being told, without being thanked—she went back into harness again, fretting and suffering all the more for her vain hopes of freedom—freedom that seemed within her grasp.

She did not even have any friends to go out with, to relax for once in a while. Two former chums, both of well-to-do families, had one day come upon her while she was on her knees, scrubbing the floor, with her dress tucked up like a charwoman, and since then they had never been to see her again, nor did she ever attempt to renew the friendship herself.

It was, to be sure, a comfort to have that Russian book to fall back on, which Mottel had lent her. He had taken her into his confidence and told her all his secrets. He was studying Russian, surreptitiously, and one day he had met her in the meadow and gone over Pushkin's verses with her. By now she very nearly knew the whole book by heart. Mottel himself was bubbling over with enthusiasm.

"The Russians," he said, "are wonderful. They write marvellous stuff. Why, you wouldn't find poetry like this in any other language!"

Books took her out of herself. The drab surroundings became festive. She lived in a new and spiritual world. But she could hardly find the time for such diversion; there was always something to do in the house. She did not protest. What was the use, since there was no one who could possibly step into her shoes? It sorely grieved her, nevertheless. Why should she, above all, bear the brunt of the hard times they had fallen upon? It would not have hurt so badly if the family had shown her some appreciation, instead of taking it for granted that she was their lowly maidservant who must have aspirations for nothing better, whose dreams were the dreams of a fool. Such thoughts had been tormenting her for a long time past, and she was forever seeking consolation in the moth-eaten yellow pages of Mottel's books.

Sometimes, however, even the poems failed her, her harrowed mind would not be soothed, and then she would run out of the home and post herself in the gateway of the house. Or she would lean up against a lamp-post which stood a few yards away and which had not been lit up for years, and she would watch the children at play, gaze after the passers-by who came and went, intent on their trivial tasks, completely absorbed in their humdrum, humble lives. Healthy-minded people. They got on with their work steadfastly, and it never entered their minds to ask what was it all about? What did they live for? Why? Why?

CHAPTER VII

The High Festivals were over. Gone was the sacred, sweetly mournful atmosphere, and in its stead came trivial, commonplace gloom. All was quiet within the *Tsadik*'s Court; sickly quiet. At times a soft, drowsy sing-song issued from the ancient little synagogue, but it sounded as though a weary mother were lulling her sick child to sleep, or as though a half-sobered drunkard were wistfully singing to himself.

From morning to night innkeepers lay dozing on the benches outside their establishments, or roamed the streets of the town sighing that business was bad. . . . The sun shed warmth and light. Ignoring the calendar, it blazed away day after day; the sharp cobblestones of the winding alleys were burning hot to the touch of bare feet, and it seemed as though the obstinately lingering summer would never make way for winter. But little by little, time had a telling effect on the seasons. Dawn would be late in coming, the day would rise sluggishly with sticky eyes: drops of dew were poised on every window like tears. Although it would still be stiflingly hot in the afternoons, the sun never rose high in the sky, but hugged the rooftops as if it were slinking away. . . .

A dread spirit of hopelessness haunted Reb Avram Ber's home. Quite suddenly Reb Avram Ber had become the most practical-minded member of the family. He could plainly see the approach of winter. (There was no such season as autumn or spring to Reb Avram Ber's way of thinking.) Coals were needed, warm clothing—and a hundred and one things besides. Slowly, without haste, the grip of winter was going to close its hold, and he found himself powerless to lift a finger in self-defence. If the *yeshiva* had not been burnt down, there might still have been a little hope. As things were now, the *Tsadik* could wash his hands of Reb Avram Ber and could leave the family to their plight—a sorry plight indeed! And while they had become inured to hardship, Reb Avram Ber clearly realised that a new chapter of destitution was opening—a chapter that would be darker than ever before, for not only was all their money spent, but their strength, too, was spent. Here was Raizela so feeble—like a guttering candle which needed but a breath of wind to blow it out! How would she survive it all? Reb Avram Ber was terribly downcast, and he could only pray to God for mercy.

The *Tsadik*, to be sure, had pledged himself on more than one occasion to have the *yeshiva* rebuilt. But that was not much use, when the family stood in need of instant relief. Reb Avram Ber, after a lengthy and bitter inner conflict, had again brought himself to approach the *Tsadik*. Whereupon the *Tsadik* had declared that a remedy must be sought, that the Lord never forsook any of His children, and, with these words, the interview had come to an end. . . .

True enough, Raizela's father had begun to send in a little money from time to time. But there is an old Jewish saying that "You cannot fill a torn sack."

Winter set in The rooftops put on their gleaming blankets of snow. An orphaned little tree in the *Tsadik*'s courtyard grew stiff; its poor frozen twigs pointed like helpless, accusing fingers at the rime forever lying in the gutter. The cobbles glittered in the coldly brilliant sunshine. And all day long crows kept cawing in front of the windows, lending even greater emphasis to the wintry atmosphere in the homes of the poor.

Reb Avram Ber was hardly ever to be found at home nowadays. Raizela never stirred from her couch. She was always reading. Deborah began to look haggard and tense, and her expression held something of nervous fear in it. She was easily exasperated, fretting terribly over every trivial mishap, while her mind seemed too numb to take in the really substantial troubles. Even Michael had, in the course of a few weeks, turned far too taciturn and grave for a boy of his age and more particularly for his nature. If ever he did crack a joke, it was so biting, so cynical, it made his companions wince. Quite suddenly he had grown into a man—a bitter man of fifteen.

Reb Avram Ber tried hard to secure a new benefice, but without success, in spite of the proverb which he kept repeating to himself— *He who searches shall also find.* . . .

And, as ill-fortune would have it, the winter turned out to be most severe. The slippery pavements and heaps of snow, frozen hard as iron at intervals along the gutters, helped to remind Deborah when-ever she ventured forth that her flimsy little coat was most unseemly.

There were occasions when Michael would tear himself away from it all and go down to the river to have a slide. But it was not like olden times. Even his mirth was joyless now. He had reached the age of understanding—he could no longer pretend that life was a game. He had begun to think seriously of earning a living for himself, but did not know which way to turn. For his part, he would have become an apprentice to a tailor, or an errand boy, but at home he did not even dare breathe any such suggestion. It would only have created a scandal. And it was really a weird notion: was he, Michael, going to become a common drudge? Still, the desperate urge to do something remained, giving his early-matured brain no rest. His face had become pale and gloomy. Somehow he looked very much taller than he had done only a short while ago, and his habitual stoop had become very pronounced.

The panes in the windows and doors were everlastingly adorned with the handiwork of Jack Frost. The home was bitterly cold. Whenever a fire was lit it refused to burn properly. The coals seemed to know that they were in a poor man's grate and, therefore, took no pains. The winter went on and on, but—like all earthly things—it came to a finish at last.

It was early spring. Already the snow was thawing and forming puddles and streamlets everywhere. In the river on the outskirts of the town huge lumps of ice were afloat. Once more Jews were to be seen about, with their gabardines spattered with mud up to the waist. A Passover atmosphere was abroad. Spring's warm breath sweetened the air. Once more Jews' thoughts turned to *matzos* (unleavened Passover bread), to charity and other sacred things. And with the coming of spring, with the lengthening of the days, and the sun mounting higher and higher in the sky, a bright ray pierced also the gloom in Reb Avram Ber's home.

Quite by chance Reb Avram Ber one day made the acquaintance, in the synagogue, of a wealthy man who had come to ask for the *Tsadik*'s blessing. Introducing himself, this visitor explained that he was a comparative stranger to the place, for hitherto there had been in his own hometown a resident *Tsadik*, who, unfortunately, had passed away recently, without leaving an heir. Now it appeared that this stranger, who had attached himself to Reb Avram Ber, was a very rich man indeed—the leading light of his own community—and it was his earnest wish that a new *Tsadik* should be found, to keep up the dignity of his home-town. It was more convenient, anyway, to have a *Tsadik* on the spot, and so a search was going on for a holy man, although so far none had been found. No established *Tsadik* would dream of moving from one place to another. On the other hand, there was no room for an imposter.

"No room for an imposter!" the wealthy visitor said with an air of finality as he unfolded his story to Reb Avram Ber.

It occurred to Reb Avram Ber that if the vacancy had been for a Rabbi, this would have been a heaven-sent opportunity. He said as much half-regretfully, and thought no more of it. But there was such an earnest, simple smile on his face as he spoke that the other man was touched. At that very instant Reb Avram Ber endeared himself to the stranger for all time, and a thought, a hope was born.

"Well, actually we need a Rabbi, too, for, you see, our former *Tsadik* (blessed be his memory!) was also our acting Rabbi. But this is where the hitch comes in. Opinion among us is divided, for unfortunately there are a lot of snobs in our town—as there are in every other town. They all happen to be supporters of the *Tsadik* of Ger, and they never used to think much of our own *Tsadik*. They were his sworn enemies in fact, and used to jeer at him and ridicule him. And now that he has departed this life they don't want to have a new *Tsadik* at all, but mean to install a Rabbi of their own choosing. You would hardly believe it, but the candidate they have put up is a son-in-law of our former *Tsadik*. This upstart fellow is a man after their own heart, because he, too, is an ardent *hassid* of the *Tsadik* of Ger, and was never on good terms with his own father-in-law. Do you follow me? That's one side of the picture. The rest of us, that is everybody except the handful of snobs, dislike this upstart son-in-law, and we won't have him at any price." Here the narrator's gorge began to rise. "Of course, we're more numerous and powerful than the arrogant scum that always floats on top, and, believe me, in the end we'll have our own way. The snobs don't stand a chance. What we want is not merely a Rabbi, but a Rabbi and *Tsadik* combined. Now tell me, would you care to assume that position? Will you come and live with us?"

"Of course I won't!"

"And pray, why not?"

"Simply because I am not a *Tsadik*."

"All right, we'll appoint you as one."

"God forbid! *Tsadikim* are not appointed by their fellow-men, but by God!"

"Well, then, allow me to inform you that you have as much right to be a *Tsadik*, and are as holy, as any *Tsadik* on earth," the stranger unhesitatingly declared his ardent faith in Reb Avram Ber. "I know that you are. However, if my first suggestion doesn't appeal to you, how about this? Become our Rabbi, and as for being our *Tsadik* you will decide about that after you have been living among us for a while."

Being a shrewd business man, this wealthy visitor had a clever little plan at the back of his mind for outwitting the snobs. He interrupted Reb Avram Ber, who had begun to speak.

"Yes, yes, I know. I know more about you than you imagine. For a number of years you were the minister of Jelhitz, and you were very highly esteemed there."

"Yes, but who told you?"

"Never mind! There are a lot of people who have spoken to me about you in this place, and they all think just as highly of you."

Reb Avram Ber smiled; he strove hard not to succumb to this flattery, but to no avail.

"I take it that you would be willing to become our Rabbi pure and simple," the stranger went on in his masterful way. "As for my original proposal, you could decide about that later on. Meantime, it would put the snobs in their proper place!"

Again he began to foam at the mouth about the "snobs."

"No, but I would never dream of settling down to strife and discord,"

Reb Avram Ber protested, unhappy at the thought that what might have been a chance of salvation should turn out to be no more than a wretched temptation.

The stranger fell more and more deeply under Reb Avram Ber's spell. He had quite lost his heart to him. But he kept his head, and inwardly dismissing Reb Avram Ber's objection to strife and discord—life was all strife and discord!—he begged Reb Avram Ber to hold himself in immediate readiness to travel when summoned by the elders of the community.

"On receiving our invitation you will know for certain that all opposition has been eliminated, and there will be nothing for you to fear," he said in conclusion.

By now Reb Avram Ber had an unpleasant taste in his mouth, but as he did not imagine there was anything serious in this man's talk, he answered casually:

"Well, when matters have progressed thus far, we shall think it over."

"Please God, they will progress thus far, and a good deal farther! I assure you! And now you have my word of honour that when we do send for you, all difficulties will have been removed."

A fortnight later Reb Avram Ber received from his newfound friend a letter that bore also the signature of several other member of the community, to the effect that they wished to appoint him as their minister; that they desired the honour of a visit from him, and if he were willing to come, two members of the congregation would be sent to escort him; that these two estimable members would bring to Reb Avram Ber an official letter of invitation signed by the whole congregation, and, moreover, in the unlikely event of his ultimate rejection of their offer, all the expenses he had incurred would be refunded to him, and that willingly! . . .

At home there was great rejoicing. Reb Avram Ber, of course, was not a little pleased, but one point sorely troubled his conscience— was he not depriving another man, the "upstart" son-in-law, of his livelihood? Raizela knew nothing about the "upstart" or the "snobs," since Reb Avram Ber had omitted all mention of them. He sent back a letter to say that he was willing.

The next thing was that one fine morning a comfortable carriage, drawn by two prosperous-looking horses, drove up into the court-yard of Reb Avram Ber's house and two men got out who were muf-fled up in their greatcoats as if it were mid-winter. The carriage immediately made off again, and it was a long time before the neigh-bours at the windows could stop staring at the gateway through which so rare a sight had come and gone. . . . The two muffled-up men enquired after Reb Avram Ber.

Raizela was taken by surprise. She climbed down from her couch, asked the visitors into the sitting-room, begged them to take a seat and motioned to Deborah to go and fetch her father at once.

On hearing the news Reb Avram Ber quite forgot his pangs of con-science about the "upstart" son-in-law. He was full of glee.

"So they've really come, have they? Thank God!"

He added something in an undertone, which sounded like a prayer, and he made straight for home, beaming all over as he entered.

"Pray be seated, be seated!"

The visitors sat down again.

Reb Avram Ber asked Deborah to get the samovar ready. Raizela stayed where she was for courtesy's sake, but after a little while excused herself and returned to her couch. Meanwhile Deborah had picked out the best spoons and had polished the tumblers until they glittered like crystal. It was with the utmost zest that she poured out the reddish, transparent tea, and watched the visitors imbibe it. They were both very diffident, and needed Reb Avram Ber's gentle persua-sion before they would take off their coats. Each of them unwound an incredibly long blue scarf from a bashfully rigid neck. Reb Avram Ber then pressed them to take lunch with the family.

That morning Deborah asked for more groceries on credit than she had ever done before, and in return she was obliged to answer all the shopkeeper's searching questions as to who the visitors were, was it their own carriage they had arrived in, what business brought them hither, were they or were they not relatives, when were they likely to leave or did they intend to stay with the family for good, and

no matter how niggardly Deborah tried to be, in the end the shopkeeper's thirst for knowledge was well-nigh satisfied.

After lunch the carriage reappeared in the courtyard. The visitors
donned their long scarves once more and advised Reb Avram Ber to
put on the warmest clothes he had, for the cold was bitter, they said,
out in the open country. Helping him to climb in, they wrapped him
up as cosily as they could, not forgetting themselves, and off they
went.

Michael had got wind of the visit and rushed home hotfoot, but
he was too late. The carriage had gone.

"Serves you right!" Raizela teased him. "If you hadn't been wasting your time, but had been in the synagogue studying as you should
be, you would have seen and known all."

A fortnight passed without word from Reb Avram Ber, apart from
the brief postcard which he had sent off on arrival at his destination.

Meanwhile it was getting close to the Passover. Raizela received a
few roubles from her father, and was quite at a loss what to do with the
money, for there were so many ways in which she could have used it.
However, the grocer was pressing strongly for payment, and Deborah
flatly refused to go into the shop unless she was given the money to
clear the debt. Matters had come to such a pass that she would have to
hang around watching newcomers being served while she was ignored,
and in the end the goods would be flung at her like charity. So
Deborah had her way, and again the family were left penniless.

Already the mild spring breezes were heavily laden with the
savoury odour of hot *matzos*. The Jewish quarter of the town was full
of soap and water, of beetroot soup, of all manner of vegetables, of
anxiety, distress and headaches as to the wherewithal for the sacred
celebrations—in short, full of the coming Passover. Every cobblestone, every shrivelled-up bush and tree seemed to be in Passover
mood. The porters of the town had all washed their faces clean, and
wore paper hats on their heads, with new pieces of sackcloth round
their shoulders. Whistling tuneful ditties, they were to be seen coming out of underground bakehouses with immense baskets of *matzos*
on their head, followed by flushed, anxious-looking housewives. Very

orthodox Jews were to be seen with little bags of *shmira*, which they nursed tenderly like coddled babes.

The town was full of cheerful bustle. Even the everyday cares and troubles gained a new flavour of their own. Jews hurry-scurried with their gabardines flapping in the breeze. The peasants that came to market made a splendid profit on their cartloads of potatoes, live poultry and eggs. As for eggs, the prices that were being paid on that Passover eve were positively fantastic! The crush was terrific in the market-place. The stallholders were shouting frantically. The peasants who brought their produce to town were besieged by eager buyers.

In Raizela's home, however, there was no hint as yet of the coming Passover. Taciturn as usual, she lay on her couch, poring over a book, with her little feet tucked under her as though she were quite oblivious of the fact that there were only ten more days to go. The air was full of a silent sorrow—it hung there like a curse, which everybody thought fit to ignore. One question tormented everybody: What could have happened to Reb Avram Ber? Why had he not answered any of Raizela's letters?

At last, only six days before the Passover, Reb Avram Ber came back. Now, as once before in Jelhitz, he sat down on a stool in front of Raizela's couch and said—but this time with bated breath—that all would be well, the Lord be praised, if only . . . if only . . . she, Raizela, were willing. . . . Whereupon Raizela's eyes opened wide in astonishment, and she gazed at her husband with a terrible suspicion: did this man mean to drag her through the mire again?

"Let me explain the position," said Reb Avram Ber, feigning composure, but the extreme uneasiness that possessed him was betrayed by every wrinkle in his face. "It's not a Rabbi the community are looking for after all, but. . . ."

Raizela's eyes opened wider still.

"But? . . ." she echoed.

It was quite five minutes before Reb Avram Ber found his tongue again.

"But . . . a *Tsadik*."

"What?"

"Well you see, this is the position. Their former Rabbi also served as a *Tsadik*. He made a very comfortable living, and was highly respected. What they're after now is someone to take his place."

"So what of it?" Raizela cut in impatiently. All this talk about the former *Tsadik* seemed quite irrelevant.

"So they have asked me . . ." Reb Avram Ber resumed, in such a gentle whisper that Raizela had to incline her ear to catch what he was saying. "They have approached me. . . . In fact, they tell me that they have heard say that I come of a very illustrious family, and I may add that my own reputation is not unknown to them either; indeed, they are very favourably disposed to me, and they promise me a comfortable living. Really, they treated me with the utmost respect and consideration. The whole community absolutely begged me to come to them as their . . . you see, they want a new *Tsadik*."

"And still I don't know what you're driving at," said Raizela. "What if they do want a new *Tsadik*? How does that concern you? You don't mean to tell me that their official invitation to you to become their new Rabbi was no more than a scrap of paper, or is that what you're trying to say?"

Reb Avram Ber felt the blood rushing up into his head.

"Not exactly, but the difficulty is this: a son-in-law of the former minister has staked his claim as the sole rightful successor, and says he is not going to make way for a stranger. To try to oust him would mean settling down in an atmosphere of strife, and what's more, this son-in-law has a small, but voluble, following in the town. He is himself a Ger *hassid*, and all the other Ger *hassidim* in the neighbourhood are strongly on his side. Whereas they used to scoff at the father-in-law, and mocked him at every turn, they think highly of the young man, and they say they'd sooner have bloodshed than see him go. With the exception of this small opposition, the official invitation to me was actually signed by practically the whole community. And these good people tell me that in the long run they will triumph over the dissenting minority, but patience is needed. Meantime they want me to come and live with them. All our troubles are going to be over

soon, thank God! I can trust these people, they are all honourable
men, and I have nothing to fear from them. 'To begin with, you will
be our *Tsadik*, or rather our leader,' they say to me, 'and then in due
course you will become our Rabbi.' At first I wouldn't hear of it, but
after a while I became convinced that I would not really be compro-
mising the son-in-law's chances, because he's quite unacceptable to
the congregation as a whole. Whatever happens, the benefice is certain to go eventually to an outsider. There can be not the slightest
doubt about that. And don't for one moment imagine that these
good people are trying to deceive me. No, they're in dead earnest! In
fact, do you know what they did? They gave me fifty roubles to help
us over the Passover holidays. Of course, I didn't want to take the
money. But it was no use my arguing. They absolutely forced the
money on me, although I never gave them any definite decision,
because I wasn't sure of your attitude. 'Please,' they said to me, as if I
were doing them a favour, 'please accept this and prepare a Passover
festival fit for a king!'"

Raizela was steadfastly silent.

Reb Avram Ber at last got tired of sitting down. He stood up and
began pacing the room, mopping his brow with his spotted yellow
handkerchief as he went. A quarter of an hour passed by. Half an
hour. Still she said not a word, did not even attempt to say anything,
but only followed his every movement with a melancholy look in
those big grey eyes of hers, which scorched him like growing embers.

Deborah came in. She had been out shopping. On catching sight
of her father she became flushed with pleasure.

"Hallo, Papa! When did you get back? Why don't you take your
coat off? It's quite warm in here. Shall I pour you some tea?"

And without waiting for a reply she busied herself at the samovar.
Soon a gleaming glass of tea stood at the head of the table.

"How are you, Papa?"

"I'm all right, Deborah, I'm all right," said Reb Avram Ber, gratified to find himself spoken to at last.

"Is everything fixed up?" she asked, unable to curb her curiosity
any longer.

"More or less!"

And at this Reb Avram Ber stole a glance at Raizela, who still lay on the couch in the same position as before, with that strange, far-away air, which gave him the creeps. There was something unnatural in the folds round the corners of her mouth. They seemed to betoken a peculiar smile, or was it an expression of anguish? Or did that grimace mean that she was crying? Or maybe she was smiling and crying at the same time? Her whole body was trembling palpably.

A sensation of warmth filled Reb Avram Ber's breast, and soon this excessive warmth made him feel sick. He began to choke. Spluttering, he asked Deborah to fetch him a glass of water. She handed it to him, and wondered what on earth could have happened. Only now did she notice that her mother was all a-quiver. Reb Avram Ber sipped a little water, then folded his hands behind his back and began to march up and down the room once more as if he had broken a journey and must resume it in haste.

"Oy, oy, oy! God Almighty, I pray to you to save us! Oh, merciful Father, what else is there left for me to do?" He turned suddenly on Raizela, as if she were his merciful Father. "Would you rather see us starve to death? Be reasonable! You know quite well that I don't think myself a *Tsadik*. They have asked me to become their spiritual leader, that's all, their leader. Surely I'm good enough for that, good enough to teach simple honest Jews the rudiments of the Talmud and to be to them a sort of spiritual leader. . . ."

Still Raizela was speechless.

"Tell me, what harm is there in that? Speak, is there anything else left for me to do?"

He pleaded with her as with a hard taskmaster, but she ignored him. In those two deep folds around her mouth there reposed a smile which seemed hard, cynical even; yet at the same time it was also pitiful and full of entreaty, like a childish pout. Suddenly, quite unlike her usual self, she burst out laughing, and laughed boisterously like a woman possessed.

"Oh dear me, it's funny to hear you! You have only just entered the profession, and already you have all the cards up your sleeves. You're up to all the tricks of the trade," she said with so much derision, with such deep contempt in her voice, that Reb Avram Ber squirmed like a mean little worm. "To begin with you said that these *good people* wanted you as a *Tsadik.* Now your memory has failed you and you have changed it round to a 'spiritual leader.' You've made a very pretty display of yourself. And now tell me, how can you complain about the *Tsadik* of R— if you're of the same kidney as he is?"

As she put this question to him she eyed him with the severity of a judge preaching at a prisoner.

It was Reb Avram Ber's turn to be speechless now. He did not know what to say in reply. He felt disgusted with himself. He realised that she was quite justified in speaking to him the way she did. It was sickening of him to have ever contemplated doing such a thing. A host of persuasive tongues and his own wretchedness had nearly succeeded in seducing him. And he was touched with gratitude towards her for having saved him from such a mean temptation.

"She is always in the right," he said to himself. "Always! Her good sense never fails her!"

And with a sense of relief, as if a heavy burden had been removed from his breast, he sat down and began to sip the tea with enjoyment, although it had long since grown cold.

"Are you asleep?" Reb Avram Ber enquired a few hours later, rousing Raizela in the other bed.

"No!" Raizela whispered, still in her uncommunicative mood.

"You know, you're perfectly right. Listen, I've thought it all over very carefully, and I've come to the conclusion that there can be no doubt about it: you're perfectly right! I'm only human, and knowing the terrible plight we're in my head was turned. I'm going to turn down their offer, and as for the money they've given me, I'll borrow a bit of it to tide us over the holidays, and I'll send the rest back immediately. I suppose something will turn up. God won't forsake us. And maybe you could go away with the children and live with your father until something does turn up. It'll make things a lot easier for you, and it will also give me more freedom to travel and look for a new position."

Raizela was reconciled. . . . And Reb Avram Ber, tired out and relieved, fell asleep with a great sense of comfort.

It was only on the following morning that Deborah and Michael were told that their father's journey had been fruitless. Deborah considered it a "pure misfortune," but she had little time to spare for idle speculation. The Passover festivals were right on top of them, and there was much to be done. Moreover, her father handed her a sum of money to do things in style, and that was certainly a comfort. After a long and assiduous search for a domestic help she led home in triumph a decrepit old charwoman, and combining their efforts they set to work with a will. . . .

The woman shuffled about the rooms with an aimless air, but there was great skill in her bony misshapen hands—like the leafless branches of a tree—as she scrubbed the tables, the chairs and the floors. Her every movement was accompanied by the quivering of her fleshless, wrinkled second chin and by an everlasting sigh. Now and again she stopped to wipe her red, diseased eyes, and told Raizela her troubles, complaining how poor she was and how her miserable little home was devoid of all trace of the coming festivities.

"If you can't go about begging, you've only yourself to blame, is what I say! You work yourself to death, and no one's going to thank you for it, neither! Such is life!" she philosophised, and as she wiped her fingers on her livid face the smears she produced on her nose were for her the sole trace of the coming festivities.

Reb Avram Ber ordered *shmira* for himself and for Raizela. *Matzos* were delivered in good time. Everything was got ready in the twinkling of an eye. It all happened in the nick of time. Nor was the charwoman forgotten by Raizela, so that in the end the smears on her nose were as nothing compared with the many good things she took home.

Michael kept aloof from all the turmoil. He lay at his ease on a synagogue bench (in a different neighbourhood far away from the *Tsadik*'s establishment) and diligently tried is hand at "making faces"

DEBORAH

(which was how Reb Avram Ber termed Michael's efforts at portraiture, to which he had recently taken with great enthusiasm.) When he came home for his meals he did not stay for very long, because the charwoman simply drove him out of the place. However, in the evening, when she had finished and was preparing to go home, she afforded him ample compensation. He happened to wander into the kitchen and found her, with her dress still tucked up, gloating over her numerous parcels in brown paper stacked on the newly scrubbed floor. It occurred to him that she would make a splendid study, and no sooner had the thought struck him, that out came his pencil and paper. No one paid any heed to what he was doing, least of all the charwoman. But when he no more than asked her to turn her head a little and to raise her skirt somewhat, she fixed such a startled gaze upon him, and her face became so expressive, that Michael had reason to thank her for the rest of his life, for this was his first and last sketch which he never destroyed.

Immediately after the holidays Reb Avram Ber sent back thirty roubles, together with an apology. He wrote to say that he was sorry he could not accept the congregation's friendly offer, and was even more sorry about his inability to send back the money in full. He promised to make good the deficiency at the first possible opportunity. In response to his letter, the two estimable gentlemen who had visited him once before came again in person; but all their arguments, all persuasion, failed utterly. Reb Avram Ber gave them a categorical refusal. The men went away deeply mortified. Heavens, what a humiliation! They could not for the life of them see what good reason Reb Avram Ber could have for turning his back on plain, but honourable Jews who wished to appoint them as their *Tsadik*, who sincerely wished to pay homage to him and to provide him with a comfortable living. He had objected to being named a *Tsadik*. That was a detail about which they would raise no difficulties. He had preferred to be called a "spiritual leader." Very well, then, a "spiritual leader" he would be! But now, it seemed, no concession would satisfy him.

"We're not good enough for him, that's what it is! If only the snobs had asked him to be their *Tsadik*, he would have fallen over himself for joy!" the two disappointed men told each other, with no little ill-feeling, as they drove away.

Two days later there was an exchange of correspondence between son-in-law and father-in-law. Reb Avram Ber began by writing a very long letter. Apart from the usual respectful title, he now addressed his father-in-law as "One of the most illustrious Children of Israel," and so on and so forth. He described fully the plight the family were in. He then made it perfectly clear that he, Reb Avram Ber, had always done everything that lay within his power to provide for his wife and children, and that he was in no way to blame for what had happened, for everything in life was predetermined by Providence, which no man, no matter how strong he was, could resist. Therefore, Raizela and the children would have to go and stay with her father for a short while, until matters would improve, and Reb Avram Ber had faith that they would improve before long. God would surely not neglect him. This epistle elicited a reply in which Reb Avram Ber was merely addressed as "My esteemed and worthy son-in-law" —and the rest of the usual title was lacking. The reply then went on to say briefly that "my beloved daughter" and the children would be welcome—God forbid that it should be otherwise—only the fact of the matter was that Reb Avram Ber had been born a simpleton, had remained a simpleton, and would always be a simpleton. . . .

CHAPTER VIII

The following week a strange thing happened. On the very day that Raizela and the children were to have gone away to stay in her father's house, Reb Avram Ber brought home a visitor—a swarthy, bright-eyed man with a long, well-cared-for and, as it were, sensible beard.

"Good afternoon!" said the stranger in a very pleasant tone of voice.

His friendly greeting met with a chilly response from Raizela. She imagined that this was another of those bright specimens with whom Reb Avram Ber was always getting himself into trouble. Not that it mattered, for she was returning to her parents' roof, and it would be a very long time indeed before Reb Avram Ber would induce her to come and live with him again. Her cup of bitterness had overflowed! But when Reb Avram Ber called her into the next room she could not be rude and refuse, so, hiding her reluctance, she joined the company. Reb Avram Ber pulled up a chair up for her and began to tell her in his enthusiastic way that Reb Zalman (this being the visitor's name) hailed from Warsaw, but had come down to R— for a few days to see the *Tsadik* on a certain matter touching the *yeshiva*, and that this same Reb Zalman was of the opinion that Reb Avram Ber could, if he so wished, get an appointment as a Rabbi in Warsaw.

"Which would, of course, be splendid!" said Raizela, smiling her most sceptical smile, but, in spite of herself, the very suggestion gladdened her heart, even though she had as much hope of its coming true as she had of the samovar, that stood upon the table, joining in the conversation. Still, she found it rather pleasant to listen to Reb Zalman as he held forth over his glass of tea. According to him, there was in Warsaw a certain neighbourhood in which a Rabbi was badly needed. It had a dense Jewish population, and as none of the "official" Rabbis—that is, those appointed by the central rabbinical authorities—lived within reasonable distance of this district, orthodox Jews found themselves greatly inconvenienced. For instance, if any doubts arose as to whether food was kosher or not, a mistress might order her maid to consult a Rabbi. But this maid, being lazy—and most servants were lazy—might not do as she was told and then—horror of horrors!—the holy laws of Moses would be transgressed. Now Reb Zalman had a great many friends in this particular neighbourhood, and he was more than certain that with a little persuasion from him they would willingly subscribe towards a stipend for Reb Avram Ber. Incidentally, being an arbiter in Jewish law Reb Zalman was well acquainted with some of the official Rabbis, and a possibility not to be ruled out was that he might even obtain a grant for Reb Avram Ber from the central authorities. He would draw their attention to the evil practices at present rife in the neighbourhood through the lack of a Rabbi, and so on and so forth. . . .

Within a very short time Reb Zalman was perfectly at home not only with Deborah, who had meantime refilled the glasses, and not only with Michael, who sat opposite him and made a poor pretense of studying a religious tract, but was familiar also with the four walls, and with the tea on the table, and was familiar even with Raizela, who listened to all he said, having come to the conclusion that he was by no means a fool.

"Finally, I'm going to make the *Tsadik* do his bit to help. He needs my favour, as it happens, and if I press the matter on him he won't refuse. Not that he's likely to quibble with me, in any case," he added with complete self-assurance. "What I'm going to ask—or rather demand of him—to do is to circularise his many *hassidim* in the neighbourhood, telling them to give me their full support. Believe me, if you take my advice, you'll never have cause to regret it. Warsaw is a thoroughly Jewish city, if ever there was one! What's the good of your hiding yourself away in a poky little town like this?"

The latter remark came as a shock to Deborah. How could anyone call R—a poky little town? Surely he would not have said any such thing if he had ever been to see Jelhitz!

"I don't mind telling you Warsaw is a wonderful city to live in," Reb Zalman went on with an expansive air, as if he owned the place. "Good old Warsaw! It's the city of golden opportunity. If a man can't do any good for himself in Warsaw, he's not likely to prosper anywhere! There are quite a number of 'unofficial' Rabbis in Warsaw. We call them 'private' Rabbis. And they all manage to make a comfortable living. And there's no reason why you shouldn't do the same. In fact, you would be in a better position than the others, because the need for a Rabbi in your district is very real."

Reb Zalman did not leave it at that, but carried on as if his own future were at stake, as if his very existence depended upon whether or not Reb Avram Ber was to be happily established in Warsaw. And he spoke with so much forcefulness, withal so quietly, and there was such unshakeable confidence in his candid brown eyes, that his plan unfolded itself like a living thing, like a flower opening its petals in the sunshine, and everybody at the table was seized with a sudden urge to get up and run off to Warsaw at once. He spoke with great reasonableness, measuring every detail carefully, leaving nothing to chance, and in the end there was no room left at all for argument or doubts. It was decided that Reb Avram Ber should travel up to Warsaw with Reb Zalman and there try his luck. Meanwhile Raizela and the children were to postpone their departure for the time being.

"I'm sure you're not in a hurry to get back to your father's house. That always remains as a last resort," declared Reb Zalman.

Deborah was delirious with excitement. It was all like a dream which could hardly come true. But what if her father was really to return from this new trip and say: "All's well, the Lord be praised! We're going to live in Warsaw!" What then? It would simply be wonderful! So much better than going to live in grandfather's house! No, she had not forgotten the holiday she had once spent there with her mother some years ago. What a life it had been! There was grandmother always on the go, always busy making jam and fruit juice, and gooseberry tarts and preserves. There was that old-fashioned oven in the kitchen, in which a tremendous fire was kept going from morning to night; it was never allowed to die down for a single instant.

Of course, it was a house full of plenty, but it was more than that—a house full of untouchables. All the cherries, the gooseberries, the black currants, all the plums, raspberries and blackberries were put away for the winter time and were not to be touched. Anyone might have thought that summer-time was a season of slavery, and that all the delicious things which grew ripe in the sunshine were only intended to be left over and enjoyed in the winter. It was so silly!

In other respects, her grandmother was not really a bad sort. Anyway, she fed her family on the fat of the land—fish and meat and soup in plenty. And she seemed to take real pleasure in seeing everybody stuff himself like a turkey. It quite upset her if ever a dish was refused. But no tit-bits on the sly! Oh, no, she wouldn't stand for that! And that was just what Deborah loved best of all, preferring it above all the elaborate dishes served so plentifully at table. If ever Deborah helped herself to a solitary gooseberry she was at once denounced as a greedy wretch, a hopeless case, a puss, a cat, and, in fact, all sorts of things!

And to make matters worse, first thing every morning grandmother would march off to say her prayers in the synagogue—and where grandmother went there went her bunch of keys. All the cupboards would be locked. And if Deborah happened to be starving, well, she could go on starving! There was nothing to do but wait for grandmother to finish saying her prayers. Of course, when breakfast did come up, it was a meal fit for a king—black currants and cream, delicious hot rolls and coffee with a really glorious aroma—but the maddening part about it all was that Deborah must never take anything of her own accord. . . .

Then, when Thursday came round, discipline would become so very strict as to turn the home into a veritable prison, for that was the day when "Long" Malka, the outside domestic help, took charge, and she was not a woman to be trifled with in any form or fashion. To think of all the work that woman had to get through on a Thursday! Grandmother was not much good at baking, and she simply had to have the assistance of "Long" Malka. And "Long" Malka knew it, and how she lorded it in the house! She behaved like the Czar. For not only did she bake the plaited loaves, she also had the butter cakes to do, and the fruit cakes, and the egg cakes, and the oil cakes, and the rolls, and the gingerbreads. And when that was finished, she had to knead still more dough, and roll it flat and cut it up into macaroni. Well, a woman who could do all that was a perfect treasure in the house. So ill-betide Deborah if she got suspiciously close to the kneading-trough, or was suddenly tempted to make off with a hot gingerbread. That treasure of a woman could not have created more fuss if it had been her own property that was being pilfered. Not that the fuss finished there. In fact, that was where it began. After "Long" Malka had done shouting (and could she shout!), grandmother would start moralising. Then came a sermon from an aunt who had been supported under the parental roof with an ever-growing family ever since she had got married twenty years ago, and for this reason—or rather in spite of it—considered herself one of the household authorities. Next, uncle would indulge in some good-natured chaffing, and, last of all, came a terrible reprimand from mother.

And just by way of a finishing touch, every Friday morning her grandmother would give her a big basket of victuals and tell her to distribute them to the respectable poor of the town. There would be a loaf—as big as "Long" Malka's head—for each family and half a pound of meat. It might be raining cats and dogs, or the sun might be scorching like the fire in the kitchen hearth on a Thursday, never mind that, she must sally forth with the basket, get rid of its contents and come back for more—sometimes there would be a few pieces of boiled fish as well, for the very respectable poor—and God help her if she tried to wriggle out of this noble and charitable deed!

Now the trouble with grandfather was quite of a different order. He spent every moment of the day in his private study, poring over the Talmud and composing his books, and no one ever saw anything of him. On those rare occasions when he came out to stretch his limbs she simply longed to have a word with him, or at the very least to hear him speak (for, as it happened, she loved him passionately), but he had a strange incomprehensible language all of his own, made up entirely of "Nu!" and "Nu-O!" These "Nus!" and "Nu-Os!" had something very profound in them, which would quite overawe the love she bore him, so that in the end her respect for him would outweigh her love. Raizela was the only person in the house he ever spoke to. And in the presence of him who was so wise, so exalted, Deborah, who was so small, so frivolous, could only feel deeply ashamed of herself. If he ever smiled at her, she only felt like going away and hiding herself in a corner, for the moment he condescended to notice her he could not but see how mean she was—just a mere worm by comparison with himself. . . .

Then, again, there were her cousins to consider—the cheeky brats! Throughout her stay they had treated her like an imposter, as if they alone, having been born and bred in the house, were the genuine grandchildren, whereas she was only a stranger, and what did she mean by intruding? True enough, she *was* a guest, and as such her grandmother thought fit to present her with a complete new outfit of clothes. But that was a blessing in disguise, for thereafter the air turned hot for her. Her cousins dropped all pretense of politeness, and quite overwhelmed her with their envy. They mocked her, and ridiculed her, and made her life a misery, so that she came to detest the fine new clothes, and would much rather have gone without. And in the end, when Raizela was sent away by her parents to a watering-place to take the cure, and Deborah—poor child!—was left to fend for herself, she might just as well have gone and hanged herself on the highest bough of the highest tree she could possibly find! . . .

Of course, things would be changed now. Even so, the prospect of going to live in Warsaw was infinitely more attractive. . . . But why fool herself? Was such a thing really possible? Certainly, she had heard people speak a great deal about the wonderful city of Warsaw. For instance, "Little Mendel always went to Warsaw to get the best materials for his shop. And Joseph Cahn's son, it was said, was a student in the university at Warsaw. But that a Rabbi should be wanted in Warsaw, and that none other than her father—a man whom both her grandfather and her mother rated as being a homely simpleton—should fill the vacancy, now surely that was a crazy notion. And yet Reb Zalman maintained that it was a possibility—nay, a probability. Well, perhaps it was, and perhaps it wasn't!

Michael took it all for granted, and he was exceedingly happy. As a matter of fact, he had lately had a lot of funny ideas in his head about going to Warsaw on his own. He had quite made his mind up to throw up his studies, run away from home and find a job for himself in the big city. But now, it seemed, without waiting for him to act, opportunity had come knocking at the door quite unexpectedly. And by way of celebration he began to whistle aloud. Reb Avram Ber looked up with a startled air.

"Who's that? Is that you, Michael?"

Michael hung his head a little and apologised, with a gentle smile on his reddening face, saying that he was quite unable to account for his whistling; it was in no way deliberate, and he was just as surprised to hear the sound as they were. Both Reb Avram Ber and Raizela assured Reb Zalman that this was the first time the boy had ever done it in the home.

"Well, is everything settled?" Reb Zalman asked, pushing back his chair and rising to his feet.

Reb Avram Ber eyed Raizela for confirmation. She began to ponder. After all, it seemed a feasible plan, and they had nothing to lose. Further, if it were to materialise, they would not have to be dependent for their livelihood on such a narrow circle of people as they had been hitherto. As for returning to the parental roof, that could certainly wait. Reb Zalman was perfectly right.

"Tell me," said Reb Avram Ber, rather losing his patience, "shall we take a chance?"

"Yes, I think so. No harm in trying."

Deborah fluttered. Perhaps, when she got to Warsaw, she might come across that brainy student with the lean face and the luminous eyes, that young man whom she had first seen when she had gone to catch a glimpse of the *Tsadik*, and who would always bestow such a strange look on her. She had almost forgotten his name. *Simon*—that was it! Shortly before the *yeshiva* had been burnt down he had suddenly disappeared, and Mottel told her that he had gone away to the capital. The memory of him was so painfully vivid, that she quite lost her presence of mind and she asked her father if Simon was now in Warsaw.

"Whom do you mean? Oh, I know! I've no idea where he's got to at all. Someone brought him a letter at the *yeshiva* one day, he went off in a hurry to the station and that was the last we saw of him. He did not even trouble to come back and say good-bye. I imagine he must have received some bad news. Perhaps someone in the family was taken ill. I often wonder where he is. But tell me, what do you want to know for?"

Deborah crimsoned.

"Oh nothing, I only asked!"

"Well, that's settled. We shall make the trip to-morrow morning," said Reb Zalman, bidding the family good night.

"He's a sensible fellow," Raizela observed, after the door had been closed behind him, "but how he loves to exaggerate!"

"He's a man you can trust implicitly," said Reb Avram Ber. "Kind-hearted and clever. And a very shrewd business man. Knows everything, knows everybody, goes everywhere and has never let anyone down. In fact, he's always willing to lend you a helping hand. He's ever so popular. We've known each other for years and years."

"Is he a *hassid*?"

"No, he isn't. It's business that brings him here to see the *Tsadik*. The two of them have been associating for years."

Raizela gave a grunt of disapproval. Her confidence in Reb Zalman was suddenly dissipated. However, the suggestion was still worth trying. She was none too keen on going back to eat of her father's bread again.

About ten o'clock on the following morning Reb Avram Ber, shepherded by Reb Zalman, took the train for Warsaw, and in a fortnight's time he returned with the glad news that he had actually rented a flat for them to move into.

"Really? Without asking?"

"Well, Reb Zalman said there was no need for me to ask," Reb Avram Ber apologised. "And honestly, I think it was best not to. 'To delay is fatal,' Reb Zalman says to me. 'Decision is everything. Don't dilly-dally! Once a man starts to hesitate, he usually spoils all his plans.' You know, Reb Zalman tells me that the *Tsadik* is going to pay all the removal costs. He made the *Tsadik* promise. I say, Deborah, could you give your father a glass of tea?"

"So we have a promise from the *Tsadik*? Now *that* is something to bank on," said Raizela with a laugh.

"You wait and see! This time everything is going to turn out for the best."

"I hope so!"

As he sipped his tea, Reb Avram Ber recounted his experiences.

"The type of Jew you meet in Warsaw is more genial, more generous in every way, if you know what I mean."

"Not so narrow-minded and less self-centred," Raizela hazarded.

"Absolutely!" said Reb Avram Ber, his enthusiasm bearing on Raizela's good sense rather than on the noble qualities of the people he had met. "Money is to them of little consequence. They can make it and they can spend it. Now you saw Reb Zalman! He's a typical example. If they conceive a liking for anyone, they'll go to any lengths to help him. I think I was lucky, because they all seemed to take a liking to me. You should have seen the reception I was given in the synagogue. They got out a bottle of brandy and drank my health. And everybody welcomed me with such warmth, there was so much good fellowship all round, anyone might have thought these people had known me all their lives. They were honestly delighted to see me. I could tell by their faces. . . . And, you know, they really must have a Rabbi in that neighbourhood, for they tell me the present state of affairs is simply shocking. Shocking! One man, who seemed to be rather important, came up to me and said, 'Glad to meet you! It's a good job we're going to have someone at last to set our house in order, because it's wicked to be without a Rabbi. And I think you're just the right sort of person for us—an honourable man with no hypocritical nonsense. You know, not the sort of Rabbi who cares only for his fee, and who when someone turns up for a free consultation sends out word to say that he's asleep and can't be disturbed. Not that sort! You're a man after our own heart,' he says to me, 'and I hope you will be comfortable with us and make a really good living.' And, God willing, so we shall!

"Reb Zalman has no end of influence with these people. He's quite one of the exalted. Everybody respects him immensely. He spent the whole evening with me in the synagogue getting up a list of subscribers. There wasn't a single person who dared refuse him, and he carefully avoided one or two people who looked rather doubtful. It was a real pleasure to watch him. He has all his wits about him, has Reb Zalman. And he has a high sense of dignity too. A great-hearted man! You can't imagine how helpful he was. I didn't know how to thank him!

"To begin with, he insisted on putting me up. And he introduced me to his wife. Now she's a wonderful woman, a perfect angel, that's

what she is! The things she did to make me feel at home and comfortable! She was after me all the time—'Help yourself to this, and
help yourself to that!' And the bedclothes she gave me were fit for a
king to sleep in. Even after I had gone to bed she sent her boy in to
ask if I could do with an extra pillow. She couldn't do enough for me.
And as for Reb Zalman, he actually devoted a whole week to flat-
hunting. I got quite tired going about with him, because no matter
how many flats he saw, none of them was good enough. Very particular man, Reb Zalman. He kept picking and choosing, he couldn't
have been more finnicky if the flat had been for himself. He was out
to find a place that would have every convenience, at a low rental.
And that wants a bit of finding! He went to no end of trouble and he
didn't seem to care a bit that while he was taking care of me, he was
neglecting his business to his own detriment. At last he discovered
just what he wanted. 'You see,' he says to me, 'he who searches shall
also find.' He was so exultant, anyone might have thought he had
found some hidden treasure. Of course, I suppose this flat really was
better than the others we had viewed. But to tell you the truth, I
never saw any difference myself."

Raizela smiled a patronising smile which seemed to say, "Heavens,
what a terrible simpleton you are!" Nevertheless, it now dawned
upon her for the first time that her own sceptical outlook on life led
to stagnation, to nothingness, and only such strong faith as animated Reb Avram Ber led to the highroad of life; it was only by utter
simplicity and a childish belief in one's fellow beings that one could
gain the whole world, with these qualities alone could one savour
the true delights of life; indeed these qualities were in themselves the
most beautiful thing that life had to offer, and a truly wise man was
he who could accept this offering. What was the use of for ever sitting in judgment on Life and never being able to pass any sentence
on it?

For a whole fortnight Raizela kept away from her couch and
resumed the use of her legs. She helped Deborah to get everything
ready for the journey, even taking the trouble to check up the linen
when it was returned by the washerwoman. (They had specially

hired a washerwoman for the occasion.) Deborah and Michael had never seen their mother so active before, and they wondered what had suddenly come over her. It rejoiced their hearts. Michael, inspired by her example, willingly lent a hand and he did not spend a moment in idle lounging as he had done before leaving Jelhitz. He simply worked wonders. At one moment he cut short a piercing whistle and burst forth into song instead. At the next he smashed a jug. Then he picked up a heavily laden trunk and ran all round the room as fast as he could go. Deborah, as usual, did most of the work, and all the while her mind was feverish with extravagant pictures of what Warsaw would be like, although even at this late hour she could not settle down to the thought that it was there they were really going to live.

But at last the great day dawned. Quite early on Tuesday morning a large cart drove up into the courtyard and the furniture was packed into it pell-mell. Then a second cart arrived for the rest of the household goods. When the flat was all empty and every voice there raised an echo, the finishing touches were put to the tarpaulins on the hoop frames of the carts, and after vainly scraping their hoofs against the cobbles—to the accompaniment of loud shouts of encouragement—the horses finally got going and the carts rumbled away out of sight. The family put on their wraps. Raizela went downstairs wearing a black velvet jacket over her long black dress and with a black silken shawl over her head, which overshadowed her face and made it appear gaunter than ever. Reb Avram Ber joined her, clad in his winter coat (although the weather was very mild) and with his old rabbinical hat on his head. It was good to see him wearing his rabbinical clothes again. He shook hands with the neighbours, and even gave the womenfolk a nod.

"Did you say good-bye to the *Tsadik*?" asked Raizela.

"Yes! I have forgiven and forgotten. Let us hope that God will forgive him too," said Reb Avram Ber, apparently not without his doubts. "Although I must say that he has taught me a useful lesson. Only now do I understand the true wisdom of 'Put not thy trust in men, for thy support lies not in them.' Naturally, the world is full of good and kindhearted people, but we have only one Being to look to for support and that is to our Father in heaven. He is a loving and generous Father. . . ."

Reb Avram Ber glanced up at the sky which was of a deep summer blue.

Now here came the *Tsadik*'s carriage and thoroughbred pair, which all the townsfolk knew so well. The *Tsadik* had particularly insisted that this, his own carriage, should convey Reb Avram Ber to the station.

"And have you said good-bye to his wife?" asked Reb Avram Ber.

"Why, of course!"

"And his mother?"

"No, I didn't feel like it."

"Didn't Deborah say good-bye to her either?"

"No!"

"Never mind!"

Laizer Nussen and old Baruch were in the *Tsadik*'s carriage, and Reb Avram Ber and Michael joined them. Raizela and Deborah got into a trap behind, a hired vehicle drawn by only one horse—a cumbrous-looking animal with fat bandy legs and bushy grey fetlocks.

The family nodded farewell to the small crowd which had gathered in the gateway. Deborah did not even forget to wave good-bye to those horrid women who had once taken such keen relish in teaching her the art of scrubbing floors. A brief shower of blessings—and they were off!

Deborah turned her head for a last lingering look at the familiar scene for which she knew nothing but loathing. Suddenly she caught a glimpse of Mottel standing a little apart from the crowd. How pitiful was the smile on his face; he seemed on the verge of tears. It was a smile of bitter protest—protest at having been left behind, deserted. A great wave of pity surged over her; so, given the chance—and had she not been ashamed—she would have rushed back to say good-bye to him all over again and to explain to him that they themselves were no more than travelling into an uncertain future. But Mottel was soon out of sight, and in his stead came the image of

Simon. Simon! Perhaps she would meet him in Warsaw, hurrying as he always hurried with his threadbare gabardine wrapt closely round his lean frame, with his eyes blazing, so dignified in spite of his shabby clothes, so spiritual!

Just as they were setting off, Michael had called out a friendly word of encouragement to Mottel, but Mottel had seemed quite deaf. He now stood stockstill, gazing down the narrow street as if he half expected to see the carriages, which were bearing Reb Avram Ber and his family away, turn back to pick him up. . .

Michael was in great spirits.

"Gallop on, my good horses, and may you drop dead ere you take it into your silly heads to turn back!" he hissed through his teeth after the dramatic fashion of a hero of a novel which he had recently been reading on the sly. "Gallop on, you fat devils, you've only got a short distance to go. Take us to the station and no further!"

Then, relapsing into a more humorous mood, he said to Faivish, the coachman, "Ever thought of treating your horses the same way as you treat the *Tsadik*? If you put your mind to it, you could make the mob worship your horse as they worship the *Tsadik*, and they'd all come flocking round the animal to obtain its blessing. Bet you never thought of that!"

Faivish turned a pair of stupid startled eyes on him, and then a few minutes later he burst out into a loud guffaw.

"I say, you don't mean to tell me that you've digested that joke at last?" said Michael.

"What's that chap jabbering about? What joke?" said Faivish to himself and then he laughed again, as if he would split his sides.

"Ain't she a beauty," he gasped. "Can yer see 'er?"

"Whom?"

"Over there!" said Faivish, pointing his whip at an emaciated mare with an ugly sore patch on her flank harnessed to a heavily laden, rickety cart with an improvised top made up of torn sackcloth. She was a terribly dejected looking animal, holding her head very low, and her foaming mouth seemed to be doing more work than her legs which moved sluggishly as though loath to leave the ground.

"Beauty yourself! You ought to be ashamed of yourself laughing at a poor old skeleton that ought to be in its grave! Faivish, my boy, you won't be much more than a skeleton yourself by the time the *Tsadik*'s finished with you. You'll have a sore behind to sit upon, you'll be all skin and bones, a real old crock!"

However, there was no denying that Faivish was a first-class coach-man and knew how to handle his horses.

They pulled up with a flourish outside the station. With a very ceremonious air Laizer Nussen wrested from Reb Avram Ber a suit-case containing his manuscripts and took it into the waiting train, where he deposited it on the luggage rack. Then, fussing about over nothing in particular, he scolded old Baruch for being a lazy wretch; he asked the family again and again if they were quite comfortable and—with a last sweet smile at them all—took his leave. Baruch remained behind, and handed over to Reb Avram Ber a parting gift—a few pinches of snuff which he transferred into a little piece of paper with shaky hand, spilling some on the floor.

"There you are! Here's something no man can do without on a journey. You'll find it very stimulating. Look here, Michael, I've got some for you and all. I'm not so sure you deserve any, you rascal, but I'm going to give you the benefit of the doubt"—and he extended a pinch between forefinger and thumb—"Come on now, sniff it up like a man. Come on, stop fooling. Will you put that trunk on the rack for me, Michael? That's the idea!"

Michael sniffed it right up, and sneezed and laughed so much, he came near to choking.

"Atchoo! Atchoo!"

"You won't forget an old friend, will you? Drop us a line now and again, don't forget!" Reb Baruch shook hands with Reb Avram Ber. "And you,"—he turned to Raizela—"don't let's have any more of your nonsense! From now on I want you to keep well and strong. As for you, Michael, you've got to become a reformed character. There'll be no *Tsadik* where you're going to, and I want you to concentrate on your studies, see?"

Michael chortled.

"Well, I'll be going," Baruch said at last. "Godspeed!"

He clambered down the carriage steps, his body sagging as though he were a rag-doll. The train moved off, as if all this time it had only been waiting for Baruch to get off.

"Good riddance!" said Michael, but Reb Avram Ber silenced him.

"How they all ignore me! Even Baruch didn't think it worth his while to say a word to me," Deborah mused, and though she tried to dismiss the matter as of no importance, it hurt her to the quick. "Everybody dislikes me, everybody! . . ."

"Michael, get away from that door! Deborah, don't put your head out of the window!" Raizela kept saying, first in a tone of entreaty, then snappishly; but they just could not tear themselves away, for there in the distance was the spreading town, and with its grey little houses like so many toys, with here and there a splash of red, and the whole dominated by three lofty steeples. All around the green countryside was on the move, as though bewitched. The trees with their branches a mass of reddish buds, had such a strange air of stupid beauty as they rushed by frantic with haste: one might have thought they were late for an important appointment. Just overhead the smoke drifted past, puff after puff, and beyond that the sky showed a cool, pellucid blue. No wonder Raizela's nagging passed unheeded!

"Deborah!"

"What?"

"Mamma's asleep!"

"Hush, I know."

"Isn't it a grand view?"

"It's wonderful! What, are you trying to sketch it? I shouldn't waste my time if I were you. You'll only tear it up afterwards. You could save yourself a lot of trouble by tearing the sheet in the first place."

Strangely enough, Michael took no offence.

"Look, Deborah, you see that line where heaven and earth meet, that's called the horizon. Now you follow that right round as far as you can go. The more you keep your eyes fixed on it, the drowsier you get, and in the end you're sure to go to sleep."

"I bet you won't find me going to sleep!"

"Don't be a fool! You've only just started. You wait and see!"

"Hush! Daddy's asleep now."

"There, what did I tell you."

Michael, it seemed, no longer heard the call of art, for with sudden impatience he stuffed his pencil and the sheet of paper back into his pocket, and now they were both standing with their noses flattened against the window. Someone behind them shut the window opposite. They both turned their heads, and then as hastily resumed their former positions. By tacit agreement they were vying with each other to see the most sights; neither of them meant to miss a single ditch, or a bush, not to mention that green little hillock with its funny hump or the stagnant pool nearby, with its surface all covered in deep green moss.

"There must be a village close by," said Deborah.

"Why must there?"

"Don't you see those cows over there, and what about that flock of sheep? Look, there's the shepherd boy!"

The engine ahead suddenly emitted a piercing whistle. A cloud of smoke came gliding past the windows and drifting into the carriages. All the windows were shut to with a bang. The train came to a standstill with all the couplings jolting in succession. They had come to a station. Reb Avram Ber suddenly woke up. So did Raizela. A number of elderly men and women also woke up with a start. An inspector came on the scene, his official face all puckered up with official ennui.

"Tickets please!" he called out with a break in his voice, as though he were too weary even to clear his throat. Discovering no bilkers in this compartment he passed on to the next, hoping to meet with better luck there.

An old woman, with a huge shopping basket in her hand, got out of the train, holding on to the iron railing for dear life as she negotiated the three steps. At long last both her shopping basket and herself were safely deposited on the platform. An old man with a sack over his shoulder followed her just as cautiously. Then a bold youth, who was quite empty-handed, made a brave jump for it, but he caught his foot on the edge of the steps, and when he scrambled back to his feet a stream of blood was spurting from his nose.

"Serves him right!" said a huddled up old man, scratching his thin straggly beard.

The train moved off. It met with a very long goods train passing in the other direction. There was a change of scenery—scraps of woodland interspersed with numerous clearings. In one of them stood a small group of peasant huts. They were so diminutive that their chimney pots seemed to be almost on top of the ground, but there was life within, for every chimney had its fluttering ribbon of black smoke—deep black in contrast to the bright white of distempered walls. Michael was actually waving to a peasant lass. . . .

And now, in the distance, a host of monster chimney stacks could be seen towering up as though they were leaning on the sky. These, too, were tipped with ribbons of smoke. A maze of grey buildings loomed up close at hand, and into this maze the train rushed headlong at full speed. On all sides passengers began hurriedly taking the luggage off the racks. The train stopped short with a spitting and hissing of steam. It seemed to Deborah that they could scarcely have left the village behind yet, for they had only travelled a very short distance. But all around were immense buildings—far bigger than anything she had ever seen in R—. Could this be Warsaw?

"Where are we, Papa?"

"If I'm not mistaken, we're in Praga—a sister town of Warsaw."

"And have we got very far to go before we get to Warsaw?"

"No, we're practically there. This is where we get out."

"And does Warsaw look anything like this?"

"Yes, very much the same."

"Well, that's funny! It was only a short journey. And, do you know, I always used to think Warsaw was hundreds of miles away!"

"Yes, that's just like you! You're a great thinker, only you always think the wrong thing," said Michael with a laugh, and Deborah blushed.

What a terribly busy station! And it was all paved with smooth flagstones—just like the description of a big railway station in one of the novels she had been reading. The crowd was seething with excitement—all in a tangle like a swarm of bees. And no one ever stopped, except for a brief instant to snatch a paper from one of the newsvendors. Why all this hurry? Had they all gone mad? Why couldn't they walk along sensibly like normal people? They were a queer lot!

Michael took the luggage off the rack, aided both by Reb Avram Ber and by Deborah. Raizela stood adjusting the shawl on her head. By now everybody had left the train, and the family got out on to the platform, where they huddled together with the luggage at their feet. An endless succession of porters came up to offer their services, but Reb Avram Ber shook his head at them, with a most apologetic smile, as if he craved their forgiveness for declining.

But here came Reb Zalman, a smile of welcome tucked away in his trim, long black beard. He was upon them before they could recognise him in the dense crowd.

"Hallo, how are you? Hallo, everybody! I only managed to get here in the nick of time. My droshky was held up in the traffic. I hope I haven't kept you waiting."

"Not at all. We've just got out of the train."

"That's splendid! I timed it perfectly. I don't mind telling you, I know all the railway time-tables by heart. Now if you'll wait here for me, I'll go out and get a droshky," said Reb Zalman as breezily as ever, and he hurried off again.

Reb Zalman's arrival lent a homely little touch to the strange and, as it were, official atmosphere of the station. His very appearance somehow put the family at their ease, and it added firmness to the ground underfoot. They would not have dared to move away from this little haven where he had asked them to wait for him: to leave it was to step into the dread unknown.

"Isn't he a wonderful man? A blood brother couldn't have been more devoted! And don't forget that he's a busy man. He is putting himself out for our sake," said Reb Avram Ber.

"Yes, he's an extremely kind and sensible fellow," Raizela agreed.

It was not long before Reb Zalman was back. Business-like, he picked up a suitcase in either hand, refusing to call a porter.

"You don't want to throw your money away, do you? Instead of arguing, let's get going!"

He made Michael carry the remaining case, while Deborah took possession of the small bag. Reb Avram Ber and Raizela were left empty-handed, and thus they marched behind Reb Zalman as he strode on well ahead of them. Outside the station they were helped into the droshky by a cabby in a shabby uniform and with a weatherbeaten face which looked as though it had been boiled tender. . . . Raizela and Deborah occupied the rear seat, with Michael sandwiched in between, while Reb Avram Ber and Reb Zalman faced them on the narrow tip-up seat opposite—a precarious perch for two grown men, but fortunately neither of them was on the bulky side. The cabby stood scratching his head a while, as if he were about to protest at having to take five fares, but in the end he said nothing, and, climbing on to the box, set off at a brisk pace over the bumpy cobbles.

Soon they came to a bridge. The roadway across it seemed to be exceedingly well paved, for the droshky now sped along with the utmost smoothness. Before they had gone far, however, there was a hold-up in the traffic ahead; their own droshky stopped, and so did a long line of trams, lorries, motor-cars, droshkies, bicycles and peasant carts coming up behind. What a great number of peasant carts for such a big city, what were they doing there? And what was the meaning of this sudden stoppage? A little while ago everybody in the station and out in the streets had been hurrying along like mad, so what good reason could they have now for halting as if possessed of a single body and soul?

"Goodness gracious," said Raizela, "what queer goings-on! At one moment you see everybody racing along as if we were in a gold-rush, at the next everybody stops as if time simply didn't matter at all."

Deborah was delighted. Her mother and herself had been thinking alike. And as for the sudden standstill, nothing could have pleased her better, for on either side of the bridge lay the mighty River Vistula, its placid surface stained a deep red by the late afternoon sun. Then a boat sounded its horn. The sheet of sunlight was cut in half, and from under the bridge a pleasure steamer entered into view, bit by bit, with white foam frothing angrily all round it. A few dinghies, no bigger than toys, which she had not noticed in the water before, were caught up in the wake of the passing vessel, and how they bobbed up and down merrily, as if they were not in the least frightened of this terrible river! It all seemed quite unreal, like a dream. And now another steamer was coming up.

"Coo, what a big ship!" she said to Michael.

"A whale of a ship!" said Michael, and then he added with an air of bravado, "I wouldn't be afraid of climbing up its rigging. I bet you I wouldn't!"

Deborah laughed like a grown-up sister.

The waterside was lined with strings of barges. And as far as the eye could reach there were stacks of timber, heaps of rubble, assortments of scrap iron and no end of casks—casks of a monstrous size, the like of which she had never seen before. The barges, of course, were at anchor, but all the dumps of material lining the river bank looked as if they might drift away at any moment—they had no visible support. . . .

There was a sudden stir in the tangled line of traffic, and, as if by a pre-arranged signal, it all came to life. They were on the move again, and a few minutes later they had crossed the bridge. The river was lost to sight, and now they came to broad streets with imposing houses rising up on either side.

"This is Warsaw proper," said Reb Zalman with a grave and important air. "How does it strike you? Some people, you know, think Warsaw the finest city in the world. That they do."

Reb Zalman was mentally clapping his hands for joy, but he could hear no echo, so he turned to the cabby:

"Well, driver, would you describe Warsaw as the finest city in the world?"

"Sure I would. Sure!" said the cabby with a sarcastic grunt, in plain Yiddish.

Deborah looked round as if she could not believe her own ears.

"What, is that fellow a Jew?" she gasped.

"Evidently," said Raizela, herself rather taken aback.

"He's a Jew we can be proud of, to judge by his looks—a man of real intellect," Michael put in, but Reb Avram Ber protested.

"You mustn't judge a man by his looks. Everybody has his redeeming features. And anyway I'm sure it's his uniform which is to blame for his coarse appearance."

"Maybe he's a Gentile who has just picked up a few words of Yiddish," Deborah reflected in a loud voice. She could not persuade herself that the cabby with his clean-shaven chin and sanguine complexion was in fact a Jew.

"Nothing of the sort," the driver suddenly spoke up for himself, without turning his head. "I'm a Jew all right! And don't I know it! I 'ave to work like a 'orse to earn me miserable living, I do. I 'ave to be out in every lousy weather, I do! No wonder I look like a brute. 'Ave to work to earn me blooming living," he whined, and furiously lashed his horse. . . .

"A good job he's taking it out of the horse. He might have taken it out of us," said Reb Zalman with a smirk.

Deborah was all eyes. She jerked her head this way and that. There were so many wonderful sights to be seen, she could not properly fasten her attention on any of them. At one moment she was pointing out one of the marvels, but at the next her eye was caught by another and even greater marvel. As the streets filed by, she felt a pang of regret at having missed so many good things. And opening her eyes wider than ever, she determined to see everything! As for Michael, he simply sat still and stared straight ahead of him. He had no alternative, for he was jammed in and could not move. But he had a vision of indiscriminate hustle; the town was like an inferno, in which humans swirled about endlessly, aimlessly, as though they had been placed by Satan himself in a boiling cauldron. If Warsaw had been hell, however, Michael would have rejoiced to go there. . .

"Market day in Jelhitz!" said Deborah, addressing no one in particular and bouncing on her seat. She had no time to spare for idle conversation. They had been driving along for quite a while, and still there was no slackening in the fierce city current—more streets, more shops, more crowds, more traffic. Where did it all begin, and where did it all end?

Then the droshky pulled up, and the cabby jumped off on to the pavement.

"Well, well, here we are! Let me introduce you to your new home. No, this isn't it! I say, driver, it's twenty-four we want!"

"All right, you've no need to 'oller at me! I ain't deaf," the cabby retorted sullenly, and tugging the halter he brought the droshky to a standstill at number twenty-six.

"No, twenty-four, my good man, twenty-four!" Reb Zalman shouted.

"All right, keep your wool on, keep your wool on!"

Michael, squeezing his way out between Deborah and Raizela, was the first to alight, and he helped the others down. He almost had to lift his mother out, as Raizela found that one of her legs had gone quite numb. When the neighbours first saw her they thought she was lame. Deborah, carrying the bag in one hand and a shawl in the other, kept guard over the luggage piled up on the pavement. Michael put his head into the droshky to make sure that nothing had been left behind. Meanwhile, Reb Zalman was engaging in a lively argument with the cabby, who was asking for more than his due. The cabby swore volubly, but finally clapped his big red hands together by way of assent, then examined the coins which Reb Zalman dropped into his palm, and after spitting on the money for luck, he buttoned it up in his large wallet, thrust it deep into the back pocket of his shiny trousers, buttoned up his blue greatcoat, climbed on to his box and, with a farewell flourish of his whip, drove away.

"Look everybody, a lot of country yokels are moving into our house!" cried a little girl of about twelve, with a feather-speckled pigtail.

Her companion, a red-haired girl with a freckled little face and a sore nose, which she was in the act of wiping with the back of her freckly hand, burst out laughing.

The newcomers gathered in the gateway also attracted the attention of the gossips chatting in the inevitable little grocery shop tucked away in a corner of the courtyard.

"D'ye know who that is, Malkela? It's our new Rabbi, God bless him! Ain't it nice to have a Rabbi in our own house, ain't it an honour for us?" remarked an old woman with her livid face a network of wrinkles.

"Sure it is! They're movin' in 'cos I live 'ere. Ain't I an attraction?" said Malkela coquettishly, and tickled by her own waggishness, she waited for some response, but none came. "Ha, ha!" she chortled, all by herself; then drawing her tattered shawl firmly around her fleshless, narrow shoulders, she vanished into one of the doorways in the courtyard, with a jug of milk in her hand.

"I say, who's that skinny young woman over there, poor thing?" inquired a huge fat woman, pointing to Raizela; this fat woman had been busy picking a Dutch herring and had missed the conversation. "You ought to know," she went on when the shopkeeper merely answered her question with a scowl.

"I don't know nothing!" the shopkeeper declared venomously. "What I do know is that you're taking too much liberty in picking and choosing around here. Hi, take your fingers out of that sauce. If you don't think my pickled cucumbers are sound, you can go elsewhere. Ah, so you want me to book it up, do you? I thought so! Curse you, and go to hell!" the shopkeeper added when the fat woman was out of earshot. "Some of these here customers are about the limit."

Reb Zalman led the way into one of the innumerable doorways in the courtyard and up a dimly lit flight of stairs, then another and another, until everybody was quite out of breath. After a while they got accustomed to the gloom and could plainly see the steps—dirty grey steps worn smooth by countless feet and littered with rubbish. Once or twice the party paused to rest, then went on again, slipping on the refuse, until at last when they had reached yet another landing Reb Zalman announced that this was their destination. He fumbled in his pockets and produced the key. He inserted it into the lock of an impressive-looking brown door, and flinging it open as wide as he could, he cried:

"You are at home!"

Reb Avram Ber placed a chair for Raizela and she dropped on to it quite helpless.

"Well, isn't this a wonderful flat?" said Reb Avram Ber with his eyes fixed on Reb Zalman. "For this and for many other things indeed, and no man could have a better friend than Reb Zalman."

Reb Avram Ber could not resist paying Reb Zalman this little compliment. It was very unlike him, for he invariably praised people behind their backs. The sincerity of it went to Reb Zalman's head, and also to his legs, for although he said "Pshaw!" and waved the compliment away with his hand, he felt his knees giving way for joy.

They all sat down to rest, either on chairs or on the luggage. Then Reb Zalman went away, taking Michael along with him, and in about half an hour's time he returned with a big parcel in his hands wrapped up in brown paper full of greasy stains. He told Michael to pull the table up into the centre of the room and to set the chairs all round it—this was an unfamiliar table with unfamiliar chairs. Where did they come from? Reb Zalman spread a prosperous-looking starched tablecloth.

Just then there was a knock at the door. Reb Zalman admitted a portly woman in the early forties wearing a blonde, neat wig in which a costly clasp was fastened; her hands were white and smooth, and when she smiled her childish dimples showed very prominently, as did her artificial golden teeth. When Reb Zalman gave her a smile, she flushed like a child—even her double chin turned red—and she became quite flustered. Raizela tried to be pleasant to her, and asked her to take a seat, which she did, still completely at a loss, but in the end she managed to pull herself together; she rose to her feet again, held a whispered conversation with Reb Zalman and began to lay the table with a dinner-service which she had brought along in a basket. Then she went into the kitchen and returned with a big dish containing soup, which she ladled out; without a word, she set down a cooked yellow fowl—a plump one, and like herself it had an embarrassed air; as though ashamed of its utter nakedness—not forgetting a cruet, sliced bread, a syphon of soda-water and pickled cucumbers.

Finally she laid the cutlery—all of massive silver, resounding on the table in massive silvery tones—and she begged Raizela to take every possible care of all these domestic treasures.

"You know how easily things get broken and mislaid . . . when everything's topsy-turvy . . . you know what I mean . . ." the woman apologised with a guilty air.

Raizela reassured her and endeavored to thank her, but could not think of anything to say. She was herself disconcerted to see this woman so embarrassed and ill at ease.

"I'm ever so grateful to you," she brought out at last.

"Not at all!" the other woman replied, and backed away to the door with obvious relief.

"She lives next door," Reb Zalman explained. "You'll find them a very nice couple. Extremely well off and ever so religious. Her husband is by no means an ignorant man, and what's more, he's an extremely decent fellow. Most generous. No one in need has ever been turned away from his door. If only they had a child, they'd be as happy as the day long. It's a pity they can't have any children, such a pity!" Reb Zalman shook his head regretfully. "When she saw me the other day she promised she would get everything ready in good time, and as you see she has kept her word. Don't think, though, that she's an exception. The Jews of Warsaw are all like that. They're kindhearted, and know how to live and let live."

Once again Reb Zalman waxed enthusiastic over the nobleness of the Jews of Warsaw.

"Quite! Quite!" Reb Avram Ber exclaimed, stroking his beard to his heart's content.

Reb Zalman had dinner with the family, and as a matter of fact he seemed to be famished.

Soon after nightfall the menfolk went away to the synagogue, returning without Reb Zalman. Then late at night the removal vans arrived and the furniture was brought up by the dim light of the gas jets flickering on the brick walls of the staircase. The kindhearted husband of the kindhearted woman next door put in an appearance. He was short of stature, had a massive gold chain across his comfortable, gently heaving belly, and wore a grey coat which was a cross between a gabardine and a frock-coat, and he padded about noiselessly in gleaming top boots. He smiled a good deal, and as he did so—like his wife—he revealed a mouthful of artificial gold teeth.

He greeted Reb Avram Ber with much warmth, and even shook hands with Michael, but treated the womenfolk to a mere nod of the head—it was a short, broad and friendly head. After a little polite conversation, in the course of which he praised Reb Zalman to the skies and reassured Reb Avram Ber that they would do everything they could to ensure his well-being, he divested himself of his coat, rolled up the starched cuffs of his immaculate shirt and helped to put up the beds, a task at which Michael had been struggling in vain for some time. A big blue vein came out on his low forehead, but at last he was finished. He put his coat on again, glanced at his massive gold watch, gave everybody a friendly nod and took his leave.

"Just past midnight," he remarked as he opened the door. "Good night, everybody!"

The family passed the night in a trance, so that they were very startled when, in the midst of their slumbers, they heard a loud, persistent banging at the door.

"Who's that? Why, look, it's broad daylight!"

They dressed in haste and opened the door to Reb Zalman.

"Well, you were certainly sound asleep," Reb Zalman greeted them with a laugh. "I've never known a night to pass so quickly myself. I see the furniture's come."

"Yes, it came late last night."

"Now this young man is going to put things straight for you," Reb Zalman declared, at which all eyes turned on a youth with an unwashed, pimply face, who had slipped in unobserved. Hearing himself introduced, the youth shuffled up from the door and began to shift the furniture about. Reb Zalman never budged until everything was in ship-shape order. The jobber cursed him under his breath for being a "finnicky old woman," and for wanting everything done in his own way. But at last Reb Zalman could find no more complaints to make; he went away to attend to his own business, and once more the family were established in a new home, once more they were strangers in a strange city.

"Hark at all that shouting down below!" said Raizela as she settled down on her couch.

"Yes, I wonder what it's all about. We never heard a sound last night," said Deborah, greatly puzzled. Putting her head out of the window she could see down below a number of men and women in rags and tatters who came into the courtyard to cry their wares and then went away again, usually without finding any customers.

"Hot rolls, hot rolls! All hot!"

"Old rags! Old boots, galoshes, hats, old rags! Don't throw your rags away, sell them to me!"

"Any windows to mend? Any windows to mend? Windows!"

"Cakes, cakes, cakes!"

"Good God, it's maddening!" Raizela cried, losing all patience.

"You won't notice it after a time. You'll soon get used to it," Reb Avram Ber pacified her. "Reb Zalman asked me to warn you about it beforehand, so that you shouldn't be upset, only I forgot to mention it. You see, all these good people are very poor and are trying to make an honest living. Most of them are Jews," Reb Avram Ber added with a sigh.

"So there's no lack of poverty anywhere—not even in Warsaw! Ah, well, you'll find plenty of misery everywhere . . ."

CHAPTER IX

In the flesh the Jews of Warsaw bore no resemblance whatever to the superhumans that peopled Reb Zalman's fancy. They seemed to be wholly ignorant, in fact, of the mighty reputation which Reb Zalman had built up for them, and never even pretended that they could earn money with the same ease as they could spend it. Deborah had imagined that they all lived in the lap of luxury, were all fabulously rich. But she was soon to be sadly disillusioned. She was soon to know that it was only a myth. . . . Now here was Deborah herself a citizen of Warsaw, but so hard up she could not afford to buy a hat, could not scrape together a few coins for such a simple thing as a hat, and was, therefore, obliged to stay indoors for three weeks on end, like an eager dog chained to its kennel. By the end of that time she was just about disgusted with the Jews of Warsaw. . . .

Reb Zalman's eldest daughter, Miss Rushka, who—according to her father—was of the same age as Deborah and was, therefore, expected to be her friend, had made it quite clear, when she paid her first call on the Sabbath after the family's arrival, that in the city of Warsaw it was most improper for a young lady to venture forth hatless into the streets. It would be counter to all the unwritten laws of decency. Consequently, Deborah stayed indoors. Funds were low, and anyway, her coat was too shabby for her to go out walking in it.

In the early days Miss Rushka had come again and again to find out how the hat problem was getting on, but one day her father, butting into the prim conversation like a boor, declared vehemently that Rushka herself had not worn a hat when she first came to Warsaw from the dear little village of Jilkovka, although at the time, some eight years ago—and here Reb Zalman put his foot into it badly—Rushka had been quite a grown up young lady. At this she had almost burst into tears, and nothing more was seen of her again. Deborah was left to her solitude, and instead of getting fed up with Miss Rushka, she got fed up with herself.

It was all very well for Michael. He had no hat problem. He could go wherever he pleased. And even though his gabardine was out-at-elbows he was not the sort to care. He had settled down in a little synagogue in the Gnoina Road, where he devoted himself to the Talmud, when he was not otherwise engaged in matching his wits against his fellow-students. The rest of the time he spent sauntering over the streets of Warsaw, like a tourist, never knowing where he was going, but always finding his way home again. And that suited him to perfection!

Then one day Reb Zalman turned up with a broad-chested youth who had a remarkably expressive, swarthy face with large mournful eyes, and a big hump on his back that pushed his gabardine out to a sharp point, around which streaks of shine radiated like rays of light. Michael, who had just tucked his forelocks into his mop of hair and had brushed his gabardine in readiness for his daily stroll round the town, was stopped at the door by Reb Zalman, who declared that in future Michael must join forces with Joseph (this being the hunch-back's name), who was going to make it his business to collect the subscriptions towards Reb Avram Ber's stipend.

"You see, things can't go on as at present," said Reb Zalman, explaining the deep logic of the situation. "The subscribers mean well, but very often they can't find the time to call in with their sub-scription, or else it slips their memory, or maybe they're hard up, but if you go to their door and ask for it, then you bring them face to face with realities and the cash comes rolling in. . . ."

Michael did not resent the proposal. On the contrary. Here was a wonderful opportunity of getting to know a multitude of strangers in a strange city. As for going round the houses, knocking at the doors and pocketing other people's money, Michael could imagine nothing more enjoyable. Certainly more enjoyable than poring over the dry pages of the Talmud. But he soon changed his mind. After a couple of weeks, he met with ugly looks from the womenfolk, who protested that they knew nothing about their husbands' affairs; and servant girls would give both Joseph and himself a no uncertain piece of their mind for being so importunate and sceptical when told that there was no one at home. Sometimes Joseph and himself would take turns at knocking at a door which remained obstinately closed, and in the end one of the neighbours might appear on the scene and order them to clear out and stop disturbing the peace. As for climb-ing up the stairs and down the stairs, there was nothing very delight-ful about it after all. Moreover, an unsavoury whiff of decay and poverty assailed the nostrils in every courtyard and on every stair-case. And as the sun grew hotter, as spring changed into summer, the whiff changed into a stench that was positively sickening.

The uproar out-of-doors became more and more deafening. More and more children came pouring out of their squalid, overcrowded homes and refused to return until long after sunset. All day long they played games in the courtyards, all day long their shouts and cries resounded through the length and breadth of the city. Their shrill voices, happy and carefree now that dreary winter was over, almost stupefied the grown-ups, who were pretty noisy themselves. And there was still the endless procession of ragged men and women that were still as eager as ever to sell hot cakes and buy old rags and mend broken windows. The massive towering walls trembled under the impact of their assaults. Then the music! No sooner did the scratchy strains of a gramophone record issue forth from one of the windows, than inevitably a beggar turned up in the courtyard and set up his own gramophone in opposition. Military marches and arias, waltzes and ragtimes blared away at each other, striving with might and main to drown one another, and as they wrestled furiously, first one would come out on top, then the other. During the interval an old beggar woman might enter and burst into song like a nightingale. She would be followed by more beggars, who all warbled the same melancholy Yiddish songs, and only varied their chanted appeals for charity:

"Kind folk, have mercy on a destitute ailing widow with six children; have mercy on my poor mites, they're waiting for me, waiting to be fed at my breast. Don't let them starve. Throw down all you can spare! . . ."

"Throw down all you can spare! I'm a cripple and an orphan. Look me over, but don't overlook me!"

Begging eyes—eyes dim and mournful and eyes bright and crafty—would be upturned to the wide-open windows from morning to night.

Now and again a slut might sling her rubbish through the window into the courtyard. . . .

Before long Michael had had more than enough, and he washed his hands of Joseph. A lone figure now, the poor hunchback bore his heavy lump from door to door, trudging through interminable streets and courtyards, climbing up endless stairs and down again, while Michael, relieved of all responsibility, strolled about with his hands in his pockets, enjoying the peace and quiet of elegant residential neighbourhoods where the streets were lined with trees in blossom, where flowers were blooming in vases at the windows, and where every drawn blind told the same tale—the inmates had taken up residence in their country estate or had gone abroad. . . .

Deborah's heart was filled with longing to see for herself those dreamlands where Michael could wander so freely, while she was kept a prisoner in her own home—all because of a miserable hat!

How happy she might have been if only she had been born a boy! It was not without good reason that her father had insisted, way back in Jelhitz, that girls were inferior creatures. Now why on earth could not men and women wear the same clothes? If she was to wear a gabardine like Michael, then, like him, she could go wherever her fancy took her. . . . However, instead of having to wait for so sweeping a reform, she found her hat problem solved one day.

It all began early one morning, when the family had passed some two months in their new home. There was a loud knock at the door, and when Deborah went to see who it was, she shrank back in amazement, for at first glance she thought the caller was the *Tsadik* of R— disguised in a lounge suit and with his chin clean-shaven.

"Can I have a word with the Rabbi?" he boomed at her in a voice that was like the blast of a double-bass. He had a belly that started halfway up his chest and finished halfway down his legs; his backside was like the dome of a great cathedral.

"Pappa is at the synagogue."

"When d'you expect him back?"

"In about half an hour's time."

"Will it be all right for me to wait?"

At this Deborah turned deathly pale. Terror-stricken she conducted him into her father's study and asked him to take a seat. He raised a clenched fat fist, pushed his sleeve back, revealing a wide leather strap round his wrist, then compared the hands of his wristwatch with those of his big golden pocket watch hanging on a tremendous golden chain across his waistcoat, and after stroking his purple jaw awhile, he carefully lowered himself on to the chair, which croaked hoarsely as though it were in great pain. He eyed Deborah with a goodhumoured twinkle in his crafty, thievish little eyes.

"I think you're afraid of me, Missy," he said.

"No, not at all. I mean, it's ridiculous, why should I be afraid of you?"

He looked her up and down with an expert air.

"Go on, tell the truth! Aren't you afraid of me?"

"Of course I'm not," Deborah protested, backing out of the room, and she fled into the bedroom, where Raizela was still abed.

Speaking in a whisper she told her mother about the caller and what a fright he had given her. She begged her mother to get up at once, but Raizela only gave her a scornful look.

"Stop playing the fool! There are no cannibals living in these parts, and he won't eat you. Now go in and join him. Don't you know it's rude to leave a visitor all by himself?"

"But Mamma, you've never seen such a terrible-looking fellow in all your life. Why, he's even bigger than the *Tsadik*!"

Raizela laughed noiselessly.

"Off with you now! Run in like a good little girl, like mummy's little darling!"

Deborah fussed about in her father's study, setting the books straight in the bookcase, dusting the table and collecting the scattered manuscripts which Reb Avram Ber had been working on during the night and which he had been too tired to put away before retiring. She pretended to be very busy, so as to avoid the visitor's gaze, but all the time she was intent on listening to the muttering of the chair as it groaned under its cruel burden. Luckily Reb Avram Ber had forgotten his praying shawl, so he put in an appearance sooner than expected.

"Good morning, Rabbi!" the man bawled at him, rising to his feet with an exaggerated air of reverence, while the chair uttered a gasp of relief.

"Good morning!" Reb Avram Ber responded quietly, himself rather overawed. "Well, and what can I do for you?" he added as an afterthought, with eyes averted. And he motioned the visitor to a seat at the table. But as if to atone for his momentary lapse, he now looked the man full in the face, without a trace of restraint and so sweetly, that the visitor was instantly put at his ease and was both like a brother and a father to him now—a kindly father who was going to listen to a terrible confession from his erring son.

"Don't hesitate! . . . I'm prepared for the worst," Reb Avram Ber's kindly beard seemed to say. And his kindly eyes seemed to add: "Well, after all, even the best of us are only human, and we must learn to understand each other and to forgive. Yes, forgiveness is all! . . ."

The visitor, who was the chief of a powerful gang of criminals and a notorious figure in Warsaw's underworld, was suffering from a secret sorrow which he was eager to share with someone. Reb Avram Ber's expression was encouraging, and the gangster felt the words welling up to his tongue of their own accord. Still, it would have been easier to begin if he could only undo his collar and take a deep breath of air. Putting his finger down his neck, he found that he was in a sweat. However, when once he had got started, he knew, he would not stop until he had gone the whole hog. But the problem was, how was he to begin? He had another look at Reb Avram Ber's face, then cleared his throat, and just as he was putting his snowy white handkerchief back into his pocket, he had a brainwave. He would approach the matter in a roundabout way:

"Your holiness, what brings me here to you to-day is a question of Jewish law. . . ."

"Ah, that's good! Proceed!" Reb Avram replied with gusto, rubbing his hands at the thought that this brutish creature was sensitive to questions of Jewish law. The Creator invested even the ugliest of creatures with a sacred soul. It was wonderful! . . .

"This is the position," the gangster continued, endeavouring to speak in a whisper, but every word he said could be plainly heard all over the flat. "You see, Rabbi, I'm a godfearing Jew, that's what I am! A Jew every inch of me, and I run my house on strictly kosher lines. That's me! Home life is home life, and business is business! That's why I never let any of the boys come anywhere near my home. And let me tell you, that if they were to try and interfere with any of my children, or if they tried to play me yeller, I'd wring their necks and dump 'em in the Vistula. Get me? What I says to them is this: 'Boys,

you all know me. My name's Berel Fass . . .' and that does the trick
with them. They know that I'll always give them a square deal. I
know that they'll always give *me* a square deal. Honesty, I says, is the
best policy. So there you are! But you can't always be too clever. No,
sir! You can go on dodging trouble all your life, till you think yourself the most artful dodger in town, and then—like a bloody fool—
you go and trip up. That's what you go and do, you go and trip up!
Now I'm not new at the game, and as for me being a booby, ask anyone you like: whatever they may say about me, they won't call me a
booby. No, sir! But I'll tell you what happened.

"A couple of weeks ago a nice bit of stuff came up from the country—and I jolly well had to hide it away somewhere or other. After
all, it's my bread and butter. And 'tain't like old times, you know. No,
sir! The police are pretty strict nowadays. They'll take a bribe all
right, but it's got to be a big 'un. That it has. They've got their jobs to
think of, they say, and the lousy sort of argument they put up to you
nowadays is this: 'We want our fair share of the swag, and if you're
not going to play the game, we'll jolly well answer the call of duty!'
It's become a regular racket. I never liked the police, but if I was to
tell you what I think of them now . . . Anyhow, a feller has to use his
wits, and I decided to ask no favours of these here new-fangled coppers, and what I did was to lock the stuff up in my own house. D'you
get me?"

"Yes, but how does all this relate to Jewish law?" asked Reb Avram
Ber. He could not follow the story at all, and he looked Berel Fass up
and down with unconcealed curiosity.

"Now I'm just coming round to that. I was just going to tell you
of the hot water I got into. Did I get myself into a sticky mess!
What a sticky mess! You see, I had a young feller working for me,
you know, one of these here smart handsome blokes, and his job
was to keep the girls in order. He knew his work all right, all the
girls were crazy about him. He's a well-set-up young feller, with a
mop of black hair and a beautiful little moustache. He has a little
cane under his arm, and swaggers about like a bloody lord. . . . You
know the sort I mean! He can make love to a girl quicker than you

can wink. And what does my own daughter do? She goes whoring with him, that's what she does! Brings shame on her own father, makes a fool of her own father, that's what she does! What a misfortune! And when her husband gets to hear of it—and he didn't have to go far to find out, 'cos the other feller actually had the face to tell him about it, boasted about it, that's what he did—as I was saying, when her husband got to know, he went up into the air, just like that! He will have nothing more to do with her! He's finished! He's had enough! All he wants is a divorce, and nothing else'll satisfy him. But that's only the beginning of the story. The rotten part about it is that my daughter's expecting a baby. And what her husband says is, that he doesn't believe he's the father. He doesn't believe it a bit. He doesn't want to be the girl's husband, and he doesn't want to be the kid's father. So that's that! And it's no use trying to cajole or threaten him. He doesn't care if I stick a knife into him. And to think that only a year ago I spent a little fortune over a grand wedding reception. Lovely affair it was! I made my mind up to marry her off to a respectable, honest working man. A real decent fellow. You'd do the same for your own daughter, wouldn't you now, if you were wallowing in the mud right up to your neck? [Here he paused and placed his hand under his chin to illustrate how high the mud reached]. Well, it just shows you, you can't be too clever! You can't go on fooling God Almighty all the time. He's like the police: if He doesn't catch you now, He'll catch you some other time! No, you can't be too smart! And when you get what's coming to you, all you can do is go and kick yourself. I said to her, with tears in my eyes, 'You lousy bitch, what have you gone and done to your poor old father? What d'yer mean by playing your own father yeller, you dirty hussy?' She doesn't say a word, but just looks at you and looks at you, till it breaks yer heart. After all, it's yer own flesh and blood! The dirty double-crosser got round her 'cos he wanted to have the laugh of her husband, who was too stuck up to speak to the likes of him. Too standoffish, you know! It's a good explanation, but it makes no difference to the sticky mess we're in now. I don't mind telling you, I've had a bit of my own back already. I've given that double-crosser something to remember me by, and he's in the horspital now. As soon as he's out, I'll get one of my boys to finish the job for me. He'll be pushing up the daisies before the month's out. I'll fix him, I swear to God I will! But is there anything I can do in the meantime to put things right, that's what I wanner know! My son-in-law, the silly boob—he should have kept his eyes open—insists on having a divorce. All right, he can have a divorce! For all I care he can go and hang himself, if he feels like it. But what about the poor little mite? Why should the innocent little babe suffer? 'Tain't its fault! The poor thing's going to become an orphan, so to speak, with its father and mother both alive and kicking. . . . What can we do about it?"

Reb Avram Ber spat into his handkerchief and had a good mind to show his visitor the door. But in the first place he was very much afraid of him, and—more important still—it was his bounden duty to divorce the woman both from her lawful husband and from her paramour. It was an extremely serious case. Although Reb Avram Ber had been unable to make head or tail of the first part of the story he understood only too well the nature of the sin committed, and that by a married woman! Good God, it was monstrous! He felt sick at heart.

"How old is the child?" he asked.

"Not so fast! She's expecting it any day now. What I want your holiness to tell me is this: supposing it's a boy, can we go on with the circumcision ceremony without the father being present?"

"Of course you can! In fact, you *must* go on with the ceremony! Meanwhile, your daughter will have to obtain a divorce from each of the two men," Reb Avram gave his ruling. "And she must do it immediately, understand? There must be no delay!"

Berel Fass promptly got to his feet, growling like a wounded beast. Then, mopping his brow, he sighed aloud.

"Your holiness, will you do me the favour of seeing this business through and giving her the two divorces? Lord love us, I never knew I had two sons-in-law!"

It was some time before Reb Avram Ber gave his reply. He sat with his face buried in his hands.

"Very well then! Be here with your daughter and her husband at ten in the morning, in four days' time. By then I shall have all the papers ready. Later on, you can bring the other man along."

"Thank you very much, Rabbi! I'm much obliged to you, I'm sure! God bless you, and may you never have any such trouble come your way as long as you live!"

And with this parting benediction, Berel Fass strode from the room with two great big tears filling his tiny little eyes.

Reb Avram Ber paced the room with his mind in a turmoil. It was unbelievable! What an abomination! Was flesh and blood really capable of sinking to such low, despicable depths? He could not get over it. He even felt disgusted with himself at having agreed to officiate at the divorce proceedings, although to refuse would have been to neglect a solemn duty. What harassed him was the thought that he would not have dared to say no to that ugly beast of a man, whatever the circumstances. . . .

"What's worrying you?" asked Raizela, when Reb Avram Ber joined her.

"Nothing. Someone called in to consult me on a question relating to Jewish law," and suddenly he smiled in spite of himself—a fleeting smile which left no trace of mirth in his ruffled beard.

"But what on earth made him shout at the top of his voice?"

"Nothing to speak of!" Reb Avram Ber said with an impatient gesture, and Raizela guessed at once that it was something unfit for Deborah's ears.

Later in the morning she heard the whole story. Reb Avram Ber began to grumble about Warsaw.

"That's the sort of thing that can happen only in a big city. You never hear of such goings-on in the provinces. When so many people are herded together, they lose sight of their own individual value as human beings with a sacred soul. . . ."

"I wonder why he picked on us, anyway?"

"I suppose he asked some stranger for the address of the nearest Rabbi, and I was the unlucky one. I don't like it a bit!"

Reb Avram Ber heaved a sigh and offered every excuse he could think of, for having agreed to officiate.

"Still, it's wonderful, when you come to think of it: seemingly a brute, yet he believes in God and thinks it necessary to consult a Rabbi. An evil man, a wicked man, but he still has a divine spark in him somewhere or other," Reb Avram Ber wound up on a more cheerful note, and away he went to the synagogue, this time with his praying shawl safely tucked under his arm.

Four days later Berel Fass showed up precisely at ten. Within this short time he seemed to have aged quite a lot. In spite of all the fat on his face, he bore a haggard expression. Even his belly seemed to have shrunk. Shuffling along behind him came his daughter, a woman of about twenty-two—possibly rather younger than that—with a pale oval face and blazing jet-black eyes, her lips half parted under her retroussé little nose. Tastefully dressed in a blue cape, with a little black bonnet on her head, she looked very attractive and dainty. There was something very gentle about her expression and her gestures. She was followed by her mother, a woman in the forties, with a long pinched nose, with freckles and warts all over her face, with an ugly set of decayed teeth and with her bleary eyes a vivid tear-stained red.

Reb Avram Ber closed the book he was reading, and told Berel Fass to sit down. A few minutes later the scribe arrived accompanied by Susskind, the beadle, who, although he was attached to the local synagogue, yet found time to help Reb Avram Ber out now and again. Susskind transferred a long wooden bench from the table to the back wall for the women to sit on. At last the lawful husband turned up—he was a powerfully built young fellow with a massive chin, which, clean-shaven though it was, bristled with the black roots of his beard. He greeted the group at the table, but took good care to ignore his father-in-law and the two women opposite. Few words were spoken, as the possibility of a last-minute reconciliation was altogether ruled-out. The husband obstinately refused to sit down, but kept pacing to and fro, only stopping with a sudden jerk whenever he was addressed by Reb Avram Ber. He seemed terribly embittered, and if his demeanour was cold and dry, it was only because he was steeling himself with fists clenched, for there was an unholy little light in his eyes which betrayed his deep agitation, pain and fury. His young wife, for her part, was perfectly calm; only her mother kept snivelling and blowing her nose till the end, and till the end a large drop of moisture was suspended on the tip of her nose, as if that, too, were a tear.

Directly the proceedings were over the two parties dispersed. Berel Fass turned his head in the doorway to say that he would call in with the other man as soon as he had recovered sufficiently to leave hospital. After he had paid off the beadle and the scribe, Reb Avram Ber had four roubles for himself. Never before had he done so well out of a divorce case.

Some weeks later the other man limped into Reb Avram Ber's study, leaning on a stout stick and his head all swathed in bandages. The young woman had meanwhile had her baby, and she was now very much paler and thinner. Clad in a close-fitting black costume she looked more girlish than ever. She did not have her mother with her this time, but her father was there, and there was nothing subdued about him now. A triumphant expression flashed and sparkled in his tiny eyes within their pockets of fact. Two burly men wearing caps took up a watchful position at the door. One of them kept fingering a bulky object in his trouser pocket, while his companion, a swarthy fellow with very short legs and extraordinarily broad shoulders, kept treading on the other's toe by way of a reminder that it was out of order to whistle here. So every now and then a merry whistle would trail off into a grunt of pain.

"This is the bloke I was telling you of, Rabbi! Ain't he a beauty? You wouldn't believe it, but he never wanted to come on this trip at all. He says she suits him grand the way she is now, without having any Rabbis to put her right. That's what he thinks. But I got him to see my point of view, that I did, and he'll be seeing a lot more funny things by the time I've finished with him. Take a peep at those two kids at the door! You see them, Rabbi? I can trust 'em like I could my own father!"

Only now did Reb Avram Ber become aware of their presence. "Please be seated," he said.

The two men exchanged an amused look.

From time to time the lover stole a peep, from under his bandage, at the young woman, who was unable to check the flow of tears coursing slowly down her pale cheeks. He did not seem to take much interest in what was going on, but did as he was told. (He had no option.) When all the formalities had been completed, Berel Fass triumphantly snapped his fingers at the two men in the doorway, who exchanged a knowing look, and then gave their chief a wink that spoke volumes. They had girdled their loins for the slaughter.

"Well, Rabbi, that's that! And when I'm satisfied with a nice bit of work nicely done, money's no object to me! Nossir! Here you are, Rabbi, take ten roubles, and don't argue!" he exclaimed, putting the note down with such a mighty thump of his fist that all the furniture in the room jumped. "Don't argue!" he cried, although Reb Avram Ber never said a word. "You've earned every bit of it, Take it!"

"So long, Rabbi!"

"Good day!"

Berel Fass got hold of his daughter by her arm and bundled her out of the room.

"Come on, you bitch. And you, fellers, seize him!"

The limping man was hustled out by the two gangsters at a half-run.

Reb Avram Ber looked all around him, as if to convince himself that the place was really empty. He sighed with relief. As he was on the point of passing into the next room, he was called back.

"You've forgotten the money on the table," said Susskind, the beadle, his eyes sparkling oddly from out of the hairy depths of his eyebrows and beard. Reb Avram Ber gave him a tip, producing the coins from numerous pockets all over his person (he never remembered to put his possessions in the same pocket.) The beadle went away doubly satisfied, for he had the funeral of a rich man to attend later in the day.

"All over?"

"Yes, thank God!"

Raizela caught sight of the ten rouble note which Reb Avram was holding gingerly between his fingers.

"What! He gave you ten roubles?"

"Reb Avram Ber deposited the note on the couch at her side.

"I really ought not to have accepted such a big sum, but I didn't dare breathe a word to him, because he behaved like a devil to-day. I do believe he has the devil in him."

"In the old days they used to stone a woman if she committed such a sin," said Raizela.

"It's terrible! I do hope that God will send us our daily bread through different channels. . . ."

And Reb Avram Ber cast his eyes upwards, as though in prayer.

He returned to his study. Deborah brought him in a glass of tea. He eyed her tenderly, and eager to keep her at his side, he asked her to tidy up. She flicked the cigarette ash off the table, swept up and put the chairs straight.

"You're a darling! Do you think you could let me have another glass of tea?"

Deborah fetched him a second glass. He had taken a volume of the Talmud out of his book-case, and only when he had become absorbed in its parched yellow pages did he find peace of mind once more.

Deborah had bought herself a hat. She need not stay indoors any longer and need not look to Michael for descriptions of the marvellous sights of Warsaw. In any case, she never believed a word he said: all he did was to spin fantastic yarns out of his head, so as to lend an even keener edge to her pangs of longing. On the Sabbath there was never any washing up to do after dinner (for this was the days of rest), and as for clearing the table, that was child's play, especially as there was a smart new frock hanging in the wardrobe, waiting to be put on for the first time, not to mention the hat which was breathtakingly *chic*—its beauty no one could deny, not even Miss Rushka. This young lady, in fact, was going to call on her and take her out for her first walk through the select part of Warsaw, the "real" Warsaw as Michael called it. And Deborah was in a great flutter and more exultant than she cared to show. Now here was a knock at the door. That, to be sure, was Miss Rushka!

"Hello, how are you? Won't you sit down?"

"Oh, no thanks, I don't mind standing," said Miss Rushka, promptly sitting down. "Oh, please don't bother! I've only just had my tea."

"Well, won't you help yourself to some fruit, then?" Deborah pleaded, as she put the hat on in front of the mirror.

Miss Rushka came to her aid.

"Not like that! Like this! There, it suits you much better that way," she said, jerking the hat into a rakish angle. "Don't you think so?"

Deborah solemnly nodded her head. The new hat solemnly nodded assent, and away they went down the stairs like a whirlwind. Miss Rushka was hard put to it keeping up with Deborah, who finally moderated her pace; it was only by a supreme effort that she succeeded in hiding a little of her impetuous excitement.

Out of doors the sun was shining brightly as if it appreciated the importance of the occasion. The street was full of animation, full of the breath of life. Carefree strollers thronged the pavements. While the elderly folk sauntered along at their leisure, young couples elbowed their way past in a hurry. There were girls with their boy friends, and girls without their boy friends. Girls with young men wearing the orthodox gabardine, but with new-fangled smart little caps and gleaming black top-boots; girls with young men wearing lounge suits—anyone might have thought they were Gentiles; and other girls with young men who looked like half-breeds, for they wore coats that were a cross between a gabardine and a frock-coat, and had on stiff collars and stiff cuffs, which none but the wearers knew to be of papier mâché. There were women with their husbands and women without their husbands. Thin women and fat women. Men with long beards and short beards. And there were children of all ages and sizes.

Among the jostling crowd there were many sinful young people who were going to break the Sabbath; hurrying away into an unfamiliar neighbourhood they would furtively mount a tram that would take them to the distant Bagatelle Gardens. The unorthodox were heading for the magnificent Saxon Gardens, where a notice "JEWS WEARING GABARDINES AND DOGS NOT ADMITTED" barred the way for others. Only the chosen subjects of the Czar could enter there. As for the working men, for the most part they were off to the Kreszinski Gardens, where they had their traditional rendezvous. Nor was a mere stroll round the streets of the town to be sniffed at! This was the holy Sabbath, when work, unemployment, cares and troubles, creditors and all other pests were forgotten, when every man was his own master, and almost every home was supplied with food for the day. As for the evil city smells, no man in his proper mind took any notice of them. As for the dust that blew into one's eyes, and the awkward cobbles that harassed the feet, these things were so familiar that no one could have really and truly enjoyed his stroll without them.

The street they were in was like home to Deborah. The scene it presented on a Sabbath was, in particular, so familiar to her, that she thought she could recognise every single face, every crack in the wall, every cobble. She could see it even with her eyes closed, after having spent so many watchful, wistful hours at the window. She knew by sight all those bareheaded, big-bosomed girls with the painted faces and the multi-coloured shawls on their backs, who paced up and down on a weekday, and now, on the Sabbath, although they still wore the same clothes, yet had a festive air about them. These girls had strange habits: they beckoned to every man that passed them by. She often wondered why, and not knowing anything about rouge, she also wondered how they came by their high complexions.

To-day Deborah's own cheeks were coloured a deep red. She was quite giddy with joy. All that she had been longing for week after week was now within her grasp. Only . . . coming up to meet her was the old woman who kept the wineshop, and this old woman had a lot to say:

"Hallo, Deborah! I like your new clothes. Wish you well to wear them! How's Mamma? Did I tell you the other day. . . ."

Deborah scarcely listened to the old woman's prattle, and only hoped it would not go on for ever.

"Well, I won't detain you any longer," Deborah blurted out after a while, and escaped from the old gossip's clutches.

"This is Krulewski Street, you know," Miss Rushka announced.

"It's beautiful! And look how clean it is!"

"The best is still to come. We shall soon get to Marszalkowski Street, and I tell you that's going to thrill you! Let's turn the corner. Now, here we are! It's wonderful, don't you think so?" Miss Rushka asked with deep pride.

Deborah did not know what to think. She was quite dazed. On the sunny side of the road the windows of the stores and shops were one blaze of reflected golden light, with pier-glasses sparkling like slabs of crystal. From high velvet pedestals, streams of crêpe de chine, batiste and delicate lace, fine as a spider's web, came gushing down like waterfalls in a fairy-tale. Lengths of cloth, tapestry, velvet, silk and muslin floated gently down to the floor from on high, as though supported by nothing more substantial than a gentle breeze. It seemed inconceivable that all these things would in time be cut up and used, still less that there were so many people wealthy enough to consume all these luxuries.

Deborah and Miss Rushka passed from shopwindow to shopwindow, each with its regal display of costly stuffs, flowers, furniture, objets d'art, paintings, jewellery. All was magnificent. Again and again Deborah found that she could not tear herself away. The brilliance was positively dazzling.

And how restless the traffic seemed by way of contrast! Wheel upon wheel, wheel after wheel, rolled by, with automobile drivers tooting their horns, with coachmen cracking their whips, with the continual patter of horses' hoofs on the smooth roadway, and elegant ladies and gentlemen leaning back so daintily in their coaches and carriages, coming and going, till it made Deborah's head reel. Without speaking a word, she feasted her eye on all these marvels, and the more she feasted the hungrier she grew. She now realised that Michael had not exaggerated in the least. On the contrary, his descriptions paled before the reality.

At twilight the scene, as Deborah saw it, surpassed all bounds of the imagination. Quite suddenly the shops lit up. The stuffs in the windows became fantastic to look at, unreal. The illuminated globes high up on the standards lining either side of the street trailed away into the distance like two strings of milky pearls suspended in mid-air. The luminous advertisements outside the cinemas kept vanishing and re-appearing as if they were winking at the passers-by. And from out of the cafés, which she had given scant notice before, issued the gentle strains of narcotic music.

The advertisements and signs detracted somewhat from the beauty of the scene, introducing the commonplace. And soon after the first blaze of splendour, the polish was dulled by the sudden influx of large crowds coming out of the parks. People began to jostle each other on the pavements and to gather round the shopwindows like moths round a bright light, dispersing only when the light rudely went out. In some of the shops a dim light was left burning. As if by magic, the street had changed beyond recognition. The harmony of it was dissipated. None the less, Deborah still went on admiring its many glories.

"I can tell you it beats everything that my brother led me to expect. . . ."

Miss Rushka was gratified. Like Michael, she began to boast of all the other showplaces which Deborah had never seen.

"And what about the Saxon Gardens? I suppose you haven't been there yet, have you?"

"No."

"If you'd like to go, I'll take you there to-morrow. It's ever so classy! You find all the nicest people there, people with titles and money and everything. . . . Jews wearing gabardines are not admitted, and girls can't go in unless they wear a hat, so it just shows what a posh place it is. Have you got permission to go out whenever you want to?"

Deborah stopped to think. She really could not say.

"*I* have!" Miss Rushka put in, wrinkling up her nose in triumph.

"I don't suppose Mamma would have any objection. I suggest you call for me to-morrow."

"No, you call for me!"

"I couldn't find my way," confessed Deborah, not without reluctance. It was most unpleasant to be the innocent rustic.

They parted with a handshake. Rather than tell Miss Rushka that she had not the faintest recollection of the way home, Deborah wandered aimlessly about the back streets, which now struck her as being drab and dismal-looking. She stopped several people and made inquiries, but experienced difficulty with her broken Polish and was confused by the directions given to her. She turned left and right, and right and left. In the end, when she had given up all hopes of getting home again, she ran down a gloomy alley, which seemed to have a menacing air about it, and suddenly found herself in the one street that she knew so well.

"Well, did you have a good time?" Raizela asked, smiling with amusement at the way Deborah stood staring with an air of bewilderment, as though she failed to recognise her own home, which she had left behind only a few hours ago.

Deborah was glad to hear her mother's voice. Yes, this was home! With a merry laugh she ran up to her mother to kiss and hug her.

"Oh, Mamma, I spent such a wonderful afternoon. We went to Marszalkowski Street, and it almost took my breath away. It's quite close, you know! Within walking distance. I was ever so surprised, because after what Michael told me, I imagined it was miles and miles away . . ."

"So you imagined that, did you?" exclaimed Michael, stirring behind the curtain at the window. She had not noticed him there before. "You judge all things by yourself. Because you're pretty at a distance and awful at close quarters you think everything else is the same. And even at a distance you're only pretty when you disguise yourself in pretty things. And what a disguise you've got on to-day! Phew! I say, how far did you get to-day? I bet you never went to the Allées! No, of course you didn't. That *is* miles and miles away. You'd get sore feet if you tried to walk it, and until you've seen the Allées you haven't seen Warsaw at its best, I don't mind telling you!"

Michael emerged from behind the curtain with a victorious smile, his supremacy still unchallenged.

DEBORAH

"Come on, Deborah, get yourself changed and let's all have tea," Raizela said.

Deborah took no notice. She felt not the least inclination to strip off her finery and dress up like the family drudge once more. Life at the moment was too sweet for such a humdrum task as puffing at the embers in the samovar. Again the old feeling of revolt against her mother took her by storm. It was not fair, why could not her mother ask Michael to prepare the samovar: he could do it just as well? But then, on second thoughts, she realised that she ought to feel grateful for all the splendid clothes they had given her, and without a word she went into the bedroom and returned with her sleeves rolled up all ready for work.

Reb Avram Ber put in an appearance, his face radiant with joy, as ever. He did not seem to mind a bit the passing of the dearly beloved Sabbath. Welcome though the Sabbath was, when its delights were over he found new delights. For one thing, there was the newly made tea to look forward to (of course, the samovar could not be touched on the Sabbath.) For another, there was the ceremony of blessing the new moon. And best of all, soon after sunset there was the end-of-Sabbath feast, when a man could sing and rejoice with his fellow-men, and join with them in hoping for a bright future in the days to come. . . .

"May the new week bring new happiness," said Reb Avram Ber, in accordance with old Jewish custom. "Hallo, Deborah! I see you're busy. That's good! I hope you won't forget our friends next door."

And zestfully passing one palm of his hand over the other, he went away again to join the company in his study. Deborah gave the glasses a good polish, filled them and put them on a tray.

"Off with you, Michael, and join the feast. Your place is with the menfolk, and I shall be very glad to get rid of you," said Raizela.

"Very well, Mamma, I'm off! But not just yet. You'll find me joining the feast when winter comes round. In the winter you get a lovely portion of roast beef and delicious *borsht*. Now, that's in my line. But in the summer all they put on your plate is a scrap of herring, and I turn my nose up at that."

"Idiot!" Raizela scolded him with great good humour.

. . .

The next day Miss Rushka called again. Mother did not object in the least. Deborah was duly impressed by the Saxon Gardens. Although she had seen trees and grass and flowers in abundance in her lifetime, she had never been in a cultivated park before. Its urbane beauty— the many-hued flower beds in such perfect harmony, in spite of the sea of colour; the shapely grand old trees; the long shady avenues— made a striking picture. Unlike yesterday's scene, instead of throbbing with excitement it soothed the nerves. Everybody in the park had such a calm and unruffled look, as though time were of little account. Spruce young couples sauntered along most peacefully, even if there was something in the way they clung to each other which betrayed feelings not quite so peaceful. Old gentlemen on the benches had their heads concealed behind newspapers, or sat smoking or polishing their spectacles. Tastefully dressed children played hide and seek, ignoring both their nurses and the soldiers who had their arms round the nurses. These children had no respect at all for grown-ups, not even for those wearing resplendent uniforms.

The thoroughfares around the park were far less noisy than they had been yesterday. There was less glitter also. Marszalkowski Street was half empty. Most of the shops were closed and had their blinds down. Elderly ladies and gentlemen, often with prayer-books under their arm, were taking the air with a solemn and pious demeanour. Even the students and their young ladies were more subdued, larking about on the sly. The shop signs seemed to have dwindled into insignificance overnight. Only a few luminous advertisements were to be seen here and there, and they were scarcely noticeable in the daylight. A long line of cabs waited in idleness, with no one to disturb the drowsy cabbies, for this was Sunday, a holy day of rest.

"Miss Rushka, what about a trip to the Allées?"

"No, not to-day. We can go there next Saturday, if you like. You'll find the place absolutely dead to-day, but on a Saturday it's spiffing!"

Very well, then, next Saturday it would have to be. Miss Rushka's word was law. . . .

DEBORAH

. . .

Gradually Deborah accustomed herself to life in Warsaw, until she gave it no thought, knowing that she was part of it, and it was part of her. As time went on, all things became commonplace, matter-of-fact and, at best, homely. Nothing surprised her, nothing overwhelmed her. Marszalkowski Street lost its magic. The tramps of both sexes huddled up in the porches and on the broad flights of stone steps in front of the churches ceased to torment her mind; they barely excited her pity. She never noticed them, as they lay there like shapeless bundles, and the only time she paid them any attention was when she was extra flush in money and could spare a few kopecks. Life at home settled down to a comfortable jog-trot. Reb Avram Ber's position went from strength to strength. The Jews of the neighbourhood fell into the habit of bringing their differences to Reb Avram Ber for arbitration, they paid their dues far more punctually, and there was little to complain of.

Michael drifted away from the synagogue and the Talmud, and picked up with young men, and occasionally even with girls of a different set. He began to frequent homes which would have shocked Raizela and Reb Avram Ber if they had known. But they never knew a thing, and Michael made the best of both worlds. . . .

Reb Zalman remained the close friend of the family. Hardly a day passed without a visit from him. Having helped Reb Avram Ber to comparative prosperity, he was now anxious to help him in other ways, and thinking it over carefully he came to the conclusion that the one thing Reb Ber Avram still needed, and needed badly, was a husband for his only daughter, Deborah. That being so, Reb Zalman kept a look-out for eligible young men, and almost every other day he burst into the home with a wonderful new marriage proposal. At first he was singing the praises of a wealthy merchant who had a son. Whereas the wealthy merchant was not much of a Talmudist, although it would be very wrong to describe him as a downright ignoramus, the son was a man of great learning, or, at any rate, would be one day if he kept up his studies. This son was perfect in every way, only just a little bit simple in the head, but that, Reb Zalman argued—and Reb Avram Ber concurred—could not be regarded as a fault, for the father was so wealthy that the son would be provided for amply for the rest of his life. Then, a few days later, Reb Zalman turned up with a discovery that beat everything: an absolutely priceless young man—no, verily a saint; a young man who really and truly was a great Talmudist, and had so far lived the life of an ascetic; his father was said to be a close friend of the great *Tsadik* of Ger; the father was by no means a wealthy man, but it was an honour—a great honour—to marry into his family. Ay! And then, by the end of the same week, Reb Zalman arrived triumphant: he had found the right match at last. A Lithuanian Jew, but a man one could trust nevertheless; as clever as clever could be, endowed with the gift of the gab; sure he had the gift of the gab, for he was a preacher; had pots of money; had divorced his first wife because she had borne him no children; an opportunity that would not come again. But alas, Deborah refused her suitors one and all.

She did not want to get married yet, and begged Reb Zalman to leave her in peace. She said she could wait, and could wait a long time. This was a setback for Reb Zalman. He would lie low for a couple of weeks, and then start again. After all, a girl must get married sooner or later, and better sooner than later, because if a girl never caught a husband while she was young, she might not get one at all in the end, especially if she had no dowry. Nice thing it would be for Deborah to become an old maid, a very nice thing! But what was the use of talking to her? One might just as well talk to a brick wall. . . .

"Now try to understand me," Reb Zalman reasoned with her. "You know quite well that but for me you would have still been wearing your shabby old clothes, you wouldn't have been able to show your face in the street, and the home would still have been a den of misery. You'll do me the justice of admitting that I mean well, and that I have had more experience of life than you have. Do you think I'd press you if it wasn't for your own good? Believe me, I know your value, and know just what sort of husband you deserve."

"Admitted, Reb Zalman, but you can't expect me to go and marry the sort of person that appeals to you."

"Well, tell me who you think is good enough for you," Reb Zalman said with ill-concealed annoyance.

"No, the point is they're all too good for me," Deborah retorted, with the colour coming into her cheeks. She felt the blood rushing up into her head.

"I know the sort of person you want," Reb Avram Ber joined in the conversation, losing his temper for once in a while. "You want one of those new-fangled husbands that don't wear the orthodox gabardine, is that it? Depend upon it, I'll not give you any of these new-fangled husbands that don't wear the orthodox gabardine!"

Thus all Reb Zalman's labours proved fruitless, and Deborah remained a lonely spinster.

CHAPTER X

As the summer wore on Deborah gave up her last lingering hopes of ever seeing Simon again. Meanwhile the High Festivals were drawing near, and Reb Avram Ber's home was thrown into confusion. All day long there was a coming and going of people who sought Reb Avram Ber's advice; his table was littered with reference books, and his brow was knitted in deepest meditation. Even the hunchback was in the swim: in the evening, when he returned from his daily round and emptied his bulging pockets, the pile of copper coins was larger than usual, often containing a sprinkling of silver. . . .

However, what was at first no more than confusion developed into a perfect riot when Reb Zalman suddenly gave the family short notice of his determination to organise a temporary synagogue in their home for the high Festival services.

"Now, you listen to me," said Reb Zalman. "It's good advice I'm giving you. We'll work out the seating accommodation, the you'll print some priced tickets, I'll distribute them among my friends, and if we don't sell them I'll eat my hat. You, Reb Avram Ber, will conduct the service. The little congregation will just love the intimate atmosphere, and it'll be a good thing all round. Now take my advice, and you'll never regret it!"

Raizela dubiously shook her head, raising all manner of objections, but in the end Reb Zalman had his own way. Reb Zalman inevitably had his own way. Thereupon bedlam was let loose. All the furniture was dumped into the bedroom, hired wooden benches and tables were introduced; loud-voiced workmen in aprons made themselves at home, rapping away with hammers for all they were worth and leaving all the doors wide open. Deborah toiled unremittingly. Even Michael was given some work to do. As for Reb Avram Ber, he kept passing from room to room, voicing his approval of all the tasks accomplished and gladly giving his blessing to all the suggestions made.

Raizela took no part in the proceedings, which were to her reminiscent of an unpleasant incident in her girlhood, when, passing through the village high street one day, she had been caught up in a crowd of wildly excited people, and although she was not in the least interested in the pig on the rampage which was the cause of all the excitement, she had nevertheless had to endure all the commotion, shouting and pushing. It was not at her behest that the home was being turned topsy-turvy (as she stated quite definitely on more than one occasion.) But when Reb Zalman, who was sacrificing his own time and personally had nothing to gain by the enterprise, assured her (with nods of approval from Reb Avram Ber) that a little fortune was at stake, and no one could afford to throw away a little fortune when winter was coming and provision must be made for it in all manner of ways, she pretended to see the light of reason. All the same, she never budged from her couch, except when it had to be moved from one place to another (and that was a most frequent occurrence).

The confusion which always prevails at that time of year became worse as the holy days approached, casting their shadows before them. . . . Reb Avram Ber had an endless procession of visitors. The home was bleak and bare. And the serried rows of tables and benches bore witness to the fact that the solemn festivals were at hand; very soon the Day of Atonement would break in all its fearfulness. This was a time of spiritual uplift, when every man must raise his soul from the sloth of the impure flesh and cleanse it. Such was the tale the unvarnished tables and benches told. As for the tickets pinned down on the tables, they told an altogether different tale. They bore witness to the fact that so far only very few seats had been booked, and the whole venture seemed doomed to failure. Instead of making a little fortune, Reb Avram Ber seemed likely to lose money: with only a few more days to go, no more than a handful of worshippers had reserved seats. The bedroom was crowded like a second-hand shop, and the family had to do a lot of climbing to get into bed at all. There was no comfort even in the kitchen, where space had been made for needy folk who could reserve a seat for nothing if they wished, or could get one for next to nothing if they were proud as well as being poor. . . .

Raizela eyed the unreserved seats (it seemed that the more expensive ones, in particular, would be quite deserted) with mingled mockery and grief. Reb Avram Ber was crestfallen at the unexpected fiasco, and keenly felt his wife's contempt. He rued his weakness in yielding to Reb Zalman's advice. It really was a shame to create such an awful disturbance in the home all to no purpose. The holidays would be spoilt, and more than ever he marvelled at Raizela's wisdom and foresight.

"Foresight and wisdom go together," said Reb Avram Ber, when Reb Zalman called in to see how things were getting on.

"So they do," said Reb Zalman, "and I wouldn't lose heart if I were you. You just wait and see! At the last moment you'll have a tremendous throng come clamouring for seats. They'll be falling over each other for seats. And I'll tell you the reason why. Only people who move about a great deal, and are not firmly established, are likely to come here, as they can't be regular members of any one synagogue. And usually they're busy people, their minds are occupied in other ways; but at the last moment they suddenly wake up, they go hunting after a seat like mad, and that's when the money comes rolling in. . . ."

Reb Zalman's words were prophetic. In the end most of the seats were taken, yielding an appreciable sum of money (but not a little fortune, by any means). Reb Zalman rubbed his hands with profound glee. He had only one regret.

"I must tell you, Reb Avram Ber, it's a pity you decided to offer free seats in the kitchen. Your duty to yourself and your family is more important than your duty to strangers," he said rather wistfully, but now that the harm was done, Reb Zalman did not actually take it to heart—far from it. "And now I'm going to tell you a little secret. Seeing that things were going badly, I put on an extra spurt, and knowing the ins and outs of Warsaw I got talking to the right sort of people, and that did the trick. Where there's a will there's a way, and when I buttonhole a man and put up a suggestion to him he never refuses."

Raizela smiled, for only a few days ago Reb Zalman had stated that strangers would come flocking in of their own accord. But Reb Avram Ber saw nothing to smile at; it never occurred to him that Reb Zalman was contradicting himself; all that mattered to him was that indubitably Reb Zalman was as good a friend as any man could wish to have, and pleasurably stroking his beard Reb Avram Ber asked Deborah to serve tea and biscuits.

It was only on the eve of the Day of Atonement that Raizela began to lend a hand. The poultry, which had been offered up to God with ancient ritual, now had to be cooked, and supper had to be ready before sunset, for at sunset the fast began. There was plenty to do. Meanwhile there was the soul to think of, for on the awesome Day of Atonement all its blemishes would be written down in the great book of judgment up in heaven. . . . Reb Avram Ber was like a man possessed! On that one day poor Michael atoned for all his past sins, because his father kept a sharp eye on him; and how he chafed under the pious paternal yoke! His love for mischief went unrequited all through the day, for it was the eve of the frightful Day of Atonement. . . .

The family had partaken of the ritual supper, drinking their fill of tea, soda water and tap water to tide them over the fast. And evening was coming on. Worshippers began to arrive with their praying shawls and prayer books, handkerchiefs and slippers, smelling salts and sins. Every man had his own bundle and every woman had hers. . . .

The sun was on the point of setting . . . Reb Avram Ber's study, where the holy ark stood up against the easterly wall, draped with a green velvet curtain richly decorated with golden embroidery, was full of the noiseless flutter of mysterious holy spirits. On the lectern, beside the ark, a cloth of the same material as the curtain was spread. The burning tall wax candles, embedded in sand-containers, projected large vague shadows on the brown walls. Shreds of scarlet light, remnants of the setting sun, were fast losing their identity in the candlelight—at one with the rippling, watery shimmer.

Reb Avram Ber, clad in flowing white robes, with a white silk skull-cap on his head, stood swaying over the lectern softly chanting to himself. His lips scarcely moved, as though he were in a trance. His whole being was filled with raptures of holy fear and joy. There was something godfearing even about the Gentile whom Michael was showing round the place, and to whom he was explaining the tasks to be performed on the morrow. . . . Raizela wore an old-fashioned white silk dress (her wedding gown). Her demeanour was grave. Her tiny face, with its large, wide-open grey eyes, looked wonderfully innocent; her skin had become strangely translucent. Her frailty was painful to look at. Deborah, in a white little pinafore and with a white bow in her hair, looked like a big serious child. As for Michael, he was a picture of devoutness in his black silken gabardine and black velvet cap. He had not tucked his sidelocks away to-day, and they dangled very prominently in front of his large red ears.

At the last moment an old woman came tottering in, panting for breath. She was dressed in the clothes of a bygone age, and the green spangles adorning her black velvet spencer reflected the last fading gleams of sunset with a ghostly light. The black fringes of her ancient, beaded bonnet surrounded her tiny pinched features like a somber black frame—black for mourning. Picking a free seat in the kitchen, in front of the open door leading into the study, she hastily brought her wrinkled long fingers into play—tremulous, ineffective fingers which struggled painfully to undo the knots in her handkerchief, in which she had tied up her prayer-book. It was a musty old volume (quite as ancient as herself), and came to pieces in her hands. After she had put its yellow leaves together again, she produced a bottle of smelling-salts, and having convinced herself by a single sniff that the scent was strong enough to revive a corpse, she carefully wiped the one and only remaining lense in her spectacles that were suspended on a long black cord, and all was ready. . . .

There was a sudden hush. The first prayer, *Tfilla Zaka*, was begun and soon over. Reb Avram Ber turned to the congregation, raised his forefinger and motioned to several of the male worshippers. They rose and surrounded the holy ark, pausing for an instant before they drew the curtain, as though they were steeling themselves for their sacred task. Stretching out their hands with great reverence they picked up a scroll each and posted themselves round Reb Avram Ber, who began to sing in a rich, pure voice, with everybody chanting after him:

"*Al daz hamokem vaal daz hakool*. . . ."

and there was never a stray sound to mar the solemn chorus.

Next Reb Avram Ber intoned *Kol Nidray*. A sound of weeping rose up in the living room, where the women were gathered; but of all the lamentations none was so mournful as those issuing from the kitchen. Those wretched-looking women on the cheap and free seats sobbed as if their hearts would break. The woman in the black spencer wailed loudest of all. Incidentally, she was the only one among them who could read the prayers, and all through the service she sang a duet with the cantor. Reb Avram Ber was a baritone, the old woman in the spencer an alto. To hide their poverty, the worshippers in the kitchen had put white bows into the shabby hair of their wigs and had covered their tatters with new white pinafores, and now to hide their ignorance they clustered round the woman in the spencer to repeat every word after her, but try as they might, they could conceal nothing. Although the old woman kept screaming at the top of her voice, it was impossible to hear a word of what she was saying. She might have been more distinct if only her tones had not been so shrill. . . . For lack of guidance, her companions began to mumble prayers of their own composition, and fell a-weeping whenever she did.

On the morrow Reb Avram Ber delivered both *Shahris* and *Musif.* He was on his feet all through the livelong day, but was almost oblivious to the strain. His voice flowed into attentive ears like pure, sweet wine into parched throats, revivifying, strengthening and intoxicating. The womenfolk wept and wept, and were all agreed (in between prayers) that this was the best cry they had ever had, every new outburst bringing new solace, as though the Lord Himself were lifting the heavy burdens from off their hearts. Raizela forced back her flow of tears, only dabbing her eyes with the handkerchief that lay in readiness on the desk, when the tears brimmed over suddenly. Also Deborah kept wiping her eyes.

As the day wore on, the atmosphere indoors became more sultry. The candles softened, and when the streams of melted wax went dripping into the sand-containers the candles, too, seemed to be weeping. The worshippers were all in their stockinged feet, and the odour of sweaty feet was blended with the scent of smelling salts. Faces turned deathly pale, and in the stifling heat vision became blurred, the walls began to turn round and round. But no one paid the slightest heed to bodily discomfort: the soul alone was being ministered to, and that day the flesh was sadly neglected. At last the scarlet tints of sunset were mingling once more with the yellow candlelight, and *Nilla* was being recited. At this point the womenfolk broke down completely, so that even the menfolk became infected and now and again one of them uttered a sob. But he stifled it as best he could, and soon regained his self-control. It would never do for him to go off into paroxysms like a mere woman!

The final evening prayer was a more ordinary affair, and soon over. The flesh now came into its own, and it rallied strongly.

"Come on now, get out of my way," the flesh said in its brutal fashion to the soul. "You've had all the attention you deserve, and a bit more than you deserve! You go to sleep again, and let me fend for myself. . . ."

The soul said not a word in reply. With sweet reasonableness it appreciated the justice of the insolent demands of the flesh.

Immediately the service was over, the congregation hurriedly exchanged good wishes and broke up, making for home as fast as their enfeebled legs would carry them.

Deborah laid the table (also as fast as she could go). Strangely enough, Raizela, who usually felt too weak to stand, found new strength to-day. She actually helped Deborah to serve up supper. Reb Avram Ber was beaming. Michael was eating. Deborah was munching as she brought in the dishes.

When they were all seated round the table and had reached the last course, Deborah made an announcement that her leather belt was missing.

"I've looked for it everywhere, but I can't find it."

"Never mind," said Raizela. "You're sure to come across it sooner or later. I saw you wearing it this morning."

"Yes, Mamma, but later on I took it off. It was rather uncomfortable, so I put it down on a chair in the kitchen, and I think it's been stolen."

"Rubbish! As if anyone would steal on the Day of the Atonement! I think the girl's crazy!" Raizela flushed with anger.

But Deborah keenly felt the loss of her belt, and she persisted:

"I don't care what you say, but I have my suspicions, and the person I suspect is that old woman who sat down next to the door in the kitchen and kicked up such a row over her prayers!"

"Deborah, for God's sake stop it!" Reb Avram Ber intervened, greatly upset. "Fancy making such an accusation when you have no proof at all, and fancy doing it on the Day of Atonement! Dear me, I'm surprised at you!"

"But Pappa, you must remember that the Day of Atonement is over now," Michael corrected his father.

"Hold your tongue! Listen, both of you, I won't have another word!" Reb Avram Ber was quite angry by now.

"Yes, Pappa, you can depend upon me to keep quiet. All I want to say is this: it's disgraceful to suspect that woman. What on earth would she steal a belt for? I'm sure that if ever she was to yield to temptation, a spencer would be the cause of it, and then only if she could find a replica of the one she'd got on," said Michael, pretending to cough.

"And pray, how is it you know what she had on?" Deborah exclaimed triumphantly. "You were sitting next door and had no business to make eyes at the old women!"

"Idiot! How could I help not noticing her? After all, she was the assistant cantor. . . ."

Michael could contain his mirth no longer. He could plainly see the comical woman in his mind's eye, and he hurried away into the kitchen to laugh it off in solitude. Meanwhile, poking around the saucepans he came on some stewed fruit which had been left over for dinner next day. He tasted it, found it delicious, and ate it all up.

On the morrow, when the workmen came to collect the benches and the desks, the belt came to light, very much trampled and soiled.

"Mamma, I've got it!"

"What?"

"The belt."

"Didn't I tell you?"

"There, that just goes to show that you have to make certain of the facts before you can cast any suspicions," said Deborah.

This gave Michael his chance:

"Well said, Deborah! Well said! The average person leaves off suspecting when he knows for certain, but you just begin!"

"Always poking his nose in where it's not wanted!" Deborah said with a laugh. In spite of herself, she admired his ready wit. Even as she had said it, she had realised that she was getting muddled, but how quick he was on the uptake!

Raizela also was laughing, quietly, and again Michael was pleased with himself.

The festive season was over, and this was the time of year when an old folk song haunted the air in town and village—an old familiar melody that evoked a smile here and a sigh there:

"Father, my Father, winter is drawing near,
And Father, O Father, a Jew should know no fear,
But look, O look, the snow is falling fast,
And hark, O hark, at the spiteful wintry blast.
See, there goes my roof, the water's coming through,
Hurry, Father, hurry, send succour to a poor old
Jew!"

It was a Jewish leap year and nearly end of October. In the early morning the window-panes would be covered with hoar frost. And now and then a little snow came fluttering down.

"We've laid in a supply of coals for the winter, our greatcoats are back from the tailor's," said Reb Avram Ber, "the nights are growing longer, and in the long winter evenings I shall be able to concentrate more than ever on the Talmud. All's well, the Lord be praised!"

Raizela wrapped herself up more tightly in her velvet jacket, and she, too, could concentrate better on her reading. The gems of wisdom in her books sparkled more brightly than ever in the wintry light.

Michael went on with his studies in a desultory way. He only came home for his meals, for all day and every day he was very busy doing nothing in particular with a set of friends who were occupied in the same way. He enjoyed the company of his boon companions, gaining their respect by his keen sense of humour, and he was perfectly satisfied with life in general and with himself in particular.

Deborah was the exception. She could not come to terms with the world around her. She was alternately gloomy and restless.

She felt that there was something lacking in her life. What that something was she could not tell. In former days her great obsession had been the glamour of city life. That passion was now satisfied: she had come to the greatest city in Poland. Soon after her arrival there, her one burning desire had been to get a hat and a new outfit of clothes, so as to go forth freely in the streets of the town. That desire, too, was satisfied. What else did she desire, what was it that gave her no peace?

How was it that her mother managed to strike such deep roots in life, although she hardly ever moved from her couch and fed her mind on her own thoughts? As for her father, he knew how to play with life and laugh with it. Then again, Michael found all things of absorbing interest; he never had to flounder about like a lost soul, but knew always what he wanted and took the shortest cut to get it. She alone was afflicted. She alone could find no place for herself.

When she did the housework she felt she was wasting her time. She hated to be a common drudge. But whenever she went on strike and sulked in a corner, she was just bored to death. Of course, there were books to read. But somehow they had lost their magic, they no longer afforded her that complete sense of escape as of old.

As for Miss Rushka, that girl was a terrible bore. Deborah got on much better without her, and was highly pleased when Miss Rushka went off into one of her sudden tantrums and stayed away for no reason at all. However, when Deborah could stand the loneliness no longer, she would pay her a ceremonial visit. And one day she learnt from no less a person than Miss Rushka that there were evening classes in Warsaw, which were open to the public. So Deborah joined, and that gave her new zest in life. She would look forward to the evenings. She did not merely listen attentively to the lessons, but drank them in. Whenever the class was given to learn off by heart, Deborah was invariably the first to master it. Moreover, she struck up an acquaintance with a girl who, although much older than herself, treated her like an equal. This friendliness Deborah very much appreciated, especially as Bailka (as she was called) was such a good-natured, cheerful soul, so interesting and clever. Gradually they both became friends and were much attached to one another.

From time to time Bailka would vaguely allude to some sort of "association," which was engaged in very important work and had a sacred mission to perform. Then, after a while, she began to speak more openly and asked Deborah if she would care to join the movement. Deborah knew nothing about the movement, but she was certainly prepared to join. She had complete confidence in Bailka. In fact, she began to look forward impatiently to the great day when Bailka would introduce her, as promised, to the comrades of the party.

"If you impress the comrades, as I hope you will, we shall be ever so pleased to have you in our ranks. We need men and women capable of the deepest loyalty and capable of great sacrifices. Democratic inclinations, while good in themselves, are not enough. Strength of character and firmness of will are wanted to back them up. . . ."

Deborah was all eagerness. She had only the haziest idea of what it was all about, but as there were comrades, loyalty and sacrifices in it, it was in all probability a good thing. After all, she had read something about the comrades in Mottel's books. They were all great, noble men and women.

"For my part, I'm certainly going to recommend you," Bailka reassured her. "I tell you what, give me a call about six o'clock on Saturday night, and we'll talk things over, we'll go out for a walk and generally have a good time."

Deborah accepted the invitation with wide-open arms.

One last puff at the embers of the samovar just before the end-of-Sabbath feast, and she was off to Bailka's!

"Hullo, Deborah, I'm glad you've come. Would you mind very much if I took you out for a walk. You know on weekdays I'm so busy that the only time I can take a bit of fresh air is on Saturday nights," said Bailka, as if to apologise for not asking her in, and for having come to the door all dressed up in her hat and coat.

They went for a stroll, Bailka talking and laughing vivaciously all the way. She told Deborah a great many jokes (which were far funnier than any of Michael's wisecracks). And she imparted such a strong sense of vigour, both mental and physical, that Deborah was carried away with enthusiasm. She was infected with her companion's gaiety, infected with her healthy laughter, and was even tickled to death when Bailka trotted out the stalest of stale jokes.

"What a wonderful creature you are!" Deborah addressed Bailka in her thoughts, and almost said it aloud.

Soon after seven o'clock they went indoors. Bailka lodged in a tiny room that was poorly furnished but scrupulously clean. It had one window and a small square table that was spread with a red cloth. She asked Deborah to sit down on the bed as the solitary chair was "feeling out of sorts to-day." They both had a good laugh at the expense of the poor broken chair, and then Bailka got busy at the gas-ring. She poured out the tea and perched on the bed next to Deborah. As they sipped their tea Bailka told her more about the party, its programme and the means they used for achieving their ambitious ends.

"We have comrades at work all over the country. Many of them are very young, but we also have elderly and highly experienced men, also elderly women. And, it may seem rather strange to you, but we also have many comrades from wealthy families, people who have sacrificed an easy life itself if needs be. We have among us the sons and daughters of Rabbis and even of *Tsadikim*. But, of course, the working-class is our mainstay. They are the life-blood of our movement: that goes without saying! You've heard of Karl Marx, haven't you?"

"Yes, to be sure, and I've read a little of his work."

"Tell me, what have you read?"

"Well, a good few chapters of his *Politische Oekonomie*. But it made very difficult reading. I went over some passages again and again, and even then I must confess that there were certain points which rather confused me."

"And what else have you read besides that?"

"A good deal about the Nihilists. All about Mihail Bakunin and his comrade Maria, who was a dressmaker. And then the Czar's own brother . . . or was it his uncle? I'm not quite sure. . . ."

"And how did those books impress you? Did they convey any message to you, did they ever make you stop and think of the life going on all round you?"

"Yes, ever so often. But to tell you the truth, it seemed rather strange to think that only a small handful of people could ever defeat so much wickedness."

"And that, I suppose, is why you never thought of joining the party yourself? Or maybe you had another reason? I want you to be perfectly frank with me, because before you take the jump—and it can turn out to be a very dangerous jump for yourself and for others—it's best to know the whole truth and face up to it."

Deborah gave an account of herself, how she had been brought up in a tiny village and had recently been living in a provincial town, where she had never come into contact with people outside her own class; her mother was an ailing woman, and for that reason the entire responsibility of keeping house devolved on herself; it was only a few months ago that books of a revolutionary nature had first come her way; she loved her parents very much indeed, and felt very sorry for her mother, who was only in poor health, but was, in spite of her incessant suffering, the most interesting and the cleverest woman in all the world. . . .

They had a long and earnest conversation. Deborah eagerly drank in everything that Bailka said. It was only now that she realised how insignificant was her own mental equipment: Bailka was so vital, full of intelligence and extremely well-read; at the same time she was such a jolly and sensible little person, a wonderful mixture of common sense and idealism. Apart from her political activities, she had to work for a living, had to find her own food and clothes and rent, all of which she managed so well that she could even afford to pay for evening classes and to offer a friend a cup of tea. Deborah saw Bailka in a new, a glorious light, and unhesitatingly told her what she thought of her. Bailka chuckled.

"Oh, you're such a baby, so naive, but I like you all the better for that. Well, there's only one thing left for me to tell you now, Deborah, and that is to preserve complete secrecy. And when I say secrecy, I mean it—silent as the grave. When you've recovered from your first flush of excitement, when you're quite calm, think it over carefully, remember the risk you're running, and if you still feel you'd like to join, then you can count yourself as one of us. Now for some more tea, and, better still, something to eat. I bet you're hungry. I know I am. I could eat a horse! Will you join me at supper? Say yes or no. Don't be backward. We don't stand for ceremony here; if we never say much among strangers, we make up for it by being perfectly among ourselves.

"All right, then, give me some supper, please," said Deborah, showing her mettle.

"Bailka cut up a Dutch herring, flavoured it with vinegar and sliced a loaf of bread. It was ages since Deborah had partaken of a meal with so much relish. As for Bailka, she, too, seemed to enjoy her supper, so much so that her bulging cheeks turned a bright red as she munched and munched.

"I say, Deborah, you've forgotten to tell me who gave you all those books to read. Was it one of our members?"

Deborah turned uneasy.

"You'll have to excuse me, but . . . but when I borrowed the books I promised never to tell anyone." She crimsoned with an air of guilt. "You understand, don't you? It's not my own secret, so I can't very well speak about it, can I?"

Bailka smiled a little humorously.

"That's the spirit. And if you have any secrets of your own, you must guard them just as jealously," she added in a more serious vein. "Now you take this pamphlet, read it through and then let me have it back to-morrow, or else burn it. Yes, you'd better burn it, when there's no one looking, of course. Well, I have your promise that whatever happens you'll never breathe a word about all this to a single living soul, is that right? Mum's the word, even if in the end you decide not to join the party. In a more sober mood you may not think it worth your while, or you may disagree with our policy, but even then you must be silent, because I want you to understand that a single thoughtless remark may mean torture and Siberia to countless comrades. Once the secret police swoop, there's no knowing how many lives will be wrecked. . . ."

"I swear to it that I'll never say a word, even if it should mean torture and Siberia for myself. And as for joining, my mind's made up. I've set my heart on it. I feel that I am on the threshold of a new life, a beautiful life."

Bailka gave her a quick glance. No, there was nothing false in those false-sounding words. They expressed genuine emotion, they were the utterance of a person who was capable of real enthusiasm, who was possessed of a great store of pent-up energy, and who, if properly guided, could render real service to the cause. Here was a youngster who only needed to be roused from her sickly stupor to start a new life and to do honest-to-goodness work side by side with the party comrades.

Bailka saw Deborah home almost to her doorstep. They parted with an appointment to meet the next day, which was a Sunday, at about five in the afternoon.

"So here you are! What makes you so late?" said Raizela.

"Late, am I?"

"Why, of course, it's half-past eleven!"

"I suppose I was so busy talking, I never noticed how the time flew. Well, well, I never thought it was as late as all that. Is there anything you'd like me to do for you, Mamma, before I go to bed?"

"No, nothing!" said Raizela, and getting off the couch she went into her bedroom.

Reb Avram Ber had one of his reference books on the table, and after settling some query in his mind he, too, went into the bedroom. Evidently, the end-of-Sabbath feast had come to a close that night earlier than usual. Even Michael was abed, snoring loudly, and with a book tucked under his pillow. Secrets everywhere! . . .

Deborah scrambled into bed. Reb Avram Ber's footsteps, as he paced up and down reciting the prayer *Hear, O Israel,* were beginning to trail off. Yes, they had ceased, and now the home was all in darkness. She lit a candle on a chair at her bedside, and draping the back of the chair with her frock, threw the rest of the room into shadowiness.

She settled down to read. She consumed eagerly the contents of the booklet. It was a small tract, which summoned her to a stupendous struggle against the enemy. It described the fate of those comrades, who, devoting all their energies to the cause, devoting the best intellect and the fairest ideals in the land, to the sacred task, had fallen victims and were languishing in Siberia, repining in the prisons and fortresses, stricken men and women who were being driven to madness, whose lungs were being destroyed, whose nerves were being methodically shattered, who were becoming epileptic through the never-ending horrors and blind through the eternal darkness in the dungeons. It described the fate of heroic men and women who would not acknowledge defeat even in the throes of torture, and to whom the modern Inquisition was but a cruel passing joke. She read on. Her heart bled. Her eyes flashed. Her cheeks burned. Her breath was hot. She was filled with passionate hatred of the enemy, an overwhelming longing for revenge, and with love and enthusiasm for those men and women who struggled and suffered so bitterly. . . .

When she had finished reading she felt that it was unthinkable for her to carry on with her present useless life, it was impossible to remain indifferent. Good God, how the storm was raging over the land, and all oblivious to it she had simply been eating and drinking and sleeping like a senseless brute, never lifting a finger to liberate the people from their yoke, never giving a thought to sweeping all the misery, filth, injustice and pain from off the face of the earth. . . . Good heavens, compared with the rulers sitting in high places the *Tsadik* of R— was quite a harmless, even a noble creature! For her the past was now dead, quite dead. The party would have to admit her into its ranks, she would refuse to take "No" as an answer. If they doubted her strength, she would swear to them by all that was holy that she would remain discreet, nay dumb! She would not spare herself in her task, she would make a superhuman effort. Yes, they would have to accept her, and there could be no turning back from the road that was clearly marked out for her.

She writhed and tossed about in her bed, and at long last, when she dozed off, sinister dreams haunted her slumbers. Every now and then she started up violently, her hand reached for the booklet under her pillow, and when she found that it was still there she was overcome with joy.

In the morning she built up the fire in the kitchen range as usual. The booklet went up in flames on top of a pile of newly chopped wood drenched in paraffin. As she watched the flames at work a gloomy nervous frown distorted her face. She half imagined she could see the victims of the new Inquisition burning at the stake before her very eyes. The burning pages curled up. One or two letters suddenly showed up white. Ghostly though they were, the words could be plainly distinguished. Deborah recoiled, terror-stricken. Her whole body was taut with gooseflesh: she shuddered. The charred remains of the booklet began to crumble.

By now her father was astir. He was coming in, probably to wash. Steeling herself, she approached the grate and poured more paraffin on to the fire which had died down after the first flare-up and was on the point of going out. It occurred to her that she had forgotten to clear up last night before going to bed. That might kindle suspicion! Thenceforth she attended to her household duties with greater diligence. In the first place it would not do to arouse suspicion . . . and then again, it was her bounden duty to help her mother who was feeble and unable to fend for herself. Seen in that light, her work was no longer drudgery, and it actually afforded her a certain feeling of comfort, even of pride.

Ten days later Deborah's name was enrolled on the list of members of the Socialist party.

Now Deborah had been a comrade for fully a month, and with Bailka's guidance had become initiated into the workings of her "cell." She had taken her place in the ranks and was conversant with the daily routine. However, there was nothing hard and fast about the routine; the tactics required high individual judgment and the resourcefulness born of experience, because there was the constant possibility of police raids, accidental discovery, betrayal, espionage and other dangers. So Deborah had not up to the present been entrusted with duties of any importance. All the same, she was popular with her comrades, especially the young male comrades. . . .

One Sunday afternoon the group foregathered in Bailka's tiny room to receive an important leader, who was coming up from the provinces to address a conference which was going to be held later in the week and to which he was bringing much vital information. At this conference also he was to obtain revised instructions for a big scheme that was then afoot. For hour after hour Bailka kept talking about this comrade, his supreme qualities as a theoretician and his ingenuity in flouting the police under their very noses. She extolled him to the skies, and promised Deborah to introduce her to him, although it was doubtful whether Deborah would be allowed to stay on after the meeting proper had begun, because it was highly confidential and she was only a newcomer.

"But I'll ask our comrade when he arrives, and if he says 'Yes,' that will be good enough," said Bailka, and the rest of the company echoed her words: "If he says 'Yes,' that will be good enough. . . ."

So there sat Deborah, perched on the rim of Bailka's bed, and, clutching the rim with her fingers, she listened attentively and solemnly to the conversation that flowed all round her: it flitted from one subject to another and always returned to the visitor whom they were expecting. He was late.

"I don't suppose anything can have happened to comrade Draiskin?"

"No, I'm not worrying about that. What does worry me is his health," said Bailka.

"Why, what's the matter with him?"

"I couldn't tell you. But he looks an awful sight, although he won't admit that there's anything wrong with him. 'Bailka,' he says to me, 'you're brain's gone wrong and I despair of mending it.' He's full of jokes and carries on with his work as usual, but I don't like his looks."

"Well, it's up to him. He doesn't need a wet-nurse," said a young girl who was of very slender build, frail as smoke, but who had a very determined, even grim-looking fold round the corners of her mouth. She rarely joined in the conversation, but when she did she spoke in a tone of complete finality.

"Here he is, he's coming!" Bailka exclaimed, and she pushed her way to the door.

"Whoa-back, Bailka! Not so fast! You want to be sure what you're doing," the grim-lipped little girl warned her.

"Don't talk rubbish. Don't you think I know his footsteps by now?"

She unbolted the door. A tall, stooping young man with a bony livid face walked in. He had wrapped his grey overcoat about him tightly so that it clung to his frame; he seemed to be doubled up with cold. His nose was pinched as though frost-bitten. His jawbone was clean-cut and sharp as a knife. But his eyes were very big and were blazing with warmth.

"Good evening, comrades!"

"Good evening!"

They moved up to make room for him.

"Thank you, comrades! Well, and how's everybody?"

"Fine!" they answered in chorus. "And how are you?"

"All right, except. . . ."

The company held their breath.

"Except for the cold, it's bitter to-night. Sorry to have kept you in suspense. You can take it from me that everything's perfect. The machinery's well oiled and running as smoothly as may be. We're going to bring off a big coup this time, comrades. But we've suffered one terrible loss this week. Old Hans suddenly had a stroke and died."

He took off his hat and coat and flung them on to the bed, at which everybody smiled.

"Oh, he did, did he? Poor fellow, he won't be able to go and tell any more tales out of school. Still, I suppose when he gets to hell he'll offer his services as an *agent provocateur* to the devil," said Bailka, and then giving Draiskin a look of remonstrance mingled with unbounded love and respect she took his hat and coat away and hung them up on a nail in the door.

"I'm sorry, Bailka! Fancy me forgetting to put my things away properly!"

"Yes, fancy that!" said the grim-lipped little girl sarcastically, and they all laughed.

"Look here. . . ." Draiskin was about to say something, but he stopped short on catching sight of Deborah. His eyes turned questioningly to Bailka. Maybe Deborah would not remember him after all this time; but no, there was not much hope of that.

"Excuse me," he addressed Deborah, "Haven't I seen you before, in R——?"

"Yes, that's right."

"Well, what brings you here? Or, rather, how are you?" He quickly changed his tone.

"I'm very well, thank you," Deborah replied mechanically. Her surprise in recognising, in this revolutionary leader, Simon, the brilliant Talmud student of the *yeshiva* at R—, had left her mind a blank.

"Well now, tell me more about yourself. And how's your father and your mother?"

"They're all right, thank you!"

"I take it you're in Warsaw now with your people? How's Michael getting on? Still has his keen sense of humour, I trust?"

"I don't think he'll ever lose that."

"Good! I like him, he's a bright lad."

Deborah kept silent.

"Bailka, where have you put my coat? What a nuisance!" he cried with a sudden show of impatience.

Bailka took the hint: she led the way to the door. While he was rummaging in his pockets he held a hurried conversation with her.

"What the devil is she doing here?"

"She joined the party."

"That's obvious, but how long has she been a member?"

"About a month."

"Extraordinary!" said Simon Draiskin, showing his displeasure. "Anyway she will have to go now. Can't have her here at the meeting. See that she leaves before we start! She's a nice kid, her intentions are certainly of the purest, but we can't have a newcomer butting in."

"I promised her that I'd try to get your consent."

"That settles it. Tell her I refused."

"Let her stay on my responsibility. I assure you she's absolutely reliable," Bailka pleaded.

"I don't doubt it. But see that she goes home immediately. Don't serve tea until she goes."

"All right!"

"Well now, tell me," he said, turning to Deborah, "how is life treating you?"

Deborah could think of nothing to say. Her head was quite empty. God, if only she could find her tongue! . . .

"Tell me," Draiskin went on, "who converted you?"

"Me? Bailka did!" (Thank goodness for that!) "I'd like to know who converted *you?*"

"Me? Bailka did! She could convert anyone. But speaking seriously I'm an old hand. Well, how do you find things here?"

"Fine! Only I'm a terrible greenhorn, I've been no more than a passenger so far."

"All in good time. Meantime you must adopt our policy of keeping ears and eyes—open; mouth—shut. Never mention my name to anyone at home, or anywhere else. You won't forget, will you?"

Deborah shook her head.

"It would be great fun, though, to see your father's face if he were to be told that his daughter and his disciple were both . . . both . . . *Lord have mercy on us!*"

He untwined his sidelocks from out of his mop of hair and turned his eyes upwards, as though in prayer. The company roared with laughter.

"Ha, ha!"

Deborah felt a burning sensation shoot through her breast. Her love for him at that moment was so painful!

"I suppose you weren't really in earnest when you used to come home with my father and carry on those discussions . . ."

"There you go supposing! That will never do!"

"Sorry! I'll learn sooner or later."

"But what till you do learn?"

"Till I do, silence!" Deborah responded, almost bursting into tears with humiliation.

Simon was anxious to be rid of her, and did not even trouble to hide it. Despite his sneering manner, he could not conceal his motives from Bailka! She guessed them by her feminine instinct, and she, too, was on the verge of tears—angry, jealous tears. There were innumerable comrades as young as Deborah, who were staking their freedom, their all for the cause, and likely as not they, too, had friends and dear ones to care for them, to love them.

Deborah began to put on her things. Simon brightened up.

"Going? Already?"

"Yes, I'm wanted at home. Mamma's none too well."

"Is she still ailing?"

"Yes, still ailing."

Bailka had told her that she must leave. She would so much have like to stay on. Why could he not make an exception? Simon wrapped his roomy overcoat about him again, turned up his collar and saw her down the stairs.

"Good-bye! And once more, Deborah, not a word about our having met here. Not a whisper! You understand, don't you? The consequences might be very, very serious."

"Don't worry. I'm not the baby you think I am."

"Splendid, Deborah, splendid!"

All this while he was clasping her small, warm hand with his long, burning fingers. She knew forgiveness now. Most likely he had some very good reason for treating her the way he did.

"After all, how can I be so bold as to judge his actions?" she pondered. "Look at Bailka! She kept telling me again and again about comrade Simon, his heroism, his drive, his unswerving strength of character, but when I asked her where he lived she dried up and said, 'Everywhere and nowhere.' I soon recognised him, but it wasn't till he detached his sidelocks that he ceased being a stranger somehow. Then I saw him properly, *properly*! . . ."

His warm handshake had not only sent the blood racing in her veins, had not only made her flesh tingle, but had stirred her to the depths of her soul. He loomed up large in her mind's eye, dwarfing all else. Superficially facetious, he was, in fact, an earnest and a deep man—a great man, as Bailka had called him. She had sensed it long ago. Her first glimpse of him as he had hurried through the *Tsadik*'s courtyard had been sufficient to convince her of that. Even so, he was modest, had himself seen her down the stairs and had called her "Deborah!" like an old acquaintance; although as far as party matters were concerned he treated her with severity; he was the leader and she the novice in whom he could place no trust until she had proved herself.

It was, she thought, nothing but Fate that had brought her into contact with Bailka. There were plenty of other revolutionary circles in

Warsaw, where she might never have met him. Bailka said that there were more comrades engaged in underground work than most people imagined. By good fortune their paths had crossed. Under his inspiration she would work unremittingly for the common cause. Their ideal would be achieved in their lifetime. As they would sow, so also would they reap. She would faithfully serve him, fondly look after him. She would give him the strength for his great task. He seemed to be in a wretched state of health, much worse than in R—. He needed to be taken care of. The time would come when his name would resound through the world. The masses would point him out: this was the man, the great and holy man, who had devoted the work of a lifetime for their weal, this was the man who had suffered selflessly for their sake. And always she would be by his side. . . . God only knows to what dizzy heights her soaring fancy might not have taken her, had she not suddenly come to earth with a bump: all at once she found herself sprawling on the pavement and close by she heard a voice, a lusty voice that was both strange and yet familiar, bawling through the night air:

"What d'yer mean by doing that, you big lousy stiff? Hey, what's the big idea?"

Just then she became aware of two large fleshy hands gripping her thighs, and these hands lifted her to her feet with so violent a jerk that she would have tumbled over again had not one of the hands caught her by the arm and steadied her.

"Thank you!" Deborah said to the man who had helped her up. He was a gigantic fellow with a tremendous belly, and he had curious, thievish little eyes, which, while blazing ferociously, yet held a merry twinkle in them.

She tried to detach herself from his grasp, but he seemed to be unaware of her convulsive efforts to free herself.

"I've a good mind to break yer bloody neck for you, that's what I've a good mind to do! I could break every bone in yer bleedin' body for doing that, I could!"

By now Deborah had recognised the man: he was Berel Fass, the gangster chief who had once come to see Reb Avram Ber on a point of Jewish law. And her heart sank. She felt sick. She shivered. She racked her brains for some means of escape from this loathsome creature, and the cluster of men surrounding him. But she was powerless to move. He was clutching her tightly by the arm. What was she to do? Should she scream for help? The pressure of his fleshy fingers was relentless. This physical contact overwhelmed her, nauseated her, and she was almost paralysed with fear.

"I beg your pardon, Missy," said Berel Fass in his most genteel tones. "None of the regular boys would have done such a thing to you, that they wouldn't. Only this one here is a new one, just up from the country; he's just an ignorant piece of flop, that's all he is!"

Deborah would gladly have pardoned him many times over if only he had let go of her and allowed her to run away. Actually, she was not aware of the fact that she had been tripped up. She imagined that she had slipped on the icy pavement. It was a frosty night and the slush had frozen hard.

"Boys, let me introduce you! This 'ere Missy is the Rabbi's daughter, that's who she is! And if any of you guys was to come cocky with 'er I'd flay you alive and rip yer bellies open! See? What you do with any other girl ain't no business of mine! Nossir! Play abaht with 'em as much as yer like! Do to 'em what yer like. I ain't of the interferin' sort. But keep yer paws off the Rabbi's daughter, get me? That's friendly advice, that is, and anyone as doesn't want friendly advice, will get something else comin' to 'im! And now, you come 'ere, you country yokel!"

He turned to one of the men, a lanky, pale-faced youngster with a murderous glint in his watery eyes. They were smiling eyes, cruel and mocking. This newcomer to the gang was leaning up against a lamp-post, nonchalantly twirling a straw between his tobacco-stained bony fingers, but beyond that he gave no sign of life. The twirling straw seemed to absorb all his attention; he stood his ground and never as much as batted an eyelid. Berel Fass gave him a shrewd scrutiny. He observed the mocking little smile, and all at once flew into such a rage that his face turned purple and his eyes became bloodshot.

"So you won't talk, ha? There's gratitude for you! After all I've done for 'im, picked 'im out of the gutter. Well, well, that's just too bad!"

Berel Fass let go of Deborah's arm, and before she realised what was going on two immensely powerful slaps resounded through the clear, frosty night.

"And now sling yer hook! Why, if 'e'd a been one of my regular boys I'd 'ave murdered 'im, honestly I would! I'd 'ave stuck a knife in 'im! I ain't got no room for troublemakers. 'E's fired! Who's the boss 'ere, me or 'im?" said Berel Fass, turning to a one-eyed fellow, who was short but abnormally broad-shouldered, and who seemed to be the second in command. "Who's the boss 'ere, hey? If that feller starts any tricks, I'll squash 'im like a bug, that's what I'll do! Blimey, I've met 'is sort before, and what did we do to 'em? Tell me what we did to 'em!" Berel Fass went on, playfully jogging the one-eyed man whose face bore a perpetual expression as though he were winking knowingly. "We did 'em in, that's what we did to 'em! He, he, he!" he went on, chortling. "D'jer see 'im laugh, did yer? 'E's laughin' the other side of 'is face now!"

Berel Fass roared with satisfaction. He had suddenly sensed danger in the taciturn newcomer. The youngster's smile and, above all, his quiet manner testified to a strong ruthless character, deep cunning and leadership. Here was a possible rival. And Berel Fass rejoiced in the knowledge that he and no one else but himself was the undisputed boss, still in possession of his full powers, and he would see to it that no one stepped into his shoes in his lifetime.

"Ha, ha, ha!" he roared, and his mighty gust of laughter followed Deborah down the street.

"Goodness me, how pale you are!" said Raizela. She noticed, too, that Deborah was shivering all over.

"Pale, am I?" Deborah feigned surprise.

"Come here, let me have a look at you."

Raizela felt her forehead.

"Why, I think you're feverish! You must have caught a cold."

"Me feverish? No, but I fell over on my way home. It's so slippery out of doors."

"Dear me! It doesn't do for a girl to walk out late at night all by herself in a big city like Warsaw. What's the matter with you? You look so scared; what's happened?"

"Nothing, mamma, I think you're imagining things."

"Come here and lie down! As if we never had enough trouble already!"

"No, I'll get the samovar ready. There's really nothing the matter with me."

"It's all right, we'll manage without you to-night," said Raizela, tucking her in.

Indeed, Deborah needed that rest badly. She was all a-tremble.

Reb Avram Ber also came up to her to feel her forehead. He, too, thought that she had a bit of a temperature; he, too, declared that she must not think of getting up; and assisted both by Raizela and Michael, he tackled the samovar. Thus Deborah reclined on her mother's couch and comfortably watched them at their labours. In spite of her fright she could not help laughing at their industrious air as they all struggled with the solitary little samovar. These were revolutionary times, to be sure! She had changed places with her mother, and now Raizela was actually bringing her a steaming glass of tea. . . .

CHAPTER XI

Soon after Deborah had taken her leave, a few more comrades—men and women, most of them very young—arrived singly, rapping at the door in the same prearranged fashion. Before long Bailka's little room was shrouded with smoke, and the atmosphere became unbearably hot and stuffy. Simon's cheeks flushed a peculiar red, and he kept struggling to overcome his suffocating little cough. For his sake, the company stubbed their half-finished cigarettes, but the window had to remain closed and veiled. The frail, grim-lipped little girl jotted down the minutes of the meeting in shorthand, and also took down some dictation from Simon. Bailka distributed the little packages of propaganda leaflets which Simon had brought in the lining of his coat, and with monotonous insistence she warned each comrade to use the utmost care in passing on this illegal literature to the public.

One by one the comrades said good-night, going abroad at the peril of their lives, until only Bailka and Simon remained, together with another comrade who had come up from the country specially to attend the meeting.

They had tea, and here the brewing of it was a complicated process, Bailka was preoccupied with improvising a bed on the floor-boards. In the end she managed to share out equally the two pillows, the quilt and their three overcoats in accordance with the best Socialist principles . . .

She turned the light out, removed the heavy cloth from the window and admitted the frosty night air through a tiny chink at the top. Now that the room was in darkness it seemed to be bigger and loftier. Simon settled down on his back, with legs propped up, in anticipation of a sleepless night. Bailka stretched her overcoat to its full length and patted it, as if to coax it into growing; but in the end she was obliged to curl herself up instead. The hour was late and not a sound was to be heard.

How she had grown, Simon's thoughts turned to Deborah. She was no longer a child, but a woman, a tempting and sensible little woman at that. He wondered: had it ever occurred to her that it was only for the sake of seeing her that he used to frequent their house at R—? Would she guess now? . . .

"What a splendid Romeo I would make!" he suddenly interrupted his own train of thought to indulge in self-mockery. "Well, well, Romeo, it's a good job for you that your Juliet doesn't care a hang for you, never did and never will. Credit her with more sense than that!"

But after all it was only natural for a poor fool to fall in love the moment the doctor told him that, for the sake of his health, he must cut women out of his life. Now to be sure, was the ideal time to fall in love, he was overwhelmed with work, and on the verge of a physical breakdown. Ideal! Damn those gaolers! They had well-nigh knocked the life out of him during his last term in prison, and here he was actually thinking of love, romance. . . . He coughed.

But there it was—one simply could not help falling in love with her. For that matter, he was even in love with her father! Anyhow, she would never know of his feelings for her; however strong his passion might be, he would not betray himself. But, since he must deny himself all the joys of life, did that mean he must also endure all its suffering? Did that mean that the fear of what might happen to her because she was in the party, must henceforth haunt all his thoughts? Why not get her pushed out of the party? All at once he was overcome by a fit of anger—and a fit of coughing. His bed-mate stirred uneasily, as though he would wake up, but turned over instead and slept on peacefully. No, no, he was being less than just to himself. If he were certain that she would be of real service to the cause, he would be satisfied to let the matter rest. But the fact was that she would be of no value in any case. She would not be able to conform to strict discipline. Terrorism would sicken her. She loved humanity too indiscriminately. She was a reincarnation of Reb Avram Ber—in petticoats . . .

Now Bailka's bed was creaking. She kept moving about. And his own bed-mate was snoring away rhythmically, repeating himself endlessly. Lucky fellow, thought Simon, dead to the world! But just then, as if to refute this, his comrade cocked up a leg and put out his hand with a comical gesture, as though he were waiting for someone to fall into his arms. Simon chuckled. Bailka turned over in her bed. The sleeper then uttered a grunt of disappointment, and snored on . . .

Bailka dressed with the first pale flush of wintry dawn. At six o'clock she was astir, padding about with quick, short, noiseless steps like a kitten. It would be a pity to disturb Simon, for he had only just fallen asleep. She knew, because she had been awake most of the night herself. She put her own scant bedding over the two men, draping it over them gently like a loving mother. They could do with a little extra warmth, for the early morning air was very raw. Softly she closed the door behind her.

Downstairs, in a tiny shop tucked away in a corner of the courtyard, there were all sorts of sweetmeats to be had, early though the hour was, if only one could afford the money. Bailka bought a small loaf, a buckling, a jug of milk for Simon, and a quarter pound of granulated sugar.

"Good morning, comrade!" the young man up from the country greeted her from under the blankets.

"Good morning! Tell me if you want to get dressed. But it's ever so early, you know, and if I were you I'd go back to sleep. Or have a lie-in and get yourself warm before you dress."

She spoke in a whisper, so as not to rouse Simon. It was he who was snoring now, but not very loudly and by no means rhythmically —the snores came in fits and starts. Bailka discovered that she had run out of tea. By the time she got back the young man up from the country was all but dressed and Simon was wide awake.

"Good morning! Did you have a comfortable night?"

"Fine, thank you!" said Simon, and then he grinned at his bedmate. "That was a good performance you put up last night. You sound like a symphony orchestra when you snore, don't you?"

"Do I? It's no good asking me."

"Well, I'm telling you. You do! And I know a good symphony when I hear one. Simon laughed. "Now, Comrade Bailka, may we have a little privacy."

She went out.

Simon hurriedly pulled on his trousers, put on a pair of slippers and, readmitting Bailka, began to help making the bed. She laughed as the two men disputed hotly how it ought to be done, each demonstrating his own—the only proper—method: the result of their combined operations was that the bedclothes finally looked like a camel's hump.

"Go on, get away with you, you sluts! You just watch me. See? I say, Comrade Simon, you'll catch cold. Why, you're running about half naked."

"Stop nagging!"

"Simon, be reasonable, stop splashing about in that icy water."

With the obstinacy of a child, Simon dipped his hands in the freezing water; with great relish he washed his emaciated neck and chest, bathed his yellowish face in handfuls of water, and plunged his black mop of hair under the chipped tap, splashing the water all over the place.

"Aah! Lovely!"

Bailka protested.

"Stop nagging, Bailka, and don't be so stupid! D'you think I'm going to knuckle under and walk about all day like a man in a dream, with a fuddled head and sticky eyes, just because you've taken it into your head to treat me like a deathbed case? Here I am alive and kicking, and believe me I'm not going to degenerate into a frowsy old tramp."

"No, that's past history," Bailka retorted laughingly, and the young man up from the country, who was busy pouring out the tea, applauded gleefully.

It was time for Bailka to go to work. She shook hands with the young man up from the country and wished him *bon voyage*.

"Of course, you're staying, aren't you?" she said to Simon, and she stood stockstill feasting her eyes on him. "Don't forget, I'll be home at eight sharp." With a hasty glance at the clock hanging on the wall she closed the door behind her and flew down the stairs.

Simon's comrade scribbled down some notes in his diary, and after a short discussion on the mission he had been entrusted with, he set out on the long return journey to his home village. Simon was left by himself.

He did his hair. It would be a good thing if he could persuade Michael to join the party. That youngster had guts whereas Deborah was a waverer. It would probably be as easy to talk her into Zionism as it had been to convert her to Socialism. She was the sort of person who had to cling to something or other—anything would do, but, of course, a lover would be best of all! True, she had the makings of an idealist—an idealist without a definite ideal. Could he be sure, though? Maybe she knew her own mind perfectly well? But oh, how she must be able to love! How she could love! She was born for that.

He completed his toilet. He did not fancy any food. He began to go through a stack of papers, some of which he crumpled up and put aside for burning. No, she must not remain in the party. Girls like Deborah were not wanted. Deborah and company were the martyrs of the movement, they always ended up in the torture-chambers, without doing any real good. He put the kettle on to boil and poured himself out a glass of tea. He walked up and down the room, taking three steps each way, sometimes two. The tea was getting cold on the table. His throat was parched. He sat down to drink and to resume his reading. But her image kept staring at him from out of the documents. That girl had taken complete possession of his senses. She was everywhere now. Damnation! Those papers were a nuisance! After all, life was not all work.

"What if you were to put your arms around me and kiss me? Wouldn't that be lovely? Do be honest!"

Simon started. It was almost as if he had really heard Deborah's voice. He sipped his tea again.

"She'd never say a thing like that, because she doesn't care a damn for me. God, what a fool I am!"

There was one thing he knew for certain: he would get no work done to-day. A whole day would be wasted, and there was nothing he could do about it. He had had a bad night; maybe that had something to do with it. His bed-mate had kicked up a hell of a row. However, there must be no repetition of this sort of thing, he must recover his grip on himself. "Simon, think of all the gaols you've been in at His Majesty's pleasure; think of how many seats in your trousers you've worn out in prison cells; remember the beatings, the damp and the dark; and remember above all that you're consumptive, and it would be worse than a joke if you started playing the great lover now. Be yourself!" Anyway, it was all nonsense, this business of falling in love. It was the sort of piffle a woman could indulge in, when she had time hanging on her hands. It was rubbish pure and simple. What if Deborah was a very pretty girl? Was that sufficient reason for him to go off his head? She and everything about her appealed to him. Very well, next time he saw her he would look her over and rejoice . . .

What did the clock say? Half-past ten! Was that all? Phew, it was a long morning! The time was passing at a snail's pace. Damn it! He might just as well look in on Reb Avram Ber and sound Michael. Michael would be a big fellow by now. He had always been on the tall side. And it would be a joke to see the old man again. Cheerful old boy, he was! Did your heart good to talk to him. He radiated good-fellow-ship and could put new life into you. Nice chap, old Reb Avram Ber!

In this frame of mind he changed into his *hassidical* clothes. He donned his topboots, the parched leather crackling as he thrust his thin legs into them. He put on his black velvet cap, detached his side-locks and, glancing at the little mirror on the wall, saw himself broken up into many fragments in the cracked glass. The broken reflection was grinning at him. A pity he had no mud to splatter on his gaberdine; that, to be sure, would have lent the finishing touch.

He tried the door after him, and set out on his hunting expedition, with Michael as his intended prey. On the staircase he encountered an *hassidical* Jew, who hailed him with a loud and familiar good morning, as though they had known each other a lifetime. Simon returned the greeting in a similar tone.

He wandered about the streets aimlessly. It was damp and messy weather, and the biting cold soon pierced him to the bone. His face turned a bluish hue. A public clock showed the hour at a quarter-past eleven. He might as well drop in now. Even if it was a bit on the early side, there would be no harm done. Reb Avram Ber would make him just as welcome.

On that particular morning Reb Avram Ber was apparently making preparations for a very busy day, for he was actually at breakfast—long before his usual time—when Simon entered. The living-room was warm and shadowy; its homely atmosphere savoured of wintry comfort and snugness. Reb Avram Ber was in the act of stirring his coffee. He had only just given up a hopeless struggle with the piece of butter on his fried egg; this frozen, slippery piece of butter refused to melt, and even Raizela had failed to make any impression on it. She sat at the table, absorbed in a book, with a shawl over her angular shoulders and her face deathly pale.

Simon knocked at the door, which stood ajar.

"Good morning, good morning!" Reb Avram Ber exclaimed, holding out his hand long before Simon had reached the table. "Peace unto you!"

"And peace, also, unto you!"

"What a rare visitor, to be sure! Pish, pish!" Reb Avram Ber was exultant. He pulled up a chair for him.

"Sit down, Simon!"

"Thank you!"

"Well, well, and where have you been hiding all this time? So you've been living with your parents? And when did you reach Warsaw? You came up by train last night? Bless my soul, what a rare guest! It's quite a time since I saw you last. You think it's two years? No, no, not as long ago as all that. Now tell me, how are you?"

"So-so!"

"How about your health?" said Reb Avram Ber, casting a suspicious eye over his visitor.

"Oh, nothing to worry about! I'm perfectly fit."

"Do you mean to tell me you don't recognise him," said Reb Avram Ber, turning to Raizela. "It's Simon—you know, he was at the *yeshiva* in R— the best student I ever had."

Reb Avram Ber's best student smiled.

"Why, of course! I just couldn't place you at first. How are you?"

"Very well, the Lord be praised. And how are you?"

"Poorly, as usual."

"Of course, you'll take breakfast with us, won't you? I suppose you said your morning prayers before you came out?"

"Why, of course!"

"That's good! Now, won't you say grace and bring your chair up closer?"

"Thanks, but I've had my breakfast and I just couldn't manage another meal."

"Are you sure?"

"Quite sure!"

"All right, then you'll have coffee with us. No one ever refuses coffee. Dear oh dear, oh dear, what a pleasant surprise," Reb Avram Ber kept murmuring over and over again; he could not get over it. "Have you been going on with your studies all this time? Don't I know how much you love the Talmud!"

By way of reply Simon undid his overcoat and instead of removing it he threw it across the back of his chair. The sudden change of air, this indoor warmth after the bitter cold out-of-doors, had taken his breath away and he was half-choking. But he had no regrets.

"The very image of his daughter," he kept saying to himself as he contemplated Reb Avram Ber's good-natured face, which expressed such genuine pleasure at this unforeseen visit.

Raizela went into the kitchen, her shawl slithering down from her stooping shoulders. She brought him in a cup of coffee herself.

"How is your father?"

"These are trying times for him."

Reb Avram Ber groaned:

"Can't he make ends meet? What a shame! Is he keeping in good health, though?"

"Hardly!"

"Oy, oy, oy!" Reb Avram Ber sighed with deep-felt grief. "Life is one long struggle for Thy chosen race," he exclaimed, addressing Jehovah. There was not a trace of complaint in his voice; he was merely bringing a fact to the Almighty's notice. But that it pained Reb Avram Ber, of that there could be no doubt.

"Have there been any changes since I saw you last? I shouldn't be surprised if you were engaged, or even married?"

"No, no," Simon replied, and his face turned red. "Damn it," he thought, "the old boy is giving me a hint; I only wish I could take it! Come to think of it, he always did covet me as an eligible husband for his daughter. It would suit me perfectly. But no such luck! . . ."

"What the devil! Here I am blushing like a maiden! What's come over me? I've degenerated into a regular softy. A little while ago I had firmly made my mind up that this business of falling in love was all moonshine, and now here I am starting to play the fool all over again. However, if I have to blush, this is the best place for it . . ."

The beadle burst into the room in a great state of excitement, crying:

"He says he's not going to attend the arbitration. He says he won't have anything to do with it, and he's not going to waste his time by coming here."

"You should have explained to him that, as a Jew, he is in honour bound to attend an arbitration when summoned."

"Yes, and when I said that he pushed me out and slammed the door in my face, the boor! The ruffian!" the beadle fumed.

Reb Avram Ber grunted.

"Never mind, he'll think better of it."

"How's your daughter?" the beadle asked, as he helped Raizela to clear the breakfast things off the table. "I hear she was taken bad last night."

Simon's pulse quickened. He very nearly committed the mistake of asking Reb Avram Ber what was wrong with her, and that would never have done for a pious young man.

"You see, when she was coming home last night after visiting her friend she slipped over, and as we thought she was rather feverish we decided to keep her in bed for the day; but its nothing serious."

"Michael asked me to get here as early as I could because Deborah was ill, and when I heard that I was quite alarmed," said the beadle.

"That's right, that's right!" Reb Avram Ber nodded his approval, not in reference to the beadle's alarm, but to Michael's initiative.

Simon was furious with himself.

"Don't you know that you're going to peg out soon?" he taunted his other self that had risen up within him in revolt. "You'll soon be in your grave, and no matter who much you protest you'll never be able to satisfy your wishes. You're a miserable dreamer. I tell you again that all your longings are so much nonsense, sheer lunacy! A delusion! And I'm going to knock some good common sense into you, even if I have to smash you in the process . . ."

Reb Avram Ber indulged in a little small-talk with Simon, then eagerly passed on to a Talmudic dissertation. At first Simon felt very little relish at the prospect of being drawn into a debate. These theological quibbles were so remote from life, and he had long since washed his hands of them. His links with the past were broken. His last term of imprisonment had been his undoing. Although his chest had given him trouble before then, his lungs had still functioned. In those old days he had it in him to lead a life of make-believe with complette conviction. He was his own master, and could dismiss at will any absurd little thoughts or temptations that might willy-nilly creep into his mind. He had known how to hate like a full-blooded man and how to strain every nerve in the struggle against the parasites of society. When his duties took him to the town of R——, where he kept up communications with Gentile comrades who would come to see him in *hassidical* garb to deliver reprots sewn into their silken gabardines, and to taken away intelligences and instructions in the lining of their fur caps, and time had hung heavily on his hands, he had it in him to concentrate seriously on the Talmud, and he actually found it a not uninteresting way of whiling the time away. Of course, in those days he had a pair of lungs to breathe with—oh, if only he could take a deep, painless breath of air at present, just one breath!— and he had been able to lead a dual life without much effort. Now everything was changed, and this Talmudic discussion soon revealed how dull his brain had since become. It all sounded rather weird and wonderful, and he got quite flustered. Bit by bit, however, the cells of his memory came to life again, and towards the end his arguments gained in swiftness, power and coherence.

Reb Avram Ber could not but notice the transformation. He led the discourse on to a higher plane, and the two men became more and more involved in its intricacies. Gradually Simon entered into the spirit of the thing. The taut skin over his cheekbones flushed an unhealthy red, as though bloodstained. His large black eyes were blazing beneath his overhanging brows. He eventually detached himself altogether from immediate realities, and gesticulated violently as he spoke, and his fingers grimly clutched the edge of the table while he listened to Reb Avram Ber's rejoinders. Reb Avram Ber was fighting back for all he was worth. He reached for his beard, his trusted comrade in arms, and the two of them—Reb Avram Ber and his beard— struggled valiantly to set Simon's disquisition at nought. But they found it a very difficult task. Obviously Simon was determined not to yield, never would he suffer defeat. Then the argument ended as these arguments always did end, with victory for Reb Avram Ber. All covered in perspiration, Simon leaned back in his chair and he smiled the familiar wry smile of the vanquished. Reb Avram Ber resumed his seat, and he, too, smiled—a pleasant smile of victory!

"I have the impression that you do not study quite so intensively as you used to do when we were together," said Reb Avram Ber with a shade of reproach in his voice; but this sounded so fatherly, that for a moment Simon forgot that he was only acting a part, and he began to excuse himself in all earnestness.

"Not that it matters, because it's never too late to mend," Reb Avram Ber added hurriedly. This was by way of a tactful reminder to Simon that he must not neglect his studies in the future.

A woman knocked at the door; she had a slaughtered chicken under her arm, which she wanted Reb Avram Ber to examine, so that he might tell her whether it was kosher or not. And hard on her heels followed the man who had so boorishly refused to attend the arbitration, and who had now changed his mind. Simon put on his overcoat and buttoned it up.

"Well, good-bye, Simon, and don't forget to call in again to-night. I should like to have another chat with you," said Reb Avram Ber, seeing him to the door, and then he turned to the two newcomers who were waiting for him impatiently.

Simon said good-day to Raizela through the half-open door of her room, and only when he reached the bottom of the staircase did it occur to him that he had forgotten to ask about Michael, the very thing he had come for. He wondered how he could make good his omission. Should he retrace his footsteps? No, he would have to call back later, in the evening. But he was not so sure that he would, for he suddenly sensed a wave of pity in himself—pity for Michael. Reb Avram Ber's home, that sweet home and all that was in it, he cherished now above all other things. After all, no great harm would be done if he were to drop Michael. The world was full of people, and one Michael more or less in the ranks of the party was not going to make all that difference!

He bent his steps homewards—the little home he shared with Bailka for the time being. When he got there he found it bitterly cold. Without troubling to change, and keeping on his overcoat, he sat down on Bailka's bed. A great many thoughts, all rather blurred and incoherent, went flitting through his brain; some of them would not go away, and they all became entangled. They were mainly memories of R——. It had been good to be alive. He had been a real man then, high-spirited, strong and healthy. Although he had already done two terms of imprisonment as a "suspected character," he had emerged with nothing worse than a slight cough and occasional twinges which were easily ignored. What did he care about a little pain when he had all the air between heaven and earth to breathe? But now, now that air was denied to him, everything had changed. It was no use his trying to deceive himself. The fact of the matter was that his burning enthusiasm had faded, and he was doing party work now only because his reasoning-powers, his plain common-sense, prompted him to do so. He understood the cause, but did not *feel* it. And also the conviction of ultimate success was lacking, now that he saw the struggle in all its stark reality . . . "the going was bad, the mud was axle-deep, and the horse was weary"—oh, so weary!

Without troubling to change he set off for another ramble through the streets and singled out a restaurant which seemed to be fairly clean while having no pretensions to elegance. He went in and ordered dinner. The man who took his order wore a rather mysterious preoccupied air, for he too led a dual life—he was by turns sole proprietor of the restaurant and its sole waiter. He was short and rotund; on his comfortable paunch he wore an apron of a doubtful white, and he wore a big smile on his double-chinned face of a doubtful pink. He recited the menu by heart, all in one breath. Simon ordered a plate of soup, a portion of roast beef and a glass of tea with lemon.

The fat man nodded his head knowingly, and departed, leaving Simon firmly convinced that dinner was about to be served. But for ten minutes nothing happened. To while the time away Simon picked up a newspaper from a chair nearby. Gradually it dawned on him that the news he was reading was all-too-familiar, so he glanced at the date. He laughed. The paper was of historical interest . . . well over a month old. Well, by the clock on the counter, he had been waiting for quite fifteen minutes. There was nothing for it, but to go on waiting. Then some minutes later he rose and went in search of the lost fat man. He tried all the doors at the back, gazing down dark passages. Then he opened a curious little door, which he made haste to close again, but there was no sign of the man anywhere. Except for a kitten frisking about with a ball of paper, and a speechless, sore-nosed infant that stood warming its tiny hands upon the cast-iron stove in the centre of the restaurant, there was not a living soul in sight. The scanty assortment of cakes and pastries displayed on the counter had such an uninviting air, that there was no risk of their being pilfered (and of this the fat man was apparently aware).

Simon lost patience, and just as he was about to walk out, in trotted the fat man with a plateful of potatoes and peas, which he set down with a great show of haste, and before Simon realised that this was not the dish he had ordered, the restaurant was again deserted. Simon was minded to protest that this was not what he wanted, but there was no one he could lodge a protest with. Even the child had vanished, and as for the kitten, it appeared quite unconcerned. Having no choice in the matter, he tackled the potatoes and peas, and then sat waiting once more; but this time the fat man reappeared after an interval of only five minutes. Having no more roast beef left for to-day, he had brought some nice fried liver. Simon was afraid it would give him indigestion; but restaurateurs are born, not made, and the fat man was master of the art of persuading diners to eat dishes not of their own but of his choosing . . . Now tea with lemon was different: that was something the fat man was prepared to serve at any time, and he therefore set it down on the table before Simon had scarcely started on his liver, so that when he came to drink it, it was ice cold. But that was his own fault.

"Look at him, taking all day to eat his dinner!" the fat man muttered to himself, as he watched Simon trying to cut the tough rubber-like liver. "What a nincompoop! I thought he'd finish it in a jiffy, and I never wanted to keep him waiting for his tea."

Simon paid for his meal and left the stuffy restaurant for the ill-lit streets. It had grown quite dark. The strips of greenish wet light that came tumbling on to the pavements from the square windows of green-walled soda-fountain parlours, which now in the winter were given up to the sale of galoshes, only emphasised the general gloom. What next? Eight o'clock was a long way off yet. He was beginning to feel the cold acutely. As he sauntered along, the scattered dimly-lit little shops and the huddled-up shabby old women with eyes tearful from the frost, who either sat selling hot *baygel* or held their hands out for alms as he passed, and the bright red of swollen cheeks and hands of a woman behind a pile of wrinkled red apples, all seemed to lend a keener edge to the cutting wind.

He went indoors again and changed. He felt his normal self, if rather less festive now. Good-bye to the Talmudic student! Yes, it was time he got down to some honest-to-goodness work. But how was he to keep the cold off? He wrapped himself up in the blanket from off the bed, and to make things more cheerful, he turned up the wick of the paraffin lamp. But it gave off sickening fumes, and he had to turn it down again. Only now did he observe that he had forgotten to destroy the pile of crumpled up papers which he had put aside on the table. That was bad.

"Half a mo', we'll soon get nice and warm," he said to himself. He put the papers into the small iron stove. He found a few pieces of wood and managed to build up a fire.

Now he would be able to get some work done. But no, his mind was not functioning. He had a splitting headache. And the fried liver he had eaten was already giving him trouble. He could feel its pressure between his nether ribs. He should not have touched it.—Damn those merchants! For the sake of profit they'd give you a dish of boiled pebbles and make you eat them. That species, that class must be exterminated ruthlessly, he said to himself aloud . . . Meanwhile the fire had developed into a merry blaze.

"But even merchants have to make a living," said a voice inside him.

"Well then, they must find productive work to do."

"But there's not enough work to go round," the voice inside him protested.

"Oh isn't there? Then there ought to be! And a remedy must be found. In a properly ordered society all natural resources will be fully exploited. There will be work and wealth and leisure for all. Poland, for example, is a fertile and rich country, and managed scientifically, it could easily be self-supporting. The same is true of other lands. If only we could change the system . . . I wish I hadn't eaten that liver!"

Bailka knocked, and he let her in.

"Good evening, comrade!"

"Good evening, comrade!"

"Well, how did you get on?" asked Bailka, taking off her hat and coat.

Simon made no reply.

"Wasn't he interested?"

"Look here, Bailka, I have decided to leave that blessed family alone. I don't want to get them mixed up in this business. I have my reasons, very good reasons. Before I convert others, I'm going to renew my own life and get down to work with my old driving-power. D'you remember the bygone days? It would be a good thing if we could launch a really nation-wide propaganda campaign—on new lines."

"What do you mean, new lines?" Bailka inquired, as she turned the minced meat, which she had brought home with her, into the frying pan. Very soon a savoury odour of fried onions, homeliness and healthy hunger filled the tiny room. "So you've had your dinner out, and you ate fried liver? And it was tough, eh? You'll have some tea with me? All right then, I'll pour you out a glass. You know, you should have refused that liver. You're just like a big baby!"

"Of course I'll have tea," Simon rejoined absentmindedly.

"Have you still got a lot of work to do?" Bailka asked, as she keenly munched a mouthful of meat. Her cheeks were flushed and glossy, and her eyes feasted on Simon, as if to season her plain fare.

"Look, if we were to adopt new tactics, if we were to change our strategy entirely . . ."

"What do you mean, new tactic?" Bailka demanded as before.

"What do I mean? Supposing we were to abandon terror as an instrument of class struggle . . ."

For a moment Bailka stopped chewing.

"Yes, drop the old slogan that the end justifies the means. There is nothing in the doctrine of the Jesuits that is worthy of imitation. It's an old and obsolete idea and is as good as played out. Yes, long practice has proved it a failure."

"And what are the new tactics?"

"We must make a fresh start. A slow process, maybe, but a sure one. I'll give you a primitive example. Take the average man. Explain to him in a friendly way the injustice, confusion and absurdity of the present way of life. If he cannot understand you at first, don't lose patience, be tolerant, and carry on with the good work, convincing him with hard facts and logical theories. And when you have done this, remain on friendly terms with him, let him feel that you're his comrade, although your views differ from his. He'll come over to your side much sooner than you imagine."

"Yes, and meantime the downtrodden masses will groan helplessly in chains, and starve, while high society makes merry and carouses, enjoying perfect security."

"Why, of course, Bailka, that was the sort of answer I was expecting. But you can't devise a big plan like that and make it sound feasible on the spur of the moment. Anyway, it was no more than a passing thought. Although what I was trying to get at was this: if we could gain widespread sympathy for our cause by peaceful means, if we acted as an irresistible magnet attracting all the healthy elements of society, then the present social order would crumble in ruins and we could build up something worth while in its stead in a comparatively short time."

"Who's going to sponsor this new plan? Who's going to handle it."

"Bailka, your naivety surprises me. You're being perfectly childish. I was only thinking aloud, so please don't pose silly riddles!"

"All right, but if you're going to preach tolerance, you'll have to be a bit more tolerant yourself and permit me freedom of speech," said Bailka with a merry laugh.

"Well said!" Simon felt pleased with Bailka. "You know, sometimes a single thought gets into your mind and no matter how stupid it is, you can't drive it away. It nags and nags."

"I think you're not feeling any too well to-day."

"Yes, as a matter of fact I am rather queer. I reckon it's the liver up to its tricks."

"Tell me, do you mean to stop in Warsaw for any length of time?"

"Yes, I'm going to settle down for a while."

"Well then, I know where you can get a nice little room at a reasonable rent, and since I'm looking after you so well, may I give you some sound advice?"

"Don't bother, I know exactly what you're going to say: Abstain from washing in cold water, abstain from eating liver, abstain from smoking, abstain from everything! In fact, don't move without Bailka's permission!"

"Well, if you want to treat it as a joke, you can, but I will say this much: you have no right to squander recklessly what little strength is left to you. It's not purely a personal matter. Your strength is our strength. We can't afford to lose it. That's the position, quite frankly. You must look after your health, not for your own sake, but for our sake. It's a pity, you know, that my mother isn't living in Warsaw. She'd take good care of you, she'd coddle you, and in a short time you'd be your old self again. You'd be able to get twice as much work done, and she'd simply love the idea of waiting on a godfearing man, serving a Talmudic student. She'd feel like she was reserving a seat for herself in heaven. You'd be like a son to her, taking the place of that wretched daughter of hers who ran away from home to become a dressmaker, a common seamstress. Poor me, I'm the black sheep of the family, and in my home village if ever they mention my name they speak it with a curse."

"You forget, Bailka, that I'm not going to play the Talmudic student any more. There may be exceptional cases when I shall have to do so, but as a rule I shall be my own normal self."

"Well, if that's how it is, then all you can expect from her is a torrent of curses for being a miserable sinner like myself," said Bailka, and she laughed till her bosom was all a-quiver, so that Simon, who was gazing intently at her across the table, saw the woman in her as if for the first time, and he found that she was not really altogether unattractive.

"Have some more tea?"

"No thanks!"

They kept up the conversation for some time. Then Bailka made the beds. Having had so little sleep on the previous night they were both tired and eager for bed. She put the light out. But again sleep would not come to her; Simon dozed off almost instantaneously—she could tell by his breathing.

Bailka struggled pitifully with her passionate longings. She felt hot and kept wriggling about uncomfortably. How painful it was to lavish so much love and to receive no response, to labour on barren soil. She lay awake for a long time. It was past three in the morning when she left her bed. In her long nightdress she looked a tall and slim figure. She seated herself on the edge of Simon's bedclothes. She gazed into his pallid face which showed up strangely white in the darkness—it was more like a spectre than a human face. For a long while Bailka kept gazing at it. She was carried away by an ecstasy of love that was almost too powerful for her to bear, and a warm, motherly sense of compassion encompassed her, such as might move a mother watching over her sick first-born child on the threshold of death. She brushed his hair away, stroked it tenderly, and planted a light kiss on his forehead. Simon started up.

"Bailka? Is that you? What's happened? Why aren't you asleep?"

Bailka burst into tears like a helpless child.

"Is anything the matter? Aren't you feeling well?"

"Simon, don't try and pretend. You must know! Not that I have anything against you. But don't go out of your way to hurt me by ignoring my . . . my agony!"

"Now, now, Bailka, don't be childish!" He took her in his arms, gently stroked her hair. "Bailka, you know perfectly well that I'm . . . a sick man. You and I are working shoulder to shoulder for the same cause. You know perfectly well that I think very highly of you—in fact, I'm interested in you, ever so interested. You're a very nice comrade to have, one of the best. Your sound common-sense, and your straightforward attitude to people and affairs . . . I like you for those qualities alone. Look, you'll catch cold. Go back to bed, Bailka."

He gathered her up closer in his arms, covered her over with the quilt which she had given him that night, having taken the overcoats for herself. She was trembling from head to foot with the cold, with tenderness that had for so long been pent up inside her common-sense, with passions and emotions that would not yield even to the strictest of common-sense.

They both forgot for the time being that he was stricken with a contagious disease, or wanted to forget.

Bailka rose at an early hour. She thought of leaving a note behind to say that she had not wished to disturb him. But it was not in Bailka's nature to play the coward. She did not go to work before her usual time. She prepared breakfast. They drank coffee together and spoke about the furnished room he would have to find for himself. They both behaved, hitherto, without any trace of restraint, as if nothing had passed between them.

Simon made his home in Warsaw. He carried on with his regular party work. By giving lessons he was able to make a fair living, eking out the small allowance which he received from the party.

Deborah learnt to love him more and more with each passing day. But Simon did not play the part of the lover at all.

His attitude to her was rather absent-minded, like a grown-up trying to be friendly to a well-behaved, if rather unintelligent, child. Finally, deeply shaken by each renewal of contact with her, he decided to exclude her as far as possible from the day-to-day routine of the party. In the end she would lose heart and stay away altogether. He argued with himself:

"She can never be yours, that much is certain. You have your work to do, and it is infinitely more important than hers—that's plain—so you must get rid of her."

In the early days Deborah persuaded herself that there was a good reason for her being barred from the confidential meetings: she had not had sufficient experience. Then it occurred to her that possibly she was under suspicion because her father was a rabbi and all her ancestors were clerics. As for Simon, who was tarred by the same brush, he was a man of great ability. His talents were indispensable and the party would have been so much poorer without them. But who was going to worry and take chances with a mere nobody like herself?

The fact that it was all Simon's doing did not once cross her mind. It only grieved and pained her to be ignored by him, to find herself spurned by a great man who had no patience for the lesser fry. Occasionally she even imagined that he was assuming this attitude towards her expressly to make her suffer. But if only she could bring herself to believe that, how she would have rejoiced! The plain truth of the matter was that he was scarcely aware of her existence. It was terrible to have to confess this to herself, but it was obvious. Of course, they had no common meeting ground. He was so much above her. But in what way did she compare unfavourably with the other comrades of the rank and file? What fault had she committed to lose that little prestige which she had held on first entering the party? And why had even Bailka cooled off towards her so suddenly? Why did Bailka go out of her way to avoid her? Why? Why?

Questions such as these harassed her mind all through the winter. Nowhere could she find any place for herself. And to make matters worse, at home they kept pestering her with marriage proposals which wore down her last lingering shreds of patience. The family and friends of the family began to look askance at her. Raizela came to regard her as an eccentric.

"Honestly, I don't know what's become of Deborah. She behaves so unnaturally. All day long she goes about with a vacant stare on her face, as if her mind were blank, or full of queer, faraway thoughts, and then suddenly she will start to cry and then in the midst of her tears she will burst into song like an imbecile. And she stays out very late of nights. And I don't know if you've noticed it, but she's turned into a brazen-faced little hussy. At the slightest provocation she'll fly into a terrible rage and jump down your throat. It's all very, very strange. I hardly dare to say in so many words what I fear has come over her. You think her nerves are on edge? Don't be silly! I don't think anybody could be more nervous than I am, yet you don't see me going about crying at one moment and bursting into song at the next. It's perfectly disgraceful. Very soon all the neighbours will be wagging their tongues. I do wish we could find a husband for her— marry her off and bring her to her senses. . . ."

Deborah learnt to detest her home. She realised only too well that the family had come to look upon her as an hysterical, irrational creature. She began to brood, and her every thought was—how to run away. Young people often left home on account of differences with their parents. When the rift between the old and the new generations became unbridgeable, a parting of the ways was inevitable. That was the course Bailka had taken. But she, Deborah, was not made of the same stuff as Bailka! Now, Bailka was a prominent member of the party, but as for herself, she was being spurned by the movement. It was one thing to contemplate action, but quite another to accomplish it. Anyway, she had nowhere to go, no means of escape.

Gradually, of her own accord, she held more and more aloof from the party and its members. She imagined she could detect something of derision in Simon's treatment of her, something that amounted to contempt. Finally, when she approached him one evening and asked him point-blank why the party thought fit to pass her over, when more recent recruits than herself were being entrusted with duties of one sort or another, he told her nonchalantly:

"To be perfectly candid, you do not quite fit in with our requirements . . ."

This after days of self-torture, of agonising vacillations before she could find it in her to throw caution and pride to the winds!

Moreover, as he made this "candid" reply, he averted his head and scanned a dog's-eared magazine which happened to be lying on the table, as if he did not so much as care to set eyes on her. At the time, also, Bailka sat reading a newspaper with unblinking absorption, as if she too wished to take part in this demonstration of complete indifference. It was the last straw. It was more than Deborah could endure. She could never understand how it was she managed to check herself from bursting into tears like a child in their presence. Possibly it was her perpetual fear of appearing childish that saved her. At any rate, she shed no tears while in Bailka's room.

The moment she got home she had a good cry. After the storm came calm, and she vowed never again to give him a single thought. Her love and affection gave way to hatred, not only for Simon, but for the whole clique around him. And her Socialism perished. . . .

If only she had been able to use her hands and could earn a living, no matter how meagre, she would have flown from Warsaw, from her parents, from herself and above all from Simon. She had no wish ever to see him again, had no wish to live in the same city as he. And, as a matter of fact, in all probability she might never have met him again, for only a few months after he had settled down in Warsaw he was recalled to R— to re-organise the party machine which had broken down there.

CHAPTER XII

Meanwhile Reb Zalman, all undeterred, was arranging a match for Deborah, and one evening he arrived with a brand new proposal, one that was—in these hard modern times—almost too good to be true.

"I have a remarkable story to tell you, Reb Avram Ber, of the strange workings of Providence," said Reb Zalman, beside himself with excitement at the strange workings of Providence. "But before I begin, Reb Abram Ber, do you know Reb Baruch Laib, the principal of the Berishlitz *yeshiva?*"

"I should say so," replied Reb Avram Ber. "Everybody knows Reb Baruch Laib!"

"And tell me, did you ever make the acquaintance of his son?"

"Let me see now . . . I did meet him once in R—. He was going away to Belgium, I believe, and he came down with his father specially to say good-bye to the *Tsadik*. That's right, and I invited him to dinner. Yes, I know the young man you mean."

"Aha, now you just listen to this funny prank of Providence! Here you are, Reb Avram Ber, with a daughter on your hands, who is, shall we say, an up-to-date young lady, one of those modern young ladies who insists on having a husband dressed up in the new-fangled European style. You, for your part, would not dream, of course, of considering any such suitor in a new-fangled get-up. And for this reason all our proposals have been foredoomed to failure. Here you are, just about beginning to lose heart. So what must happen? Well it so happens that the other night Reb Baruch Laib drops in for a chat. We get talking about one thing and another, and suddenly it comes to me in a flash—just like that. The funny part about it is that I fancy Reb Baruch Laib was thinking on similar lines himself. Anyhow, guess what I did, Reb Avram Ber? I suggested a marriage between your daughter and his son. How's that for a brainwave? It's the old, old story of satisfying the wolf and saving the lamb, so to speak. Ha, ha, ha! Really, I must say that Providence weaves a very cunning net. I suppose you know that the town of Antwerp boasts of one of the most deeply religious Jewish communities in the world?"

"Well, I have heard something to that effect."

"No, but I beg you not to take it from hearsay! You take it from *me*! There is more true religion to be found in Antwerp than anywhere else. Here in Warsaw a great deal of wickedness is hidden away under orthodox gaberdines. Now in Antwerp, where everybody dresses in the modern style—after all, it's a foreign country, and when in Rome one must do as the Romans do—as I say, whereas they dress differently, at heart they're more orthodox and infinitely stricter than most of the people here. They are Jews in the best sense of the word, and Antwerp is a thoroughgoing Jewish city if ever there was one. Everybody there studies the Talmud. The place is full of synagogues and *hassidical* circles—in a word, a replica of Warsaw! Take Reb Baruch Laib's son! He devotes several hours to the Talmud in an *hassidical* circle every evening as soon as he's finished his day's work."

"What's that? Do you mean to tell me he's a working man?"

"A working man, if you please! You don't imagine he's a tailor or a cobbler or something low-down like that! Allow me to inform you that by profession he is nothing more nor less than a diamond-cutter!"

"What?!" Reb Avram Ber was left almost breathless.

"That's it, a diamond-cutter! I need hardly tell you, therefore, that he does not exactly have to struggle to make a living. How goes the old tag? The man who chops the wood gets the splinters. And believe me, the man who cuts great diamonds gets the little diamonds. Besides, it's a gentle art, a noble profession. I must make a confession to you, Reb Avram Ber—I envy you greatly. I only wish Reb Baruch Laib had chosen to marry into my family. But no, Providence would have it otherwise! What Reb Baruch Laib has set his heart on, is marrying into your family. He has heard say that you have a really fine daughter, good-looking and clever. And maybe you, Reb Avram Ber, will guess who it was imparted this knowledge to him. . . ." Here Reb Zalman smiled a significant smile. "The point is, Reb Baruch Laib is anxious to give to his son a wife who will be a good influence, who will help to keep his son the same as he's always been—a pious, upright and honourable Jew. That's the idea! After all, a girl that springs from such good stock as yours, Reb Avram Ber, is bound to set a shining example to any young man. . . ."

Reb Avram Ber's hand reached for his beard. It was all very odd. But who could tell? Maybe there was something in it! The ways of Providence were inscrutable. At any rate, he would call in Raizela. She found the proposal quite reasonable.

"But does he know that we have no dowry to offer?"

"That's a detail, which you need not worry about! I have already made it clear to Reb Baruch Laib what an honour it would be for his son to marry into your family. I'll even go a step further and say that, with a little management, I'll induce Reb Baruch Laib to provide the dowry himself. In fact, I'll go a step further than that, and make him bear the wedding expenses and all. You leave that to me. Once my mind's made up, nothing can stop me. I don't believe in delay, and to-morrow morning, please God, we shall write a letter to the young man asking him if he is willing to be married, and if his answer is yes, if only he gives his consent, then the whole thing will be almost too good to be true!"

The young man in far-away Belgium readily gave his consent. And why not? What could be better than marriage on such terms? Here was his father beseeching him to accept a fine dowry, wedding gifts, financial support after the wedding, and whatnot, with a wife thrown into the bargain! Better still, his father was accompanying the offer with a handsome remittance. And the girl was good-looking, too, because he remembered having seen her in R—. Not at all bad! He would have been a dolt to turn the proposal down. No, he would never do such a silly thing as that. He was going to be a bridegroom! It was a soft job. He liked soft jobs. He hated hard work, and, above all, he hated looking for work!

When they approached Deborah on the subject, she considered it as a means of escape. If she could go abroad, then she would be able to live her own life. She would be under no more obligations as the daughter of an orthodox Rabbi, everything would be left behind, all her ties with the past would be severed. The past would be dead. So frantic was her impatience, so feverish her condition, that she failed to see any alternative to the dramatic gesture of giving herself away to a man whom she had never set eyes on—at least she could not remember him—an utter stranger about whom she knew nothing. She was conscious of only one thing: she must run away. And when Reb Zalman talked and talked, until she could bear to listen no longer, she said "Yes."

Her consent obtained, Reb Avram Ber waxed jubilant. Raizela was less effusive than he; she well concealed her satisfaction. But Deborah was the more deeply pained by her mother's attitude. It showed plainly enough that Raizela would feel no pangs at parting with her. It showed plainly enough that her mother was eager to see the back of her. Well, that being so, there was only one thing left for her to do, and that was to clear out! She had been given notice to quit! Did that really mean that her mother would never care to see her again, would never miss her? Yes, that was what it meant. It could mean nothing else, and her sense of surprise was even greater than her grief. She was a pariah. Simon wanted to have nothing to do with her. Her parents were quite willing, nay happy, to send her away to a distant land. The party had unceremoniously kicked her out. And she, poor fool, had been deluding herself all along that, despite all appearances, Simon was not really indifferent to her, that there was a mistake somewhere, that her parents loved her, that her mother's habit of preaching at her was prompted by motherly affection.

"Of course, the real truth of the matter is that she hates me, always has hated me, and is perfectly delighted at this opportunity of getting rid of me. That's what it all boils down to. I'm not good enough for her, I'm not her clever, artful sort. Not that I had to find it out for myself, for she's always telling me as much. And she's right! I am a fool! A sentimental idiot, I pity and trust those who taunt and perse-cute me, I live in a world of make-believe, and they can see it all as a grand joke. My own mother pokes fun at me, so does Michael, and Simon, and everybody. . . . Everybody!"

She would go away and get married. As a means of escape from a home which was only a home in name, and which she hated like poi-son, as a last resort of getting away from parents who were eager to disown her, a marriage of convenience was surely no worse than the cowardice of dying by her own hand! As for the man whom she was going to marry, he did not matter at all! Why, not even her father had flinched. She could almost hear them all shouting at her, "Get out! We don't want you here!" And even her father did not care a damn. That her father loved her dearly, was something she had never doubted. Now she saw the hard truth: she was all alone in the world. She began to weep and sob in a loud voice.

Raizela came running in from the bedroom as fast as her feeble legs would carry her.

"What is the matter, Deborah?"

For the moment Deborah really hated her mother. She wished for nothing better than to make her suffer. She did not trouble to reply, and finally when Raizela had repeated her question many times over and had become quite alarmed, Deborah calmly declared that she was not crying and would her mother oblige by leaving the room. Raizela gaped at her. She had never known Deborah to address her in this manner. She became furious, and without a word trudged back to her bedroom.

"It's too bad," she said to Reb Avram Ber, who had joined her to discover the reason for Deborah's sudden outburst. "That precious daughter of ours is doing her best to kill me. I shall be very glad to see this marriage through, and have her go away—in peace (she added)."

"Of course you'll be glad, for it's a wonderful match, for which the Lord be praised! It's a very serious matter nowadays, finding a husband for a girl without a dowry."

"What's more, she picks and chooses. No one's good enough for her."

"Yes, thank God she has not disgraced us by running off with a freethinker, or doing something of that sort!" Reb Avram Ber rejoiced. "And at the same time she'll be marrying a man dressed in the modern style, just as she has set her heart on doing. Reb Zalman tells me that this young man in Antwerp is as good a Jew as you could wish for, godfearing and a Talmudist. He's well off and will make a splendid husband. The Lord be praised!"

A few days later the family received a formal visit from a short, tubby woman wearing on her huge bust a jacket of black cloth trimmed with innumerable silk ribbons and with a very broad, prosperous-looking shawl of fine lace on her head. Behind her, and overlooking her, came a tall, lean, red-faced woman, likewise wearing a black jacket with silk ribbons, although her trimmings were far fewer and less glossy, and her shawl was narrow and rather mean-looking. And trotting along at their side like a puppy, came yet another woman in a black jacket; but she was very skinny and tiny indeed, and she had no silk trimmings to boast of at all. The shawl on her head was as narrow as a thread, and her pinched little nose was even narrower still. She had watery little eyes, a pitiful little mouth with wrinkles and a pitiful little chin with more wrinkles. These three ladies were Deborah's prospective mother-in-law, the mother-in-law's sister and the sister's sister-in-law respectively, and they had all come to inspect Deborah.

The sitting-room had been tidied up for the occasion. Raizela was wearing her black gown. The skin over her cheekbones was flushed.

Deborah's face was glowing with fever. And the big paraffin lamp diffused its mellow light over her with a radiance such as befitted a young, innocent bride.

After a strenuous effort her prospective mother-in-law managed to climb on to a chair. However, she did not succeed in getting comfortable, and appeared to be only half-way up. But this was all to the advantage of her lanky sister opposite, who was able to claim all the space for her long legs under the table. As for the sister's sister-in-law, she perched on her chair with her short legs dangling playfully like a child. Deborah took note of all these details. Suddenly she burst out into an uncontrollable fit of laughter. The three newcomers exchanged a look of amazement, and the marriage quest might have ended there and then if Deborah had not retrieved matters by responding sensibly, tactfully and modestly to all the questions which were later put to her, and if Raizela for her part had not informed the visitors that during the morning a very comical incident had taken place, which Deborah could not forget, and which kept provoking her laughter again and again.

Deborah passed muster. Some days later an engagement party was held.

Deborah's prospective father-in-law was a big, fat man with a very long and fiery red beard, and with a shiny forehead and beefy face in which his eyes were scarcely visible, lost in a tangle of fluffy side-whiskers, jutting eyebrows and puffy lumps of flesh. All through the ceremony he did nothing but stare at the bride-to-be. The more he saw of her, the more he wanted to see, and he had his eyes glued on her to the very end. On the other hand, his wife, who once again was unable to get the best part of herself on to the chair, had her eyes glued on *him* to the very end.

When they presented Deborah with a long, golden chain and hung it round her neck, she shivered at the touch of the cold metal and at the thought that the most vicious of dogs might safely be tied up with a chain such as this. She made no attempt to follow the flow of talk at the table, nor did she pay any heed to the shower of congratulations and blessings which fell all round her. Her thoughts all moved in one narrow channel: she was taking revenge on her parents, on Simon and on herself. Fully persuaded though she was that Simon cared for her not in the least, she experienced a perverse pleasure in this mean trick she was playing on him. At the height of the celebrations, however, when a plate was smashed to pieces on the floor and everybody began screaming, *"Mazal tov, mazal tov!"* a gloomy cloud, so dark and horrible, settled upon her, that even the guests suddenly noticed it for all their rejoicings. Everybody began to ask what was wrong: was she, God forbid, ill, or did she feel faint, or would she have a glass of water, or take a sip of brandy? And they begged her not to hide the truth from them. She reassured them that there was nothing the matter with her, but the deathly pallor of her face and the expression in her eyes belied her tongue.

At last the party dispersed. At last even Reb Zalman had taken his leave. And now the lamps were being put out. Deborah lay in her bed, fixedly gazing at the darkness enshrouding her. Her mind was a blank. She was incapable of thought, incapable of feeling. She had no regrets. She was not fully conscious of what had happened that evening. Already a clock somewhere in the distance was striking five. All things about her dwindled, growing smaller and smaller till they faded out of sight. She fell asleep. In the morning, as soon as he was awake, Reb Avram Ber hastened in with beaming face to renew his congratulations.

"Mazal tov, Deborah! May this be the beginning for you of a long, long life of happiness! Listen, Deborah, I cherish you in my heart now more than ever before. The Lord be praised for His graciousness! Well, Deborah, why don't you say something? Aren't you happy?"

She remained silent.

He brought a jug of water into her bedroom and slithered an enamel basin over the floor up to her bedside.

"Come, Deborah, hold out your hands and I'll pour the water for you."

"But what do I want to wash my hands in bed for? Can't I do that when I get up?"

"Don't you see, I want you to have breakfast in bed. I believe you were feeling rather faint last night."

He gave her a piece of honey cake which had been left over from the engagement party, and he brought her a glass of tea in bed. Deborah looked at the cake and winced, as if its sweetness were poisonous and its honeyed aroma stank in her nostrils.

"I can't touch it, papa, I just can't. Take it away and leave me alone."

"What's the matter with you, Deborah? Don't you feel well?"

"Of course I'm feeling well, I feel splendid! And now let me go to sleep again, please! No, I don't want any tea either. No, I want nothing. Nothing at all."

"Maybe a little more sleep will refresh you," said Reb Avram Ber, and he went off to tell Raizela that for some reason or other Deborah was looking very pale and was refusing food.

"She must be tired," said Raizela. She was going to have some more sleep herself, and turned over with her face to the wall. "By the way, how did you manage to make tea?"

"I asked the beadle to buy a jug of hot water in the shop downstairs."

It was two o'clock in the afternoon when Deborah got out of bed. She moved noiselessly about the home, clearing up the mess of last night's party. Her face was extraordinarily pale, and her eyes were in mourning, sparkling with gloom and despair.

From that day onwards she felt like a stranger in the house—a superfluous stranger. Her father, her mother, her brother—she regarded them all as acquaintances who were accommodating her as an unwanted guest and were looking forward to the hour of her departure. She began to look forward to it herself. That sense of resignation, oppressive and bewildering, never took leave of her no matter where she went or what she did. She was bowed down under her burden of ponderous thoughts, of weird and hideous notions, which from that morning onwards harrowed her brain without cease, distorted her vision, poisoned the blood in her veins. A thousand times over and over again she reasoned with herself—she could easily break off the engagement; and a thousand times over and over again she refused to listen to reason. If her parents wished to see the back of her, she must not miss the opportunity of quitting. It was only bare self-respect. There was but one alternative, and that was for her to find a way of earning her own living. But how? What was she to do? She had never been taught a trade. She was a useless ornament. Stubbornly, and with ever-growing bitterness, she let things slide.

Her parents were puzzled. Raizela was inclined to think that Deborah's speechlessness had come about by way of a reaction to her former frivolous talkativeness. She was growing up. After all, she would shortly be a wife, and was probably feeling the responsibility. As for the colour having gone out of Deborah's cheeks, Raizela gave this little thought. Herself always ailing and engrossed in her books, she scarcely noticed the change. She did mention it once or twice to Reb Avram Ber, but he thought that there was no ground for worry.

"I think it's more or less the normal thing. This is a difficult period in a girl's life, you know what I mean," he half explained, waving his hands in an effort to convey his thoughts to Raizela. "The only pity is that she seems unable to grasp how fortunate she is. Thank God, though, that things have turned out so well. Reb Baruch Laib, you know, travels all over Russia collecting donations for his *yeshiva*. The money pours in. He's a very good speaker, you see, and he gets very well paid for his work. . . . The great difficulty had been to find a suitable husband dressed up the modern way, that being what she had set her heart on. Well, that's the sort of husband she's going to have. So there you are!"

"But papa, how on earth can you presume to know what I have set my heart on?" intervened Deborah, coming in from the kitchen, where she had accidentally overheard the conversation.

"Aha," said Reb Avram Ber with a smile, "we old people know more than you imagine!"

In the family circle they began to treat her with rather more deference, as if she were an independent person. Everybody tried to show her greater consideration, and her mother in particular was anxious to see her always well dressed. Her prospective father-in-law lavished many costly presents on her, but both he and his gifts left her quite cold. This peculiar attitude puzzled him and hurt his pride. His own womenfolk in particular were greatly astonished. Deborah's unmaidenly conduct formed an everlasting topic of conversation with them.

"What a queer girl!" they murmured. "She's very clever and all that, but so unreasonable. I was a good girl in my time, to be sure, but I wasn't above taking a present if it was offered to me. Why, she's such a funny creature, she won't even put her jewellery on. She just doesn't seem to care a hang whether she gets a present or not. . . ."

"She's shamming, that's what it is. You stop giving her presents, and then I bet she'll come begging for them. You take my tip," said the long-legged sister-in-law to Reb Baruch Laib.

Winter drew to a close, and gone were the long nights which afforded Deborah such ample opportunity to brood and brood, without her being able to hatch a single new thought. Spring was here again. . . . The streets of Warsaw thawed in the sunshine, and the slush coating the pavements and roadways became like one vast swamp. The Passover holidays were muddy, warm and sultry (that, at any rate, was how they impressed Deborah). And, like all earthly things, they, too, came to an end, and inevitably in keeping with the season the days began to grow longer and longer. The sun climbed ever higher and higher, gaining in power. And from out of their musty homes, where they had been hibernating, townsfolk came flocking into the open, to breathe, to fill their lungs with the summer air. Children were again everywhere in evidence, kicking up a shindy. Again the courtyards began to stink in the glowering heat. Once again the rag-and-bone merchants turned out in full force, filling the air with their monotonous cries from morning to night. The baker's wife again sat cursing in her corner at the gateway, where she sold hot bread-rings from a huge basket. Deborah once more took up her position at the wide-open window, looking out into the courtyard. She rarely ventured out of doors. She had only one interest in life: to watch the children at play. For hours on end she would follow their restless movements, their excitements and frequent little quarrels; there were occasions when she entered absolutely into the spirit of their lively games.

She declined to touch any of the housework. She did not mind a bit the confusion all round her; the home was in a terrible muddle, and for her part it could stay like that. Actually she was unfit for work. Of late she had begun to suffer from pains at the heart. The doctor who saw her said her heart was not affected—nerves were at the root of the trouble, merely that. Plenty of fresh air was what she needed, he said, and nourishing foods, and—above all—she must refrain from worrying. He prescribed a medicine, but it made no difference. Sometimes the pains eased, then again they grew more acute.

"An early marriage will cure her of all her ills," said Reb Zalman, when Raizela took him into her confidence. "As soon as she has a husband and a home to look after, nerves will be a luxury for which she will have no time to spare. It's a good job, I'm thinking, that her future father-in-law knows nothing about it. He would certainly break off the engagement at once."

"God willing, she will soon be herself again. Nerves are not a real illness," said Reb Avram Ber, by way of soothing Reb Zalman, and Raizela herself was somewhat comforted.

"Deborah, I hear you have become engaged to a wealthy young man abroad. Allow me to congratulate you!" were Bailka's first words at a chance encounter in the street. Her eyes were full of mockery.

"Well, he's not wealthy," Deborah managed to bring out after a long pause. "And nothing definite has been fixed yet. My parents are eager to see me married. You know what parents are, always trying to provide for their children's future. But I'm going to have some say in the matter myself."

"Oh, really? It's funny that I should have been told you were already engaged."

Deborah crimsoned.

"Who told you?"

"Oh, someone you wouldn't know."

That was a lie! But it clarified a great deal that had been obscure to Deborah. It explained why Bailka had been giving her the cold shoulder of late. "She thinks I am selling myself for money. I suppose she looks down on me as a future capitalist."

So that was why Bailka had shrugged her shoulders so impatiently at their last meeting, when Deborah had asked how comrade Simon was getting on. "How should I know?" Bailka had answered almost sullenly. Why not put an end to all this falsehood, this misery, and call the marriage off?

"By the way, Deborah, I've just received a letter from Draiskin. He tells me he's going to spend the summer in Warsaw. Last week, you know, he paid us a flying visit."

"Indeed?" Deborah blurted out. Then checking herself, she went on more calmly:

"Did he spend the day with you?"

"No, only a few hours."

Bailka was scanning her face, as if eager to detect something. Deborah tried to persuade herself that she was only imagining things. Surely Bailka could not have guessed, and yet there she stood gazing into her eyes as though searching for some sign of emotion. "I believe I'm going mad. I'll finish up in an asylum. I'm moving in a crazy world full of mad fancies and with a mad longing to do myself a great injury."

"Listen, Bailka, I'm trying to find myself a job. Do you think I could get work at a dressmaker's? Could you help me in any way?"

Bailka burst out laughing.

"Well, it's easy enough to find work at a dressmaker's. But you have to know the work first, don't you see?"

"Bailka, tell me why you've turned against me in this strange way. If you're angry with me, why don't you say so? Don't you think it would be much better than playing this double game?"

"But, Deborah, don't be silly. I'm not angry with you, not at all. I'm rather upset about party matters, and believe me I have plenty of personal worries besides, so perhaps I don't appear quite as friendly as I might. But whatever else I may be, I'm not angry. You're not really to blame!" She immediately repented this latter remark. Deborah was asking:

"Why, what do you mean?"

"Nothing, of course! Don't be so suspicious, Deborah. There isn't a hidden meaning behind everything I say, as you seem to think. Now let's change the subject. Tell me, how is it you're looking so ill, not a bit like your old self? And how is it we never see anything of you these days?"

"*You're* imagining things now. I'm feeling perfectly fit. And as for why I keep away, probably you could explain that better than I could. It's surprising you should affect such complete innocence."

"Believe me, Deborah, it's no fault of mine. If I had any say in the matter, everything would be quite different. The others don't seem to understand you as well as I do." Bailka made excuses. She was moved to compassion by Deborah's appearance.

Deborah promised to call on her one evening, as of olden times, and never kept her promise, even though many a time she felt that it would have been a comfort to take Bailka into her confidence. She still had a great liking for her.

One day one of the comrades agreed to teach Deborah how to operate a silk winding machine. When she broke the news at home, there was an outcry of woe and a wringing of hands.

"What madness is this? Do you mean to say you're going out to work just when you're about to be married? Why, the girl's gone crazy, absolutely crazy!"

"Let them talk themselves blue in the face!" she thought. "All they care for is their own precious selves." When once she had learnt the trade and could learn a little money, they would have no one to talk to.

During the first few days of her new venture all went well. Everything was perfect. The comrade who was giving her tuition, a frail young man with, as it were, solemn-looking shoulders and good-natured drowsy eyes, toiled unremittingly from morning to night. He had two assistants, an apprentice girl and his own sister, a plump little girl of about sixteen, both of whom sang at their work. Noisily the cog-wheels turned round and round, beating time to the incessant songs. And the colourful silk threads whirled round and round to the music, gleaming and glittering and forever changing hue. At first all Deborah had to do was to follow closely the swift progress of the leading silken threads: to see how they responded to the action of the treadle, how they snapped whenever there was a sudden jolt, how the loose ends were caught between thumb and forefinger and knotted together again. Tying the knot seemed rather a ticklish business, yet even that was simple enough. Not only the young man, but his sister and the apprentice-girl performed all these operations with apparent ease and great deftness. When the young man told Deborah for the third day in succession that she must still stand by as an onlooker, she thought he was merely wasting her time. She was convinced that she had learnt all there was to know in a matter of hours.

She was highly delighted when he finally called on her to try her skill at the machine. But, as she soon discovered, there was a world of difference between merely watching and actually tackling the job. Whenever the thread snapped, the loose ends escaped her, no matter how strenuously she tried to catch hold of them, and even when she succeeded in grasping them after many exertions, she could not tie the knot properly. It would keep coming undone. When she at last made the knot secure it was always ugly and clumsy. And there was worse to come: as soon as the silk began to run strongly, without any breakages, and her hopes soared high, it refused to pass smoothly on to the bobbins in orderly fashion, as it did effortlessly with the other operators, but jumped about zig-zag and got into a hopeless tangle. Neither patient determination, painstaking concentration, nor repeated demonstrations and coaching by the comrade were of any avail.

"It's just as I thought—no one can possibly hope to pick up a skilled trade in a few short days," the comrade's aged mother commented as soon as it was plain that Deborah was at long last resigned to a true appreciation of the circumstances: they were only poor people, all dependent on the bread-winning eldest son, whose time was too precious to waste and certainly his stock of silk was too valuable to be spoilt.

"Well, well, do you mean to tell me your career has come to an untimely end?" scoffed Michael. "Or have you gone on strike? No, I know what's happened: you've already made your pile and have decided to retire."

Deborah bit her tongue till it bled. She made no reply.

She began to look for a situation as a nursemaid. She had many interviews and was given countless promises, but never an engagement. Always she received a polite letter containing some excuse or other. But surely to goodness some girls did find employment as nursemaids, and wealthy ladies did need nursemaids for their pampered infants? It was a mystery.

Meanwhile time was growing short: the marriage was due to take place at an early date. Raizela took a very lively interest in getting the trousseau together. For once in a lifetime she all but denied herself the pleasure of reading. Day in, day out, a loud-voiced tradeswoman darted in and out of the house with endless samples of cloths, linens, silks, velvets, feathers, eiderdowns, trimmings and many other things besides. Deborah moved about the home like a stranger. She had no patience for the samples. What did matter to her were the newspaper advertisements under the heading, "NURSEMAIDS WANTED." And all the time she was afflicted with pains at the heart.

"We'll never get ready for the wedding if we wait for *her* to come down to earth," said Raizela, and she ordered lengths of material entirely on her own judgment, all of the highest quality. She was convinced that no one knew better than herself what would best suit Deborah.

Next Deborah had to pay a long succession of calls on her dressmaker and tailor. They took her measure and gave her innumerable fittings. Mechanically Deborah did all they asked her to do; she no longer consulted her own wishes and had lost all her will power. So she was going to get married after all, and yet it was sheer madness! If she were to decline even now, what could her parents do to her? And even supposing no one would accept her as a nursemaid, nor yet as a servant, could she not remain as she was and cling to her home?—Thus the trend of Deborah's thoughts as she stood in front of the mirror, while the dressmaker adjusted the semi-finished clothes on her living dummy, putting pins in and taking them out again, undoing seams and sewing them up again, basting and chalking and talking. Deborah lifted her arm, lowered it, rested her foot there, rested it here: she obeyed orders.

"Dear me, you will be a radiant bride, to be sure!" the dressmaker hissed her flattery at Deborah from between clenched teeth, for she had a pin in her mouth.

"So I'm going to be radiant, am I?" said Deborah, with only a hazy notion as to why she had spoken.

"Bless your little soul, of course you will! Now just have a good look at yourself in that mirror. Why, you look like a born princess. Honestly, a queen at her best couldn't look any prettier. I hear you're going to settle in Germany. Am I right?"

"Belgium!" Deborah corrected her.

"Go on! Isn't Belgium somewhere in Germany?"

"No, of course it isn't!" Deborah smiled.

There was nothing to smile at, as far as the dressmaker could see. One was entitled to ask a question and receive a polite answer. All the same, it was not policy to argue the point with a client.

"Surprising your parents should let you go that far," the dressmaker resumed, taking the pin out of her mouth.

Deborah was silent. All at once she felt she was going to tear off the half-finished frock, dash it to the ground, and herself fall to the ground weeping and tearing her hair. She forced back a tear which sparkled in a corner of her eye for a fleeting instant, and then she turned her right shoulder towards the mirror (as requested by the dressmaker).

"Must be a love match, that's what it is," the dressmaker went on, trying to draw her client into conversation. Finding that she could get no information, she formed her own conclusions. "Nowadays parents have absolutely no control over their children. I hope you won't think I've been putting my nose in where it's not wanted, only knowing your father was a Rabbi, it seemed rather funny he should allow you to go away and live in Germany."

"Shut up and go to hell! Fool, idiot!" Deborah fumed in her thoughts. "Please hurry up!" she said aloud, by way of reply.

The dressmaker said not another word, but she was most curious to know how the lovers had first met; she was simply burning with anxiety to find out. Some girls had all the luck. Here was a slip of a girl, there was not much to her, really, and yet she had had her love affair and was going abroad to marry him. Probably *he* was of the passionate type. Some girls had all the luck. Others, like herself, had no luck at all.

Deborah's reserve of patience finally gave out. As each passing day brought her closer to the impending wedding, her nerves became more and more inflamed. Now at last she began to protest, to entreat her parents to break off the engagement, or at least to arrange for her to meet the man she was supposed to marry.

"What's that? You want to put us to shame now that the wedding is only a few days off and all the arrangements have been made and everybody knows? Stuff and nonsense!"

At last she quietened down; she ceased tormenting herself; her strength deserted her, and she took to her bed with a nervous break-down. The home was plunged into chaos and utter despair. Raizela stooped like an old woman as she went about her work. She fumbled all she did; everything she touched slipped through her fingers. And there was more to be done now than ever. Michael became her right hand, and he did for the remaining crockery. Reb Avram Ber walked about like a man in a dream: he was in a continual state of alarm lest Reb Baruch Laib, Deborah's prospective father-in-law, should get to know how things were.

But they succeeded in hushing the matter up (for which the Lord be praised!). The doctor, without actually saying so in as many words, led Reb Baruch Laib to believe that Deborah was indisposed with a feverish cold. After a while the doctor reached the decision that his patient's nervous disease was not to be cured by keeping her in bed. On the contrary, she must get up, take plenty of fresh air, mingle with the crowd, shun solitude of any kind, and—very impor-tant this—she must avoid dwelling on any painful thoughts which might be afflicting her; plenty of fruit was what she wanted, plenty of vegetables—and most important, said the doctor, pulling out his watch—on no account must she worry. In his opinion her indisposition was due to some trying experience, such as would leave a deep impression on a highly-strung adolescent mind. That was why she must do everything within her power to banish foreboding thoughts. Her condition did not give rise to anxiety; the illness could now be nipped in the bud; but to do so, it was essential that his advice be acted upon rigorously, and then he went on to give the most unprofessional sort of advice, the sort that left one flabbergasted, coming as it did from a medical man. . . .

Some weeks passed. Deborah regained the merest semblance of a young, healthy woman. This, therefore, was the appropriate moment to marry her off. There had been several postponements of the wedding, but the happy event could not be put off for ever.

"Do you mean to say you're worrying about what the doctor said? Can't you see the man's crazy?" said Reb Zalman at the family conference, scornfully shrugging his shoulders and flinging out his hands in mock despair.

Raizela and Reb Avram Ber were both obliged to acknowledge that the doctor was as mad as a hatter. Obviously no sane man would say to a bride, who had completed all her arrangements for the wedding and had her trousseau all ready, that she must find a job as a saleslady so as to keep her mind occupied, and if the man who said such things—a doctor at that—was not sane, clearly he was insane.

"*Goyim* will be *Goyim!*" said Reb Zalman.

Again Reb Avram Ber and Raizela were both obliged to acknowledge that *Goyim* will be *Goyim*.

"Have you ever heard of such a thing? Here's a girl on the threshold of her married life, with all her life before her, and some silly fool of a doctor comes along and has the impertinence to tell her to. . . . Why, it's monstrous! Monstrous! As if we wanted his advice! A doctor's job is to give you medicine and pills," said Reb Zalman, "and if we stand in need of advice, we shall know where to get it: we'll go and consult a *Tsadik!*"

"You're quite right. And, please God, she will be all the better for an early marriage."

Meanwhile, there were rumblings of revolt from another quarter: Reb Baruch Laib was greatly perturbed to see that Deborah had grown so much thinner. She had not been plump to start with; he now felt that he was being badly cheated. He voiced his protest vehemently, without beating about the bush.

"And you should see my other daughter-in-law, the one that's married to my eldest son. Why, she's a perfect beauty. I've never seen anyone with a rounder face and a rosier complexion—just like an apple . . ." Thus Reb Baruch Laib.

"Yes, it's a pleasure to look at her. Why, her countenance is so handsome and bright and cheerful, you feel quite dazzled when you look at her. She's like a full moon." Thus Reb Baruch Laib's wife.

And the couple shook their heads in despair over Deborah.

"However, let's hope she'll impress the bridegroom favourably. That's all that matters, really," said Reb Baruch Laib. He wondered, though: would she impress him, and how?

It was determined that they should all leave for Berlin on the following Sunday, and the wedding was to take place on the Tuesday after.

When that fateful Sunday came round, only six weeks after her nervous breakdown, an excited, jostling crowd of bosom friends, not to mention neighbours, assembled in Reb Avram Ber's home, to bid farewell to the happy bride. They all drank a toast to the lovely bride and to the proud parents, and they ate and they drank and made merry (after first complying with the prim formalities of refusing to eat and drink and make merry), and they renewed their congratulations again and again to Deborah, her family and in-laws. They stood about laughing and joking and talking and jabbering, till the very walls seemed to be swaying dizzily. But it was the kisses that the womenfolk smothered her in which sickened Deborah most of all. Her cheeks and mouth were aching, limp and slobbery, and still the endless succession of smacking lips came on and on. Tireless lips, wet, ugly lips, that deafened her with kind hopes and blessings. They trusted most sincerely that Deborah would be very happy, and that her husband would prosper in that far-off land; one day, perhaps, he was going to be a millionaire—who could tell? Everything was possible with a man who dealt in diamonds. Why, they knew of girls who had been brought up in poverty and had found themselves outlándish husbands and were now living in the lap of luxury. Even so, all the guests were surprised that Raizela should agree to part with an only daughter, and all the guests said as much in very plain language.

Deborah pricked up her ears. Surprised, were they? Well, granted that her parents were eager to be rid of her, why on earth should she oblige by running away? How on earth had all this come to pass? Surely it was not too late to change her mind even now! Why not scream her refusal now, at the top of her voice, and dumbfound these hateful people who called themselves her parents, her well-wishers, her friends? Why not undo their wicked machinations and put them to shame? But what was it all about, anyway? She was not being sent into the wastes of Siberia. She was going first to Berlin, and then on to Antwerp. And possibly when she got to Berlin he might not like the look of her and might refuse to have her. There was still that chance of escape as Reb Baruch Laib had pointed out only a few days ago. But on that occasion, when she had offered to break off the engagement, Reb Baruch Laib had declined to hear another word, and had told her not to take every passing remark so seriously. So now she was travelling out to meet him. What would she do if, as ill luck might have it, he said "Yes"? *He*? Who was this *he* to whom she was going to give herself away?

"What a mad whirl my mind is in! If Simon were to know how things really are, he would save me from myself. God, what makes me always do the contrary of what I *want* to do? I know quite well that I am doing the wrong thing, and yet the moment I make up my mind one way, I act the reverse way. One mistake after another, one folly after another! Don't I know that I'm acting the fool, and yet I can't help myself. I just go blundering on and on . . . I must be raving mad!"

"Deborah, here's Mrs. Barski to say good-bye to you."

Deborah's throat was parched. She dreaded kissing Mrs. Barski. She kissed Mrs. Barski, and even smiled back sweetly at her.

No, there could be no turning back now. After yesterday's foolishness, she felt too sick at heart to care what might become of her. What an idiot she had been to go to the café and solemnly break the news to Simon that her parents were forcing her, against her will, to marry a man in Antwerp whom she did not know. Now he looked up and caught sight of her, what a tender expression had entered his eyes, how they had fondled her. As he gazed at her and sought her eyes, and his hand moved forward as if to clasp her own, she felt sure that he loved her. He spoke to her, and his voice was even gentler than his words:

"I wonder, Deborah, if you have ever suspected how strong even the frailest of us can be?"

He still went on looking at her in that ecstatic way, and she said jerkily:

"I don't understand. What do you mean?"

She was quite certain then that her instinct had not betrayed her when occasionally it prompted her to believe that Simon cared for her, that he loved her. Just then, however, some comrade joined them at the table, and she waited patiently, hopefully. At last they were alone again, and she blurted out the whole stupid story, trusting that he would be sorry for her, that he would try to dissuade her, or might even protest—now at length he would speak his mind—but, instead, she heard Simon say quite cheerfully:

"So you're going to be married. Ah, let me congratulate you!" She wondered if she had heard aright. But then he added: "You did very well to accept, Deborah. Yes, you did very well! . . ."

So here she was again kissing an old woman whose face was disfigured with warts—brown warts and black warts, and some of them had hair growing out of the centre. How disgusting those hairs were! She was dying to wipe her hand across her mouth, but for some reason the old woman would not look the other way, the beast!

Was she really justified in throwing the blame on others? They had their own point of view, and she ought to have hers. It was all her own fault. What if Simon had shown indifference? That surely was not sufficient cause for her to run away from herself. Scorning all opposition, she could simply say, "I refuse to go!" and the whole terrible nightmare would end instantly.

But no, her parents would not have thrown her out bodily. She would go of her own accord. Now, what would Bailka have done in her place? Bailka would not have wavered.

They were helping her to climb into the droshky. They were off, heading for the station.

She had not even said good-bye to Bailka. What was Miss Rushka doing in the droshky? Surely it was unnecessary for the whole of Reb Zalman's family to see her off to the station. And what had come over Miss Rushka to-day that made her look so different from her usual self?

The procession of droshkies was speeding through the streets of Warsaw. Trip-trap, trip-trap! went the patter of the horses' hooves. A feeling of bliss, so exquisite that it hurt, took possession of her all at once. She had a strange craving to drink in all she saw, as if she had been away from the city for years. Every sharp cobblestone, every muddy stretch of pavement, every shabby building, every panting porter bent double under his staggering load, became suddenly a precious part of herself. Even the beggar women, who sat on the doorsteps nursing babies in torn shawls, and who kept pinching the flesh of these babies to make them howl piteously, were like dear, old, loving friends, from whom parting was difficult. And how quaint those red-nosed, aged-looking little girls with the swinging pigtails were to-day; how worried the expression on their faces, poor things!

The droshkies were held up in the traffic. A little distance away an old woman in tatters, her face a furrowed, formless jumble of skin and bones, was sitting over a basket, on a doorstep, calling out her wares. Sighting the droshky, she lifted up her basket appealingly. The contents were a sticky mess, for all the world like a heap of dung.

"Buy my gol'en fruit, ladies, buy, buy!" she droned feebly in a scarcely audible, nasal voice. She fingered the mess in the basket to make it look inviting, but only succeeded in squashing it the more.

Deborah peered into the basket. She wondered very much what the contents might be. It quite teased her. She hazarded a guess just as the droshky began to move on—over-ripe apricots. She felt so sorry for the old woman. Alms would not come amiss, even though Bailka was of the opinion that charity only helped to bolster up the existing rotten social order. Anyway, who was to blame for its rottenness?—Miss Rushka and Reb Baruch Laib! She tossed the woman a coin. The droshky gathered speed. She turned her head, and saw the old woman squabbling with a ragged urchin. The boy grabbed the money, spat the woman full in the face through his thick lips, and lifting one leg hopped away in triumph. What an outrage! But the droshky was now going at full speed.

"Well Deborah, you can say good riddance to Warsaw now," observed Miss Rushka.

"What do you mean, good riddance?" Deborah exclaimed hotly. She continued more calmly: "On the contrary, I think Warsaw a splendid city."

"Sure, Warsaw is the finest city in the world! There is no other city to compare with it, anywhere!" said Miss Rushka. "Why, I wouldn't leave Warsaw for all the diamonds in the world!"

Deborah moved away on her seat.

Miss Rushka's mother coughed uneasily, and lightly pinched her daughter in the fleshy part.

"I don't know so much! Some people love nothing better than to travel," she said, trying to make amends for her daughter's spitefulness, and then, to demonstrate her friendly feelings, she added: "Why, when I come to think that soon you will no longer be with us, it simply breaks my heart. . . ."

Deborah was silent.

CHAPTER XIII

What a mighty contingent of uncles, aunts, brothers, sisters, cousins, nephews, nieces and bosom friends were gathered at the station to give the bridal party a right royal send-off! How they all overran the platform, talking and shouting and kissing and sending their love to all the other relations that would be waiting at the journey's end!

"Remember me to the bridegroom, remember me to Rebecca, remember—."

Slowly the train moved off, with the engine roaring and spitting like a furious monster. Puff, puff, puff!

And the uncles, the aunts, the brothers, the sisters, the cousins, the nephews, the nieces and the bosom friends were left behind, waving their hands, their handkerchiefs and their umbrellas like mad. They were on the verge of exhaustion, but still they went on waving farewell and blowing kisses, as if they were quite insatiable. How they all loved to kiss and kiss again! Why did they address her with the familiar "thou," Deborah wondered. How was it that she had never addressed Simon as "thou"? The absurdity of this thought, which entered her mind so unexpectedly, both shocked and sobered her. She was waking up to the realities of the situation. With every fleeting instant the train was drawing closer and closer to a strange city, where a stranger would be waiting to claim her as his own, and she was leaving Warsaw, her home and her past. But, in spite of herself, she did not very much care now. It was all so false.

"Deborah, what about having a little lie-down?" her mother was saying.

That caused her to lose her temper suddenly. Would they never give her a moment's peace?

So it had come to this, after all. Somehow they had laid hands on her and were disposing of her just as they pleased, as if she were a corpse. And yet, here was she alive and in full possession of her senses. How had it come about? But perhaps—and at the thought, an icy shudder ran down her spine—she was not really in the full possession of her senses? Maybe she was living in a kind of trance, so that although she was able to see and hear and feel, she lacked the means to resist. What was to be done? One thing was certain: the train was bearing her on and on. Soon it would be too late. As if it were not too late already! She was helpless. Again she shuddered.

Someone was asking her something about smoking.

"No!" she said.

The gentleman in the corner seat opposite gave her an astonished look.

"No, I don't mind if you smoke. Not a bit!" she said, collecting her scattered wits.

"Thanks!" said the gentleman, politely doffing his hat, and now that he had removed it from his head he went a step further and tossed it on to the rack. He lit a cigarette, leaned back in his seat, crossed his legs, and having made himself quite comfortable emitted a large puff of smoke through his dark-red lips. The smoke coiled upwards and vanished in a faint white haze. There followed another pig puff, this time dense and bluish.

"Pardon me, Miss, but may I enquire what is your destination?"

"Berlin," Deborah responded peevishly. Why didn't that fellow keep to himself? What was the matter with him?

"Ah, so we're both going to the same place. I think Berlin is a wonderful city. Have you ever been there?"

"No!"

"Ah, then you've something to look forward to. I love Berlin. I once lived there for four solid years; that was when I was studying for my degree. What a time I had there! The best years of my life! Honestly, I feel quite excited when I think that just a few more hours and I'll be stepping out into the same old station, the same old streets! How we old people long to revisit the haunts of our youth. Of course, at your age you can't imagine any such thing. But as for me, I'm all eagerness to see my old digs again, where I once spent a few really happy years. It will be a pleasure to meet old friends again, and would you believe it, I'm even anxious to see the old professor again. He was a sarcastic little fellow! Ha, ha, ha! How everything changes and grows sweet in your memory after you've left it behind for years and years!"

Deborah was lulled into good-humour. It was a pleasure to listen to his boyish talk. So frank and good-natured. She wondered where he was now living. His words had a ring of sincerity. She would speak to him. Of course she would. It would bring on forgetfulness. It would take her out of herself.

"May I enquire," she said, using his own expression, "where is your home town?"

"Why of course you may!" he exclaimed with a smile, pleased to see that he had broken down her reserve. "My home is in Harkov."

"So you're a Russian?"

"Yes, that is so. I'm only going to Berlin for a short visit, to get myself some new instruments—surgical instruments. Berlin is the place for instruments—the best the world has to offer. Germany's ambition, you know, is to conquer the world, and one day I believe she'll do it. The Germans are making such tremendous progress in all the sciences, they march ahead with such gigantic strides, no other country in the world can keep abreast of them."

"I get it: *Deutschland über alles!*" said Deborah, recalling how Simon had always scorned the Germans for their chauvinism.

"Well, they certainly know their own strength. They are fully conscious of their own power. They feel proud of themselves, and not without justification," said the doctor in his enthusiastic way.

"You certainly are passionately pro-German, aren't you?" said Deborah, the colour mounting to her cheeks.

"No, I don't think I am. I love Germany, and I love Russia, only in a different way. Russia has got something big, something epic about her, if you know what I mean. But I will say this: after a taste of Western European civilisation, you begin to wish that Russia were not so backward, so primitive. Anyway, I am a Jew first and last. And if I'm really interested in any country, that country is Palestine. If it ever becomes our own, however, I would prefer to see it developed on the German, rather than the Russian model. Russian soil, Russian natural resources—wonderful! Czarist policy, Czarist barbarism—no thank you! Please let me continue. In some respects this country's way of life borders on complete lunacy, and unless we have a radical change, and that pretty soon, Germany will teach Russia a severe lesson."

"I take it you are a Zionist?"

"Of course I am! No Jew in his right mind can be anything but a Zionist."

"I don't agree with you. But to return to the point, I must say I'm very much surprised at the beautiful rosy picture you paint of the Germany of blood and iron. To my knowledge, the Germans may be wonderful instrument-makers, but what they most excel at is militarism and anti-Semitism. I've been told, and I'm quoting a person of real authority now (Simon again!), that the Germans are the world's worst reactionaries. Really, I don't know how you can tolerate their slogan *Deutschland über alles!* We all know that Russia is unruly. But Russia as she is to-day is a diseased country. And surely wrong-doing in the case of a healthy country, as of a healthy person, is less pardonable than in one that is ailing?"

"Yes, you're perfectly right there, Miss, perfectly right! Of course, from my own point of view Palestine really ought to be *über alles*. Not that I'm so arrogant as to want even that," said the doctor, rather amused.

Deborah was carried away by that passionate zest for life and affairs which mostly lay repressed within her and which used to well up so irresistibly whenever she heard Simon speaking at party meetings.

"I wonder how you can say and think such things when you profess to hate tyranny and brutality! Do you really imagine that if Kaiser Wilhelm were to free the Russian people of their antiquated yoke and were to rule them with his own civilised iron rod, a new and a better Russia would be born? Would you care to see Germany perpetuate tyranny and brutality by modern scientific methods? For my part, I think that if any such thing were to happen, life would not be worth living!"

Deborah's tone became heated, her cheeks flushed and her eyes were flashing. Her blood was up and she appeared ready to proclaim war on the Kaiser single-handed.

"Yes, Miss, but please, I beg of you, do not get so excited. After all, my personal views are of little account, and believe me I don't really care a hoot if we have Rasputin or Wilhelm as our ruler. I have no politics, and my only political concern is the welfare of our own people. For the rest, all tyrants can go to the devil. Moreover, it is far safer not to discuss such delicate subjects on Russian soil, for walls have ears, and whatever our views, we had best keep them to ourselves, for to Russia we must return."

These last words touched Deborah to the quick.

"I won't be coming back," she said softly.

The doctor did not hear her remark. He helped himself to another cigarette.

"Now, now Deborah, what manner of conduct is this? What on earth put it into your head to enter into conversation with a man you've never seen before? And of all things, fancy speaking politics to a complete stranger? How do you know he isn't a spy? For all you know, he may be an informer. Really, no respectable girl ever dreams of picking up casual acquaintances in a train. It just isn't done!" Reb Baruch Laib admonished her, the moment the doctor had withdrawn with a most affable bow like a man of true western culture, and had gone off down the swaying corridor intent on doing himself some good in the dining-car. "Why, as I sat there listening to the conversation, I felt my hair rise on end. I felt I was about to have a fit; but I didn't dare interrupt in case I made matters worse. Good God, supposing we got ourselves into trouble with the authorities, that would be a nice thing, wouldn't it? Wouldn't it?"

Did that beast, who was supposed to be her father-in-law, presume to address her as though she were his own property? Did he too imagine that he was free to bully her and trifle with her life? Oh, oh, one more word from him and she would make him pay for all the persecution, all the humiliation she had ever suffered.

"Deborah, why don't you say something? You wouldn't like your father-in-law to feel that you're ignoring him, would you now?" Reb Avram Ber interceded.

Her father's gentle voice reminded her of her love for him.

"I have nothing to say Papa. Any time a passenger speaks to me, I shall answer him. It's not a crime, only common courtesy."

"Yes, but remember you're a grown-up girl. A grown-up girl mustn't talk to a strange gentleman," Reb Avram Ber reasoned with her.

She smiled.

"Look at her, look, she's laughing at us!" cried Reb Baruch Laib. Beside himself with excitement, he was attempting to pace up and down the compartment.

"All this is quite uncalled for," Raizela put in, detaching herself from her book.

"Please, mamma, you keep out of it. Why worry? You're soon going to get rid of me!" Deborah addressed her mother with unconcealed bitterness.

"Yes, thank God!" Raizela retorted, and she returned to her reading.

Reb Baruch Laib's wife, Tertsa-Roisa, was having a nap. As usual, she heard nothing, saw nothing. Her breath came easily, unctuously, and in the midst of her slumbers a good-natured little smile was playing on her parted, whitish lips—lips that were a wee bit askew in her fleshy face. Deborah happened to rest her glance on these tranquil features, and suddenly it occurred to her that if the bridegroom was anything like his mother, then at this very moment he too would be snoozing and smiling in his sleep while the train rushed onwards from Antwerp to Berlin . . .

Sated and beaming, the doctor ambled back from the restaurant-car. He resumed his seat and one could tell by his amiable expression that he was hankering for an opportunity to launch out on another heart-to-heart talk; however, he would not repeat his first mistake, but would confine himself strictly to topics that were pleasant and happy and romantic. Not by any stretch of the imagination could he guess that the fat old man with the great belly, fiery red beard and glowering countenance, with blazing pin-point eyes, was puffing and blowing so furiously all because he—a doctor and a gentleman—had chatted, innocently enough, with a fellow-passenger. In fact, he was not even aware that the young lady in question was a member of the fat old man's party. What he did notice was the fact that she was wearing her morose and unapproachable expression again . . .

For her part, Deborah was only too eager to continue the discussion and to broaden it, if only to teach her father-in-law a lesson. And, besides, it was a joy to converse with a person who treated one as an equal, who was intelligent without being self-important. Unlike most people he did not inspire in her that unaccountable embarrassment which created a barrier between thought and speech—an impassable barrier which fostered unnatural silence and misunderstanding. She watched the doctor light a fat cigar. He addressed a few words to her. Her answer came abruptly. Inwardly raging, she rose, went out into the corridor, and then, instead of returning, she sat down in the next-door compartment. Reb Avram Ber joined her.

"Thank you, Deborah, you're a darling. You have saved the situation. And now your father-in-law has gone and made it up."

"Oh has he? How wonderful! Hip, hip, hurrah!"

"What is the matter with you, Deborah? Just think! You're going to get married to a very nice young man, who will give you a comfortable home, and you will be able to do just as you please . . . Any other girl would think herself extremely lucky to be in your position, especially if her father were poor and could not provide her with a dowry. Really, Deborah, I don't know why you treat your father-in-law the way you do, as if he were dirt. He's a very nice man indeed, I think. And I can prove it to you, Deborah. Guess what he's been telling me! He tells me that he has bought a pair of ear-rings costing no less than three hundred roubles. And they're going to be the bridegroom's wedding-gift to you in Berlin. Isn't that wonderful?"

Deborah only smiled.

"Words are cheap, Deborah, but how can you doubt Reb Baruch Laib's affection for you when he does such extraordinary things. Honestly, I think you're a very fortunate girl. The Lord be praised!"

Deborah heaved a sigh.

For all his shortsightedness, Reb Avram Ber perceived that his daughter was sad and that her sadness was not to be dispelled by any glittering trinkets.

"Perhaps you'd feel better if you were to lie down?"

"Yes, I'm tired, ever so tired."

"All right, I'll ask mother to keep you company. Isn't it strange that this compartment should be absolutely empty?"

Raizela joined her. After a little while they both fell asleep, and it was only when the train drew to a standstill in Berlin, at

Alexanderplatz Station, about half-past seven in the morning, that they opened their eyes. With her face deathly pale, her frock crushed and a mist before her eyes, Deborah swayed feebly as she rose to her feet. Through the window of the compartment she caught her first glimpse of the station—an immense place teeming with activity. With her mother she rejoined the others in the next-door compartment. Tertsa-Roisa was sitting up, wide awake.

"Good morning," she said. "Good morning! Hope you had a good night's rest. Oh, Deborah, just take a look at yourself! How rumpled you are! Dear me!"

Deborah obligingly took a look at herself and forced a smile.

Mingling with the hurrying throng in the station, yet distinct from this throng, were certain tall, clean-shaven Germans with proud mien and fat cigars and fat walking-sticks, who held their heads high and their bodies erect—great hulking bodies such as were seldom to be seen in Warsaw. Firm as rocks in a troubled sea, unperturbed by all the hubbub and bustle around them, they marched forward with measured gait and their every movement had an air of deliberateness, of pre-meditation.

Reb Baruch Laib pulled the luggage off the racks. Reb Avram Ber did his best to help. Having negotiated his wife through the all-too-narrow doorway of the carriage, Reb Baruch Laib could now afford to pause and mop the perspiration off his shiny brow. The party waited, with the suitcases piled up at their feet.

A porter approached and comparing Reb Avram Ber with Reb Baruch Laib, unhesitatingly selected the latter as the leader, to whom he offered his services in a very guttural and unintelligible German. His business-like trolley told its own tale.

"Do you mind telling him, Deborah, that we want to take a taxi," said Tertsa-Roisa, with an enquiring look at her husband. He nodded his approval, and Deborah acted as spokesman. She informed the impatient porter of their destination—The Kosher Hotel, Grenadierstrasse.

No sooner had he ascertained that it was in fact Grenadierstrasse they wanted and that all the other streets which he erroneously volunteered were unacceptable, he heaped the luggage on his green trolley and dashed off helter-skelter at such a pace that Tertsa-Roisa broke most of the fishbones in her corset in the chase that ensued. In vain they called on him to halt, in vain they shouted and hissed at him. Out of sheer desperation, Tertsa-Roisa somehow succeeded in keeping up with the rest, puffing and blowing and snorting.

It was a bright morning. Outside the station stood a long line of gleaming taxis. The porter raised his hand, and instantly the foremost cab drove up to the kerb. The driver inclined his ear, and learning from the porter that his passengers were Polish Jews and whither they were bound, he rubbed his nose with a show of contempt. Reb Baruch Laib wondered how much the journey would cost, but the driver ignored him and meanwhile the porter stood waiting with outstretched palm. Reb Baruch Laib was thrown into confusion.

"What, two marks?" he gasped.

"*Jawohl.* Two marks! And you'd better look sharp! Time is money! *Verstanden?*" the porter snapped back at him with great severity.

"Daylight robbery, that's what it is! Still, it can't be helped. God willing, he'll spend the money on a doctor's bill. I wonder what sort of appetite this fellow has got," added Reb Baruch Laib, indicating the taxi-driver, as the car moved off and he rebuttoned his back trouser-pocket; his wife who sat opposite him, with Raizela and Deborah squeezed in on either side, just smiled.

Berlin was throbbing with life: the pulse beating in its veins had the regularity, the power of a vital, self-confident being.

"So this is Berlin! Well, it's good to be alive!" was the stranger's first impression on passing through the city that morning, all steeped as it was in sunshine. The streets were teeming. The cafés were besieged with workers, with impatient men and women at the bars and on the terraces, waiting to get their glass of beer. They gulped it down unceremoniously and hurried off to their work. Clanging and screeching on the rails, the crowded tram-cars followed hard upon each other in endless processions. Early though the hour was, many private cars were to be seen winding their way furiously through the traffic. On the swarming pavements men and women were gabbling away at each other as fast as they could go. The city was bestirring itself with a will.

"Isn't it a magnificent sight?" cried Deborah, seemingly oblivious—for a breathless moment—to the fact that she was soon to be married. She felt she must share her joy. "Do have a look, Mamma!" She was oblivious, also, to the fact that soon all this human energy would be consumed by insatiable, smoky factories.

Raizela turned a critical eye on Berlin.

"I don't know how the people can stand it. The racket is absolutely maddening!" was her verdict.

Grenadierstrasse was certainly not so select as it might have been, but it was nothing like the slums of Warsaw. In its own way, it was clean and fairly quiet. The Kosher Hotel was run by a Polish Jew, Herr Berger, or Reb Haim as he was more familiarly known to the *hassidical* Jews and Rabbis who patronised his establishment. Herr Berger heard the taxi drive up. He hastened out to welcome his guests, whoever they might be. Opening the door of the cab and taking stock of its occupants, he gave vent to a joyous cry of "Peace unto you!"—a cry that was so jolly and friendly, withal respectful, one would have thought he had known these newcomers all his life. Then he paused and reflectively stroked his smooth white forehead, framed in a gleaming black skull-cap, as if he had forgotten something that he badly needed to remember.

Reb Avram Ber was the first to alight. Deborah followed and she helped her mother out. Then came the hardest task of all. Reb Baruch Laib summoned up all his ingenuity in extracting Tertsa-Roisa from the swaying cab.

"Will you please ask him what the fare is," Reb Baruch Laib panted at the hotel-keeper.

"Right! You leave it to me, I'll square him!" Herr Berger exclaimed with a great air of authority, and simultaneously he flicked back the white starched cuff that had worked its way down his wrist—flicked it back smilingly, deftly, like a man who means to see that all things shall stay where they belong. He had it out with the driver, clinching the argument by pointing an accusing finger at the taximeter. The driver foamed with rage. His face, his ears and even the nape of his neck turned scarlet, and his eyes became bloodshot. At last his breath failed

him, and wrathfully grunting "Dirty Jew!" he pocketed his due and
made off in a cloud of smoke from the exhaust.

"Well, of all the dirty Germans!" said the hotel-keeper, still smiling unctuously. "He tried to do one on me. *Me*, mind you! Anyone
would think I was green, anyone would think I was a foreigner who
couldn't read a taximeter. The miserable cheat, someone ought to
give him a thick ear!"

Saying which, Herr Berger ceremoniously opened the door of the
restaurant that formed part of his establishment. He posted himself
in the doorway and with a flourish of the hand ushered his guests in.
His boiled shirt gleamed proudly, the skirt of his coat—a cross
between tails and a gabardine—fluttered bravely. He ordered a weedy
lad of about seventeen to carry the luggage up.

"Go on, get a move on!" he said with an amused smile by way of
encouragement.

Reb Baruch Laib beckoned to him confidentially and they held a
whispered consultation. When their two heads parted, both faces wore
a knowing expression. Herr Berger counted the party's strength on his
fingers, then he asked them to follow him upstairs. The house echoed
to Tertsa-Roisa's gasps:

"Phew! Ugh! Phew!"

Entering a large bright room on the first floor, with three windows—all of them wide-open and overlooking the Grenadierstrasse—the weary travellers settled down peacefully on the rather
weary-looking upholstered chairs and sofa.

"You see, this is our best room. Look how bright and airy it is! It's
a rest-cure, that's what it is, believe me! Tell me would you like to
have some refreshments brought up? Or would you rather have a
wash first?"

"Well, we haven't said our morning prayers yet," Reb Avram Ber
spoke up for the first time.

"Haven't you really? Allow me to inform you then, that you
couldn't have chosen a better time for your arrival, because we're
just about to hold our morning service."

"Do you mean to tell me that you have sufficient Jews here to

make up a full congregation?" Reb Avram Ber gasped in utter astonishment.

"Exactly," said Herr Berger. "In this hotel you will find everything
you want. If it's a full congregation you're looking for—no need to look
any further, here it is! And what a congregation! Believe me, when you
see the type of guests I have staying in my hotel, you'll be surprised.
Some of them are Rabbis (God bless them!), and as for the rest, I have
no reason to be ashamed of them either (God forbid!), not a bit!"

Reb Avram Ber rubbed his hands with deep satisfaction.

"Oh, God!" he rejoiced. "What a wonderful race Thy Jews are! One
finds them everywhere, everywhere. And even in these foreign parts,
there are Jews we can be proud of, upright and godfearing!" he
enthused over his new-found friends, friends whom he had not even
met yet. The sight of a *hassidical* Jew like Reb Haim in the modern
style of dress was very reassuring and reminded him of all that Reb
Zalman had said about the bridegroom.

A Gentile maid, blonde and rosy-cheeked, with a powerful bosom
which was quite cramped within her tight bodice and which at every
breath strained upwards as though eager to gain its freedom, conducted the womenfolk to the bathroom, where she initiated them in
the use of the hot and cold water taps, and after having made certain
that her services were no longer required, she went tripping down
the stairs, whistling cheerfully.

Reb Avram Ber and Reb Baruch Laib took breakfast with Herr
Berger's ten Rabbis (God bless them! although ten was rather an
exaggerated figure) and with the rest of the guests, of whom Herr
Berger had no reason to be ashamed (God forbid!) They opened a
bottle, drank to each other's health and treated each other to a great
many benedictions. The new friends were promptly invited to attend
the wedding, and the invitation was as promptly accepted by one and
all. Before long it came to light that one of the Rabbis, a skinny little
old man with a straggly goatee, was one of Reb Avram Ber's long-
lost, distant relations. And there was great and prolonged rejoicing.

Deborah felt quite carefree, even buoyant. Ever since she had set
foot in Berlin, her constant gloom and despair had given way to utter

calm. It was all very odd, but she had no particular wish to find out why—all that mattered to her was the fact that she had at last found peace of mind. She now had only one interest in life, and that was to discover who dwelt in that curious house across the road with the white, motionless, starched curtains. What sort of people were they, were they a large family or a small family, Jews or Gentiles? She had had a wash and a change of clothes, and with her hair neatly combed, she stood at the window waiting patiently to catch a glimpse beyond those elegant curtains, as if the knowledge she hoped to glean thus was of vital importance to her, as if it were indeed the sole object of her visit. The maid was clearing away the breakfast things. Deborah was pleasantly aware of this. It was so good to be waited on, and to be free, utterly free! Now here she could stand without lifting a finger, and she could leave everything in the capable hands of the maid. It was charming, the maid was charming, and hopefully Deborah kept gazing out of the window . . .

The non-arrival of the bridegroom was the cause of some anxiety and surprise. He ws due to get in by the early morning train from Antwerp, but the family consoled themselves with the reflection that there might have been a delay *en route*. The only person who showed complete indifference was the bride! She was in a state of perfect apathy. If the house had suddenly come tumbling down, it would scarcely have disturbed her. Such complete calm, such wonderful serenity had never been hers before; she felt as if she had been born again, remembering nothing of the past and caring nothing for her future. Her in-laws, her parents, they all kept talking and brooding and wondering what had happened. Not so Deborah. She neither talked nor brooded, nor wondered: would he come, would he not come, what type of man was he, how was he going to impress her and how would she impress him? Not a thing did she worry about. Her head was altogether empty, devoid even of a stray thought.

Night came on. Last thing before going to bed they despatched a telegram to Antwerp. Did that concern her? Surely, it had nothing to do with her!

On the following day, about nine o'clock in the morning, a smile blossomed forth on Tertsa-Roisa's face, such a great smile that her features could scarcely cope with it and they became all contorted.

"That's him! I can recognise his footsteps! It's him! He's coming!"

She made as if to run out to meet him, but was spared the pains. The door opened, and the maid admitted a tall plump young man with a smiling, self-satisfied, good-humoured face framed in a circular, fiery-red beard; he had on an obviously new, grey overcoat and held a new leather suitcase in his hand.

Deborah turned deathly pale.

The young man looked about him bashfully and quite bewildered. The sight of his mother struggling to rise from the sofa gave him his cue.

"Good morning, Mother!" he bent down and kissed her on the cheek. "How are you, Mother?"

"Thank God, I'm all right!" Tertsa-Roisa was beaming. "And how are you? This is your future mother-in-law."

The young man turned his head, with a rather furtive look in his eyes. His anxious gaze rested on Raizela. How pale and thin she was, as though she had just risen from a sickbed . . . He greeted her. He was not so sure that it was the proper thing for him to shake hands with her, as she was sure to be extremely pious. On this assumption he withheld his hand.

"And now I will introduce you to your bride."

Deborah made some sort of effort to smile.

The bridegroom blushed, so that even his circular beard seemed to turn from ginger to scarlet. A sunny smile settled on his face. He tried hard to articulate, but failed, and when finally he succeeded in mumbling something or other, no one took any notice anyway.

"What next?" he wondered, and then he had a brainwave. He decided to sit down on a chair that his mother had pulled up for him. The scene was heartrending. He had broken out into violent perspiration, and in his embarrassment he took refuge in the most sublime wisdom of all, the wisdom of silence . . .

"Hello, Berish, how are you?" His father saved the situation by arriving at a point where silence was becoming ridiculous, in fact impossible. Reb Baruch Laib's meaty old hand clasped the plump youthful hand of his son. "Have you seen the bride?" he enquired in a businesslike tone.

"How are you father?" the son hedged.

"Not so bad! *Well?*" Reb Baruch Laib was getting impatient.

"All right!" the young man gulped, his face turning an even deeper red than his beard.

"Ah, peace unto you! How are you?" Reb Avram Ber exclaimed at the threshold. He approached and shook the young man's hand so hard, he almost wrenched it off his wrist. "Well, well, we were getting very worried about you, but we'll forget all about that, now you're here. Have you said your morning prayers?"

"Yes, I said my prayers on the train."

Reb Baruch Laib smelled a rat; but he could do no more than glare at his son with a withering sceptical gleam in his crafty little eyes.

"Well then, we must be getting on with our own prayers," he said. "Look here, Tertsa-Roisa, tell them to lay the table in this room. We'll all have breakfast together. Are you coming Reb Avram Ber?"

"Why of course I am!"

No doubt it was Reb Baruch Laib's purpose to bring the bride and bridegroom together—he was anxious to break the ice, encourage them to exchange a few words; however that may be, at the breakfast table he made a proposal that they should all sally forth to Tietz's on a shopping expedition. Reb Avram Ber was left out of the party, as a matter of course, while Raizela excused herself on the plea that she was much too tired.

The weather was glorious. Berlin was radiant in the sunshine. The silks on display in the shopwindows, catching the sun's brilliance on their folds, were like flowing molten gold, disturbing and dazzling to the eye. On the shady side of the street the costly fabrics showed their charms more demurely, flowing gently, coyly beckoning to passers-by. The flagstones of the pavements sparkled as if studded with myriads of gleaming little diamonds. A leisurely throng filled the streets; the women kept stopping in front of the shop-displays.

The city bore a festive air now, quite different from the hurly-burly early yesterday morning. Loud, garish, posters and commercial signs screamed their messages from the rooftops. All this evoked memories for Deborah of her first visit to Marszalkowska Street.

She had been paired with the young man; but she never said a word as she walked by his side. He too was silent. Confound it, if only he would leave off smiling in that sickly sweet little way of his! It was unthinkable that this young man was to be her husband. He did seem quite a decent fellow, but . . . but there was something dead about him. There was something dead about the way he walked, the way he smiled. Here her lips curled up in amusement: how he had come to life at the breakfast table, though, how energetic he had been with his knife and fork! . . .

Suddenly the living image of Simon arose before her, blotting out all else . . . There he was, majestic of presence, tall, with stooping shoulders. His face was radiant with intelligence, with a deeper intelligence than ever before. "Simon, don't you see that it's too late now, too late!" "*Why is it too late?*" "Because it is!" No, that was not the way he had spoken to her in reality. He had not tried to deter her from running away, but had goaded her on. "I congratulate you, Deborah!" that was what she could hear him say over and over again. Why, then, did he not cease tormenting her? What justification had he for haunting her thus? She was not fit for party work. She was no good at repartee. She was an utter fool. She was a wretched girl without a dowry! . . .

Anyway, what on earth was her companion smiling at? Wasn't that fellow ever going to stop? Confound him! Really, Berlin was a most exciting city, it put Warsaw in the shade . . . There, he was at it again, smiling once more! Yet he did not look a fool. Actually, of course, there was no reason why he should look a fool!

"I beg your pardon?" her fiancé spoke up all at once, conquering his shyness. He knew full well that she had not said a word, but he hoped to entice her into doing so, and meanwhile he smiled patiently, goodnaturedly. Deborah felt sick at heart. What the devil was he so pleased about?

"Deborah, will you please find out whether we're on the right track. Somehow I think we've lost our way," Reb Baruch Laib said, turning his big head.

Deborah stopped an elderly gentleman clad in a loosely fitting overcoat, every stitch of which looked typically German.

"*Königstrasse? Gewiss!*" he exclaimed in a very loud voice.

Deborah did not quite catch the gist of his staccato words, and after bearing left they turned to the right, only to come back where they had started. She inquired again. At last the name of Wertheimers stared at them in bold letters, and across the road was the house of Tietz. Within its portals there was an air of dignified calm. The interior opened up an immense perspective—a city within a city . . .

Reb Baruch Laib led the way from department to department, past interminable counters. At each stop, the display of colourful goods changed, yet retained a certain artificial symmetry and uniform beauty, like the patterns in a kaleidoscope. The variety of wares seemed inexhaustible . . .

Deborah's glance lingered for a fleeting instant on a pair of long white silken gloves. Her fiancé immediately bought them for her, together with a blue and white scarf which rather resembled the Zionist flag, and later on he presented her with an umbrella. Then he bought another umbrella, for himself, and a pair of brown kid gloves. It seemed very strange to her that a pious young man who wore a beard—and a ginger beard at that—should think of putting on elegant kid gloves that were obviously designed for a dashing dandy. Surely the people of Antwerp must be a queer, hybrid crowd!

Tertsa-Roisa made a number of purchases too. This was by no means her first visit to Tietz's; two or three years ago she had been there on a similar errand. The occasion then was the marriage of her eldest son who was living in Antwerp. This eldest son, unlike Berish, knew his fiancée, having been betrothed to her before he left Warsaw; but, like Berish, he was also wed at Herr Berger's Kosher Hotel. Tertsa-Roisa was therefore no stranger to this outlandish departmental store. All the same she could not for the life of her believe that the prices marked up were genuine and unalterable. And she lustily haggled over the lace neckerchief which was to be a present for her daughter in Antwerp, over the serviettes which were for her daughter-in-law, and again over the trinkets which were to delight the hearts of her grandchildren. The young shop-assistant was about to lose her temper, but, changing her mind, she pressed a push-button instead, and a tall young man appeared clad in a long black frock-coat and striped black trousers; his sleekly brushed head of black hair positively oozed brilliantine, his teeth were whiter than driven snow. Lightly touching the neckerchief, he smiled a gracious smile, bowed, and said in honeyed tones:

"Very sorry, Madam, but our prices are not subject to bargaining."

As though his words were law, Tertsa-Roisa opened her purse and paid the bill without any further ado.

They returned to the hotel with many neat little parcels; the smiling bridegroom was given charge of the two wrapped-up umbrellas, which he tucked under his arm. They all had dinner together. Deborah ate frugally, much to Reb Baruch Laib's disappointment.

"Why, if that's the way you eat, you'll soon be no better than a skeleton," he reprimanded her as gently as he could. Reb Avram Ber concurred, pointing out that eating was an essential function of living. Tertsa-Roisa argued that eating was merely a habit; if one lost the knack of eating, then one would never feel hungry, and anyone who did not eat could not expect to be strong and healthy. This statement was endorsed by all present (except the bridegroom). So Deborah ate her full portion, even though she felt she would choke.

The wedding ceremony took place on the morrow. The bride and bridegroom saw nothing of each other all day.

Again Deborah felt perfectly calm. She was as lighthearted as a child. Again she had not a care in the world. She had even left of caring who dwelt in the shuttered house across the road. But when evening was drawing in, and her mother told her to put on her wedding gown, she was overcome by a perfect frenzy of despair. All at once the horror of her situation became clear to her in a piercing agonising light. And as if salvation lay that way, she began to plead desperately with her mother for a respite.

"Please, please, don't hurry me! And haven't I told you all along that I won't, I won't put on a ceremonial wedding gown?"

"Don't be childish, Deborah! You're just like a baby!" said Raizela. "When I tell you to put on your wedding gown, do so. You know quite well that if this wedding had been celebrated at home you would have had to be dressed up in white all day long."

"Don't say white! Say black!" Deborah burst out.

Raizela clapped her hands over her ears.

Deborah stood praying at the wall facing east. A higgledy-piggledy train of memories, strange memories, went straggling through her brain. Old Hannah crossed her mind, and the kitten that Hannah had taken away when the family left Jelhitz. Did she see Joel before her now? Yes, but what was he doing in this faraway place? It was an apparition, but try as she might she could not get rid of it. His crafty old face obstinately refused to go away. "Congratulations, Deborah! Be a good girl and say your prayers!" It was Simon speaking. . . . Then Deborah recalled how Tertsa-Roisa had tried to bargain in broken German with the wide-eyed shop-girl who had so despairingly, so naively protested her innocence—*she* was not responsible for the prices charged, *she* was not to blame. . . . Suddenly Deborah burst out laughing.

Raizela and Tertsa-Roisa looked up with startled faces.

"What on earth is the matter with you? Have you lost your reason? Don't you realise what a solemn prayer this is?"—Raizela spoke as calmly as she could, concealing her exasperation, but it was preposterous for a bride to indulge in ribald laughter in the midst of her prayers. And there was no apparent cause for laugher: it was sheer madness!

Deborah heeded the rebuke. She stifled her mirth. She took three paces backwards, in accordance with the ritual, and then suddenly, against her own will, against her better judgment, she broke out into another uncontrollable fit of laughter. This time she laughed louder than ever, laughed hysterically. Raizela bit her tongue, deeply ashamed and angry.

Two hours later, beneath the nuptial canopy of red velvet upheld by four poles, beneath the night sky stretching far and wide over the courtyard of the hotel, Deborah stood trembling as with the ague; a crowd of onlookers—purring with self-content—all round her. Reb Avram Ber himself officiated. Everybody, including the maidservant, assumed a solemn expression.

The man at her side was holding a ring in his hand. All bewildered, Deborah struggled in vain to remove the glove from her fingers. At last, in her confusion and forgetting that her wedding gown had detachable sleeves, she peeled the long glove, which the bridegroom had bought for her at Tietz's, violently off her arm, and in doing so ripped away the sleeve inside. She was left with a naked arm dangling for all to see and be ashamed of. The blood came rushing up into Reb Baruch Laib's head. His beefy face became inflamed, his tiny eyes kindled. But he held his peace. Deborah managed somehow to pull the glove back on to her arm again, and with the sleeve crumpled up in her hand ascended the stairs followed by the crowd.

Upstairs the tables were all spread for the banquet. The guests drank a toast to the newly-wed couple; congratulations and—where proper—kisses were generously exchanged.

Reb Baruch Laib, for reasons of his own, was burning with fury; but he exercised sufficient self-control not to explode prematurely. He was biding his time. The disgraceful incident of the naked arm had given him the pretext he wanted. And when the guests were all seated round the tables, and the first course was being served, he calculated that his moment had come.

"This wedding ceremony," he bawled, "has been the greatest humiliation of my life. To think that the wife I have chosen for my son, the woman who I fondly hoped would walk with my son in the ways of God, should dare wear a sleeveless wedding gown and make an exhibition of herself on this night of all nights. Just think of it! What a fool I have been to spend all this money on her, what a fool! Did *my* daughter wear a sleeveless gown on her wedding night? I should say not! It's no use arguing. I saw everything! Everything!"

And then Reb Baruch Laib let himself go. It was like a bolt from the blue, and there was complete chaos. The bridegroom felt so ashamed of himself and of his father that he would gladly have jumped into his grave and buried himself there and then. Tertsa-Roisa burst into tears. Deborah turned an inquiring look on the people around her, as if she were studying their faces. She did not seem to be greatly upset. Apparently she did not grasp what it was all about. Reb Avram Ber had not seen the naked arm, and, therefore, refused to believe in it. . . .

"I shall take my daughter away, and we shall leave at once!" he screamed at Reb Baruch Laib. "We're going home this very instant. The idea! Do you think I shall allow you to slander my poor child?"

Raizela bit her nails. She succeeded, but only by a supreme effort, in suppressing the tears that welled up within her. Her large grey eyes bore such a mournful expression, they shone with such grim despair, they might have been the symbol of eternal grief.

In the end Herr Berger's rabbis, and more particularly Herr Berger himself, brought about a reconciliation and peace. The party drank another toast, and blessings were exchanged all over again. Reb Avram Ber was radiant. What an occasion this was for rejoicing, the Lord be praised! A momentous occasion in a father's lifetime! (The recent unpleasantness was quite forgotten and forgiven, so far as he was concerned.) The company regaled themselves and made merry. The rabbis vied with each other in the telling of fascinating *hassidical* anecdotes. Reb Avram Ber was a good listener, but he was also a good raconteur, and he told some of the most breathtaking tales of all. Reb Baruch Laib contented himself with descriptions of life in Antwerp, not forgetting the wealthy diamond merchants. The bridegroom smiled knowingly, as if to confirm all that his father said. Raizela, at the lower end of the table, was rather flushed. Her eyes sparkled with festive gloom. Tertsa-Roisa kept shaking her head enthusiastically. She listened only to the words of her husband, and was simply flabbergasted by his pearls of wisdom. How did he manage to think of so many clever things? Her face was like a bowl of dripping, circular and shiny. Deborah was astonished to discover that she was not waiting at table, as usual, but was being waited upon. The hotel-keeper's wife was dressed up to the nines. As each new course arrived she appeared on the scene like a joyous herald of good tidings.

The company ate and drank; the menfolk swayed happily from their hips, left and right, as they sang *hassidical* songs. And from time to time they left their seats to dance round in a ring like children.

The bride felt numb. The heated atmosphere was stifling. It was sultry, terribly sultry. She felt out of place, she felt that she did not belong here, and did not know what to do with herself.

When they called on her to join in the ritual wedding dance, she tried to make some protest, but it passed unnoticed. She shrank back from the crowd that summoned her; yet she found herself whirling round with them in a ring—an enchanted circle of strangers to whom she was absurdly joined by the end of a stranger's pocket-handker-chief. Round and round they went, until she was overcome with gid-diness. And in the centre of the ring stood Simon. He, too, was dancing, clapping his hands and mocking her.

"Congratulations, Deborah! On with the dance, on with the dance!"

She felt sick. She knew that if they did not release her this very instant she would fall into a dead faint. Perhaps the ordeal would have been less terrible if the hotel-keeper's daughter, a slim, olive-cheeked girl of about her own age, had not come to the door to watch the spec-tacle in a stupor of amazement.

The next morning, when they clipped her curly hair to the roots, she offered no resistance. Her hair would grow again, in time. But the wig which they put on her head gave her an awkward feeling. Casting a shadow over her eyes, it lent emphasis to the deathly pallor of her face. Also the ring on her finger was uncomfortable, like something super-fluous—and cold to the touch. . . . She said not a word, but meekly did all she was asked to do. Soon after breakfast the hotel-keeper's daugh-ter came running up the stairs with two belated telegrams.

"Please don't think me inquisitive, Madam, but . . . er . . . could you tell me, what is the name of that dance you all entered into after supper last night?"

"It was . . . a devils' dance!"

"Beg your pardon? I didn't quite catch that."

"Even if I were to tell you, you wouldn't know. The dance is quite peculiar to Polish Jewry."

"Yes, but do tell me what it's called. I'm so interested, for it's the strangest dance I've ever seen. So beautiful, though; so fantastic!"

"It's a ritual dance," Deborah said, on the verge of tears.

"So it's a ritual ceremony! I see! Oh, how original, how beautiful!"

Deborah studied the girl's brown tresses. She felt like a clumsy old woman in the presence of this slim, vivacious, olive-cheeked girl, who was in fact two years older than herself. The girl went away satisfied with the information she had gleaned.

"*Madam*! She calls me *Madam*!" Deborah thought. She was alone now, and no one witnessed the outburst of pent-up anguish which brought a little solace to a heavily burdened heart.

A little later, when Deborah was dozing, completely exhausted, on a sofa in a tiny room divided off from the sitting-room by a plush curtain, she was suddenly roused by her mother's voice. The familiar tones had a new and hard ring in them, such as Deborah had never heard before.

"So now the cat is out of the bag!" Raizela was saying. "The mystery of Reb Baruch Laib's unprovoked and scandalous outburst last night—in the presence of strangers, mark you—is a mystery no longer. Oh, what a mean despicable creature that man is! And oh what a terrible mistake we have made, what a terrible mistake! . . ."

"Why, what's happened?" asked Reb Avram Ber.

"Everything has happened! I have had my eyes opened, but unfortunately too late, too late! We have given our daughter away to the wrong sort of people. That's what has happened! Do you remember that when we were on the train, Baruch Laib told us that he had spent three hundred roubles on a pair of ear-rings which were to be the bridegroom's wedding gift to Deborah?"

"Yes, that's right. I wonder why he hasn't given them to her yet. It's about time he did."

"I can tell you why," said Raizela. "It's because Baruch Laib is a liar and a scoundrel. That's the simple explanation. Early this morning I was lying on the sofa in that little room behind the curtain and quite unwittingly I overheard the old man enter into a dispute with the bridegroom. 'I refuse to have anything to do with it!' said the bridegroom. 'The "diamonds" in those ear-rings are faked, mere paste, and if you wish to give them to her yourself, you're welcome! But you can leave me out of this. Having made a promise, you should have kept it. If you knew you were running out of funds, then you shouldn't have made any such promise.' Next, I heard Tertsa-Roisa join in the argument. She begged her son to be reasonable and not to be a trouble-maker. She assured him that in a few weeks' time, at the outside, Baruch Laib would get a pair of ear-rings with genuine diamonds in them, which would be a replica of the artificial pair and then he could quietly substitute the new for the old and no one would be any the wiser. That was Tertsa-Roisa's motherly advice to her son—*Be a scoundrel like your father!* But Berish flatly refused to be mixed up in this deceitful game. 'Supposing she were to find out,' he said, 'what then? Think how awful that would be!' 'So you won't give them to her, eh?' said Baruch Laib. 'All right, you needn't! I don't care. She won't even get dud ones now, she'll get nothing at all, see! Not a thing!' 'Is that what you had at the back of your mind when you started that disgusting scene at the banquet last night?' Berish inquired. Upon my word, you should have heard the language the old man used when Berish put that question to him point blank. 'Shut up, you miserable heathen, you low-down swine, shut up! Another word from you, and I'll wring your dirty neck! Speak when you're spoken to!' He bellowed away like an enraged bull, all because his son had put his finger on the sore spot. Berish had torn the mask away with a vengeance. You see, not content with having bamboozled us, pretending to us that he had paid three hundred roubles for so much worthless paste, Baruch Laib decided to extricate himself from an unsavoury position by making a bullying attack on Deborah and by humiliating us in front of all those strangers. It was a put-up affair, to provide himself with a pretext for not honouring his promise."

Raizela heaved a deep sigh.

"You appreciate, of course," she resumed after a lengthy silence, "that it's not the actual ear-rings I'm concerned about?"

"Why, of course! As if the ear-rings mattered!"

Reb Avram Ber sighed gently. If he had not heard this strange story from Raizela's own lips he would never have believed it. Was it possible? Was Reb Baruch Laib really that kind of man? Even now he could not inure himself to the thought. But Raizela herself had told him so—Raizela herself! Reb Avram Ber sat crestfallen, as though lifeless, for a long time. Then he reached for his beard and began to tug it hard. Then he combed it with his fingers, stroked it, twirled it around his forefinger and finally he was biting it furiously.

"You understand, don't you," Raizela repeated, "that it's not the ear-rings I'm concerned about?"

"Of course I understand! Ear-rings!" Reb Avram Ber exclaimed with a world of contempt.

"There seems to be no privacy in this place at all," said Deborah, drawing the curtain . . . Raizela turned her large gloomy eyes upon her. "Mamma, I don't care. Don't say another word about it, please. You know I don't want the ear-rings in any case."

Raizela's gaze lingered upon her. Then she hung her head in silence.

Reb Baruch Laib and his wife were to accompany the newlyweds to Antwerp. They had their eldest married son and a newly married daughter living there, whom they had not seen for some years, and they were planning a family reunion. But Reb Avram Ber and Raizela were less fortunate. Not only could they not afford the fare to Antwerp, they had scarcely enough money left to cover their expenses back to Warsaw. Indeed, they had to leave for home that very same evening.

Raizela bade her daughter a subdued farewell. She planted a kiss on her forehead, opened her mouth as if to speak, but sucked her cheeks in between her teeth instead. Both mother and daughter were silent. They did not cry and had nothing to say to each other. They preserved a grim silence.

Reb Avram Ber said good-bye to Deborah in gentle fatherly tones. He kissed her upon the head. For some time he gazed heavenwards, apparently calling upon the Almighty, as he gave her his blessing. She heard him murmur: "Oh Father, You are omnipotent, loving and merciful!" And then he climbed into the carriage of the waiting train.

Raizela put her head out of the window into the twilight of the station, bidding another silent farewell to her daughter, who stood surrounded by three strangers in a strange city, watching her parents leave for home. The engine uttered a long-drawn-out piercing whistle. The train began to move. Reb Avram Ber and Raizela, with their faces glued to the window, saw their daughter dwindle rapidly, and then in a flash she was gone.

"Don't forget to remember me to all the folks at home, don't forget!" Tertsa-Roisa cried animatedly at a swiftly passing carriage and they returned to the hotel.

CHAPTER XIV

On the journey to Antwerp Reb Baruch Laib went out of his way to create still further unpleasantness. The trouble this time was a book which Deborah had picked up from her mother (who had just finished with it), and to which she now turned eagerly to while the time away.

Before long she had become deeply absorbed in its pages—it was a Life of Moses Mendelssohn—and her heart bled as she followed the adventures of this poor suffering philosopher-hunchback. His indomitable struggle against his own physical infirmity and external antagonism aroused her deepest admiration. The account to how the authorities turned him back from all the gates of the city of Berlin, filled her with profound pity for the bright-eyed cripple, who, intellectually and spiritually, towered so high above the common clay that barred his way; and she was filled with hatred and contempt for the police who played such an abominable part in the drama. His ultimate triumph over untold opposition was like a personal victory of her own, and how she exulted! She was so carried away that her own life was forgotten. But Reb Baruch Laib took care that this forgetfulness should be short-lived.

"There can be no doubt about it now," he fumed. "She's a freethinker! Look, she's reading the biography of that heretic Mendelssohn! Go on, have a look!" he urged his wife, pointing an accusing finger at the title-page of the book which Deborah had laid aside for an instant.

Tertsa-Roisa duly inspected the title-page (illiterate though she was, as her husband well knew), and she shook her head with an air of disapproval. She wondered what on earth could be wrong; but if Reb Baruch Laib was shocked, then that was sufficient reason for her to feel shocked, too. All the same, by means of timid gestures and obsequious smiles, she begged him to restrain his virtuous wrath and to preserve the peace.

The bridegroom was seething with rebellion. He, likewise, fixed a look of entreaty on his father; but there was something in his eye that boded evil. And with a pang of regret Reb Baruch Laib subsided.

Deborah ignored him. She quietly resumed her reading. Within her heart, though, all was tumult. . . .

They steamed into Antwerp as the shadows of evening were gathering. The Central Station presented a picture of semi-darkness and utter desertion. The arrival of the express livened things up somewhat, but only somewhat. The streets, too, bore a dreary aspect— they were dark and desolate. The gleaming wet iron bars of the gateway to the zoo had a forbidding air, as if behind them lay a dark and wretched prison. A slight but penetrating drizzle, quite unlike a summer shower, settled tearfully on the windows of their taxicab.

The cab halted in Levrik Street, or "Boulevard de Levrik," as the wags of Antwerp humorously called it. The bridegroom in person knocked at the front door. He had to go on knocking for a long time, however, before he could make any impression on the din that was going on within. At long last the appearance of a drab greenish light in the vestibule showed that someone was coming. The door opened and the someone turned out to be a whole procession of people. It was headed by a tall woman in the early thirties, with a tremendous bosom and a flat, blonde wig on her head; after her came a short, young, barrel-shaped woman, with a face as red as beetroot and with a piled-up black wig on her head; next, a tall, young man who was the image of the bridegroom except that he had a very much bigger beard; and, finally, a horde of children of all sizes and descriptions. They immediately fell on the newcomers' necks, shrieking and kissing and voicing apologies for having failed to come to the station. After a pause for breath they began embracing and kissing all over again. In the general confusion Reb Baruch Laib laid hands on the short young woman with the beetroot face and very nearly smothered her before he discovered that she was his daughter-in-law, and not his daughter, as he had at first imagined. He then made amends by brushing a kiss on to the face of his daughter, who was the tall woman with the big bosom and the blonde wig. His eldest son, the young man with the big ginger beard, whose wife had been the victim of Reb Baruch Laib's error, proposed that they should all go inside and get on with the kissing in the light, rather than hang about in the dark. This suggestion was adopted with alacrity, and in a twinkling the guests were deposited, luggage and all, in the residence of the taller and elder of the two women.

Here the air was clammy: it smote the nose with a tang of fungus and urine. The rickety wooden table was spread with an American cloth which had so many holes and ink-stains on it that it seemed to record the events of a long and crowded lifetime. . . . The curtains over the two windows were only partly torn, but dirty all over. The chairs creaked, and the baby of the family—a fine, chubby little boy between the age of one and two—was yelling in his cradle like a perfect demon: no doubt he was indignant at having been left out of the riotous welcome.

"So this is Antwerp! This is where the ship comes to port!" thought Deborah.

The big woman and the tubby woman both got busy with the tea-things. The young man with the big ginger beard got a bottle of whisky out of his father's suitcase. His mother, Tertsa-Roisa, handed him another bottle, saying:

"Will you open this, Lipa. It's sweet cognac for us women. There!" They all gathered round with upraised glasses. Reb Baruch Laib and Lipa both proposed a toast to the future birth of a son. The womenfolk toasted the unborn son. Deborah was embarrassed, and her tongue failed her. The womenfolk exchanged a significant look, and then they eyed the bridegroom and then they smiled. Deborah smiled, too, both vexed and amused.

After the American cloth had been wiped dry they all got round the table. The young man with the big ginger beard engaged in earnest conversation with his father; he obviously had something very solemn and confidential to impart to him. And to lend emphasis to his remarks he kept plucking at his fine bushy beard. He had grown this beard for his father's especial benefit, just to convince the old boy that he, Lipa, was as pious as a rabbi, and that his, therefore, was a deserving case. Lipa knew that his father knew that man was made in the image of God, and that no good Jew would dream of interfering with God's will by trimming the growth on his chin. So this was Lipa's trump card, and he lost no opportunity of playing it. He gave the beard a tweak, and scowled. He gave the beard a tweak, and grinned. But just as he was about to lift up his chin and flourish it under his father's nose as a final demonstration of piety, the door opened and in walked the master of the house, a wiry man of about forty-five, with a really long beard that bristled with hairs black and grey.

He took stock of the whole situation at a glance. He evinced some astonishment, just for the sake of decency. He also betrayed delight, just for the sake of decency; but he did not overdo it. He went up to his father-in-law and said, "Peace unto you!" (but failed to notice the bridegroom). Then he twisted up his nose judiciously, like a connoisseur, and sniffed the air once or twice in a very suspicious way. Immediately, without the slightest hesitation, he strode across to the cradle where the baby was still howling like a creature possessed, and, again without hesitation, raised the quilt. A poisonous odour seeped over the room.

"Do you mind giving me your attention, my sweet! Will you step this way!" he said to his wife with grim sarcasm.

Meanwhile, the infant was kicking up his legs most violently, and all present instinctively reached for their noses and squeezed them tight for dear life.

However, the master of the house was soon mollified by his wife (the tall woman with the big bosom and blonde wig) when she beseeched his forgiveness. She had been terribly busy all evening, she said, and in any case she was sure the accident was of recent occurrence. He even condescended to help clean up the cradle, and every time she stooped over the sheets he gave her a friendly pinch in the fleshy part.

When it was all over the windows were opened at the top a wee bit. And in honour of the master of the house the beakers were filled again. This time the newly-wiped infant in the cradle was the toast: the hope was expressed that he would be a source of joy to his parents and to all the family. And with their noses still puckered up they all nibbled sweet honey-cake.

Reb Baruch Laib, Tertsa-Roisa, the two stout young women and the young man with the flowing ginger beard called the bridegroom aside and they all went next door, apparently for a family consultation. Deborah remained with the master of the house and the crowd of children.

"I hope you have not been misled regarding your husband's ability to provide for you," said the master of the house, turning to Deborah with an ominous and malicious little smile.

Deborah's heart sank. It was the brutality, rather than the significance of his words that stunned and angered her. What kind of talk was this?

"Pray do not be so alarmed," her brother-in-law went on. "There's no need to despair. But it all depends on you."

Her uneasiness grew.

"The point I am trying to make is this: A clever woman can mould her husband like clay. If he is lazy, she will know how to make him industrious. A resolute wife can convert the worst of men into a model husband. I hope I have made myself clear. I imagine it would be superfluous for me to enter into details."

Indeed, thought Deborah, that would be quite superfluous. He had made himself abundantly clear. But she consoled herself with the reflection that this was obviously a case of personal animosity.

He gave her a stealthy glance to see how she had taken it. Deborah's gaze strayed round the room. It positively reeked of poverty and wretchedness. The light from the gas lamp flowed down in murky waves of a miserable greenish hue. The wallpaper was full of smears and in places was hanging from the walls in tatters. The floor was sticky underfoot, and the ceiling overhead was a smoky brown. In a corner by the door a fat-bellied spider was at work weaving a web for itself. She noticed a fly on a yellow flypaper, suspended from the ceiling, struggling furiously to escape the fate of scores of its fellows that had long since given up the struggle and lay dead in the sticky mess. But this one refused to yield, and in the end by forfeiting a leg it saved its life, and the mutilated remains flew away with a horrible buzzing noise. What a foul thing to have in the home—a cemetery for flies! The sight of it, and many other things besides, made her feel sick at heart. The master of the house fitted in well enough with these surroundings. How dare he presume to give her counsels of wisdom? . . . All at once, darting another quick glance all round her, she quoted—almost involuntarily—an old Hebrew proverb:

"The wise man's wealth is his wisdom: he possesses no worldly riches."

She was herself taken aback at the suddenness with which this little-known saying had fallen from her lips. She wondered where she had picked it up. Then she remembered that her father used it occasionally in his rare tiffs with her mother.

The master of the house resented the imputation that he possessed no worldly riches. He knew, even if she did not, that at one time in his career, before he had divorced his first wife, he had been quite a wealthy man, and once a wealthy man always a wealthy man! As for his being a wise man, he took that for granted—after all, everybody in the house did the same! He felt deeply offended, and flashed a look on Deborah that seemed to vow eternal enmity. Anxious to be rid of him Deborah began to play with the baby, who chuckled most delightfully.

The family consultation came to an end. It was agreed that they were to stay where they were for supper, Deborah was to spend the night with her sister-in-law (the short one with the very red face), and the menfolk were to put up in an hotel down the road.

Deborah's two sisters-in-law got busy. Lipa went out shopping. The master of the house, his face all wreathed in scowls, refused to take any interest in the proceedings. He even refused to give the family the benefit of his wisdom, and whenever he was approached for advice, he retorted that he would deem it a favour if they shut their traps and left him in peace.

When the tall woman with the blonde wig spread a tablecloth riddled with holes and full of ugly stains, Tertsa-Roisa was put to shame, and she motioned to her daughter-in-law to fetch another. The red-faced young woman hurried into the adjacent room, where she had her own little home, and soon returned in triumph with a starched snowy-white tablecloth that was a credit to her housewifery, whereupon the other woman turned her nose up, greatly piqued.

By this time Lipa had come back with a parcel of herrings and sausages, rolls and cakes, and bottles of beer. Reb Baruch Laib sat down at the head of the table. On his right was the bridegroom, and on his left the surly master of the house. Then came Lipa and the womenfolk. The children were ranged at the bottom of the table, all in a tangle like crushed sauerkraut. At first they sat quietly enough. Gradually, however, their bashfulness wore off and they began to enjoy themselves. They reached out with their smutty hands for the herrings and the sausages, and indeed any food within range; they picked up a roll, dropped it, and decided to have another instead; they stretched full length over the table in superhuman efforts to get at the cut cake. They licked their plates dry; they swallowed their food without chewing; they let their noses run recklessly. . . . Father and mother and all the family remonstrated and asked them where their manners were.

"Ugh! Don't you know any better than that?"

"Wipe your nose! Ugh!"

But the children took not the slightest notice and went their own sweet way. Even if they were to behave like angels they would still be preached at by their elders. So why worry? For some reason grown-ups always had a habit of saying, "Ugh! Don't you know any better than that?" They seemed to enjoy saying that sort of thing. But any child in his proper senses knew that it would never do to take such admonitions seriously. All the children here were eminently sensible, they looked very well after themselves indeed. All, that is, except the eldest boy; he fared badly. He had reached the mature age of twelve. And he could not very well degrade himself by acting the way the others did. Yet he was not considered a grown-up and was being left out in the cold. His eyes were glued on the dainties with fervent yearning, but he waited in vain for encouragement from his parents. He felt very sorry for himself to the point of tears. At last he could stand it no longer, and with the fury of a rebel he began grabbing from this platter and that, like a hungry beast. The whole family were simply shocked beyond words. What! A big boy like that—it was terrible! Unbelievable! Without uttering a word in his own defence he began to take his little brothers and sisters to task, giving them first a pinch and then a dig in the ribs by way of emphasis. "Ugh!" he said. "Don't you know any better than that? I'm ashamed of you, that's what I am!"

At first the infant in the cradle seemed disposed to take an active part in the festivities. He crooned and chuckled to himself. Having finished his bottle and lying in clean sheets he was as pleased as pleased could be. But having no one to communicate with, except with his big toe, he finally fell asleep.

"What's the matter with those kids to-night?"

"Haim, d'you want me to rap you over the knuckles? Now, leave it alone! Put it down!"

"I'm only playing with it: I'm not going to eat it."

"Never mind, stop playing with it! Just put that apple back where you took it from!"

"I'm fed up! I don't know what to do! What shall I do?"

"What shall you do? Here, stick some snuff up your nose!"
"Yankela, sit up!"
"I'm sitting up!"
"No you're not! Do as you're told. Sit properly!"
"Ugh! Faigela, what's the matter with you, a big girl like you?
Ought to be ashamed of yourself! Hurry, quick, wipe your nose!"

A profusion of handkerchiefs from Uncle Lipa and auntie, and grandma, and dad; and even mamma came dashing up with a pinafore. But too late. Faigela could not wait.

"If those impudent brats don't mend their ways they'll be sorry for it!" said the master of the house, glowering at Deborah the while. "Behave yourselves!"

For a while the children sat motionless, as though petrified, but they were only bracing themselves for a renewed and even more violent attack on the cut cake.

"You're not helping yourself. What can I offer you? I guess you don't think much of this Belgian sausage. It doesn't taste half as good as Polish sausage. But what else can you expect? Polish sausage is famous the world over," said Lipa, gallantly addressing Deborah, but gazing across at his younger brother with a mocking smile, as if to say "Now look, I'm going to get off with your bride. Stop me if you can, you dumb idiot!" The bridegroom lowered his eyes with an expression that seemed to say "Go to hell!"

"No, not at all. The sausage is excellent," said Deborah, courteously defending the sausage without making any attempt to eat it.

Reb Baruch Laib was drinking hard, and so was the master of the house, who was now so absorbed in his bottle that he allowed the children to do just as they pleased. This was Lipa's finest moment for showing off his beard—and it was really a lovely beard, the sort of beard that would have done credit to a saint.

Each time he tossed off a drink he threw his head back and protruded his chin for his parents to rejoice in his hairy emblem of piety. If a beard like that was not going to make the old man fork out, then nothing would!

The bridegroom was all eagerness to communicate with his bride.

He toyed with the idea of passing her an orange or a tot of cognac, he might even have spoken a few words to her, if only to spite his brother, Lipa, the insolent dog! But he could not get at her very well, she was too far down the table. It was most annoying. When brother Lipa had got married he had been seated next to his wife, Baila. Perhaps that was because they were cousins. No, that was not the explanation. The true explanation was that everybody had entered into a conspiracy against Deborah and himself. They were a mean lot!

At last the nuptial supper—the first of a series of seven ritual feasts—came to an end, in prayer. The children had all fallen asleep on their chairs and had long since been carried off to bed, one by one. It was past two in the morning. Deborah still sat with her head drooping with weariness. All the others had gone away, leaving her by herself. At last Tertsa-Roisa reappeared and conducted her into the bedroom next-door. Here Lipa and his wife were sitting side by side at a tiny table. How Deborah wished she could tear off the bed-cover and fling herself into the white sheets. It was an inviting bed, piled high with an inflated eiderdown and surmounted by a big puffed-up pillow trimmed with lace fringes and marked with an artistically embroidered monogram in red silk.

The young couple sat at the table, however, seemingly unaware of Deborah's presence. She noticed that Lipa held a plate in his hand and flourished a stewed prune in a silver spoon which he was trying to pop into his wife's mouth. It was all very curious!

"Oh, please leave me alone!" cried the fat young woman imploringly.

"Now go on, be a good little wifey and do as your hubby says. Prunes, you know, are good for you. There, down it goes!"

She protested coyly, pulling a wry face as if she were taking a bitter medicine, but Lipa was as firm as he was gentle. He insisted on her eating all the prunes, all of them, because her health demanded it.

"And now, sweetheart, I shall leave you and you can go to bed!"

He kissed her good-night, and only on tearing his lips away did he discover that he had an audience. He became very confused and apologised, but Deborah had previously observed him peeping at her out of a corner of his eye. It was all very curious!

The fat young woman with the beetroot-red face gave her a smile and removed the bedcover.

"My husband is such a fool," she said in a plaintive voice, but with a gleeful smirk on her face. "He really is too good to me, the silly! He hangs round me all day, I simply can't shake him off. He's such a dear!"

Deborah very nearly tore her clothes off and flung herself into bed.

Tertsa-Roisa and Baila began to undress, unlacing their corsets at the back, undoing the clasps at the front, removing cotton wool padding from their hips and taking more pads off their buttocks, substantial though these were. Deborah gaped at them from under the bedclothes. What fanciful creatures these women were to enlarge their monumental backsides with cotton-wool padding! The younger woman turned the light down to a faint glimmer.

Snuggling up against the pillow and curling herself up Deborah gazed out from the comfortable, wholesome bedclothes at the wall opposite. On this wall magnified shadows of the two women were prancing about. Shadowy ribbons were fluttering about fantastically. At last the shadows went to bed and all was quiet. The peacefulness of night was intoxicating after all the fuss and excitement. But Deborah was too exhausted to fall easily asleep. Incoherent thoughts went racing through her head until she felt giddy. She tried to rid herself of these meaningless thoughts by counting: one, two, three, and four, and five . . . but all to no avail. She kept a lonely vigil for a long time and then, in the early hours of the morning, she was roused from her sickening stupor by a whispered heart-to-heart talk between mother-in-law and daughter-in-law in the opposite bed.

"Are you asleep, Baila?"

"No."

"Why, what's wrong?"

"Nothing in particular. Can't get to sleep somehow."

"Well, how is it going?"

"I expect it in a couple of months' time."

"Yes, I know that. But how's Lipa treating you these days?"

"How's he treating me? Don't ask! Ever since I've got married it's been a cat and dog's life!"

"But surely he's changed now? He tells me he's a reformed character."

"He told you that, did he? Naturally! And I shouldn't be surprised if you believed him! I never noticed him saying anything to you."

"Well, you see, just before going to bed I had a little talk with him next door. I called him in specially. He was the first to break the news about your expecting a baby. There, you'll soon be a mother, and yet you keep on complaining that you can't get on with him. You mark my word, when baby comes Lipa will be a new man!"

"I hope so! All he does meanwhile is to waste his time in Laibel's Café gambling at cards from morning till past midnight. And he forgets about me, I don't matter. I have all the housework to do, and do properly—look, you can see for yourself how tidy I keep my home, not like Rebecca does."

"Well, there's a reason for that. Rebecca has her hands full looking after the children, Good bless 'em! You'll soon find out for yourself how difficult it is to keep house when you have a baby to look after."

"What about it? Don't I work as a dressmaker? Don't I have to slave from morning to night? Don't I have to dress up all the fine ladies in town, stand all their nagging in the bargain, as if I wasn't made of flesh and blood like them? Oh, how I hate them! I could murder them! I could murder them! I wish I were dead, God forbid, rather than have to go on leading such a poor, miserable existence!"

Deborah was both amused and scared. She heard a sound of muffled weeping.

"I hope she isn't awake."

"Of course not, you silly! She's fast asleep, that's what she is. Why, she was half asleep at the table! I wish I could sleep as soundly as she does. Old age is no joy," said Tertsa-Roisa, heaving a wistful sigh.

"Well, I can't say that I get any joy out of being young. For all the fun that I have out of it, I might as well be a widow weeping over Lipa's grave."

"Stop! Don't you dare speak like that about my son!" hissed Tertsa-Roisa in a sudden fury.

"Your dear little son! And I suppose I'm not a mother's child, am I? I'm an outcast!"

"Now, now, don't start crying again, don't cry!" said Tertsa-Roisa, instantly resuming her former coaxing tone. "After all, we're always ready to lend you a helping hand. What with the allowance you get from your father-in-law and what with the money you earn at your dressmaking, you should be able to make ends meet."

"Yes, but what's going to happen when baby comes? You've just admitted that's going to make all the difference. Will I still have to be the breadwinner?"

"Tut, tut, things aren't as black as you try to paint them," said Tertsa-Roisa, anxious to retrieve her previous indiscretion. "Please God, to-morrow I'll talk things over with your father-in-law. And I'll have something to say to Lipa as well. And, believe me, by the time your father-in-law has finished with Lipa, Lipa will be a new man. You mark my word! Anyway, when baby comes Lipa will become a good family man and he will settle down to work in earnest, because once he becomes a father everything will be different."

"I hope so! Although it sounds too good to be true. Anyway, what use are all these promises? Haven't I had enough of promises? At present I have to sit up night after night, sick and pregnant, all alone, like a dog on a chain. I sit up for hours on end, waiting for him, and when the feeling of sickness comes on, I have to go and fetch myself a glass of water, with no one to lift a finger for me or say a kind word to me. Not once has he dropped in of an evening to see how I'm getting on; not once in two years has he offered to take me out. If he had any decency in him he would ask me to go with him to the theatre once in a while, but not him! No, not him!"

"Do you get Yiddish plays in Antwerp?"

"Of course we do. We have just had a marvellous company of strolling players come over from London. And do they make you laugh? They make you roar! People say there's one particular actor who sings such funny songs, that when you hear him you laugh till you get the belly-ache. Lipa once brought home a sheaf of papers with all the songs written out, so as he could learn them off by heart,

and I hear nothing else these days but him singing the same songs over and over again. One of them goes like this:
'Anna's the girl who's fat and flighty,
Ever seen her wearing her naughty nightie? . . .'
"Lipa's simply crazy about that actor. But have I ever been to see the play? Oh, no! I don't matter! I can stay at home like a dog on its chain. It's not worth living, this sort of life isn't, believe me!"

"What do you care about the theatre? Rubbish! You should worry! I've lived all these years, thank God, without ever once having been to the theatre, and I'm none the worse off for it, am I?"

"Things are different nowadays. It's a husband's duty to take his wife to the theatre. No modern woman would stand for what I stand. It's a living death, that's what it is, God forgive me for saying so!" Again she wept—and wept bitterly.

Deborah listened, stupefied. She felt amused, yet rather sorry for her sister-in-law, and this compassion was intermingled with other vague emotions which brought the tears into her eyes; but she cried so softly, that the two women in the opposite bed continued their conversation undisturbed. The younger one complained and whimpered, the elder one tried to pooh-pooh it all. At last they both fell asleep. Deborah made some attempt to review all that she had overheard, but her head was light and no matter how hard she tried to concentrate, her thoughts kept scattering like so much smoke. They were strange thoughts, as strange and incoherent as the scraps in a beggar's bag. She fell asleep, and rose early with a headache.

"Hope you had a good night's rest?" Lipa greeted her with a broad, ambiguous smile.

His wife gave him an ugly look, then she turned with appealing eyes to her mother-in-law. There, that was the sort of man he was, nothing better than a brute! The more he showed himself in his true colours, the better she would like it. Let him get on with his little flirtation, by all means. . . .

Deborah replied saying that she had slept very well. Again she noticed her husband staring across at Lipa with that unbrotherly look in his eyes that seemed to say, "Go to hell!" Much to her own surprise she was conscious of a keen sense of pleasure at finding herself the centre of these little jealousies.

After breakfast she went out on a sightseeing tour of the city with her husband. It was a perfect morning, the air was fresh and pure as though cleansed by yesterday's rainfall. Deborah looked straight up into her husband's face. But for his trimmed beard, Berish was so much like Lipa, one could scarcely tell the two brothers apart. She recalled the conversation she had overheard in bed last night, and she brooded over her sister-in-law's plight, a plight that might very soon be her own. It was only natural that she should feel grave misgivings, even dread, and she strove hard to summon up such emotions, for they would have been far, far easier to endure than that dull little pain which afflicted her relentlessly, unremittingly, like a worm slowly eating its way into her heart. Would this young man walking by her side do as Lipa did— would he pop a sweetmeat into her mouth and then go away to gamble in a café, while she sat at home, the neglected wife? She was trying hard to think on these lines, but instead she found herself wondering whether the kitchen in her parents' home in Warsaw was in a mess, now that she was gone; and she found herself passing judgment on Antwerp as a repulsive and ghastly town from which she must flee—at once. . . .

In parts the city was quite dead: one could quite safely go to sleep in the middle of the roadway, without any fear of being disturbed. The dwelling-houses were small, mainly two-storied, and they all stood spick and span like newly scoured pots and pans. The pavements were abnormally clean, too clean to be trodden on with comfort. It was like wearing new clothes. The gleaming window-panes solemnly reflected the silent streets. The motionless lace curtains traced patterns of dancing nude women and cherubs with fleshy little legs rather like the legs of her sister-in-law's baby. The luxurious blinds were of a quality unsurpassed by anything Deborah had ever seen in Warsaw or for that matter in Berlin.

They passed through thoroughfares wide and narrow, and much the same pattern unfolded itself repeatedly. Everywhere was the cleanliness of a newly washed corpse. In one of these residential streets, however, the solitude was shattered by the sudden arrival of a costermonger's little cart drawn by two large, workmanlike, fawn-coloured dogs. On the threshold of each house a housewife appeared with a face as clean as her doorstep. The beefy costermonger favoured the ladies with a sweet smile, and he addressed them with the courteousness of a diplomat. For their part the ladies smiled back at him as if they regarded him as their equal. And this was their strange greeting, which consisted of only a single word.

He: "*Madame!*"

She: "*Mynheer!*"

It was like a military salute. And their business transacted, the smiling ladies vanished at once behind their polished doors, as if the city were under a curfew.

Really, it was fortunate that a passing horse left its droppings behind in one of those soporific streets. But for that, one would never have seen the energetic little woman come bustling out of doors with a pail and shovel in her hand, nor would the excited little sparrows have flown down from the housetops. And the monotony would have been quite unrelieved.

All this while her husband made no attempt to make conversation: he was as dull and silent, as respectable and bright and shiny as the streets through which they were passing.

An elderly gentleman hailed her husband "*Mynheer!*" She listened to their incomprehensible chatter in a tongue which sounded like a cross between German and Yiddish, and although at times she felt certain the phrases had a familiar ring about them, she was unable to follow the gist of it. Her husband paused to stroke his beard reflectively, and just as he was about to resume the conversation, the elderly gentleman politely raised his hat and with a knowing shake of his fleshless double chin, vanished down a side-street.

Without offering any explanation her husband stopped, and suddenly brought one of the lifeless houses to life by rapping at a brightly varnished door with a gleaming brass knocker. The door opened cautiously, and a nose peeped out through the aperture. Behind the nose was a woman.

"*Mynheer!*" she said.

"Is the flat on the second floor to let?"

The woman opened the door another inch or two, and after sub-jecting Berish to a searching scrutiny she went on to study Deborah's new velvet costume.

"Can we see the flat?" asked Berish. Obviously it was still to let, hence the scrutiny.

The landlady gave the young couple another shrewd look before rousing herself from her reverie.

"Why, of course!"

She asked them into the vestibule and promised to be with them again in a moment, then vanished behind the broad, prosperous-looking door of her parlour. The linoleum underfoot was bright and slippery; the hat-rack had a dazzling polish; and the pedestal bearing the aspidistra was positively brilliant. The lamp overhead was adorned with a large red shade, and on the walls hung massive framed portraits of old men wearing curly grey wigs on their heads and intricate white ruffles on the sleeves of their blue coats. They were a grim crowd. And beneath them hung many smaller portraits of stern-faced dogs that in some strange way seemed to bear a fam-ily resemblance to the men above. On the strip of blue carpet run-ning the length of the vestibule a kitten was struggling playfully with a cotton-wool sparrow. The woman returned.

"This way, please!"

They followed her up the stairs. It was an imposing staircase, with a blue carpet climbing up the varnished white steps. The brass carpet rods gleamed importantly. The little window on the landing above was draped with a small curtain of a dazzling white. A young knight on horseback smiled down at the strangers from his tiny frame on the wall. From one of the doors on the landing a young brunette emerged, in a very low-cut red gown, with many sparkling rings on her slender, swarthy fingers. She, too, smiled down at Deborah and her husband—a faint smile which broadened immensely as she exchanged a greeting with the landlady.

Next came a flight of bare, rough wooden stairs. The transition was at once sudden and saddening. The unexpected sound of thumping feet struck a discordant note. But the rooms on the top floor, for all their emptiness, were not uncheerful, being bright and lofty and airy. The wallpaper was cheap, but colourful and clean. And the ceilings, although by no means as ornate as in the lower part of the house, were still profusely moulded. A refreshing draught was blowing in through the large, wide-open windows.

The rent was reasonable enough for a high class residential locality. Not that money mattered to a man like Berish, who had been promised a dowry by his father. So he decided to take the flat. Deborah told him that it was all the same to her: he was to do as he pleased. She confessed to having no opinion on the subject, which was perfectly true. The landlady interrogated her new tenants like a detective. Who were they, what were they, where did they come from, and why? It was only because they were such a nice-looking couple and would not bring any children into the house that she let them have the flat so cheaply.

"If I take kindly to people, I'm always willing to make sacrifices. I just happen to be made that way," she said, as she handed them their receipt, and so, with her good wishes to cheer them, and with the knowledge that they now had a home of their very own, they went on their way.

Berish was jubilant. What a glorious neighbourhood! What a marvellous flat! And, best of all, what a long way from his relatives' place! What a pity, though, that his wife was so gloomy, so icy cold! Nothing, not even her new home, seemed to please her. Her mind seemed to be preoccupied with all manner of things, but apparently he was not one of those things. Now how could any normal brain contrive to be so busy? It was odd, but whenever he spoke to her she seemed to start and shudder a little, as though she were dreaming.

"Maybe it's partly my fault. I ought to be more of a man," he thought. She did, when spoken to, respond after a fashion. Yes, but even then there was something faraway about her. There she was at his side, yet she wasn't there. That was a very funny thing. Now, what could a fellow do to liven her up? If he had it in him to conquer his shyness he would certainly ask her outright what was the reason for her absent-mindedness. Maybe she was feeling tired or ill. She did not act that way out of spitefulness. No, it was not spite. "I suppose she'll start taking to me when she gets to know me better. At present we're almost complete strangers"—he sought consolation—"but I think that swine Lipa has found out the way things are between us, and he'll be crowing over me like the devil. Never mind, Lipa can go to hell!"

Whatever blemishes Levrick Street may have had, a state of torpor and deadness was not one of them. Its houses were no bigger than elsewhere, but they were certainly not clean to a fault. Nor was there anything melancholy about this busy little street. A great many men, young and old, were to be seen picturesquely clad in the flowing robes of orthodox Polish and Galican Jewry. And each man wore a beard that was unique in character, whether short or long, red or black or grey. There were some beards that finished up in a sharp point, others that ended in fluff; beards that had only just been combed and beards that had never been combed at all. There was a great coming and going, endless bustle, in Levrick Street, and the little streets all round it. Men of all ages walked about gesticulating expressively in endless arguments.

Here, too, Jewish tradesmen were selling their wares from dog-drawn barrows, but the very dogs looked more human—they were more animated, they wore a more businesslike air and lent a touch of quaintness to the street scene.

Children were running wild and yelling at their play, just like children in Warsaw. One gang was chasing an elusive cat that looked as it if had been rubbed up the wrong way. The womenfolk were not shy of lingering on their doorsteps; in no way did they behave as if the city were under curfew. Shops there were in plenty, and of every description. Evidently the inhabitants of that part of the town needed something more substantial than purity of air and of flag-stones to keep body and soul together. The Jewish womenfolk bargained vehemently with the Jewish tradesmen: they raised their voices and did not even trouble to smile sweetly. The stores were small, crowded, and scarcely a shop-window but displayed the sign

"KOSHER." But even these signs were different one from the other; the letters ran irregularly, usually with one or two missing, rather like teeth in an old man's mouth.

The whole place was bubbling over with life. It brought back memories of Warsaw; but because realities are never so real and vivid as memories, Deborah's pangs of nostalgia were all the more poignant.

When Deborah and Berish got back, and Berish smilingly broke the news about the flat, his beetroot-faced sister-in-law puckered up her snub nose in disapproval, while his big-bosomed sister took him to task for having "run away" to so remote and unfriendly a neighbourhood. The master of the house was still moping, so he disdained to make any comment. But Lipa, though he was not on speaking terms with his younger brother Berish, patted him on the shoulder with mock encouragement, crying:

"Well done, brother! You're not going to live in the Ghetto, like us paupers, are you? Of course you're not! A rich man like you!"

"Really, fancy going such a long way out when you might just as well have lived locally," said Tertsa-Roisa, likewise showing her displeasure.

"I can't see what all the fuss is about, mother. The flat is ideal, the rent is reasonable, what more can you want?" Berish protested.

"Have you paid a deposit? You have, eh? Well, I suppose it can't be helped now."

"No, it can't be helped. He hates his own flesh and blood, he's an apostate, that's the trouble. Am I right?" said Reb Baruch Laib grimly, turning to Lipa for sympathy.

Lipa gleefully, proudly, stroked his flowing red beard.

"He's so refined, father, that's the explanation. When I get that refined, I too, will desert the Ghetto! . . ."

For seven nights running the family sat down to a ceremonial nuptial supper of sorts, and then at long last on the morning after the final banquet—Reb Baruch Laib and Tertsa-Roisa made ready to set out on the long journey homewards. They had finished packing their bags, which now lay stacked up on the floor of the living room, and Lipa had gone out to hail a taxi. But still Reb Baruch Laib showed no intention of handing over the promised dowry to the newly married couple. On the contrary, he seemed determined completely to ignore his obligations. Early in the morning he and Berish had locked themselves up in Lipa's room for a private quarrel, every word of which could be plainly heard throughout the house. Reb Baruch Laib roared like an angry beast:

"Don't pester me! Don't follow me about like a suspicious creditor! You needn't worry, I'll settle my accounts with you. I'll put paid to all my debts, believe me! What! You want me to furnish your home for you? You do, eh? You want a luxury home, is that it? It suits Lipa to share his home with Rebecca, but you—you swollen-headed fool!—you must needs go away to live in an expensive neighbourhood like a man of independent means. Very well, then I must assume that you *are* a man of independent means. You know your own pocket best. But please, whatever you do, don't bother me!"

"Father, how many more times must I tell you that the rent for my flat isn't much higher than what Lipa is paying. Don't be unreasonable!" Here Berish paused, as if choking with rage. "Do you think anyone in his senses is going to live in a stinking hole like this when he has a reasonable chance of getting out. I want something clean and decent."

"D'you mean to tell me, you swine, that this isn't good enough for you? Why, believe me, your wife never had a better home or a better father than Baila."

"Don't mention them in the same breath!" said Berish scornfully.

Reb Baruch Laib very nearly burst a blood-vessel. His tiny eyes became all bloodshot.

"Say that again, will you! Say that again! So I'm not to mention them in the same breath? So that's how things are!"

"Take it easy! Don't get excited! You know very well you're not on speaking terms with Baila's father, even though he happens to be

your own brother. So why pretend? It's not for you to take his or even
his daughter's part!"

"You impudent swine! Why, I'll give you the thrashing of your life!
You apostate!"

Reb Baruch Laib was just beginning to let himself go; he was just
beginning to indulge himself—for days now he had been itching and
craving for a really big scene—when, much to his disgust, a neighbour looked in to bid him godspeed. And when the exchange of
courtesies was over, he found that his fury had abated. The craving
was still there, but the time was too short for him to work himself up
again properly. Sorrowfully he realised that he would have to postpone his outburst until he got back to Warsaw. He would have it out
with Reb Avram Ber and Raizela. And, by God, were they going to
catch it!

Meanwhile his wife was annoying him. She was getting on his
nerves by her feeble efforts to act the peacemaker. If she did not
desist he would—but no, he would not do a thing. The psychological moment had passed, and now there was nothing more to be said.
He paced the clammy, malodorous floor in silence. Once or twice he
stopped and growled, but went on again, backwards and forwards, as
if to hasten the hour of departure.

However, at the last moment, when the taxi was waiting at the
front door, he plunged his hand into his inner pocket and produced
his wallet, which was still bulging with fat wads of bank-notes. Lipa's
mouth began to water, he licked his lips and held his breath. Reb
Baruch Laib picked out three 100-franc notes, and stuffed them hurriedly into Deborah's hand.

"Be thrifty! Waste not, want not! Don't spend it all on furniture,
as you will need some money to tide you over the next few weeks.
I'm very short after all the expenses I've incurred over the wedding,
and it'll be some time before I can let you have any more money.
Well, good-bye, and God be with you! May God be your only support and may you never want help from any one."

Tertsa-Roisa kissed Deborah good-bye, wished her happiness,
and even shed a tear. The old woman had wept so copiously at this

parting from her "children," that she was ready now to shed tears at the slightest provocation. The mistress of the house was unable to see her parents off because she could not leave the little one. Baila was feeling a little sick, so Deborah also stayed behind, and only the menfolk accompanied Reb Baruch Laib and Tertsa-Roisa to the Central Station.

"Any message for your mother?" asked Tertsa-Roisa, just as the taxi was about to move off.

"No!" Deborah answered, and she burst into tears like a lost child.

"Come, come! You mustn't carry on like that!" her mother-in-law chided her with a laugh. "You're not a baby now, you're a married woman!"

There was yet another indiscriminate shower of blessings. The womenfolk stood waving at the taxi as it moved down Levrick Street. They stood shrieking at the taxi as it gathered speed. The children all yelled in chorus, telling grandma what presents they wanted her to bring when she came again to Antwerp. And then the taxi turned the corner: it vanished out of sight. . . .

Deborah was unable to check her outburst. Every time she wiped her eyes, a new and mightier flow of tears came welling up. Disgraceful . . . a married woman . . . behaving like a baby . . . She vented her feelings on the bank-notes which she still clutched in her hand. She crumpled them up with all her strength. It gave her a thrill—a curious thrill of relief. She had not counted the money, but she realised that it could help her to accomplish the impossible: for instance, it could help her to run away. Already she was seriously considering how to escape, even though a few moments ago the very idea would have seemed utterly fantastic. A few moments ago she had felt that she was doomed for all time.

"If you're not careful, Deborah, you'll tear the notes to shreds," said Baila, greedily watching the convulsive movements of Deborah's fingers.

Deborah put the notes away in her handbag. Baila looked on with the intentness of a cat that has seen a mouse, and is crouching to pounce. And then, unexpectedly baulked of her prey, an expression of surprise, weariness and self-pity settled on her face. How many notes did Deborah have? For aught she knew, there were only two or as many as ten. So strong was her curiosity, that in the end she finally decided to ask Deborah outright. She would put the question in an amicable, matter-of-fact way—that was the best approach. She hit on the right sort of careless phrase, and was just about to open her mouth when, unfortunately, Berish walked in.

"Come on, put your coat on and let's go out," he said to his wife, but with his eyes fixed suspiciously on his sister-in-law.

Baila left the room in a huff. Berish was soon back from the station; but where was her man Lipa? Her man Lipa had most assuredly gone out to spend the rest of the day with his boon companions. Such was life! A worthy woman like herself was treated worse than a dog, a silly little girl like Deborah had all the luck in the world. And thinking thus, Baila swallowed a pink pill that tasted terribly bitter—almost as bitter as her own feelings. . . .

The sun had broken through the clouds and was shining brightly.

"Well, Deborah, everything's going to be all right," said Berish as soon as Baila was out of the way. "I had a world with father at the station, and he explained everything. He told me he was rather short of money at the moment, and that's why he couldn't let us have our full dowry on the nail, but he'll let us have the balance later. After all, it's no use grousing: it only makes matters worse. Just a little confidence and everything will come right. Father did the same with Lipa's dowry—he paid it in instalments."

Deborah made no reply, she was not interested. In her imagination she was visualising herself at the railway booking office buying a ticket to Warsaw. And as soon as she was home again she would refund the money she had taken, which really belonged to her husband. That was reasonable and fair enough. Yes, but what folly, what madness had possessed her to do all she had done so far? Why had she run away from home in the first place? She had been blind not to foresee the crushing loneliness that lay in store for her when all her ties with the past were broken. Life here was meaningless: it had no content, it was empty, quite empty. How fascinating her life had been! Even her sufferings had not been bereft of a deep inner relish. Now she was face to face with nothingness. She was all alone with a stranger whose presence she could not endure. Why could she not endure him? That she did not know. She was in a foreign land among new-found relatives who filled her with loathing. And how they all hated her! Why did they hate her? That she did not know. . . .

Deborah took out the three bank-notes and handed them over to her husband.

"What? He only gave you three hundred francs? Good heavens, he told me he'd given you five hundred! I hope he forks out soon, or we'll be in a jam. That's too bad! Still, I suppose the old man won't keep us waiting too long. I understand Lipa's going to get a tidy sum too. When he gets his, we'll get ours, I guess. Lipa keeps on the right side of father by all manner of tricks. He pretends he's pious, grows a long beard, tells a pack of lies, cringes, and generally makes a fool of the old man. He's cunning is Lipa, but what a blockhead!"

Deborah laughed a malicious little laugh.

Her husband looked at her with covetous eyes. What a tempting little woman, and she was his own wife!

"Before we go any further, let's have something to eat," he said, and he took her to the cafeteria in Tietz's departmental stores, in the centre of Antwerp. They lunched on sardine sandwiches, which he obtained from a slot-machine built flush into the wall.

He was in a happy mood. His wife was a woman who went in for thinking. Well, what did she think of him now? Surely, thinker or no thinker, she could not help feeling astonishment and admiration at the way he conjured up sardine sandwiches out of a solid wall! He entertained her to another of his favourite tricks. He dropped a coin into a slot, and out popped two glasses of bright, frothy beer. Deborah declined the beer, so he brought her some coffee.

Berish was radiant with joy, his face was wreathed in smiles. He took his wife round the furniture shops, where everything was terribly expensive.

"Bah!" said Berish. "These people are barmy! All fancy prices!"

However, in the end the furniture dealers turned out to be perfectly sane, so he decided to buy no more than a couple of beds for the time being—beds being essential—and a table and a few chairs.

"As soon as we get the rest of the dowry, we'll complete the home in style!"

Deborah was much amused by the whole stupid business. She very nearly told him that for her part she was willing to forego the furniture, if only he would advance her a loan for her fare back to Warsaw. But she said no such thing. She merely told him that Reb Baruch Laib had warned her not to expect any more money for some time to come, as he was out of funds.

"Really? Well, he told me something different. What he said to me was, 'I'll send you the rest of your dowry as soon as I get back home.'"

"Well, he may do."

She flushed. Yes, she liked the beds. She liked everything. The shopkeeper rubbed his hands. He chose the furniture and fixed the prices to suit himself, and the bashful young couple accepted without demur. They were just the kind of customers he dreamt of in his dreams. And now they had come true! . . .

CHAPTER XV

They had settled down in their new home. They had already had letters from their parents in Warsaw bearing the new address.

The rooms they occupied on the second floor were large and airy and empty—all the more empty for being so large, dwarfing what little furniture there was. The floors were without any sort of covering. And the flight of stairs leading down to the first floor was as indecently bare as it had been when they first viewed the flat. Emptiness, vast and depressing, filled their new home.

All day long Berish reclined, fully dressed, on the bed. He usually lay face upwards, saying not a word. But there was no mistaking his enjoyment of life. It was a good life, this! It was fine for a man to get away from his relatives and live in a home of his own.

Deborah was puzzled to see him thus idling his time away. Did he not profess to be a diamond-cutter? Then why was his diamond-cutting machine always covered up in its blue dust-sheets? The advice which her brother-in-law had tended to her on her first night in Antwerp would often recur to her now. She also recalled the pathetic conversation she had overheard in bed that night. But, strangely enough, these things never worried her. What did worry her was her husband's constant companionship. He was always with her, and she felt terribly uneasy in his presence. She felt as if a worm had eaten its way into her heart and was constantly sapping her strength away. Now she knew the meaning of the word "heartache." Not that she could have defined it, say, to a doctor. As a matter of fact, the physical pains at the heart, which had once caused her so much suffering, had stopped now. The new ache was not a real ache, yet it was more agonising. The only relief she knew was when her husband went out. Then all her cares would be forgotten. Once, when she was all by herself, she even burst into song. But it was very seldom that he did go out and leave her by herself. . . .

They had been living together for more than two months now. The money Reb Baruch Laib had left them was nearly all gone. The hope they had entertained of Reb Baruch Laib paying the rest of the dowry was completely gone. Lipa had sent a sneaking letter to his father, informing him that Berish had shaved off his beard, that Deborah was no longer wearing her wig. On the receipt of this startling news Reb Baruch Laib wrote the newly married couple a very long and very fierce letter, in which he heaped on them all the abuse and curses he could think of. He was especially angry with Deborah, whom he "excommunicated." It was her evil influence, he argued, that had led Berish into sinfulness; by himself he would never have done such a diabolical thing as to cut off his beard. He, Reb Baruch Laib, being a loving father, had gone to no end of expense to give to his son the daughter of a rabbi, as a shining example of godliness. But behold, instead of walking the ways of God, she was actually perverting and seducing the innocent boy, dragging him into the abyss. Would anybody have believed such a thing to be possible? If he, Reb Baruch Laib, had harboured the least suspicion, would he have exerted himself as he had done, all for the sake of marrying his son off to an indecent wench? And a consumptive wench at that! And so forth. And he finished up by assuring the newly married couple that they would never get any more money from him so long as they lived.

Some days after this letter had come she asked her husband how it was that he never did any work.

"Because there's no work to be done, my sweet, there's none to be had for love or money!" he said in reply, catching her round the waist and forcibly clasping her to his bosom.

Deborah tore herself from his embrace with dread and loathing. He was constantly filled with glee for no apparent reason, but surely this latest outburst was sheer craziness! Berish made as if to gather her up in his arms again. Why should he be a puny weakling, and act the shy youngster with his own wife? But he withdrew, of his own accord.

"You're just like a baby, and seem to be frightened of me, as if I were a stranger, a monster trying to assault you," he summoned up courage to administer a manly rebuke. He meant to break the ice once and for all. He hoped she would apologise, plead bashfulness—the sort of bashfulness that time alone would cure. He, himself, had been shy enough at first, but look at him now! . . . "I guess you're worrying about father's letter, but you mustn't take seriously all he says. He'll fork out. He's only trying to put the fear of the Lord into us. He has that blustering way with him. But I never take his threats to heart."

"I'm not worrying. I'm not even interested."

Tut, tut! how extraordinarily shy she was! He ought to do something about it. He might take her to the theatre. That would infuse a bit of life into her.

Deborah escaped into the kitchen to cook the dinner. But she could not shake him off. He followed her in. Making himself helpful as best he could, he grabbed hold of a pail and unwittingly splashed its contents all over the floor. If only he were less obliging, if only he would keep to himself!

"To-morrow night we're going to the theatre," he announced, gazing into her eyes.

"We can't afford to," she said, taking him into her confidence. "All we possess now is twenty francs." This, also, was by way of giving him a hint that it was high time he went out and found some work.

"Well, well, anyone would think we were broke!" he said merrily, and the hint passed him by. . . .

The days wore on. He was unable to take her to the theatre, but he still went on beaming with joy. The only thing that marred his bliss was her woebegone expression. All she seemed to do was worry, worry, worry!

"I bet she thinks I'm lazy and shy of work," a thought suddenly occurred to him. "I bet the in-laws have been at her, telling her a pack of lies about me. I'll soon find out."

"Deborah, you do understand, don't you? It's not my fault there's no work to be had for love or money. Father simply will *have* to help out, whether he likes it or not. I guess the family have been telling you the usual pack of lies about me. They even write sneaking letters to father about me. They think it's good business: the less money he sends me, they reckon, the more he'll have left over for them. You see my point, don't you? If there's no work to be had I can't produce any from under my hat. Or can I?

"Of course not!"

"Lipa's been unemployed for eighteen months now. It's only because father sends him a weekly allowance that he's able to make ends meet. And he can thank his lucky stars that Baila works her fingers to the bone to keep him. He never earns a cent, never. As for my brother-in-law, although he's so mighty stuck up and thinks himself wonderfully clever, do you think he ever turns an honest penny? Not him! He's simply a great big windbag, a helpless nincompoop. If father were to stop supporting him, he'd be out in the street with all his brats, starving, in no time. He just can't stand on his own two feet, that man! Father's constantly plying him with dire threats and 'final' remittances. And father will do the same to us, don't worry!

"Do you know, Baila would be the happiest woman on earth if Lipa was as fond of her as I am of you. She's terribly jealous because she knows I spend all my time with you—not like Lipa, who's always out on the spree till the small hours gambling away whatever money his wife earns for him. I don't mind confessing, though, that if Baila were *my* wife I'd do just the same as Lipa, and worse. Not only would I leave her to fret her heart out till the small hours—I'd leave her for good."

Deborah listened with rapt attention.

So that's how things were. Her only support in life was to be none other than Reb Baruch Laib. Meanwhile in her sweet ignorance she had infuriated the very man to whom henceforth she must look for her bread and butter. She had discarded her wig, her husband had removed his beard. What a future! To be for ever at the tender mercy of Reb Baruch Laib was, indeed, a delightful prospect. However, now she knew precisely where she stood. . . . But, why on earth was her husband so remarkably cheerful? Did he not take his father's threats seriously? Maybe that was the explanation. Anyhow, it was no concern of hers. Whatever happened she could not go on living with this man who was supposed to be her husband. The best way out—and the most honourable—would be for her to confess her true feelings: when once he knew the reason for their uneasy conjugal relations he and she would part. . . .

"It's strange," Berish resumed. "But the more callous Lipa is, the more Baila loves him. She's quite crazy about him. She nags him, curses him, and weeps, but all the same she can't resist giving him every cent of her earnings, knowing perfectly well that he'll only lose the money at cards. And look at you! You're such a baby! A sweet baby, but a very naughty one! Whenever I try to take you in my arms, you shove me away, as if I was trying to kill you. Let me be quite frank with you—I resent it. There, I'm being perfectly honest with you!"

Yes, thought Deborah, it was best to be perfectly frank and honest. For her part, she too must hold nothing back. She must tell him all about herself, the terrible mistake she had made. She was the chief culprit and deserved her punishment. She had abandoned herself, gloatingly, to an *idée fixe* that everybody, even her own mother, hated her and was anxious to be rid of her; a prey to this delusion she had deliberately brought disaster upon herself, hoping thus to inflict pain on others—a fantastic imaginary act of revenge on imaginary persecutors . . . with what terrible results!

"I say, you are easily upset," he exclaimed, "Tut, tut!" Her eyes were brimming with tears and she hung her head, as though abashed by his rebuke.

"Listen to me," she said, after a prolonged and awkward silence, "and listen carefully. I am going to be perfectly candid with you. I hope you will understand . . ." and she told him her story, concluding with the avowal "And the worst part about it is that I love him still, in spite of myself. That makes our situation—yours and mine—impossible. If I love *him*, I can't love you."

Her husband heard her out in silence, and the more he heard, the more he was fascinated by her. He was overwhelmed by such a passionate longing for her that he was willing to overlook any confession she might make . . .

She turned towards him to await his reply. She could see that her words had moved him, for his face wore a grim expression . . . and he was biting his nails furiously. She did not exactly relish the prospect of returning to the parental roof. On the other hand, if he asked for a divorce, as he was bound to, she need not return to Warsaw. How would she live? Well, to begin with, she could pawn all her jewellery . . . All manner of speculations as to her uncertain future went flitting through her brain.

But no, he was not going to ask for a divorce. Indeed, he had not a word to say for himself. He seemed actually to have regained his composure. There, he was smiling again! He had taken her hand and was patting it, trying as best he could to comfort her. How extraordinary! What a strange fellow! . . .

As time went on, all their jewellery found its way into the pawnshop. Only a few trinkets remained which would scarcely cover the price of a fourth-class ticket to Warsaw. Why did she not secretly dispose of them and go away while the going was good? Why not put an end to all this misery? As for the inevitable scandal, her parents would not eat her! Far better to face a scene, or even endure constant bickerings, than submit to this slow, relentless torture of the brain which could have only one unhappy ending—in the mad-house.

If only her husband were less angelic, how much easier her task would be! After hearing her unpalatable tale, instead of showing any self-pity, he had instead felt sorry for her. He had soothed her and said to her, "Never mind. Time heals all wounds. One day you will forget, and then, perhaps, you will learn to love me . . ." And he had even promised her that until she said she loved him, he would not molest her. Sometimes, though, he forgot his promise and sought intimacy.

"Well, well, well. What's the use of looking for work, when you know there's none to be had anyway," he would say at ever more frequent intervals as their plight grew more desperate.

Autumn came, then winter. Reb Baruch Laib for once in his lifetime proved as good as his word. He sent the "young sinners" not a cent. Berish began to search for work feverishly, but day after day he returned home with the same dismal tidings.

"Not a hope. There's an awful slump in the diamond trade, it's been like this for more than a year now. The whole town simply stinks of unemployment. What little work there is, is snatched up by the professional crawlers and cringers. They get down on their knees and lick the bosses' boots. I couldn't do that to save my life! It's the cadgers who get all the work, the others, like myself, hang around for hour after hour, only to be sent packing in the end—'No More!'"

Their home was bare and empty. Their stomachs were empty. And even her head felt empty—quite empty, yet she had not the strength to hold it erect.

And then, with grotesque mockery, the landlady began to wax indignant because the new tenants had not carpeted the top flight of stairs. Every time Deborah left or entered the house she was accosted by the stern old matron.

"How is it that you take no pride in the house like the tenant on the first floor? And you only just married! Really, young woman, it's disgraceful!" And as her tone towards the young woman on the second floor grew daily more harsh and contemptuous, it became more honeyed towards the lady on the first floor.

Deborah would promise to buy a strip of carpet "one day next week or the week after, for certain." She invented all sorts of excuses; her favourite one was that she was looking for a pattern to match the rest of the staircase. But the landlady would not be fobbed off with idle pretexts.

"I know a shop where you can pick up a real bargain, just the thing you're looking for. I'll take you there myself! Now, that's more than I would do for anybody else, but you're really such a nice girl! I like doing favours to people I'm find of. I'm just made that way! If you weren't so awfully negligent, I'd like you even better than the person on the first floor. I hate people who are stuck up and think themselves God Almighty! Now then, we'll take tomorrow afternoon off and trot along together."

No, unfortunately Deborah would be busy to-morrow. She appreciated the offer and would certainly avail herself of it some other day. And as she made her apologies, she thought: "If I had any money, you witch, I wouldn't spend it on a carpet, but on food. Can't you see I'm hungry?"

Thus the days went by; they turned into weeks and mounted up into months. Occasionally her husband found an odd job. With the proceeds he paid the rent, she settled the bill that she had run up at the grocers', and then they were left penniless once again.

In none of her letters home did she as much as hint at the dire need she was in. What was the use, for her father was himself only a poor man who could scarcely support his own little home? Even if he had been able to help, she preferred to go hungry rather than beg. And she had no wish to bring sorrow on her mother—a frail little woman whose health was failing and who had never known much happiness at the best of times. Her mother was not wholly to blame for all that had happened. Looking back on the past, Deborah found that her father too was at fault, for had he not willingly given his consent to the match? But where did the final responsibility rest, if not with herself? She and she alone was the real culprit, for she could have averted the whole tragedy simply by saying "No!" If she must point an accusing finger, she must point it first at herself.

It was only by chance that Deborah discovered how profoundly her attitude had changed. One day she received a very long letter from her mother, in which Raizela beseeched her to write home more fully and more often. "Do not make me suffer, do not keep me in nervous suspense by stinting your correspondence with me. I am your mother and I want you to confide in me. Tell me the truth, tell me if you are happy. I am terribly uneasy about you. Do not make my life unbearable. Believe me, if I have done you an injury, I now have my punishment in full. Do not make things worse for me . . ." Thus wrote Raizela—and Deborah found that her thrill of gratification was mingled with untold distress. She could never afterwards quite explain to herself what it was that impelled her to react the way she did, but there and then, without a moment's hesitation, she wrote back to say that she was completely mystified by her mother's letter, and there was certainly no justification for any remorse or uneasy forebodings. Thereafter all the letters that passed between Deborah and her parents were almost perfectly alike and almost perfectly meaningless.

"We were very glad to hear from you (her parents would write), and were indeed happy to learn that all is well with you, for which the Lord be praised. We too, thank God, are in good health. Pray God that we shall always have cause to rejoice in our mutual prosperity. With kind regards to your dear husband, etc."

And Deborah would write back in the same strain. Occasionally Raizela would renew her attempts to gain her daughter's confidence, but to no avail. There were times when Deborah yielded to the temptation of telling all. She would sit down and write endless letters; then, after filling many pages, she would stop to read what she had written, she would tear it all up and send off the usual postcard phrased in the usual way. Even when Deborah lay ill in bed, dispirited and hungry, she still insisted on telling her parents that she was enjoying good health, for which the Lord be praised, and so on and so forth . . .

So she became more and more estranged from her parents (although she still loved them in a new and aloof way), and she remained as much a stranger to her husband as when she had first set eyes upon him (although she was more and more conscious of his love for her). The iron entered into her blood. She learned to hate, to regard everybody with suspicion. All round her she saw enemies, masked and unmasked. Polite people were hypocrites. Rude people were deadly foes.

Whenever any of her husband's bachelor friends called in, she treated them so contemptuously that they withdrew quite crestfallen. When her sister-in-law with the big bosom and the blonde wig once paid a courtesy visit, Deborah openly accused her of having come as a spy on Reb Baruch Laib's behalf, a charge of which the poor woman was quite innocent. If anyone tried to tell Deborah a lie, be it never so harmless, she refused to let the falsehood pass unchallenged. Until very soon no visitor darkened her door.

When she had broken all bonds with the outside world, she found the loneliness almost intolerable. And still her husband aroused in her the selfsame loathing: his companionship tortured her. She could not endure his presence—for reasons beyond her understanding. And then came a time when her solitary confinement in the empty, poverty-stricken room played so badly on her nerves, that she would feel relieved to hear his footsteps coming up the stairs. But this feeling of relief was always short-lived. . . .

She passed the day in idleness, not that there was anything for her to do. If only she could read! But no sooner did she set eyes on a book, than a cloud of specks, like a swarm of troublesome insects, began to dart about all over the printed page, and these hovering specks would make her quite dizzy. The empty room around her would sway drunkenly, and she would have to put the book aside.

And then a host of strange fancies would take possession of her mind. She could not shake them off, no matter how hard she tried.

For instance, it might occur to her that she was really born to be a housemaid and now at last she must answer her true calling. She must go out at once and do something about it. She knew all the time that it was an absurd idea. What chance did she stand of getting a job as a housemaid when she looked more dead than alive? She knew she must chase the thought out of her head. But no, it would not budge! It clung to her like a leech, sucking the strength out of her. "False pride is your undoing," a voice whispered, "and it is better to be humble than to starve. Now is the time to act!" "No," said another voice, "it's all nonsense!" And so the crazy battle surged back and forth in her tormented brain, ceasing only when she was exhausted and everything within her was numb.

Then the next day a different canker would prey on her mind. The more it festered the more she would struggle to remove it; but soon she would have to acknowledge defeat. She would have to surrender herself to the one and only monstrous notion that nibbled and nibbled and nibbled until it gnawed through some barrier in her mind, and then a regular horde of similar thoughts, but each with a distinctive form of its own, went rampaging through her brain until everything was in a whirl. Then at last peace and quiet would descend on her.

But for her cowardice, she would have gone to see a doctor about it. That was indeed the only sensible thing to do. Yes, she would go to-morrow. But even as she formed this resolve, she knew she would not keep it, for there was one dread little word that she feared above all other words. Supposing the doctor were to utter that awesome word? Of course, in reality he would do nothing of the kind. And then she would be able to go home and laugh heartily at her own fears; she would at last be able to cure herself of this strange affliction. But she was too tired to go to-day. To-morrow . . .

So the days and the weeks and the months wore on, and each day, each week, each month was like an eternity. Nothing ever happened that had not happened before, except that Deborah and her husband had to move twice at short notice. This was a merciful respite for Deborah, although no sooner had she become accustomed to her new surroundings, than she relapsed into her old mental habits. At their first flat they were all but thrown out.

"We're not accustomed to having paupers in the house," said the landlady scornfully, having finally convinced herself that the top flight of stairs would remain bare for ever. She could see that all was not well with her second floor tenants, for Deborah was visibly shrivelling up, getting more haggard every day.

They found rooms in a tumbledown two-storied building in a working-class district.

The landlady was a poor widow who ran a little baker's shop, and she had too many worries to care whether or not Deborah carpeted the top flight of stairs. For that matter her own part of the staircase was so shabby—the linoleum was all scrappy and worn out—that the bare rough boards above looked comparatively respectable. It was not snobbery that impelled her to give her penniless tenants notice to quit. It was sheer necessity. Her young married nephew and his children, who were on their way to America from Russia, had got stranded in Antwerp, and she could do no less than put them up until such time as they might be able to resume their travels. So Deborah and her husband had to go.

They went to the cheapest place they could find on the outskirts of the city. Their front window overlooked a military installation replete with barracks and underground fortifications. The little street they lived in was made up of a row of tiny, old-fashioned houses on the one side, and of a long wall with a big iron gateway on the other.

Deborah would sit at the window all day, her elbows resting on the sill, her chin cupped in her hands, and she watched the men at their drill. "One, two! One, two!" roared the sergeant-major, and the tiny uniformed figures marched off down the parade ground with machine-like precision; at a distance they looked like schoolboys who were only playing at soldiers. These military exercises were a great attraction to Deborah, and she never voluntarily left her point of vantage for an instant. She felt that she was a little girl again, and although she was not allowed to join in the games she had the plea- sure of looking on.

Berish would be out all day. He had found himself a sweated job at twenty francs a week, a wage which enabled them to pay the rent and starve . . . She always felt very envious of the soldiers when the bugle sounded at mealtimes and bareheaded men carried across the parade ground huge cauldrons of soup that gave off a glorious steam. How it made her mouth water!

DEBORAH

Their new landlady was a Gentile—a short stocky woman with big hips and a neat coiffure, although her hair was so scanty on top that the parting down the middle looked more like a bald patch than anything else. She kept a small general stores, and sold ham and bacon at cut-throat prices. Her shop was always crammed with customers—most of them soldiers off duty—and of a Sunday there would be a regular struggle between those who wanted to get in and those who wanted to get out.

"Like moths around a candle," the neighbours would say with a knowing glance towards Georgette behind the counter. Georgette was the buxom young niece of the proprietress and according to local gossip she had not only conquered the army, but had broken the hearts of all the local shopkeepers. For them business was in the doldrums, and they were sick with jealousy. At one time they had even hatched a conspiracy to entice Georgette away and to poison Jacond, the aunt's dog, which was also a great favourite with the troops. One competitor, who was a widower, had even proposed marriage to Georgette, offering to put her behind a counter all of her own instead of having to work for a cross old aunt. He was sure she would yield to the temptation, especially as his own charms were irresistible. But man proposes and God disposes. Jacond was a wily dog, and all attempts at administering poison to him failed. As for Georgette, she would not dream of leaving her place, much less of marrying a widower.

Deborah was on the most amicable terms both with Jacond and Georgette. But Georgette never had a moment to spare the livelong day, and the old hag, her aunt, for some mysterious reason would never permit Jacond to pay any calls. Apparently she considered it beneath his dignity to do so. Whenever he did come upstairs, he had to steal his way up like a thief. Admittedly in the early days Deborah was rather scared of him. She would let him paw at her door and whimper away, until he took offence and stalked off in a sulk. But in time a tacit understanding sprang up between them. Their friendship began one day when he trotted in through the open door and set to fondly licking her heel. She did not shoo him off, although after he had gone she did brush down her leg at the spot where his fur had touched it. But by now both Deborah and Jacond had quite forgotten those early, aloof, diffident days, and they really were great pals. The moment he spied her on a Monday morning coming down the stairs with the rent-book and the rent in her hand, he would lose his head completely. He would rush up to greet her, then dash backwards and forwards across the shop, wagging his tail furiously. He fussed over her, put his tongue out and licked her and kissed her and then, quite overcome with ecstasy, rubbed his fleshy muzzle on the floor in canine homage . . .

What she feared most, had happened. Now if the landlady chose to do so, she could put them out on the street, and they might as well go and drown themselves in the Scheldt. . . .

Poor Jacond was quite distraught. Deborah had failed to put in her customary appearance with the rent on the Monday. Meanwhile he was under the stern eye of his mistress, who was determined that he should not slink upstairs. In the end, to make quite sure, she put him on the lead behind the counter, and for the second day running he was being held a prisoner there, for no good reason at all as far as he could see. . . .

The situation had become truly desperate. Berish's employer, who was himself only an "outdoor worker," had been unable to get a single job from the diamond-cutting factories during the past fortnight. There was a panic on the Bourse, and all business had practically come to a stand-still—simply because an Austrian crown-prince had been murdered in faraway Serbia.

"And yet people have the audacity to complain that there is no justice on this earth," Deborah mused aloud. "Here we are on the brink of war, all for the sake of Justice! How the conscience of the world is shocked when innocent blood is spilt, especially if that blood happens to be precious blue blood! Of course, ordinary red blood is cheap, inferior, and who cares if it is shed in interminable torments, drop by drop, day after day? I wonder if anyone would ever dream of stopping me in the street—'You look hungry. Let me treat you to a meal!' Ha, ha!"

She laughed until the tears came into her eyes. What a fool she was, talking away to herself, and pretending to be a sort of Karl Marx in petticoats! Ridiculous! . . .

But, seriously, if war was to break out, how would it all end? Might not things change for the better? After all, Simon himself had once prophesied as much during a heated debate: the next war, he declared, would be followed by a great social upheaval, there would be world-wide revolution, and then Socialism would become universal—it would even spread to Mars. . . . She remembered his very words. He always theorised boldly and confidently, then threw in a witticism, which far from detracting from his closely reasoned arguments would lend them all the more weight.

Simon! Simon! Simon! Enough of Simon! There was only one thing she cared about now—to end her present mode of life and to return to her parents before it was too late, before she went mad. She must save her reason. But how was she to get to Warsaw when she could not even afford a loaf of bread?

War was inevitable now. That was what a soldier had told Georgette earlier in the day. And Deborah could see for herself that something big was brewing. For the past few days the barracks across the way had been throbbing with activity. Flashing bayonets and flashing brass buttons everywhere! From morning to night officers were busy drilling new recruits. "One, two! One, two!" they kept roaring without cease, so that the words were now constantly ringing in her ears, and the diminutive soldiers, herded together like sheep, kept rhythmically stamping their heavy boots, "One, two! One, two!" It was beyond her understanding. By what mysterious mechanism did the threat of war between far-off Austria and Serbia galvanise these Belgian barracks into a state of furious preparation? All she knew was that if Belgium did become involved in hostilities, then her fate would be sealed—she could never hope to return home. As if she had any hopes of doing so even now in peacetime!

Her husband came in, shuffling his feet: he had been tramping the streets all day.

"War has broken out between Austria and Serbia. Some people say that Belgium is going to get mixed up in it."

"Really?"

They went to bed. Her husband's face was horribly livid. It was none of her business. Neither he nor she had eaten a crumb for two whole days.

Daylight had come once more, and again she was at her seat by the window.

If only she had the strength to go out in the streets and lose herself in the crowd as her husband did. That would be fine! There was something else she wanted to do, but it had slipped her memory. Oh yes, she wanted to return to Warsaw and join her parents before all Europe was ablaze! Of course, that was it! . . .

And then, even as she was thinking these hazy thoughts, a spasm of fear swept over her as she realised that her mind was wandering. This was her first taste of madness, sheer madness. She must pull herself together. How could she forget that she was penniless, that far from being able to set out on a long and costly journey, she could not even afford to buy herself a loaf of bread? How foolish of her to worry about the war, as if that could make any difference to her. She must remember always that there was only one thing she really wanted—food, food!

It was a shame though that she could not go along and see Meerel! Meerel was a kind soul and would surely have lent her the price of a ticket to Warsaw. Even if Meerel was to give her only a few coppers for a loaf of bread, that too would be splendid. Why not swallow her pride and try to buy some food on credit in the grocery shop down below? She ought to ask Georgette when the old woman was not about.

Meerel was such a lovable creature. Happy days! It would be wonderful if she and Meerel could go across the green meadows to the byre on the squire's estate. Meerel would give her a cup of milk straight from the cow—warm, creamy milk. And she would drink it up as eagerly as she had done in Jelhitz on those hot summer days when she was convalescing from a serious illness. Every morning, in the bright sunshine, she and Meerel would cross the meadows into the squire's estate. Oh, for those far-off days in Jelhitz! Was it very long ago? Yes, a long, long time ago!

She was only a child then of about eight. . . . It would be good to know that Meerel was still managing the dairy on behalf of the squire, who was too aristocratic and too lazy to administer his own estate.

He was a handsome gentleman, was the squire, and so courteous. He always gave her a magnificent nosegay to take home. One day he seated her on his lap, and made her feel so very ashamed of herself, but he said he would not let her go until she kissed him. How he did love to tease her!

And then his brother arrived, a mere boy, who resided abroad. That was the only visit he ever paid to the family estate in all the years that she lived in Jelhitz. He was supposed to be a law student, although he did not look it. Meerel said that he was attending a German university. Ha, ha! How well she remembered him, as if it were only yesterday, with his freckled face and great wild eyes. He followed her about wherever she went. In honour of his visit the squire held a garden party to which he invited all his tenants. The whole of the festive scene came back to her—she could see it all now; but beyond Jelhitz, beyond the fields and the orchards of the squire's estate, she could also see the barracks and the Belgian soldiers marching up and down in formation on the parade ground. The squire ordered cartloads of planks to be brought from the forest, and this timber was laid out to form a sort of floor over a large meadow. Peasants were busy with huge sheets of canvas studded with brass rings, putting up marquees. The canvas was grey. Yes, of course it was grey! A few policemen were brought in from a neighbouring town to keep order. Now the band was striking up a merry folk dance. Fiddlers were fiddling and drummers were drumming. Among the many side-shows was a Punch and Judy show. How the peasants guffawed to hear these rag dolls speak and quarrel, just like a real husband and wife, and when the husband began beating the wife, the crowd almost split their sides laughing. What a great throng of peasants. They must have come in from all over the countryside . . .

Suddenly Deborah burst out laughing . . . Now, the squire's younger brother would admonish the crowd, saying "Stop pushing! Stop pushing!" So the crowd nicknamed him "Stoppush." Before long his real name was forgotten, but his visit to Jelhitz was remembered for many years. "If only Stoppush would come back again," the people would say with a sigh of yearning. "What fun we would have." "And what a boon it would be for trade," the shopkeepers would remark, rubbing their hands in anticipation. Before her very eyes the dead past had come back, colourful and noisy. "Stoppush" tried to persuade her to accompany him into one of the marquees, so that he might show her what was going on inside; but she declined, for she was rather afraid of him. He then began to address her in German, as if he thought that by doing so he could more easily gain her confidence. At first she thought it was Yiddish.

"Haben Sie nur kein' Angst, Krausköpfchen!" he kept saying to her in a slow, deliberate way . . .

She started up from her reverie. The host of memories fled suddenly like spooks at cockcrow, leaving her breathless with surprise, but the sweet ecstatic sensation lingered on, and her lips were twitching, smiling with delight.

What now? Now that the pangs of hunger were gone, what ailed her? Yesterday, she had been so hungry! No, thank God, she was not hungry any more, not in the least. Only her head was aching more than ever.

She rose to her feet.

"Goodness, what's happened? I can barely stand on my legs. Why, I'm staggering! Hold on, hold on to the ledge! Good God, am I to become paralysed? No, it must not be! I'll go downstairs into the shop and ask Georgette. If the old woman's there, I'll even ask *her.* Maybe Georgette is on her own to-day, and she'll let me have a loaf on the sly. But no, she won't, she won't do anything of the sort. She'll just say 'Sorry!' as usual. 'I'm ever so sorry, but you know what the old woman's like, don't you? You remember the trouble I got into last time!' Poor Georgette, the trouble she got into last time! And there won't be another last time. . . ."

The sun was still shining. Was it morning or afternoon? She glanced across at the barracks' clock. Dinner hour! The soldiers were filling up their mess tins at the steaming field kitchen. They seemed to have nothing to do all day except eat, and then eat again! Not that she could have touched any of their food. By now even her bodily weariness was gone. Her limbs had ceased aching. She would try and walk, to see how she got on. Yes, it was quite easy: the stiffness had gone out of her legs and she felt as light as a feather. As light as a feather and all empty inside. No trace of a headache now. What did annoy her was the buoyancy of her head, it would not keep straight, but swayed from side to side like a leaf in the breeze. That was a very strange thing. . . .

Ah, here was her bed and she would lie down on it. Now that was better, much better!

She had not been resting for more than ten minutes when Georgette shouted up to her from the bottom of the staircase:

"Have you heard the latest? Germany has invaded us. It's war!"

Deborah heard her perfectly well, but she did not have the strength to shout back. What did she care, anyway? Still, supposing she had the money for a ticket, she would go back to her parents—at once. Before long, communications would be disrupted. The sergeant-major who walked out with Georgette every evening after shop hours had not shown up for quite a few days. . . . What had happened to him?

"What is the matter with me? Am I really going mad? Why am I obsessed with the impossible idea of getting back to Warsaw? This starvation is killing me . . ."

She lay perfectly still. Everything grew calm within her. There was not a thought in her head. She was devoid of all feeling. And then it was that a strange sense of bliss, beatific bliss, crept over her and took complete possession of her . . .

Suddenly she jumped out of bed. She feverishly assembled her whole wedding trousseau, with the long golden chain that had been put round her neck at her betrothal, as well as her husband's gold watch, throwing everything into one great heap. Her fingers were wonderfully deft and it was not long before she had done up all her spare chemises and underwear into another bundle. This she stuffed into the bright leather suitcase that her husband had held in his hand when she first set eyes on him in Berlin. She locked the door, leaving the key on top of the gas meter out on the landing. As she passed on her way through the shop, the landlady ignored her, but Jacond leapt up, straining at the leash, and he began to bark with such terrible fury that it seemed his tongue would drop out of his mouth. It was a long, lolling tongue, almost reaching the floor. No one could soothe the wretched dog. She kept drawing her cheeks in and out between her teeth. Out-of-doors a thousand suns were blazing over the city. The letter to her husband was finished. She hid it away under the pillow. Was there anything else needed doing before she left? No, nothing!

She took the suitcase and all that was in it straight to the municipal pawnbrokers. She was all a-tremble, her legs were sagging beneath her, her heart was beating violently as if, like Jacond, it was straining at the leash. The streets were busy with people hurrying home from work. She looked about her nervously. For all she knew she might run into her husband. So she began to fly along the pavements with the nimbleness of a child. She did not feel the impact of her feet on the flagstones—she was soaring onwards like a bird.

She was eager to get past the zoological gardens before closing time, when the wives of the wealthy diamond merchants would come trooping out into the streets. For this green and shady retreat was their habitual rendezvous in the summer. Too late! They were coming out now, all smiles, all jewels, all flesh. Some of them were so fat, they could scarcely waddle along. None the less, they looked immensely pleased with themselves. Deborah gave them a hurried look, then turned her gaze on the younger women, those with the flashing eyes—eyes full of sensual greed, of unquenchable voluptuousness. As they tripped along they conversed with many a coquettish gesture and mannerism. They contrived to vary the curves of their warm, pulsating bosoms, without ever losing their graceful poise. They were not women, but goddesses, for each held lightning in her hands, and when, thoughtlessly, the goddess raised her slender fingers, a streak of summer lightning flashed forth upon the world from great and lustrous diamonds. . . . They minced along at their leisure, for—unlike herself—they were not running away. No, of course not, they were only going home to meet their perfumed husbands who had spent the day speculating and profit-making on the Bourse.

What was the matter with her? She must hurry. She had no time to stand and stare. She quickened her pace. Her hands fluttered excitedly. She scurried along like a frightened rabbit.

Thank heavens, here was the pawnbrokers' shop and the door had closed behind her. She laid out her possessions on the counter, and gazed through the wire netting, which carved up the young assistant's face into a pattern of squares as he peered back at her.

"I don't know how much to ask, really I don't. Give me whatever you can, but please hurry!"

The young man's criss-cross wire-netting wrinkles widened out as he bent his head forward, and he repeated in a friendly voice:

"How much?"

She pushed the bundle towards him, and he carefully examined all her gowns, then placed her golden chain on the scales.

"All right," she said, "I'll take 130 francs."

"Very well!" said the wrinkled young man, pushing a wad of banknotes towards her under the wire netting . . .

"Number two platform. The train that's just come in over there. See it? It's due to leave at seven past. Change at Brussels."

"Yes please, a single ticket to Berlin," said Deborah, almost in a voice of entreaty, and her left eyelid flickered uncontrollably as if she were winking at the clerk behind the grating in the brightly lit, square little booking office.

Thank heavens, the train had started and she was in it, with her suitcase upon her trembling knees, and with her buoyant head turned towards the window, through which she could see the flaming sun as it burst through the trees and enveloped the treetops, touched the ponds and the meadows with crimson fire, gilded the hillocks, the church spires, the peasant huts, the bogs, the fallen leaves . . . And her spirits began to rise; the gloom that had weighed so heavily on her heart was dispelled, and life became like a song.

The train pulled up. Deborah was jerked forward. She got out on to the platform with all the other passengers. At a tiny canteen she bought herself a cup of coffee, two cakes and a small bag of acid drops. How delicious! What lovely cakes! And the flavour of the coffee surpassed anything she had ever tasted before.

Once more she was ensconced in a corner seat by the window. This was her favourite seat, the same as she had had on the outward journey a year ago. Only now everything was different. She was not travelling to Berlin to get married now—oh, no!—and she was so happy, so terribly happy. It was a boundless happiness such as she had never known before. Ah, the train was beginning to move. And all the newsboys and cigarette-vendors were hurriedly jumping off on to the platform. The train was crowded to suffocation, but surely no one was as happy as herself. She, and she alone, was possessed of that wild spirit of abandon that lifted her high above mortal cares and mortal responsibilities, she alone was experiencing that frenzy of joyous escape, which made her oblivious of the past and even of the future. It gave her strength and courage. The wheels of the train were grinding on the rails, and each distinct grind carried her further away from that strange man whose company she found harder to endure than physical pain and hunger, that strange man whose presence was even more repugnant than the abominable atmosphere that brooded over the whole city of Antwerp. She was free, and had not a care in the world. She did not even care about herself. Hurrah! Absolutely free!

The lamps in the train were all lit up. A stout man opposite her shut the window and drew the dark green blind. Resting their heads on cushions, shawls or coats, or—for the lack of anything better—on the bare boards, the passengers all sat back and did their best to go to sleep. A weedy youth, who was rather like one of the soldiers she had often seen at the barracks in Antwerp, reopened the window. But the stout man next to him gave him a withering look, accompanied by a contemptuous smile—it was an ugly smile that made her shudder—and then, without a word, he closed the window again with a bang. All the other passengers looked on unconcerned.

Where was she? It was daylight again, and she was still sitting in the corner seat. But the train was at a standstill, and the engine ahead was spluttering wrathfully, like a man coughing his lungs up. Dense clouds of smoke went floating past the window. And then the train began to move again. The stout man with the ugly smile was gone and in his place sat a middle-aged German woman with a big black hat perched on her head, and she was eating some sandwiches out of a linen bag.

Deborah glanced out of the window. Wide open spaces, a far-spreading sky, here and there a crooked tree. Near by a few children with sticks were chasing a cow. The cow was moving fast on her bandy legs, her udder swinging to and fro. There was a trace of a smile on the animal's comical face; indeed, she looked awfully stupid, even more so than the red and white cow on which Meerel used to milk in the squire's byre. Deborah laughed aloud.

She stood up, smoothed her crumpled coat with her fingers, and then, studying her own reflection in a tiny mirror, muttered to herself, ironically, "You do look beautiful!" Well, well, it was about time she went into the restaurant car and had a snack. She was ravenous. In front of her stood a cup of steaming coffee and two rolls. It only whettened her appetite and she wanted more. But she must not have any more, or she would run short of cash. Never mind, she would have another cup of coffee. She simply could not resist the temptation.

The repast finished, she returned to her compartment. But her seat was occupied. The weedy youth who had got himself into trouble the night before had taken advantage of her absence and was comfortably installed in the corner by the window. As good fortune would have it, though, the German woman with the big black hat was about to get out, and so Deborah was able to go on gazing out of the window to her heart's content. It was a great comfort to have this little window—but not great enough to make her forget her hunger. Her stomach was nagging worse than ever. How was it that the weedy youth opposite showed no signs of hunger? He had not had a crumb to eat throughout the long journey and yet he seemed to be none the worse for it. He was bearing up very well.

She must do likewise. Though she could not forget that she was hungry she would stop worrying. She fixed her attention on a solitary peasant's hut in the middle of a field. Tied up to this hut was a dog— she could have sworn it was Jacond, she had never seen two dogs so alike—and it was straining at its leash in a frenzy of despair and barking piteously. The poor dog was hungry! Now, what could that cosy little coil of smoke fluttering from the chimney-pot mean other than that the womenfolk within were busy cooking dinner. It could mean nothing else. How delightful! Now great masses of clouds were creeping over the sky. The sky became all overcast and it dropped lower and lower, until it rested upon the rooftop of the peasant's hut. At last the train was on the move again. She began to count what was left of her money, and wondered, could she afford another snack or would she be better advised to go without? She really ought to be ashamed of herself, because opposite her sat a mere boy who had not eaten a thing the whole time, yet he did not seem to care a bit. But just then, as if he had divined her thoughts and wished to confound her, the weedy youth produced a cut loaf of bread and a big piece of green cheese pitted with holes. He started to cut the cheese into slices.

"Would you car to share this with me, miss?" he said, offering her a sandwich.

She boiled over with rage. The impudence! And rising to her feet, she hurried off down the swaying corridor on her way to the restaurant car, leaving the weedy youth like a fool with the miserable sandwich still outstretched in his puny, charitable hand.

She spent two francs at the buffet, and still her throat was parched. No matter how much coffee she drank she could not quench her thirst.

Where was she? The train had stopped. Oh yes, she must get out at this station. She found herself a seat on a platform bench and waited patiently. Hundreds upon hundreds of people were pouring out of this train and another train and they were all flocking to the exits. To pass the time away, she began to read in the lamplight the postcards which she had received from her parents ever since she had been married. There was a striking change of tone in the most recent ones: they were full of hints, obscure and ambiguous phrases. "Our Father in heaven is a merciful Father . . . It is not for mortal man to question His wisdom . . . We must take courage in His all-embracing love . . . Grandfather is indisposed . . . We may have to pay him a visit . . . Circumstances may change . . ." Taken together, these postcards frightened her. No, no, she must ward off her terrible fears. She put the correspondence back into her handbag.

The express that would have borne her on to her destination if she had not run short of money, was steaming out of the station. The rain was coming down in torrents and beating down the smoke from the locomotive. A big cloud of smoke floated her way and made her cough. She got up from the bench and began walking up and down the platform with her suitcase in one hand and her hat in the other.

"Hello, curly!"

She found herself standing in the shadow of a burly man with a huge paunch and with a big, puffed-up, mauve-coloured face—a railway official to judge by his shiny black raincoat and peaked cap.

"My dear, you're freezing. Come into my office for shelter," he said to her in German, pointing towards a tiny cabin at the end of the platform. *"Haben Sie nur kein' Angst, Krausköpfchen!* You'll be nice and comfy with me. I won't do you any harm, I'm no monster. I should hate to see a nice little girl like you freeze to death. Come on in! It's always terribly chilly at this time of night."

"No, I'm all right. Tell me, when does the next train for Warsaw get in?"

"D'you mean the fourth-class train? What, is my curly little golly-wog travelling fourth-class, in a cattle-truck? Shame!" he cried, "Shame!" And his big breathing body seamed to grow bigger than ever.

A clock rang the hour. One! Two! Three! Four! . . . She moved towards the exit.

"Now, don't run away. Come into my office, and we'll look up the time-table. What? Surely you're not afraid of me? Tut, tut!" There was a wicked smile in his greedy little eyes.

She was terrified of him, and she crossed to another platform. Here she found two or three people to keep her company, but the wind was blowing the rain her way. She huddled up in a corner and waited for what seemed an eternity. Then there was the roar of a passing train. She rushed back, only to find herself once more under that same horrid shadow.

"Well, well, if it isn't my curly little gollywog! She's come back to me," said the fat, heavily breathing man, with that evil smirk in his tiny eyes; and loudly clearing his throat, he spat on the ground like a beast.

She felt terribly sick. . . . She felt the impact of his horrible little eyes as they pierced her clothing and caressed her naked body.

An inspector sauntered by. The puffed-up, mauve-faced official saluted with grotesque obsequiousness, and falling in with his superior, ambled off—the two of them, great hulking figures, both with hands clasped behind their backs.

A piercing whistle came rushing in from afar, growing louder and louder. Two gleaming red eyes approached in the darkness, growing bigger and bigger. There was a belching and sizzling of smoke, and into the station steamed the fourth-class train. She climbed up the steep steps, holding on for dear life to the rusty iron rail. She sat down near the door, at the end of a long wooden bench. It was a nightmare train, but strangely enough it answered in every detail to the mental picture she had formed of it whenever she had contemplated returning to Warsaw fourth-class. The carriage, which was not divided up into compartments, was in almost complete darkness. The air was foul and clammy. Everywhere on the floor children lay asleep on bundles done up in sackcloth. They snored laboriously through clogged little nostrils. Women sat wrapped up in huge dark shawls, as if it were midwinter.

"If only we could eat to the fill once in a while!" they moaned in chorus. "If something doesn't happen quickly, we shall starve to death."

"Yes," said a woman with a hoarse voice, who was hidden in the gloom, "that we shall. What we need is some capital to buy and sell, and make a little profit. Although that's not so easy as it sounds. Supposing you have the cash to buy poultry, well you have to pay through the nose, but when you go to market it doesn't fetch a decent price. That's the trouble."

"It isn't as if we were greedy and wanted a lot, is it now? I know there's precious little that I want! All I want is to marry of my eldest daughter and get her out of the way. And it won't be long before this one here is grown up either," said one of the women, pointing a withered finger at a little girl of about twelve, whose face was quite fleshless. The child sat chewing a piece of bread and her jawbones could be seen champing—like the jaws of a skeleton. "Look at her, she's bolting down her last piece of bread, and when that's finished she'll have to go hungry for hours and hours. . . . It'll serve you jolly well right!" The mother was a decrepit old hag—to all appearances she was over seventy, she was toothless, her skin was all shrivelled up, her face aws covered with hundreds of warts big and small.

"Shut up, you dirty Jews!" cried a tall burly fellow in an ill-fitting tweed coat. It was the sort of coat that the squire in Jelhitz used to wear. How, Deborah wondered, had he come by it? He sat puffing at a clay pipe. The fumes all but suffocated her. She moved over to the other end of the carriage, but everywhere the air was foul and clammy, everywhere was darkness, everywhere men and women lay groaning in their sleep. Those who were awake sat talking many foreign tongues.

At the frontier they all had to get out for the customs inspection. Hundreds of battered trunks were opened, hundreds of bundles were undone. A big-bellied woman, seemingly pregnant, was taken away for examination by a masculine-faced woman official whose features Deborah had seen before. The pregnant woman pleaded and protested at the top of her voice. Deborah was not even troubled to open her suitcase. The customs officer simply waved her away, but began to rummage suspiciously in a soiled little bundle, whose owner broke into a shrill cackle.

"A fat lot he'll find in there! All my jewels, and I don't think!"

Was this really Warsaw? Yes, it was Warsaw indeed! Here she was in the old familiar station; everything looked just the same as she had left it.

All she possessed now was a rouble and twenty kopecks. Should she walk home, or should she be reckless and take a droshky? She would certainly have danced for joy in the middle of the station for all to see, but her legs were failing her. They were very much enfeebled. Ah, there was the gilt-framed mirror hanging on the wall, and there the same right-angled sofa fitting so modestly into the corner!

"Hey, driver!"

The cabby whom she had hailed poked a weatherbeaten face out of his oversized blue greatcoat, his hands emerged from his long sleeves. He touched up his horse with gusto, and away they sped past the station in the heart of the city. She lay back in the droshky.

All that she beheld was hers—the cabby, the horse, the droshky, Warsaw, they were all part of herself! The familiar streets reeled back dizzily as the droshky flew onwards. The streets were alive! The cobblestones were alive! Yonder were the treetops of the Saxon Gardens. They were alive! Krulewski Street had rather an outlandish air about it; but the girl who kept the soda-fountain parlour happened to come to the door and she gave Deborah a smile of recognition. Deborah was about to return the greeting; however, the droshky was moving too fast for that. All the same Krulewski Street had now lost its outlandish air; the sudden appearance of that shop-girl imbued it with a friendly homely atmosphere.

"Warsaw! My dear own Warsaw! My very own! How I love you!"

"Whoa-back!"

"Why, we're here! Good heavens, I never realised it was such a short journey. I say, cabby, you certainly did it in record time!"

"Betcher life I did! Whatcher expect for yer twenty kopecks? Had yer money's worth, aintcher? Want me to take you to Berlin, do yer?"

"Oh no, no, don't take me to Berlin! Please don't. Leave me where I am!" she felt like screaming.

The children playing in the gateway did not recognise her. Nor did the baker's wife, who sat on her usual chair in her usual corner of the gateway, selling bread-rings out of a huge basket. She had a glass of tea in her hands, but she was not drinking. She was busy giving a piece of her mind to a man coated in flour from head to foot. Apparently he had kept her waiting a long time for the batch of hot bread-rings which he was now pouring into her basket. He gave Deborah an amused wink and went his way. Deborah followed him across the courtyard, her feet buckling under her upon the tortuous cobbles. She began to climb the familiar staircase, littered with rubbish. Once or twice she slipped.

At last she had reached the doorway she knew so well, the varnished brown double doors. She knocked, and as she waited her heart slammed madly. No answer! Again no answer!

"After all, why should I knock? Surely I'm at home now! How silly of me."

She flung open the double doors.

"Oh!"

The rooms were all empty, quite empty. The windows were smeared with whitewash. On the floor stood a pail stained from top to bottom with paint of every hue, rainbow-fashion, one layer of colour merging into the next. There was a big heap of pink powder piled up near the sink. Reb Avram Ber's study was newly decorated, as was the bedroom. There was a crushed trilby hanging on the nail in the kitchen door, together with a pair of white overalls which had large holes near the pockets and were spattered all over with green and pink.

She stopped short, utterly dazed and panic-stricken. The shock was too much for her.

Where were her parents? Why had they not written to tell her that they were moving? What was the mystery? She stood stockstill, as if petrified, powerless to move. She surveyed the bare walls, the newly-painted doors. The odour of fresh paint irritated her palate. Her tongue was trying to move in her half-open mouth; it was completely dry, as if someone had passed a hard cloth over it. What now? What was she to do with herself?

"Whom are you looking for, miss?"

"My parents used to live here. Have you any idea where they've gone to?"

"No, miss. I couldn't say!"

The decorator took his overalls off the door and began to put them on. She turned to go.

"Ask the landlord. He may know," he called out after her, buttoning up his red-and-green-stained overall-trousers. "I don't know where you can get hold of him, though. I've been trying all morning to track him down, but he's blooming well vanished. I say, didn't the Rabbi use to live in this here flat?"

"That's right. Don't you know where he's gone to?"

"No, haven't the faintest!"

She went downstairs, suitcase in hand. It was outrageous! Her parents had not even deemed it necessary to inform her of their change of address, and now, after such a long and weary journey, she found herself stranded. The disappointment was too great for her to bear. She was sinking, sinking fast. Soon she would fall headlong.

The baker's wife in the corner of the gateway recognised her.

"Heavens, is that you? Look what's become of you! Why, if it isn't our Deborah! How you've changed! What brings you here, now that your parents have moved from Warsaw? Didn't you know? Your flat's empty! It's to let. Good Good, how ill you look! What's the matter with you, are you hungry? Nothing to be ashamed of, even if you are. Far better to admit it than to starve. Come and have a cup of tea with me!"

Deborah shook her head. She inquired after her father at the general stores, but the shopkeeper was not very helpful. He did believe that he knew Reb Avram Ber's new address—he had heard it mentioned—but he couldn't for the life of him remember it now. The landlord was out. Unfortunately he had been gone all morning, and several other people besides Deborah were searching high and low for him. At her wits' ends, she took refuge in the little restaurant at the corner of the street. Possibly the proprietor, who was a member of Reb Avram Ber's congregation, might know. He did not even recognise her.

"The Rabbi's new address?" he grunted. "How the devil should I know!"

She ordered a bowl of soup. She could not afford to take any meat. Meat was not for people like herself who must consider dry bread a luxury.

The restaurateur set the bowl down with an angry bump, spilling part of its contents. He seemed to think her a pauper, and kept an eye on her, as if to encourage her to finish the soup quickly and then clear out. She lifted the spoon to her mouth, but she could not swallow. She felt that she was going to choke.

A young man strolled in and sat down opposite her.

"I beg your pardon, miss, I hope you won't think me inquisitive, but I should say that you're a stranger in these parts. Is this your first visit to Warsaw?"

"No, I live here."

"Do you really? That's funny, because you don't look like one of us, if you know what I mean. Not that that's anything to be ashamed of. Country folk are as good as us any day of the week. Well, well, and what do you think of the news? Terrible, isn't it? As if we never had enough to keep us worried, now there's this talk of war. War may break out at any moment, they say. If it does, all communications will be disrupted and lots of people will be cut off from their homes. It's terrible! The first thing I did when I heard that trouble was brewing, was to pack my parents off to the village where they belong. You never know what funny things may happen in a big town like Warsaw. The papers say it all started because some prince or other was murdered. Have you seen this?" he said, pointing a tremulous forefinger at a crumpled news-sheet.

She was unable to read it, for the print was so greasy.

So it was to be war. Perhaps in the long run some good might come of it. The common people seemed to think war the greatest of all possible calamities. Were they right? Yes, of course they were! Only a madman, a killer, could think otherwise. When war came, humanity sank to the lowest depths of misery and wretchedness. Already the men in the barracks across the road were preparing for the slaughter . . .

"Deborah, pull yourself together! Stop talking to yourself. Deborah, are you all right? Deborah, look at me! Were you asleep?"

Deborah sat up in bed.

She looked all round her at the familiar room with the familiar window, through which the half-light of evening was now peering, and she rubbed her eyes in an effort to rouse herself from her stupor, to shake off the hallucination which was only now beginning to fade. She stared hard into the gathering darkness.

"Who's there?" she asked.

"It's me, Deborah. What's the matter with you? Have you had a nightmare? I say, Deborah, I met one of my old pals and he lent me two franks. We're going to have some supper."

Her husband struck a match and applied it to the gas mantle, but he forgot that the gas had run out days ago; the light instantly went out with a pop. He put a coin in the meter and relit the lamp. A flood of greenish light settled on the bed and filled the hollows of Deborah's livid face.

Her husband handed her a cup of tea in bed, together with a few slices of bread. Deborah tried to swallow a mouthful of bread, but it stuck in her throat.

"I say, Deborah, have you heard that war has been declared? We're in for it now!"

Deborah slowly sipped her tea in silence.

She was past caring.

AFTERWORD

"Happy families are all alike; every unhappy family is unhappy in its own way." If there had been such a thing as a family crest in the impoverished, disenfranchised world of Eastern European Jewry, this resonant first line of Tolstoy's *Anna Karenina* might have served as an appropriate motto for the family into which Esther Singer Kreitman (1891–1954) was born. Kreitman's milieu and her novel, however, are distant indeed from the world of heraldry or the heroic or the epic. Nor does *Deborah*'s thinly veiled autobiographical depiction of the family dynamics in the Singer household leave much room for the nostalgia that has transformed the once vibrant community Kreitman describes into a source of jokes about Jewish mothers and Jewish families or, more significantly, a site of mourning for the culture destroyed by the Holocaust. Instead, her novel depicts a young woman's desire to escape the strictures of a restrictive religious environment, a family in which she is regarded as little more than household drudge, and the madness (or depression?) that threatens to overwhelm her. In addition to this personal and psychological turmoil, *Deborah* traces the emergence of a modern political and cultural consciousness in its protagonist, a consciousness that had long been the hallmark of modern Yiddish literature, but that was now astonishing precisely because it was associated with a female character.

Esther, or Hinde as she was called in the family, was the oldest child in a remarkable and, from all indications, remarkably discordant family of writers. Her parents, Pinchas Mendl and Batsheva, emerged from the radically different religious worlds of Eastern European Jewry represented in this novel by Deborah's parents: the father was an adherent of Hasidism, characterized by its devotion to a tsaddik (a "righteous man") or Rebbe and by its enthusiastic, emotional expression of religious devotion; the mother was the product and follower of *misnagdim* (literally: opponents; in this case, specifically opponents of Hasidism), characterized by their devotion to rationalism, learning, and a skepticism regarding what they considered the excesses of Hasidic practice. Six children were born into this family: Hinde, the Yiddish writer Israel Joshua Singer (1893–1944), two daughters who died in early childhood, the Yiddish Nobel Laureate Isaac Bashevis Singer (1904–1991, who adapted his mother's name to sign his Yiddish literary works), and Moshe (1906–1944?), the only son to remain within the family fold, following his father into the rabbinate and perishing with his mother and wife in Russia during the Second World War. The three Yiddish writers all produced autobiographical novels or memoirs, and despite their differences, they all described their parents in remarkably similar terms. The father was repeatedly called a "*batlen*," the Yiddish word for an impractical, inefficient, innocent man; the mother was consistently described as a more aloof parent, an intelligent, learned woman, more worldly and much less emotional than the father, "*a froy mit a mans-bilishn kop*," as I. J. Singer wrote—a woman "with a masculine head," a description he no doubt meant as high praise. But he also asserted what his brother and sister implied in varying ways: "My parents would have been a well-matched pair, if my mother had been my father and my father my mother."[1] According to each of the siblings, the difference in the parents' religious adherence and personalities led to a reversal of traditional gender roles so that the father's emotion was always at odds with the mother's reason.

Kreitman was, by all accounts, much like her protagonist Deborah, the unhappy product of this mismatched pair. Author and character move from Kreitman's birthplace of Leontchin, to the Radziminer Hasidic court, to Warsaw, and to Belgium. Both engage in the female and modern acts of rebellion from the religion, poverty, and misogyny that define their early years, finding at least temporary respite in romantic love, literature, secular education, and political radicalism. Both try to escape into a loveless arranged marriage to a Belgian diamond cutter. And both express their fear and hopeless acceptance of the "madwoman in the attic" role to which they have been assigned by genealogy and history. Kreitman ends her novel with the outbreak of World War I, before the period of her own productive literary career in London. She would spend most of the last four decades of her life in England, with extended visits back to Poland. A strong feminist reading of the text might suggest that the act of writing helped Kreitman elude the madness that beset Deborah, but it is, of course, impossible to verify such a provocative conclusion.

Within the Singer family, Hinde was regarded as something of an embarrassment, an hysteric subject to nervous breakdowns or, as Isaac Bashevis Singer wrote, an ill woman who was either mad or epileptic or possessed by a dybbuk, the wandering soul of Jewish legend who enters the body of another and must be exorcised.[2] That last diagnosis is the only one we can definitively reject at this distance of time and place, but it is also the most revealing one. The dybbuk signals transmigration and transgression; it is often a male who enters the body of a female and speaks through her, attempting to right some wrong done to him or, more often, by him or the human he possesses. The dybbuk is at once a sign of sexual no less than psychic transgression and of ventriloquism: the voice belongs to another; the body into which it enters has no power over it; only other religious, masculine authorities can compel it to withdraw from its victim. For Isaac Bashevis Singer, there could be no more apt image for this transgressive woman who wrote Yiddish literature, speaking in a voice that sounded strikingly like that of modernist male writers (her brothers primary among them). The fanciful conceit suggesting that she was possessed of a dybbuk was not only a way of dismissing her literary accomplishments, but also of containing the potentially disruptive power of female creative endeavors, and even of claiming some credit for them. Her younger brother made only passing reference to Kreitman's literary work. In a Yiddish retrospective written after his sister's death, Bashevis asserts that she was "quite a talented authoress and wrote several books that were not at all bad,"[3] surely a most grudging acknowledgement of literary talent. In his memoirs, he refers only to the smart, humorous letters she sent home to Warsaw, thus erasing her substantial fictional texts.[4] Consigning women to the epistolary or to diaries is another familiar mode of dismissing them from the ranks of serious writers, relegating them to genres considered more personal, fragmented, less public, and less mediated.

The obvious parallel trajectories followed by the author and protagonist of *Deborah* have led critics to read the novel as autobiography, ethnography, history, and feminist screed. Such views of the novel underscore the interpretive obstacles that writers of Yiddish literature share with women and other non-canonical writers identified with ethnic or subaltern literatures. Yet *Deborah* is more than the sum of its parts. Readers tend to create special categories for Yiddish texts, often perceiving them as simple or crude by the standards of modern (Western) literary aesthetics, but also as sociohistorical documents, "true" to the unfamiliar people and places thus introduced into the expanding literary consciousness. They are subject to a kind of protectionism that perpetuates a division between the complicated forces of the present and the simpler dynamic of the past. This is also a division between modernity and tradition in which "tradition" becomes little more than a synonym for "primitive." Yiddish literature bears the added unspeakable burden of the Holocaust, which is presumed to have destroyed it and which has certainly become the prism through which it is now read. The literature has become personified, as if, against all odds, it is a survivor to be treated sympathetically, kindly, with awe that only increases as time passes. It bears witness to destruction. It speaks—echoing the title of I. J. Singer's posthumous memoir—of "a world that is no more," thus becoming an historical and cultural artifact that it would be unseemly to question or criticize. This late-twentieth-century perspective is entirely at odds with the aesthetic, political, and cultural worldview of Esther Kreitman and precludes a more nuanced analysis of the texts she wrote. These texts are political, modernist, and psychologically astute explorations of European Jewry in the first half of the twentieth century.[5]

Kreitman was productive in the 1930s and 1940s, publishing two novels, a collection of short stories, and two volumes of translation. At the same time, she was an active participant in the London literary magazine *Loshn un lebn* (Language and Life) and in socialist politics. Her publishing career began with two translations from English to Yiddish, both produced in Warsaw. In 1929 she translated Charles Dickens's "A Christmas Carol," following it in 1930 with George Bernard Shaw's *Intelligent Woman's Guide to Socialism and Capitalism*, which had appeared only two years earlier. Her choice of texts to translate only underscores the pervasive myth of her contrariness since it could not be supposed that these titles would meet with a particularly warm reception from the Yiddish-reading audience to which they were addressed. In London, following the Warsaw publication of the Yiddish version of *Deborah*, she wrote another novel entitled *Brilyantyn* (Diamonds, 1944) and a collection of short stories, *Yikhes* (Lineage, 1950). That both of these works are appearing now for the first time in English reflects a renewed interest in Kreitman's work.[6]

Brilyantyn is a more expansive novel than *Deborah*, depicting a broader array of men and women and their diverse social and economic circumstances. It begins where *Deborah* left off—in Antwerp, in the period leading up to World War I—and follows Kreitman's own geographical path as these characters flee to Rotterdam and on to London. The novel contains an author's prefatory note explaining that it was written in the years 1936–1939 and that "all the characters in this novel are entirely fictitious" (*ale karaktern inem dozikn roman, zaynen durkhoys fiktsye*). In light of the autobiographical readings of her first novel, perhaps this disclaimer may serve as a caution against reading her earlier one, too, as entirely true. In its second half, *Yikhes*, in turn, takes up the historical period following *Brilyantn*. Its first five short stories are set in Poland, but in the final seven stories, we find ourselves in London under the quite different but nonetheless profound turmoil caused by poverty, assimilation and, worst of all, Nazi attack.

Kreitman's Yiddish stories entered a literary culture to which women were rarely admitted. Scholars have often noted the dearth of women writers in Yiddish and the fact that those who were able to publish in the lively periodical press of Europe and North and South America tended to write poetry and not prose.[7] There were, to be sure, social and cultural conditions that made prose publication in Yiddish a particularly difficult enterprise for women writers, not least of them the absence of "a room of one's own." As a woman who wrote short stories and novels, living primarily in England, Kreitman also had little access to the editors and publishers who disseminated Yiddish literature in the first half of the twentieth century. As the sister of two prolific and famous Yiddish writers, she may be supposed to have had greater access to them than many of her female peers, but it is not at all clear that her brothers were particularly sympathetic or supportive of her literary endeavors. In writing prose (like her brothers) rather than poetry, she distinguished herself from most other writing women. The valence of each genre within Jewish culture makes this choice even more noteworthy. The kind of grounding in an expansive and cohesive social world that storytelling demands may be one of the reasons that women tended to write poetry instead. Within a Jewish context, storytelling and the oral tradition have been associated with *midrash* and *aggadah,* the rabbinic and post-rabbinic hermeneutic and exegetical exploration of biblical narrative. They are thus very much part of a masculine tradition of learning. In Kreitman's novel, the very fact that her mother has some erudition in such matters is a source of much surprise and contention.

In the novel, Deborah envies her mother's learning. She envies, in fact, all learning, whether secular or religious, and reads whatever is available—psalms, secular poetry, a Russian grammar, Karl Marx, story books of every kind—whenever she can steal time from the demands of her highly regulated domestic and religious life. The quest for knowledge and rebellion against these demands are shared by her brother, Michael, but they are not a struggle for him. The difference in the treatment of boys and girls in this traditional Jewish milieu is one of the major themes of Kreitman's novel, beginning with the first words we hear her father utter. His parents hope that Michael will grow up to be a great Talmudist, but Deborah is to grow up to be "nothing, of course." Michael's behavior and his distaste for the traditional learning that comes so easily to him make it clear that he will not become the kind of learned man his parents would have him be. The novel never suggests a tone of lament for this radical reversal of expectations. On the contrary, this familiar trope of modern Yiddish literature may be Deborah's best hope. The conflict between parents and children, usually figured in these terms of masculine rebellion, become a model for Deborah as well, who is expected to be a wife and mother but who wants something more she cannot yet name. Perhaps she, too, will be able to flee her fate as her brother does physically by running out of the study house to revel in the light of summer, or intellectually by reading forbidden texts, or even by giving free rein to artistic expression. Kreitman introduces a radically new perspective on this desire for independence by extending it to the modernizing daughters of religious parents.

Deborah's mother, Raizela, is an educated Jewish woman, and she embodies the ambivalence such a figure generates. Like Deborah, she reads whenever and whatever she can. Educated by her own learned father and married, at the age of fifteen, to the equally learned Reb Avram Ber, Raizela becomes her husband's advisor in secular matters and his opponent in virtually everything except the desire to see their daughter married. Reb Avram Ber will not repeat the mistake made by his father-in-law in educating his daughter. Michael will share none of his knowledge with her. Raizela, inexplicably, also refuses to translate Hebrew passages or explain anything to her daughter. The one instance in the novel in which there is an exchange of any meaningful sort between mother and daughter occurs only after they have parted for the last time. As she travels to Antwerp after her marriage, Deborah is deeply absorbed in the pages of a book she "had picked up from her mother (who had just finished with it)" (242). The book—a Life of Moses Mendelssohn—offers a surprising insight into the character of Raizela and the ongoing internal Jewish cultural wars of the period. Mendelssohn is the harbinger of the *haskole*—the Jewish Enlightenment—and anyone found reading about him could be attacked, as Deborah is by her father-in-law, as a freethinker and a heretic. That, indeed, is the fate Reb Avram Ber fears that his own father-in-law was tempting when he taught Raizela to read religious texts. A woman who learns what she is forbidden to know will end up reading truly forbidden, secular texts. In the Yiddish version of Kreitman's novel, Deborah's father quotes the Talmudic injunction against teaching one's daughters—*"kol hamelamed 'et bito torah ke'ilu melamdah tiflut"* (whoever teaches his daughter Torah, it is as if he taught her something frivolous, i.e., unnecessary and wrong for her to know; from Mishnah, Sota 3:3) (7). Raizela escapes the label of heretic, freethinker, frivolous, or madwoman only because she is portrayed as *sui generis* within the narrative, as within the religious milieu, mysteriously absolved from carrying out the traditional functions of wife and mother, even though she is both. Kreitman protects the figure of Raizela from this despised role, but in doing so she also renders her as an invalid, symbolically containing the power of this all-knowing and powerful woman by crippling her and confining her to her couch, making it impossible for her to walk away from the conditions of her own unhappy life.

Mother and daughter are more alike than either wishes to recognize in this novel. Deborah's psychological anguish has a physical analogue in Raizela's paralysis. We are given no medical cause for Raizela's illness. On the contrary, she is able to walk and there are periodic moments of physical energy and movement in the text (e.g., her visit to the *tsaddik*'s wife, her preparations for the move to Warsaw). Yet, like Deborah, she is stricken with inexplicable bouts of infirmity. She reminds us of other powerful literary figures who are subdued and contained within a maimed body, figures such as Samson, Oedipus, Melville's Ahab or Charlotte Brontë's Mr. Rochester. Usually it is masculine power that is physically controlled in this way; female power is more commonly contained, as is Deborah's, by nervous disorders. The character of Raizela, who takes on the masculine trope of impotence instead of the feminine one of madness, is a sustained illustration of the inversion of male and female I. J. Singer described in his parents' household.

Gender roles are similarly inverted in the tensions the novel traces between the generations or between tradition and modernity. These tensions are usually figured in Yiddish literature in a son's rebellion against the law of the father and against the patriarchal religious authority that is at odds with the emerging sense of the modern self. In *Deborah*, the tensions are similar, but the conventions of the genre are re-fashioned by the daughter's rebellion, which is primarily directed at the mother who represents all authority and knowledge in the household. Raizela is following in her own father's footsteps, rejecting her husband's weak, feminized Hasidism and embracing her *misnagdic* upbringing. Deborah can emulate neither her weak and ineffectual father nor her overpowering mother.

In addition to being a condemnation of the social and religious structure that would regulate every aspect of life, the novel traces the young woman's desire to formulate and articulate her separation from the family and the familiar. Deborah barely recalls her child-hood in this narrative which begins when she is fourteen (the Yiddish text has it as fifteen, exactly the age at which her mother married) and ends, some unclear number of years later, with the out-break of World War I. Its subject is the conscious, maturing attempt to constitute the independent self and, more particularly, the female self, but the modern signs of independence—learning, sexuality, pol-itics, art—are undermined in the narrative. In particular, the body and sexuality are repugnant to Deborah after her marriage, although there are signs of their potential power earlier, with Mottel and again with Simon, but certainly not with her husband's coarse and entirely revolting advances. The clearest sign of physical intimacy in the novel concerns her beloved Simon, but it takes place in silence, with-out her, and without the slightest hint of pleasure. Simon, against his doctor's orders and the threat of contagion, makes love to Bailke and then disappears from the novel. Deborah can find no release in love of any kind. Sexuality, in this novel, is not the typical sign of freedom or modernity, but merely a different illusion of redemption.

Liberation, if it is to come at all, must take a more public, social form. *Deborah*, after all, may be regarded as a political novel in which Kreitman presents a perspective strikingly like the socialist one she encountered in the political tome of Shaw that she translated. She links class and gender, condemning the powerlessness and silence to which they consign the poor and women. She offers a resonant connection between the status of Hasidim (like Reb Avram Ber and her own father) and of women in Jewish life. Both are childlike, subject to the supervision of masterful figures; both crave belief in something; both are ignorant and need to be educated (p. 86 in the Yiddish text). By the novel's end, this naïve subjection is replaced by an insistence on individual responsibility for the self and for others, and by a clearly articulated, though not yet realizable, desire for a more equitable social order. Starving, threatened with eviction, surrounded by soldiers preparing for battle because "an Austrian crownprince had been murdered in faraway Serbia," Deborah rejects the purportedly noble justifications for war:

> How the conscience of the world is shocked when innocent blood is spilt, especially if that blood happens to be precious blue blood! Of course, ordinary red blood is cheap, inferior, and who cares if it is shed in interminable torments, drop by drop, day after day? I wonder if anyone would ever dream of stopping me in the street—"You look hungry. Let me treat you to a meal!" (280–281)

Within the narrative, such a focus on the political is constantly vying with the equally threatening focus on the individual. (Does Kreitman anticipate the feminist discourse of a later day that would proclaim the personal as political?) There can be no sentimentality about the social and family conditions that have contributed to Deborah's unhappiness. No longer relying on what she calls the "*idée fixe* that everybody, even her own mother hated her and was anxious to be rid of her" (271), she yearns to be reconciled to her parents and to return home. But, as we learn by novel's end, that desire is nothing more than another hallucination. The Great War, to which Deborah awakens from her nightmare of isolation and rejection, will resolve nothing politically or personally for those about to be caught up in its horrors, and as the last line of the novel asserts, she is "past caring" about events over which she has no control. War appears here as a kind of pathetic fallacy, an objectification on the national level of the inner turmoil the novel has been tracing and from which it can find no way out. Just as she rejects the all-encompassing religious system from which her protagonist flees, Kreitman refuses to embrace any *deus ex machina*—secular, deistic, world-historical, political though it be—that will change her protagonist's fate. She rejects the conventional happy ending and even a deliberately ambiguous one, rejecting as well the dualism of Deborah's romantic novels and her Marxist tracts. There can be no resolution, no synthesis, because the belief in concepts of good and bad, repression and liberation, thesis and antithesis is ultimately too confining for Kreitman's imagination and for her politics.

The novel's seemingly episodic plot, its fragmented characterizations of people, places, and events, enacts on the structural level what we have been primarily tracing in the thematic and symbolic development of *Deborah*. That fragmentation is more pronounced in the Yiddish original than in this English translation, produced by Kreitman's son, Maurice Carr (Morris Kreitman), ten years after the novel's original publication. Differences between the English text and the Yiddish one raise intriguing questions about the process of translating this novel, a process about which neither author nor translator left any record. Her own translations from English into Yiddish make it quite clear that Esther Kreitman's command of English was excellent and, although she may have been more at ease with Yiddish as the target language and English as the source, she could certainly have commented on the English translation. In fact, there are frequent instances in her Yiddish text where we encounter calques from English, words or expressions it would have been unlikely for her to have heard in her native Poland but that she could have incorporated from her adopted language (*Frosts kunstmoleray* [Frost's artistry],

referring to Jack Frost, *brekhn dos ayz*/breaking the ice.) Such observa-
tions make it seem more likely that she had some influence on the
English translation of her novel. In fact, at various points in the text,
one may imagine the mother peering over her son's shoulder. One—
or both—of them undoubtedly took the liberty of editing parts of
the text. One—or both—felt that the perspective of a Yiddish novel
in 1936 could not remain unchanged in its 1946 English version. It is
impossible to do more than speculate about the relationship between
author and translator or between this mother and son, but it is not
difficult to imagine that it was fraught with more than the usual
complement of translation issues.

Differences between the Yiddish and English texts attest to the editorial revisions that accompanied this process of translation. The first
and most dramatic of these revisions concerns the most basic one of
identity: the name. In Yiddish, the novel is entitled *Der sheydim
tants*—The Dance of the Demons—a resonant image of chaos. In
English, that title is relegated to a reference (on p. 238) to a mysterious
dance a servant girl sees at Deborah's wedding; it is of folkloristic or
anthropological interest.[8] *Deborah* changes the tone of *Der sheydim
tants*, encouraging a stronger focus on the eponymous protagonist
rather than the macabre world that surrounds her. It is as if, after the
Holocaust, that world must be afforded at least this modicum of pro-
tection from harsh judgment or scrutiny. There are other changes in
the English that are more clearly inspired by the decade that destroyed
the Polish Jewish milieu at the center of the novel. By 1936, the frequently heard echoes of "Deutschland über alles" were already threatening to engulf world Jewry and, in both Yiddish (222) and English
(219), these words inspire disgust. By 1936, Jews in traditional dress
were forbidden to walk in Warsaw's Saxon Gardens, but the 1946
English text links that prohibition with the horror that has just ended.
The Yiddish text has those dressed in modern garb strolling freely in
the Gardens "as if they weren't even Jews," (*vi zey voltn gor keyn yidn
nisht geven* [145]); the English text has the unorthodox heading for the
Gardens "where a notice 'JEWS WEARING GABARDINES AND DOGS NOT
ADMITTED' barred the way for others" (137). More radically, the English

text erases any sign of the German culture that had, by 1946, become synonymous with genocide. Here, Deborah takes great comfort in reading Russian and, especially, the verses of Pushkin (78), but in Yiddish (88) she is comforted and inspired by German's Gothic script and by Goethe's poetry, which she and her brother recite from memory. This rare moment of camaraderie is excised in the English text, as if to erase any hint that their exposure to German culture might unite these characters as nothing in their Jewish lives could.

Other revisions are less momentous. In Yiddish, there are chapter titles that have been elided in the English text; there are different divisions of paragraphs; a chapter break is added to *Deborah* (Chapter XIV, p. 242). The translation grapples with the embedded Slavic and, especially, Hebraic and Aramaic elements of common Yiddish speech, sometimes seeking for them an idiomatic English expression and sometimes ignoring them completely. This translation is very clearly a product of its time and place and, frequently, the British idiom or Cockney accent that substitutes for a Warsaw-inflected Yiddish, reminds us not only of the challenges of translation but also of the distance between turn-of-the century Jewish Warsaw and mid-century London. What are we to make of the allusion to "the artful dodger" (128) that is entirely missing—and meaningless—in Yiddish? Intertextuality in the Yiddish alludes to Talmudic or biblical texts; in English, the intertextual reference here is to Dickens's *Oliver Twist* and conjures the Jewish thief Fagin, with whom an English audience would no doubt be familiar. In addition, the English text contains explanations of Jewish ritual and religious references that require no comment in the Yiddish original, omitting some that are deemed unnecessary or incomprehensible to an English reader; yet it also leaves some Hebrew untranslated (e.g., *shmira* [ritual matzos for Passover, 87, 92] or *yesh omrim* ["it is said," 51]). When the Yiddish text refers to Deborah's grandfather simply as a *misnaged*, the English text erases this unfamiliar term, substituting a lengthy explanation about tsaddikim and Hasidism (9). Elsewhere, *goyim un goyes*, or the more pejorative *shkotsim un shikselekh* used to refer to non-Jews, becomes simply "men and women" or "youths."

Such adjustments are common to translations from Yiddish, but there are other, more substantive ones here that suggest subtle changes from the tenor and perspective of the Yiddish original. Although *Deborah* is intently focused on its major protagonist, it also wrests the narrative perspective away from Deborah herself, even as it emphasizes everyone else's judgment of her mental state. The English text periodically insinuates Michael into passages where he makes no appearance in the original. It is, for example, Deborah alone in *Der sheydim tants*, and not Deborah *and* Michael, who observes and is disgusted with the stranger who enters Reb Avram Ber's study (20). Deborah speaks more in the Yiddish version, both to other characters and to herself. A few telling examples change the interiority of the Yiddish text, in which she refers to herself in the second-person singular, into a more externalized third person, emphasizing even more the enormous distance she must traverse to establish a strong first-person voice. In English, "Deborah must never take anything of her own accord" (98); in Yiddish, she says to herself, "*you yourself* must never get close (*aleyn torstu zikh nisht tsurirn* [107]). Similarly the English text has her imagining her "escape from a home which was only a home in name" and fleeing "from parents who were eager to disown her" (197); in the Yiddish text she thinks of fleeing "a home from which *you* are estranged" (*vos iz dir fremd*) and parents "who want to be rid of *you*" (*vos viln fun dir putr vern* [202]). Other characters comment on her madness and her lowly status more explicitly in the English text. There is, for example, no Yiddish version of any of the following sentences, though their sentiments are certainly evident throughout.

"Everybody dislikes me, everybody!" (109)

Now here was Deborah . . . like an eager dog chained in its kennel. (121–122)

Deborah was left to her solitude, and instead of getting fed up with

Miss Rushka, she got fed up with herself. (122)

Raizela came to regard her as an eccentric. (191)

The English thus makes more explicit the judgments of Deborah's personality found in its Yiddish source, leaving a bit less to the reader's discernment. It also slightly softens Raizela's view of her daughter. Lamenting, as Deborah does in English, that she is "so little thought of by her mother" is not at all the same as feeling, as she does in Yiddish, that her mother doesn't like her (*"zi gefelt nisht der muter"* [68]). Similarly the sarcastic, dismissive *"khokhume mayne"* (my genius [135]) is changed into the surprising, anachronistic English phrase "mummy's little darling" (126), uttered by Raizela. These should not be regarded as faulty translations, but rather as deliberate changes, the result of a careful re-thinking of the original text.

The most extensive set of changes appear in the novel's opening chapter where virtually every page discloses the editorial process, the felt need to educate an English audience in Jewish lore, and the desire to redeem some part of the now-decimated Eastern European past from the harsh criticism it receives in Kreitman's novel. *Der sheydim tants*'s first chapter does not begin with the invocation of the Sabbath we have here. It offers a considerably more extensive depiction of the family, one in which Reb Avram Ber is even more dependent on his wife's practicality and her knowledge of religious texts, Raizela is even more disdainful of her husband, and Michael is even freer to roam away from this unhappy family. Here Kreitman describes a home in which may be found everything, except anything at all redolent of home (*"akhuts abisl azoyns, vos zol shmekn mit heym"* [8]). The deliberate omission of such passages moderates the unremittingly bleak view of the earlier text. It is a protective gesture, and it may also help explain the increased focus on Deborah's role in the family and on her psyche. There is, after all, some possibility for addressing, perhaps even remedying psychological distress, individual trauma, childhood unhappiness. There is, in 1946, no future change to be imagined in the world of Eastern European Jewry.

. . .

Even as *Deborah* adapts *Der sheydim tants* for a radically altered milieu, it accurately reflects the modernist, feminist sensibilities of Kreitman's novel. Indeed, Kreitman may have engaged in a process of translation rather like the one her son undertook. Her translation, however, did not involve making one language or social and historical context comprehensible to another. Rather, we can discern in this novel Kreitman's adaptation of a new perspective, which transformed her own literary, social, and political surroundings by claiming a place for women, a place for Yiddish, and doing so with neither apologetics nor nostalgia. One may be reminded, at various points in this novel, of her brothers' fiction. One may similarly be reminded of the situations in which George Eliot's protagonists find themselves, or, more pointedly, of the novels and essays of Kreitman's contemporary, Virginia Woolf. These echoes are not invoked in order to trace her literary antecedents or influences, but rather to locate Kreitman's place in the wider cultural setting of which she was a part. Like these canonical writers, Kreitman describes the obstacles encountered by the maturing modern individual. Her novel may seem disjointed or fragmented in parts, but that, too, echoes the narrative techniques of her more famous contemporaries, where interiority and social critique rarely led to realist fiction or transparent narration.

For Jews and for women, assertion of the self may have been a particularly difficult enterprise because it countered prevailing myths of the community and family. When her brothers, or other male writers of Yiddish prose, declared their independence from the strictures of traditional Eastern European Jewish life and letters, they were heralded (or vilified) as modern men creating a new literature and new forms of Jewish expression. Kreitman responded to the same influences, refracted through the differences made by such categories as gender and status, and the more fluid ones of temperament and consciousness. The changing literary reputations of other women writers—Jane Austen, the Brontë sisters, and Emily Dickinson,

Afterword

as well as Eliot and Woolf, come to mind—offer an apt model for reading Kreitman, too. Rather than analyzing her nerves or her marriage, it has finally become appropriate to analyze her literary work in its social context and to claim a place for it in an expansive apprehension of modern literature.

Anita Norich
Ann Arbor
April 2004

NOTES

1. I. J. Singer, *Fun a velt vos iz nishto mer* [Of a World That Is No More], p. 33.

2. Isaac Bashevis Singer, *Mayn tatns bezdn-shtub* [In My Father's Court], ch. 27, 152–158. Janet Hadda writes that Kreitman's symptoms suggest a rare form of epilepsy called partial complex status epilepticus (Hadda, *Isaac Bashevis Singer: A Life* [New York: Oxford UP, 1997], 43–44).

3. *"Zi iz geven a gants feyik shrayberin un hot ongeshribn etlakhe gornisht keyn shlekhte bikher,"* "Fun der alter un nayer heym" [Of the Old and New Home], *Forverts*, June 6, 1965.

4. Clive Sinclair, in his introduction to the Virago edition of *Deborah* (London, 1983, vii), cites another reference to Kreitman possibly by Isaac Bashevis Singer: a review of *Deborah* in London's *The Jewish Chronicle* (September 13, 1946) signed I. B. S. By 1946, when the review appeared, Bashevis was not yet widely translated into English. Morris Kreitman (aka Maurice Carr) had included him—along with Esther and I. J. Singer—in a volume entitled *Jewish Short Stories of Today* (London: Faber & Faber, 1938), but it is unlikely that Bashevis, writing Yiddish in New York, would have found any other English translator or publisher in London. If I. B. S. is, indeed, Kreitman's brother, might it have been his nephew—Morris Kreitman—who had a hand in translating this less than enthusiastic review? It is unlikely that we will know, but it may be one of the many literary mysteries surrounding this family.

5. For other English-language considerations of Kreitman and the novel, see: Maurice Carr, "My Uncle Yitzhak: A Memoir of I. B. Singer, *Commentary* (Dec. 1992): 25–32; Dafna Clifford, "From Diamond Cutters to Dog Races: Antwerp and London in the Work of Esther Kreitman," *Prooftexts* 23 (2003): 320–337; Ari Goldman, "The long neglected sister of the Singer family," *New York Times* (April 4, 1991); Janet Hadda, *Isaac Bashevis Singer,* esp. 39–46; Faith Jones, "Esther Kreitman: Renewed Recognition of Her Work," *Canadian Jewish Outlook* (March/April 2001): 17–18; Anita Norich, "The Family Singer and the Autobiographical Imagination," *Prooftexts* (Jan. 1990): 97–107; S. S. Prawer, "The First Family of Yiddish," *Times Literary Supplement* (April 29, 1983): 419–420; Clive Sinclair, Introduction to *Deborah*, London: Virago, 1983, v–xiii; Ruth R. Wisse, *The Modern Jewish Canon,* 2000, 147–152.

6. *Yikhes* has been translated by Dorothee Van Tendeloo as *Bitz and Other Stories* (London: David Paul, 2004) and *Brilyantyn* is forthcoming as *Diamonds* (London: David Paul), translated by Heather Valencia. *Yikhes* has also appeared in Dutch, translated by Willy Brill (Amsterdam: Vassalucci, 2000), and translations of *Brilyantyn* into other European languages are expected to follow.

7. See: Kathryn Hellerstein, "Canon and Gender: Women Poets in Two Modern Yiddish Anthologies," *Shofar*, Vol. 9, no. 4 (Summer 1994): 9–23, and "In Exile in the Mother Tongue: Yiddish and the Woman Poet," in *Borders, Boundaries, and Frames*, Mae G. Henderson, ed. (New York: Routledge, 1995), 64–106; Irena Klepfisz, "Queens of Contradiction: A Feminist Introduction to Yiddish Women Writers," in *Found Treasures: Stories by Yiddish Women Writers*, Frieda Forman, Ethel Raicus, Sarah Silberstein Swartz, and Margie Wolfe, eds. (Toronto: Second Story Press, 1994), 21–62; Anita Norich, "Jewish Literatures and Feminist Criticism: An Introduction to Gender and Text," in *Gender and Text in Modern Hebrew and Yiddish Literature*, Naomi Sokoloff, Anne Lapidus Lerner, and Anita Norich, eds. (New York: JTS and Harvard, 1992), 1–16; Norma Fain Pratt, "Culture and Radical Politics: Yiddish Women Writers, 1890–1940," *American Jewish History* 70 (Sept. 1980): 68–91; Naomi Seidman, *A Marriage Made in Heaven: The Sexual Politics of Hebrew and Yiddish* (Berkeley: University of California Press, 1997).

8. Dafna Clifford points out that Kreitman's Warsaw publisher, Brzoza, referred to the novel as Dvoyrele—the Yiddish diminutive of Devorah—in letters he sent to the author before its publication. Later correspondence calls the book by its proper Yiddish name (Clifford, 336–337).

The Feminist Press at the City University of New York is a nonprofit literary and educational institution dedicated to publishing work by and about women. Our existence is grounded in the knowledge that women's writing has often been absent or underrepresented on bookstore and library shelves and in educational curricula—and that such absences contribute, in turn, to the exclusion of women from the literary canon, from the historical record, and from the public discourse. The Feminist Press was founded in 1970. In its early decades, the Feminist Press launched the contemporary rediscovery of "lost" American women writers, and went on to diversify its list by publishing significant works by American women writers of color. More recently, the Press's publishing program has focused on international women writers, who remain far less likely to be translated than male writers, and on nonfiction works that explore issues affecting the lives of women around the world.

Founded in an activist spirit, the Feminist Press is currently undertaking initiatives that will bring its books and educational resources to under-served populations, including community colleges, public high schools and middle schools, literacy and ESL programs, and prison education programs. As we move forward into the twenty-first century, we continue to expand our work to respond to women's silences wherever they are found.

Many of our readers support the Press with their memberships, which are tax-deductible. Members receive numerous benefits, including complimentary publications, discounts on all purchases from our catalog or web site, pre-publication notification of new books and notice of special sales, invitations to special events, and a subscription to our email newsletter, Women's Words: News from the Feminist Press. For more information about membership and events, and for a complete catalog of the Press's 250 books, please refer to our web site: www.feministpress.org.